# THURSDAY NIGHTS
### *at the*
# BLUEBELL INN

# THURSDAY NIGHTS
## *at the*
# BLUEBELL INN

KIT FIELDING

CORONET

First published in Great Britain in 2019 by Coronet
An Imprint of Hodder & Stoughton
An Hachette UK company

This paperback edition published in 2021

1

A CIP catalogue record for this title is available from the British Library

Paperback ISBN 9781529378580
eBook ISBN 9781529378566

Typeset in Sabon MT by Hewer Text UK Ltd, Edinburgh
Printed and bound in Great Britain by Clays Ltd, Elcograf S.p.A.

Hodder & Stoughton policy is to use papers that are natural, renewable
and recyclable products and made from wood grown in sustainable
forests. The logging and manufacturing processes are expected to
conform to the environmental regulations of the country of origin.

Hodder & Stoughton Ltd
Carmelite House
50 Victoria Embankment
London EC4Y 0DZ

www.hodder.co.uk

To my lovely wife Debbie who will
always be Wonderful Tonight

# A DARTS MATCH ON A MONDAY NIGHT IN OCTOBER
## THE BLUEBELL VERSUS THE NAGGERS

*Katy*

It's Monday night – my night – and Jerry's sitting in front of the fire toasting his toes while I'm running around like a blue-arsed fly. I'm clearing up, washing up, sorting out Laura's clothes for the morning. I say, 'It wouldn't hurt you to help.'

Shifting himself into a more comfortable position, Jerry says, 'I've been out in the bloody wet all day.'

'You know it's darts.'

'It's always darts for you, Katy.'

'Oh, yeah? So who cooks the meals? Who cleans the house? Who looks after . . .?' Then I can't be bothered to go on and he's not listening anyway.

My lovely daughter Laura, soon to be sixteen, belt for a skirt, lolling in the armchair, rolls her eyes towards the ceiling. 'If you two are going to start, I'm off to my room.' She flounces out looking like me but talking like him.

I say, 'Look what you've done.'

He says, 'Look what you've done.' He draws out the 'you've' in a condescending, 'of course it's your fault' intonation.

I want to spit at him but I light up a fag instead, cos that really gets his goat since he gave up smoking.

'Not in here, Katy,' he snaps at me.

And because he's going bald and is conscious of it, I say, 'Okay, keep your hair on.'

And he says, 'Hah bloody hah.'

It's five minutes till I have to leave and I'm looking in the mirror, putting my face on. Jerry's still flopped in his chair, staring at the telly and mumbling 'What a load of bollocks,' but he doesn't take his eyes off the screen. And you know what? I briefly feel sorry for this deflated man, whose hair is peeling back from his temples. Is he as unhappy as I am? But the moment doesn't last because he opens his mouth and dredges up a loud belch.

'Pig,' I say.

'At least I don't look like one.'

This cuts me because I've been trying to lose a bit of weight; you know, easing down on the chips, only having two slices of cheese on toast. I'm not fat, just a bit over the ideal. What's the word? Voluptuous. That's it. Voluptuous. Like Nigella Lawson: big and beautiful. Well, dark-haired anyway.

In my reflection, I suck in my cheeks to give myself the hollow look, check that the flabbiness under my chin isn't turning into another chin. Then I work on my eyes, squint on my eyeliner, squint again for my mascara. I step back to admire my handiwork. I'm not exactly a pale-skinned sloe-eyed beauty, but it's not bad, Katy. Not bad.

'You used to fancy me,' I say to Jerry.

'Used to fancy a lot of things.'

I shake my arse as I mock-leer at him from the mirror. 'Fancy a bit of action?'

He says, with no interest, 'Maybe later.'

'When? After you've filled your guts with lager?'

He grins then. 'It deadens the pain.'

I have to laugh, and there's a second of how it used to be.

I pick up my handbag, check I've got my darts, and then I'm ready to go. I say, 'Make sure Laura goes to bed on time.' As if he will, and as if she would, but I've got to go through the motions.

So I leave Jerry, warm and comfortable and fucking selfish, to his evening in front of the fire, to his collection of porn DVDs and cans of lager. He'll come along to the Bluebell a bit later, in time for a couple of pints before closing and a couple of free sandwiches off the team's plate.

Jerry calls the Bluebell my second home because I spend so much time there, but even my crummy council house is in better nick than this pub. The Bluebell might be half comfortable inside, but the outside could definitely do with some help from *DIY SOS*. Danny the Landlord calls it his Victorian Wreck and he's not joking. There's dead weeds in the car park and withered flowers spilling over the hanging baskets that are hanging by a thread – something to watch out for on a windy night, or when I'm sitting on a plastic chair in the designated smoking area. Which is where I should be sitting now cos I'm taking a last few pulls on my fag outside the entrance – under the rusting sign of a faded bluebell – before I join my teammates.

\*     \*     \*

And in the Bluebell, my girls are practising for the game, taking it in turns to throw their darts at the board. Behind the bar, Danny the Landlord – giving his paying customers his rear view – is playing with his newly fitted toy: his CCTV monitors.

I interrupt him. 'Any chance of getting served here?'

Danny turns around, lets his wondering eyes wander up and down my body.

'There's every chance of that, Katy.'

I say that I'm fed up, not hard up, and he shrugs, says that it's my loss. I tell him that he's probably past it anyway, and he pats his stomach and says that he's as fit as a butcher's dog. He's got the dog bit right because he's the spit of an old greyhound; same colour, same knobbly joints, same way of scratching his hair for a hidden flea.

So it's six drinks I buy for the Bluebell Ladies – for Six Of The Best. For Irish (Mary O'Brian): 'Mother's ruin' and tonic. She's a shade on the blowsy side, pushing fifty and always moaning about her gobshite of a husband.

For Maggie: half a cider. 'Cos of the old man.' Won't see sixty again.

For Lena: WK Blueberry. She's twenty-five years old and the biggest flirt in the pub – short skirt, low top and big, big eyes.

For Scottie Dog aka Marie Stewart: whisky and water, 'and go easy with the water.' Lives alone with her cats in a smelly terraced house with a jungle for a garden. Must be seventy if she's a day.

For Pegs: 'Um. Same as you, Katy.' Lives in a park home on a travellers' site. Twenty years old and darkly pretty, but keeps herself that little bit apart like gypos do.

For me: vodka and Coke. Me, Katy Jones, thirty-five, heavy smoker, and thinking my life's over. Well, the fun part of it anyway.

So we sip our drinks, get in some more practice on the board, and wait for the opposition, the Nag's Head ladies' team – 'the Naggers' – to turn up.

Irish, already ordering another drink, says to Danny, 'So what's with that, then?' And nods her curiosity towards Danny's side of the bar, towards the newly set up CCTV screens that are snapping postcard views of the Bluebell.

'Insurance wanted them for security. In case of thieving,' Danny says.

'Who'd want to steal anything from this shithole?' says Irish.

Then Scottie Dog says, 'I bet the perv's put one in our bog.'

Danny laughs. 'Shouldn't think anyone's seen yours in thirty years, Scottie.'

Scottie Dog says, 'A Sassenach's never going to see it, Danny boy.'

Old Bob, standing close, but with his own conversation going on, says, 'Would have been better to spend the money on a pot of paint; place ain't seen a brush since VE Day.'

He's probably right; the ceiling is a dirty yellow from generations of fag smoke, and on the wall by the Gents is an enamel poster for Craven A cigarettes.

Our opponents – that's too strong a word, friendly rivals is better – arrive to start the game. They're a gentle team, about halfway up the table, and that's ambition enough for them.

'Bad luck in the cup this year, Katy,' says their captain as we make the draw. She adds, 'Again.' As if I didn't know.

At least we're putting in some good results in the league. We're a quarter way through the season and lying third behind the Moonies and the Battersby Babes. But you know how sometimes you get the feeling it's your turn, a time for you? Well, that's how it seems to me. I go to sleep at night playing out the games that we've got left, imagining winning – actually winning – the Division One Ladies' League. Jerry reckons I'm obsessed and I cut him a blinder and tell him that's all I've got to look forward to.

And the horrible truth is that it seems to be true.

Anyway, Danny wants some silverware for the shelf behind the bar, and ever since we've been playing here he's said, 'If you lot cut down on the boozing, you'd start winning.'

Lena, leaning forward to show off her boobs, says, 'You're a fine landlord telling us not to drink.' But Danny's not really hearing her; he's fighting a losing battle trying not to look down her top.

So that's where we are on this Monday night, recovering from being knocked out of the cup and wanting to keep this good run going for the rest of the league.

'Nearest bull then, Katy,' says the captain of the Naggers, and promptly launches her arrow into the twenty-five to start pole position in the team game.

I'm first throw on our side and I get us away with a sixty. In fact all of my side score well, but so do the Naggers, and it's a only a fluky treble eighteen that leaves me wanting double sixteen with a dart still in my hand.

Irish, in my ear, whispers, 'Give it fuck, Katy,' and the double seems to beckon my dart in, and we're out. We've won the team game.

I can hear Irish giggling behind me. 'Well, they didn't keep up with the Joneses.'

So it's been close, and gasping for a fag, I head outside for the table and chairs of the smoking area. There's a light rain falling and it's starting to get dark, and I'm thinking, 'Bloody smoking ban, sending me out on a night like this.'

I'm only there a minute when Johnny James comes out through the door rolling up a cancer stick.

'Chilly out here, Katy,' he says and lights up.

Now I don't know what to make of Johnny James. I always seem to be bumping into him. We'll have a chat, a few words about nothing much, but he has this habit of looking directly into my eyes with his deep grey ones and I . . . Well, it's a stupid thing to think, he must be five years – perhaps a little bit more – younger than me, and I'm slightly plump, and how could he possibly be remotely interested? Anyway, I've got enough trouble with one man without going off into a fantasy land with another.

Johnny says, 'How's the game going, Katy?'

'One up, Johnny.'

I'm puffing furiously at my fag, guiltily hoovering up the nicotine when I should be inside encouraging my team. I drop my half-finished habit onto the slab floor and grind it to death with my toes. 'Better get back, check how the girls are doing.'

'See you a bit later?' He holds me with those eyes.

I think he means the next fag break, but it sounds like an invitation to . . . No, it doesn't – he's just being pleasant.

I say, 'I expect you will; I'm out here every hour.' And that sounds like a confirmation to a question not asked.

Inside, Pegs – quiet Pegs – is on the board and she's struggling through her game. The chalkboard shows her inconsistency with a forty-five, a thirty, a twenty-six. When she comes back to the oche, Irish shoves a drink into her hand.

'Get that down yer neck.'

I say, 'Just slow down. Think about it.' As Pegs nervously, quickly, drains a half glass of vodka and Coke.

'That was my drink,' I say to Irish but Pegs has thrown a ton and Irish laughs. 'It went to a good cause, Katy.'

I go to the bar to order up and, from the pool-room side, Johnny James is paying Danny for a pint. When Danny serves mine, he says, 'All done, Katy. Your admirer bought you it.'

'Admirer?'

From the other bar Johnny James raises his glass in a toast.

'Don't be daft, Danny.' But I can feel myself, of all things, starting to blush.

Whenever we play at home, we have support from a quartet of regulars. These are the guys who seem to live in the pub. If I call in for a packet of fags, or if Jerry and I visit on one of our rare nights out together, some of them are always here. Danny calls these waifs and strays 'the Motley Crew', and they drink the day and night away. Jerry says the Bluebell would go bust without them. I tell him Carling would be in dire straits without his contribution to their sales.

He doesn't think this is funny. 'If you slimmed down, you could get in the door to Weight Watchers,' he says quite nastily.

I reckon that if he smartened up he could become a slob.

And that's how it seems to go on between us, this kidding that's not really kidding.


Anyway, our local support – the Motley Crew, from Old Bob, to Paddy, to Jilted John to Pikey Pete (Pegs' cousin) – are fun drunks, not nasty, falling-down, troublemaking drunks. They booze and joke and laugh at each other. Tonight they're in a singing mood, and half-cut, they drift over to watch the game.

So our local support, starved of entertainment, get behind us.

'Come on, the Bluebell girls!'

'Come on, luscious Lena!'

Lena perks up at the attention. She starts to pose on her throw – bottom pumped out, bosom thrust forward. When one of her darts bounces out of the board, and she bends over to pick it up, the whistles and cheers must be heard halfway across town. But this distraction is fatal for Lena and a setback for us. Her game goes to pieces and she's well and truly trounced.

If you couldn't see the next three games you'd know who was playing by the songs the wags of our supporters put together. Scottie Dog gets 'Donald, Where's Your Troosers?' Lead vocals by Old Bob and Pikey Pete.

Maggie gets 'Maggie May', the choir led by Jilted John – and she moans to them that Maggie may not, if they don't give her a bit of hush.

But it's Irish they love, and every time she throws her darts it's 'When Irish's Eyes Are Smiling'. This is started by Paddy, because this is the song he sings every night, without fail, at chucking-out time.

'Saves me shouting "last orders",' says Danny.

Irish tells them they won't be smiling if she doesn't win this effing game, but she keeps her cool and collects her double out as the Naggers fall at the last.

So it's drinks all round – again – and my head's becoming a bit fuzzy. The girls, my girls, are on a high. Maggie, on several ciders too many, keeps saying she 'must go home, cos he really shouldn't be on his own. Okay, I'll just have the one – only the one, mind.'

Even Pegs, our lucky Gypsy mascot, is letting her hair down. The trouble is, the more she drinks, the quicker, the thicker, her traveller accent becomes. 'Dordee, dik o racklee,' she says to Pikey Pete. (Don't ask what it means, I've haven't got a clue.)

What with it having the same effect on Scottie Dog – 'Yee canna tale me thaat,' – and Irish – 'Oi'm ater tinking dis is a greatest day in moi loif,' – there's only half the team speaking proper like.

I'm thinking that I've nearly had enough for one night when Danny lines up a round on the bar.

'For Chrissake, Danny – I'll be on my arse in a minute.'

Irish says, 'Never look a gift horse in the mouth.'

I say, 'I'm off to put a ciggie in mine.'

Outside, in the dim lighting of the leper colony, Johnny James is smoking his roll-up.

'Katy,' he says, feigning a cough, 'I've been through three fags while I'm waiting for you.'

I have to laugh, but inside me I wonder if it's true. The waiting.

As Johnny's going in, he says, 'I'll be out here again at ten. Might see you then?'

'Might do.' The way I say it sounds teasing, like I'm flirting. I make a mental note to steady up on the vodka.

Our fan club has retired to the bar to be closer to the beer, and my girls have commandeered a table to sit at.

'Been on my feet all day,' says Maggie. 'Twice, my Ken went walkabout. Second time he nearly made the bypass.'

I've seen her holding her husband's hand, leading him back to their house through the streets like a scolded schoolboy.

Maggie says, 'They want him to go in a home.'

'I wish I could put Gobshite in a home,' mutters Irish.

'My aunt Zilla had Alzheimer's,' says Pegs. 'She used to get up in the middle of the night, walk round the site like a ghost.'

Lena says to Maggie, 'It must be awful for you.'

I forget sometimes, that there's a side to Lena that's not all boobs and bum. It always surprises me.

Scottie Dog reckons the drink is affecting her waterworks and, because it's contagious, Lena, Irish and I join her in the loos.

I touch up my lipstick, check my eyeliner (can't think why) while Irish, toilet door wide open, carries on a conversation with us as she sits on the bog. Her skirt's bunched up and when she's finished, with a contented sigh, she stands and her skirt drops back to her knees.

Irish goes straight to the sink and Lena says, 'You didn't pull them up?'

'Pull them up?'

'Your knickers.'

'I'm not wearing any.' Irish lifts her skirt and, sure enough, she isn't.

I say, 'You'll catch a chill, Irish.'

Lena says, 'For God's sake don't trip over on the way out.'

Scottie Dog says, 'You'll frighten the horses, Irish.'

Irish reckons she could do with a good stallion. 'Better than the little gobshite I've got at home.' She's combing her hair through her fingers and looking at herself in the mirror above the sink.

She sets up a pose and asks, 'Do yer think I'm getting a little on the plump side?'

Scottie Dog says, 'You're an ample woman, Irish.'

'Ample? What the fuck does ample mean?'

'Fat,' says Scottie Dog, which I think is on the harsh side because I'd say that Irish was just well covered. She's a bit like me, but with a bit more.


You know how a song can take you back years? When we sit ourselves down again the jukebox has been fed and there's a tune on from twenty years ago. I look around this pub where nothing much has changed in all that time. Those words, 'I will always love you', and that gentle insistent tune, used to drift out the back door of the Bluebell as I sat, fifteen years old, on the wooden bench in the warmth of a summer evening. Then, I was desperately wishing to join in the freedom of age, craving to be older. (That one worked out all right, didn't it?)

Jerry would sneak me out a drink – a vodka drowned in Coke so it didn't look suspicious – and he'd bring out his pint. Every window of the pub would be open and the jukebox would track my crush on this laughing boy with his thick mop of brown hair. He was handsome then, Jerry was. He didn't have a paunch and I was as thin as a rake. Those long summer evenings were spent sitting out the back of the Bluebell, sharing cigarettes and talking, always talking. About anything. About nothing.

Jerry had a car – bit of a wreck, mind, and sometimes not taxed – but in that car we'd drive miles. Some Sunday mornings he'd pick me up from home and we'd just drive to anywhere that took our fancy.

And we were happy. So happy.

The day I was sixteen I walked out of school for good, got a job in the packing factory, and told Mum that Jerry and I were looking for a flat.

Mum says sadly, 'Don't you want more than that, Katy?'

But all I want is to hold Jerry every night, wake up beside him in the mornings, and live my life with him.

Mum says, 'You can do all that later, you've got all the time in the world.'

God, I know now how right she was, and suddenly I'm in one of those 'If only I could turn the clock back moods'.

Maggie says, 'Penny for them, Katy.'

I say, 'They're worth nothing,' and the bitterness in my voice surprises even me.

Irish says, 'The mood of her. You'd be thinking we'd just lost the bloody game.'

Maggie says gently, 'C'mon, Katy, buck up a bit.'

I try because I know that Jerry will be here in a minute, and if he sees my long face it'll give him something else to go on about.

So what I do is take my last twenty pound note, the one I'd been saving for midweek shopping, and buy yet another round of drinks. (Afterwards, when everything came to a head, I reckon that this is what did it: that drink.)

I take a huge gulp of my vodka and Coke and then, even more fuzzy-headed, go for a smoke.

\*     \*     \*

There's no one else out here and I sit on the damp bench under a dripping plastic cover and wonder if I'll be sitting here in five, ten, twenty years' time. I might even die out here, some old crone puffing on her last fag, while the world carries on beside her. I've started to feel really sorry for myself, and all because of that bloody song. Even now I can't get it out of my head. *I will always love you.*

Well, I fucking won't. And I fucking didn't.

And then, believe it or not, I start to cry. I put my head in my hands and I cry for a life that's being wasted, for a young girl with all her hopes and dreams standing before her. I cry for a me that was.

That's what Johnny James must have seen: me crying. Perhaps he even stood over me for a minute before . . . before he sat down beside me, put his arm around my shoulders, and drew me gently towards him.

'Katy, whatever's the matter?'

Well, I'm not going to answer that, am I?

So what happens?

What do you think happens? I kiss him, that's what I do. I put my arms around his neck and I kiss him long and hard.

'Jesus, Katy,' he says, and then he kisses me back.

'You're all woman, Katy.' Now he's kissing my neck. He's gentle and warm and his hands are caressing everywhere – and I mean everywhere.

Then he puts his mouth to mine again and it feels like heaven to be wanted so badly. But I need to take a breath, to draw air. 'Johnny,' I say, 'give me a breather.'

I'm saying this, and over his shoulder I can see a pinprick of red light, and it seems to be flickering, pulsing, and . . . and it's a bloody camera. It's Danny's security camera beaming me into the public bar.

I freeze and I've got this image in my head of me – of us – captured in this black-and-white scene of deceit. And what if Jerry's at the bar, leaning over and saying, 'A pint please, Danny'?

And what if, while Danny's pouring up, Jerry scans the CCTV screens and, forever the voyeur, thinks, 'That couple having a snog and more. They're going for it. Hang on. Wait a minute.' He squints at the picture. 'That looks like . . .'

I say to Johnny, 'The camera. The fucking camera.'

He goes, 'Shite, Katy. Do you think anyone . . .?'

Later, Irish says to me, 'He stood at the bar as still as a statue, and Danny was saying, "That'll be three pound twenty." He says it twice and Jerry doesn't move, just stares at that screen, Katy. Then Danny turns around to see what's got Jerry's attention and says "Jesus Christ, isn't that . . .?"'

Irish says, 'And then Jerry walks out, like he's a zombie. He leaves his beer on the counter and, quiet as a mouse, he walks out.' She sighs like she's disappointed. 'He just walks out.'

I say, 'Who knows? Who else saw?'

'Just me and Danny. And he's not a one for the talking.'

We've stayed behind, me and Irish, and the bar's empty, and the jukebox is on automatic, and every fucking song that's playing sounds like a requiem for an act of folly.

I'm drunk. I know that and I'm saying, 'It was only a kiss, Irish. Only a kiss. That's all.'

But inside me I know what it was. It was a little bit of excitement in this dull, boring world where all I've got to do is play darts and get pissed and look after an ungrateful husband and an even more ungrateful daughter.

Danny, washing glasses behind the bar, calls over to me. 'Your taxi'll be here in a minute.'

Irish asks, 'Can you drop me off, Katy?'

When I get home, the house is in darkness and I let myself quietly into the front room where the embers of the fire are still glowing. Jerry's voice comes out the shadows, making me jump.

'Don't turn the light on, Katy.' He's sitting in his usual chair and his words sound muffled.

'Jerry, it wasn't like it looked.'

I want to tell him how I felt, how I wanted things to be, but I don't have the words . . .

Jerry's talking quietly and deliberately, and the meaning is lagging behind his words. I'm thinking about them, digesting them slowly.

'In the morning,' he's saying, 'I want you gone.'

'Gone? Gone? What do you mean, gone? What about Laura?'

He says, 'Me and Laura'll be all right.'

I'm angry now and I'm drunk, and I'm not talking in the dark to someone who doesn't understand what I want, what I need.

I flick on the light and I can see his eyes are red and his cheeks are wet. He's been crying, and for the first time this night I wonder, 'My God, what have I done?'

Then through the drink, through my self-justifying argument, I see me from his side. And I don't like what I see.

Jerry gets up from his chair, wipes his sleeve across his face. 'I'm going up to bed. Your case is in the hall.'

\*  \*  \*

16

I don't sleep. I shovel a bit of coal on the fire, wrap myself in a blanket, light a fag and sit out the night. I wait until dawn sneaks in the window and then, not sure if I'm devastated or not, I go to Mum's.

I suppose I was in some sort of shock. But I was thinking that it'd all blow over, because I hadn't really done anything. Not really.

Mum's kitchen light is on and I can see her through the net curtains of the window. She's hunched over the sink, filling the kettle for her morning cuppa. She must hear the click of the garden gate because she's suddenly still. Listening. Then she lifts the net and peers out, but I'm already at the door, a refugee with a suitcase on her step.

Surprise is not too strong a word for Mum's reaction. 'Katy?' she says. 'What are you doing here so early?' Then her eyes drop to my case and she ushers me in before the neighbours can see.

We sit in Mum's lovely warm kitchen and I drink her sweet tea and eat her hot buttered toast. And I tell her all that's happened. I tell her what's wrong with my life. I tell her why I kissed Johnny James. I tell her everything that I couldn't tell Jerry.

And then I cry. I cry properly. I sob my heart out at her kitchen table in her one-bedroomed house while she strokes my hair and tells me not to worry.

A little later she says, 'What about Laura?'

I'm bitter then. 'She's a daddy's girl.'

Mum just says, 'Oh, Katy, she's yours as well.'

I tell her I don't want anyone to know about me leaving, not yet, but she says that Ellie will be coming round later this week. 'She'll wonder what you're doing here.'

Ellie's my younger sister. Ellie who is everything I'm not: small, slim, pretty, blonde. Six years younger than me. She looks like a china doll, but she's anything but fragile. She'll see me here, and that superior look will drift over her face. She won't actually say these words but it'll be plain. 'Messed up again, Katy.'

This first day I don't set foot outside. I sit and smoke in the front room with the window open and Mum spoiling me. I phone work and pretend I've caught flu.

My manager says, 'Take a few days, Katy; I don't want the whole line going down with it.'

I imagine the girls in assembly, clicking parts together to make a whole. There'll be talk about last night's soaps and jokes. And gossip. Gossip about me.

'Did you know she's been carrying on with that Johnny James? Been going on for months, you know.'

'Such a nice bloke, her husband.'

'Quiet ones are the worst.'

'Well, she was hardly quiet.'

'Caught on the job, round the back of the pub.'

'Having a knee trembler.'

There's a round of dirty laughter.

But I'm hoping that this is my imagination and that the secret – my secret – is kept by Irish, by Danny, by Jerry, by Mum, by my sister, by my daughter. And not forgetting the man himself.

Christ, it's hardly a secret any more.

The second day I go back to my house that isn't really my house and let myself in the back door. The house is empty of sound and I tiptoe around like I'm a burglar. I don't even light up a fag.

On the kitchen table is Laura's school work, and her English exercise book is open. Across a half-finished essay she has scrawled in angry scored words, *I hate Mum*.

If I had any tears left, I think I'd cry again.

I make myself a cup of tea and have to drink it black because there's no milk in the fridge; there's no bread in the cupboard, no veg in the tray. This gives me a feeling of satisfaction.

'Now they'll see what I did.'

So why do I make the beds, hoover the floor, put the dirty washing in the laundry basket? And why do I take Jerry's porn DVDs and dump them in the trash can?

And why do I write in soft gentle words, under Laura's condemnation of me, *I love you*?

This evening me and Mum sit and watch the soaps. We drink tea and nibble on biscuits while the world carries on outside. Just me and Mum. Like it used to be. Like I can remember before she married and had Ellie.

Mum says, 'You were only four, Katy.'

But I do remember, and now I'm thirty-five and I'm in this limbo of not knowing what to do.

'You've got to do what's right.'

It's okay for Mum to say that but I don't know what is right any more. So I say to her, 'Then why did you marry Jim?'

Because if ever there was a mistake, that was it. You know, when we left, I never called him Dad again, even when he used to pick up Ellie on a Sunday. She would come back clutching the latest CD and talk of Big Macs and Mr Whippy and toffee popcorn and rides in the theme park.

But he never took me.

'Why did you marry him?'

Mum's gone very quiet. 'Because it seemed the right thing . . . the only thing to do.' Then she adds, so quietly that I almost don't hear it, 'At the time.'

And after that there's no more chat about Dad – Jim – this night.

About eleven o'clock, just as I'm tucking myself into Mum's sofa bed, my phone rings. It's a number I don't know and, when I answer, I'm ready to give someone a bollocking for calling this late. But the voice says, 'Katy, it's me. I'm outside.'

And the voice belongs to Johnny James.

And when I look out of the window I can see the glow of his cigarette as he loiters with intent in the darkness at Mum's gate.

# THURSDAY NIGHT DARTS PRACTICE

*Katy*

Thursday nights is darts practice at the Bluebell and I've half a mind not to go, but because I'm captain I feel obliged to show.

When I get there the girls are already throwing at the board, and Irish has me a vodka and Coke on the table.

'I knew it would take more than that to keep you away,' she says.

I suppose there're a few curious looks towards me, but I'm only today's news – a little excitement to stir boring lives. What surprises me is that I don't really care what anyone thinks.

Now there's the six of us here and usually we just have a couple of drinks and go home early. But tonight my girls sit me down and keep the vodka flowing. Of course they want to know what's going on and I say, catching Irish's eye, 'Bit of a row with Jerry. Need to cool off at Mum's for a couple of days. You know what it's like.'

They all nod in understanding, even Pegs who can't have a clue what I mean.

I say to her, 'Stay away from men. They only bring trouble.'

Irish says, 'Get yerself a friendly rabbit, Pegs,' and laughs until she nearly chokes.

But Pegs' eyes are flitting to the bar where Big Dave Trinder, all of twenty-one years old, is hunching his shoulders in his leather jacket and trying to look cool. He's nursing a pint and casually flicks his gaze around the bar room.

Only when it falls on Pegs, it lingers.

'You've got an admirer,' Maggie tells her, and that word reminds me of the other night when my trouble started.

Scottie Dog, scratching her boob, adds, 'I wouldn't mind getting into his van on a dark night.'

Pegs mumbles, 'It's nothing like that.' She picks up her darts and throws at the board.

Irish says to her back, 'Nothing like what, Pegs?' and she doesn't answer.

But later, when she goes up to buy the drinks, they have a chat – her and Big Dave Trinder. I'm watching her like a mother – I mean, an older sister – and there's an easiness to their talk, as though the ice has been broken, as though they already know each other quite well. Seems like Pegs is a bit of a dark horse and perhaps she's already been in the passenger seat of his Transit van.

What am I doing? I've enough problems of my own without brewing up a romance that's none of my business. I feel guilty then because I should be worrying about Laura. I should be sorting things out with Jerry.

'Tomorrow,' I tell myself. 'I'll phone then.'

Tomorrow seems a long time away, and meanwhile I'll be practising darts as normal. I'll be drinking vodka and Coke as usual. I'll be going out for a fag as usual.

But Johnny James won't be there as usual.

I sit in the designated smoking area – that's what Danny calls it – and smoke two fags in quick succession. Then I give a Vs-up to that bloody camera and go in to my girls.

About half ten, when Paddy starts to sing, we begin to drift off to our homes: the girls to their old ones and me to my new one. We leave Danny saying, 'Jesus Christ, Paddy, why'd you do that? There's still a half hour to go.'

Mum's waiting when I get back and she makes me a mug of cocoa. We sit by the gas fire and I give her the other gossip: the stuff that's not about me. We're friends, me and Mum, and it's just the two of us. No ghost of Jim issuing his orders. No spoilt sister monopolising attentions. We sit and talk and I tell her about next Monday's league game, about Pegs, about Big Dave Trinder. Mum says that it wouldn't work because Pegs is a traveller and they live differently – she whispers it – 'than us'.

And that reminds me of Jim and his rants on everything under the sun: foreigners, Mrs Thatcher, his boss, but most of all Gypsies.

'That lot,' he'd say. 'Hitler had the right idea; stick 'em all in the gas chamber.'

He even signed the petition to move them on from the Station Yard. He and Mum had a row about that.

'They've been there for ages, coming and going. Don't do no harm to anyone.'

'You would say that.'

'What do you mean?'

Then they'd be off like . . . Well, like me and Jerry.

Only it was much worse for Mum because Jim was quick with his fists where she was concerned.

Next morning – I'm on day five and counting – I phone Jerry early and tell him I want to meet Laura.

He says, 'I'll have to ask her.'

'Ask her? She's my daughter.'

'I'll have to ask her.'

I'm angry then. He's being obstructive, deliberately making it bloody difficult. I conveniently forget she doesn't answer her phone to me.

'I'll be there when she comes home from school, Jerry,' I hiss.

'Look, you're the one who fucked about. You're the one who left us. You're the one who . . .'

He doesn't finish because I don't let him. I hang up on him wishing I was hanging him up by his scrawny neck.

I let myself into *our* house – my name's still on the tenancy book – and make a cup of tea. Now there's milk in the fridge and sugar in the bowl, and the larder is full. I check the living-room carpet. Clean. I check the beds. All made. I check the airing cupboard. All ironed – yes, ironed – and clothes stacked neatly on the shelves. The only room that's still up for slum clearance is my daughter's.

I'm downstairs again when the front door rattles open and Laura comes in.

'Mum.' She says it just like she's saying hi to someone she doesn't particularly like.

'I wanted to see you, Laura; to explain things.'

'Dad said that, but there's no need. I know what you did.'

*What I did?* Probably half the town knows what I did by now. But only I know why I did it.

And while all of this is going on in my head, Laura, my fifteen-, soon-to-be-sixteen, year-old daughter, goes under the sink for a bowl of potatoes.

Then she starts to peel them with the knife I always use.

'Laura, what are you doing?'

'Dad's tea. He'll be home in half an hour.'

She says it matter-of-factly, this younger version of me. This girl who wouldn't even lift her legs when I was vacuuming. This girl who wouldn't wash a cup, who stayed in her room night after night, streaming the same song over and over again at full volume.

And then she says, 'I'm thinking of giving up school to look after Dad.'

'You can't, Laura.'

'I can.'

'You can't.'

She looks at me coolly, like she's a woman. Like she's my equal.

'You did. You left school at my age.'

I suppose my mouth is open in amazement and I'm popping like a goldfish out of water. I want to tell her it was so different then but she carries on.

'Dad'll be back soon. I think you'd better go.'

I've cried a lot in the last few days, but I'm fucked if I'm going to let her see me cry now. I never thought that she would be so remote, so unreachable. So cruel.

My own flesh and blood throwing me out; well, ordering me to leave my own house.

I start to mumble something about coming round again in a day or two but Laura cuts me off abruptly.

'Bye, Mother.'

She holds the back door open and tells me goodbye. I light a fag and make sure I leave in a cloud of smoke like the Wicked Witch of the West. Or is it the east?

I'm so pissed off. So misunderstood. So misjudged, and all I've got to look forward to is a flat, dull weekend and darts on Monday.

# A SATURDAY NIGHT IN OCTOBER
# AT THE BLUEBELL

## Still Katy

Saturday evening, miserable and moping, I'm stuck at Mum's watching TV and criticising her favourite programmes. I'm really getting on her nerves.

'For God's sake, Katy,' she says, 'can't you phone one of your friends, get out from under my feet?'

It's almost as if I were the teenage girl again.

I walk on down to the Bluebell, my home from home from home, and the Motley Crew are there. Been there all day going by the state of them. They're crowded around a half-hearted fire, and, above the mantelpiece, the mirror on the wall reflects misspent youth, red-veined middle age and blue-nosed addiction.

But they're so happy, this alcoholic family. So nice. They might be a bit unsteady on their feet, they might laugh at ridiculous situations, but they embrace me in welcome.

'It's the lovely Katy,' says Jilted John, who got his nickname because he was dumped twice at the altar.

'The best-looking girl in here,' says Old Bob.

I'm the only female in the pub but I like the girl bit.

At the bar, Danny's poured my drink without being asked.

'How's things?'

'Not too bad, Danny.'

'No?'

'All right, they're shit. I'm living at Mum's, my daughter won't talk to me, my money's running out fast and everyone thinks I'm a tart.'

'Could be worse then.'

I have to laugh; nothing seems to faze Danny. All those years behind the bar, I suppose.

Lena comes in a bit later with a gaggle of lookalikes, all boobs and bums and bare flesh under mountains of hair. All giggles, lipstick, eyeshadow and strong perfume on a girls'-only night out.

'We're off to the club,' she says. 'Why don't you come with us?'

I look at them and their colour and youth and then I imagine me, overweight, with a hairstyle five years out of date and a dress sense stuck in the last decade. Me go with them? I'd look like a retard on a day out.

'Another time, Lena.'

'Sure. Anyway, see you on Monday.'

As quickly as they arrive they leave, drinks knocked back and quick visits to the loo over. They take their freshness and colour with them and leave me with just my envy for company.

I sit at the bar, chat to Danny, while people drift in and out. Most of them I know; as I said before, it's a small town. Some speak, some nod, and some – Jerry's workmates – pretend not to see me. About half nine, I pop out for a fag and Johnny James is sitting at the smokers' table.

'I knew you'd have to come out sometime, Katy.' He says this with a laugh in his throat.

He's smartly dressed tonight. He wears an open shirt with a light jacket over it and it reminds me of how young he is, and that's another reminder of dowdy old me.

'I'll come in, buy you a drink.'

'Johnny,' I say, 'there's enough trouble going on without making it worse.'

'I expect we're being watched now.' He looks to where the red button of light blinks in nosy surveillance at us.

I'm finishing my fag as he says slowly, deliberately, 'If you won't let me buy you a drink here, will you come back to mine later?'

I want to tell him that he's too young, too tempting, too good-looking, too dangerous for faded, jaded me. I don't want him to break my heart.

I say, 'I can't, Johnny. I can't.'

He stands up, moves close enough to touch. Close enough for me to want to touch him.

'Katy,' he says, 'the other night. It wasn't a one-off, you know. Not for me.'

I can't answer. I shouldn't answer. I can only shake my head as I brush past him.

So what do I do? I go back in the pub, throw a few more voddies down my neck till I'm past caring, and then make my way to Mum's.

\* \* \*

I'm nearly there, nearly to my new home, when Johnny James glides up in his big BMW and lets the window down.

'Do you want a lift, Katy?'

I tell him I've only got a few yards to go and he says for me to jump in anyway because it's no trouble and the streets aren't safe for a good-looking woman this late at night. I don't know if it's him and his smart car, or me and my need of being held, or maybe all of that. But I get in and I don't get to Mum's until the next morning, and by then I've done everything that Jerry thought we had.

So fucking there.

# MONDAY NIGHT DARTS IN LATE OCTOBER
## THE BLUEBELL VERSUS THE
## PHOENIX AWAY FROM HOME

*Irish*

Gobshite says, 'You won't be too late tonight?'

His thick Belfast accent that used to chant for Ireland's Thirty-Two hasn't altered a shade in the long years I've known him. Loved him.

Gobshite is lounging on our bed, smoking. His wet hair is palmed back from his forehead and he's watching me get dressed. His tongue is flicking across his lips like a snake.

'I'll be as late as it takes, Michael.' I silently add on *Gobshite*.

He slips off the bed while I'm still in my bra and stockings and makes a grab for me. I slap his hands away.

'For fuck's sake, Michael, not now.'

'So when you come back; when you're a bit tipsy?'

'Depends if we've won or not.'

I'm saying this but the burning's starting inside of me and he knows this. He knows me so well.

'Irish,' he says – even he calls me Irish – 'you'll show me when you get home?'

'Michael, I'll show you.'

I'm affected now, really affected, and I have to leave now or else I won't be able to.

'Think of me,' he says as I'm closing the bedroom door behind me.

He knows what'll be in my head all night; he's a bastard is Gobshite.

Now in the ritual of every time I leave the house, even if it's just a visit to the shops, I kiss the tip of my finger. Then I touch the cheek of my child who laughs at me from his fading image on the hallway wall.

'Goodnight, Davey,' I whisper. 'Sleep tight. Don't let the bedbugs bite.'

But there won't be any bedbugs, not where Davey lies.


I'm the last to arrive at the Bluebell. Katy has pulled the drinks in and she looks tired, a bit detached.

'How's it going?'

She shakes her head. 'Not too good, Irish. Not too good.'

'Take it out on the darts,' I say.

I join Pegs, Maggie, Scottie Dog and Lena having a few practice throws before our game at the Phoenix, before Danny, our taxi, ('Hurry up, I've got a pub to run') herds us out to cram into his 4x4.


The Phoenix is a modern pub: one big open bar, a jukebox that vibrates the glass in the windows with enough noise to drown any attempt at conversation. By the way I judge it, I think I must be getting old.

And age reminds me of sleepy country pubs, the slow tick of the clock, and halves of Guinness on hot afternoons. It reminds me of wet evenings and the bus to Dublin to the darkness of the cinema.

It reminds me of Michael and his visits from the North when we were young.

So we're not keen on playing here in this shiny new Phoenix. Well, except for Pegs, who's no age. And Lena, who actually likes it here. And Katy, who looks like she couldn't care where she was. Maggie's tapping her foot to a rap song about stabbing a policeman, or something like that, and even Scottie Dog is laughing with the barman.

All right, so it's me who's not keen on playing here.

Our opponents, the Phoenix Vixens, can only pull in four players so that gives two of us a free outing. We look at Captain Katy and she says, 'I'll stand down.'

I say, 'And me,' before anyone else can get a word in.

I keep Katy company when she goes for a fag and outside it's already dark. There's a bunch of smokers forming a circle of exiles in the doorway, drawing ravenously on their glowing cigarettes, standing in their halfway house, torn between a wanting for beer and a craving for tobacco.

Katy and I sit down, and I say, 'So are you going back then?'

'I don't want to go back.'

'Johnny James?'

'Best not go there, Irish.'

She looks miserable. It's as though the world is settling onto her shoulders.

'The thing is, Irish, I'm not even sure what I want.'

I start, 'Laura . . .'

She snaps, 'The whole fucking world doesn't revolve around Laura.'

'Sorry, Katy.'

'No, I'm sorry, Irish. Sorry for this whole fucking mess.'

Then her mobile beeps a text message, and she stares at the screen.

'Irish,' she says. 'I've got to go.'

'What about the darts?'

'I've got to go.'

And she gets up and walks away, just like that.

Inside, Lena's won her game and Scottie Dog is down to a double.

Maggie says, 'Where's Katy?'

I say, 'Bad week. Wrong week,' and they all nod with the understanding of sisterhood.

The match is over without the loss of a leg and I'm glad to be heading for home. I want to be out in the air, away from the continual throb of loud music and the shouted conversation. It's still early, well before ten, and I don't join the girls for a trip back to the Bluebell.

I say, yawning, 'I'm due an early night.'

I walk home in the evening of this English town, where a drizzle of soft rain is settling on the pavements, dribbling into gutters. I'm passing street pubs, crowded centre pubs, the alley pubs where the old boys click down their dominoes. It's become an almost familiar comfort: the roads, the buildings; but how I miss the green of County Meath.

How I miss that time of innocence when I first met Michael.

\*　　\*　　\*

He's strange, is Michael. He stays with his uncle on a lonely farm miles from town, but he's not a farm boy; he's tall and light on his feet — you can tell that he's not sat on his arse all day on a tractor.

If me and Dad meet him on the lanes, his greeting, 'Good day to yer' is in the harsh accent of the North. Sometimes he comes to the bar of the Fountain Hotel and takes the Guinness steadily for a couple of hours: Guinness and cigarettes in equal measures. He'll sit in the corner, his back to the wall, and watch the door like he's expecting someone.

The barmaid, Rosie O'Hara, reckons he's a man of mystery, and if she can't get any information out of him, no one can. She also reckons that he's too good-looking to be on his own, and if she was on the right side of forty she'd be after having a crack at him herself. But, to be sure, nobody bothers him much except to ask after the health of his uncle.

'Sure, he's fine and why wouldn't he be?' is all they'll get in answer and question.

But he'll catch me with a look, with a hint of a smile, on his way out. He'll hold my eyes and then nod. 'A goodnight to you, young lady.'

And I'm thinking he's a cheeky sod because he must only be three or four years older than me anyway. Then one night, he's waiting for me outside the hotel bar, and he says, 'I'll walk you home, Mary.'

He takes my arm.

We talk and it's not the monosyllabic young man of before. He tells me of the life in Belfast, of vibrancy, of the sights, of the clubs. He talks quickly; he makes me feel like a country bumpkin, a bog trotter.

When I ask about the Troubles, 'Is it like in the newspapers?', he thinks for a minute.

'Sometimes it's bad,' he says abruptly and I don't ask again.

We stop at the corner to my house and he turns me to him, slips his arms around my waist, tells me I'm the most beautiful girl he's ever seen. Then he kisses me long and hard. I'm telling myself that I should struggle, that I should protest, that he shouldn't think I'm easy. But the night is concealing, and his body fits the length of mine. And although I hardly know him, I want more.

I've been kissed before, gone further even – though that never comes out at confession – but this is something different.

'Saturday,' he whispers, 'I'll borrow the old fella's car and take you out.'

Then Dad's dogs start to bark and the porch light comes on and Michael melts away.

And as he melts away the yearning starts.

But Michael doesn't come for me on Saturday. His uncle says to me, after Sunday church, 'He had to go. Urgent job came up.' He passes me an envelope.

Michael has written, 'Mary, I'll be back next weekend, then we'll have our day out.'

He signs off with a single x.

And that's how it is with Michael; he comes and he goes. He works on his uncle's farm for a few weeks at a time. 'Got to help the old fella out,' he says. Then he's up to the North for a building project. But there's never a number to phone or an address to write to.

'I'm always moving about, Mary,' he says.

So it's him who contacts me, him who rings in the dead of the night, and me who answers in our cold, tiled hallway, with the nosy moon peeping through the window.

Dad calls through the thin bedroom wall to me, 'Why can't he be phoning at a decent hour, Mary?'

I catch Mam's muffled something about being young once.

And I whisper my yeses to Michael as he tells me what he's going to do, what we're going to do, when we meet up.

'Just hurry back,' I say to him and I'm sure he hears the tremor in my voice.

Then Dad bangs on the wall. 'For Christ's sake, Mary, I've got to be up at six,' and Michael signs off with a promise.

And it's that promise that's on his mouth when I meet him at the station a week later.

Oh, the drug of himself. I live for the times he's back, for our love in the secret places. But sometimes there's no waiting, there can't be. Sometimes I'll meet him off the train and in the back of Patrick O'Rourke's grubby old taxi we'll start.

And that's how it is with Michael. That's how it always is with Gobshite.


The house is in darkness when I let myself in, and I call out, 'Michael, are you there?'

There's no noise. No sound. I don't click the lights on as I feel my way from the entrance hall, up each step of the stairs and into the inky blackness of the bedroom, where the heavy curtains are drawn tight to block out the light from the street. He's in here; I'm sure I can hear him breathing.

'Michael, answer me. I'm scared.'

My voice is barely more than a whisper and I'm already trembling with excitement.

The next morning Michael's gone before I'm even up, before I've brushed the bitter taste of last night's drink from my mouth. I vaguely remember him slipping from our sleepy warm bed, vaguely remember the front door closing behind him, vaguely remember the car starting in the drive. Michael's off to do his business, of what I don't ask, never ask, because the Cause never dies. It might be hidden behind the curtains, it might slumber in a warm bedroom, it might be behind the façade of a respectable job, but it's always there.

This Tuesday morning finds me down the stairs at eight o'clock. I boil an egg, turn a bit of toast, sit in my drudgery and read yesterday's news. And I envy.

I envy Katy her affair.

I envy Lena her youth.

I envy Scottie Dog her cats.

I envy Pegs her Gypsy freedom.

And I envy Maggie a husband who's dependent on her.

So on this morning of another endless day, I do what I always do; I replay the past.

*I'm eighteen years old, and my home – our home – is a downstairs flat on the outskirts of Belfast. I've been with living with Michael for just three weeks when, of a Saturday morning, the car's outside of our door. Michael's just going for a newspaper and I'm watching him through the window. He stops, looks at the car, opens the door, looks inside. Then he looks at me through the glass and he doesn't smile at me like he usually* does. He doesn't go for his paper, he comes back inside the house.

'That car,' he says, putting on his coat. 'I've got to take it to a friend.'

I snatch up my coat and purse and follow him out.

'I'll come with you.'

''Tis all right.'

'I'll come with you.'

'There's no need, I won't be an hour.'

But lovelorn and headstrong me streaks around to the passenger side and gets in the car.

I'm laughing but Michael's not.

'Mary, get out.'

I'm not moving and he's glancing up and down the street and looking at his watch like his life depended on the time. Then he opens my door, grabs me by the wrist, tries to yank me from the car. 'Get yerself fucking out, Mary.'

He's hurting my arm and young fiery me wedges my feet in the footwell. I'm definitely not for the moving now. I don't know what would have happened next if the police car hadn't been driving slowly up our road. A row would have been the least of it.

Michael lets go of me like he's been scalded. He hisses through his teeth, 'Suit yer fucking self,' and his face seems to contain all the anger of the world but he takes himself casually to the driver's seat.

'Act normal,' he says as the police draw abreast.

He leans across and kisses me on the mouth and I bite hard onto his lip.

He flinches and mutters, 'Just wait, Mary. Just you wait.'

The police car has stopped across the road and it looks like they're checking out vehicles. Michael starts the motor. 'Jesus, we've got to get out of here.'

We edge away and he keeps his eyes on the mirror until we're in the traffic. He's sucking his lip.


So we drive into the city, into the Saturday morning traffic; Michael and me, and the baby I haven't told him about.

I'm chattering on about this lovely motor, about how big, how luxurious it is and, 'Do you think that one day, Michael, we'll be able to afford something like this?'

'One day,' he says. 'Everything will be all right one day.' He looks at his watch every few seconds; he looks at the clock on the dashboard, at every church tower we pass. He mutters to himself, 'Jesus, you'd think there'd be a second to spare.'

I say, 'What for, Michael?'

And he says, 'It's how it works.'

I'm nervous now. 'What is it? What's the matter?'

Michael says, 'You're in this now. Like it or fucking not, Mary.'

My Michael has gone. This stranger here is not my night-time lover who holds me so close and whispers of what we can do to each other.

My Michael has gone and this man is cold and hard.


We're in the city now and we slow, almost stop, alongside a block of flats where a bold sign states:

Security – Restricted Parking – Permit Holders Only.

Then a strange thing happens; a car the same colour, the same make – basically the same car as ours – pulls out from the parking lot and we glide into our twin's place.

40

*And then that's it. Our ride is over, the delivery is done. Michael opens the glove compartment, takes out a yellow parking permit and sits it on the dashboard. Then he says, short and sharp, 'Out.'*

*I grab my coat and already he's locking the doors and then he's striding away and I'm almost running to keep up with him.*

*God knows where he takes me. It's through a maze of back-streets and alleys, and walls topped in concrete, broken glass and barbed wire. There're burnt-out cars and potholed roads and an air of hard despair in shattered, derelict houses. On brick walls the legends of 'Free Derry', 'Prodees out' and 'Fuck the Queen' are spray-painted on brick, on concrete. We're watched; boys circle us on bicycles and housewives, grouped on corners, turn to stare. Then we're in a small square, and then inside a crowded dingy bar where Michael buys a pint and a half of Guinness and we sit at a small table and watch the door.*

*'What are we doing, Michael?'*

*'We're waiting for Leary, that's what we're doing.'*

*I'm feeling in my coat, rummaging through my pockets.*

*'What's the matter?' he says.*

*'My purse, Michael; I can't find it. I must have dropped it.'*

*'Dropped it? Where could you have dropped it? Christ, not in the fucking car.'*

*He says this so loud that heads tilt towards us.*

*'Michael, it's only a purse. There's a fiver in it, that's all.'*

*'That's all? No letters? No ID?'*

*'A fiver, Michael. A fiver.'*

*'Christ, Mary.'*

\*   \*   \*

*I feel like I'm in some crazy dream. Things aren't making sense. Michael's not making any sense in this bar where the tricolour is pinned to the wall and, in an ancient photo, in sunlight and dust, a ragged line of volunteers march towards the camera. The date, handwritten, marks the title and the year as 'The Boys of Killarney. 1919'.*

*Then Leary comes in and the bar's noise and bustle stutters to a halt. How do I know it's Leary? I know because he fits into the disjointed unreality of this day. He owns these moments of averted eyes and shuffled feet, and drinks stopped in mid-pour.*

*'Michael,' he says. ''Tis time to go.'*

*His eyes, as cold and hard as glass, sweep over me.*

*'You,' he says. 'You as well.'*

*He turns and I can't think to argue as Michael takes my arm and leads me after this man.*


*Outside there's a car with its engine running and before we're in the back seat there's a rumble of an explosion from across the city. The pavement shudders, the houses tremble. A startled cat leaps off a garden wall, bounces off a dustbin. Then, catching up, there's the whoomph of the blast, the blowing apart of bodies, of lives.*

*We leave the city before the sirens, before the ambulances, before the Brits seal the roads. And before an hour's gone we're over the border.*


I live this day, over and over. This day from more than a quarter of a century ago. I can't see what happened, but I know what happened: the army patrol, the squaddies who are no more than boys in big boots, who are all some mother's son. The corporal's eyes flicking across a scene where nothing is out of place. Right cars, right number plates. I bet he's thinking that it's all hunky-dory and he says, 'Okay, lads.'

But it's not, because the Watcher, from his attic hideaway, is slowly pressing the buttons into the number of the Beast and it ends the world for this pack of Brits.

And I can't tell anyone. I dare not tell anyone. There's an invisible thread that forever demands the complicity of silence. I sip my tea, listen to the radio, try and read the newspaper while that day breathes again.

Dies again.

*Leary, taking my face in his fingers, looking into me with those cold, cold eyes. 'If ever,' he says, 'if you ever tell a soul of what you think you know, it won't only be you that pays.' Then he says my ma and da's names: 'Mr and Mrs David Donalee.' And still gripping my face with those cruel, cruel fingers, he says the address: 'Ford Farm, Kinnerley, Co. Meath.'*

*Then he lets me go and thrusts a thick, brown envelope at Michael.*

*'You take this and you get yerself to England. You disappear, you understand? You fucking disappear for a while and take this stupid bitch with you.'*

*So we cross the water and for three whole years we live in a collection of first-floor flats in Kilburn.*

*Michael likes Little Ireland, as he calls it.*

*'Like a home from home.'*

*For him there's the pubs, the craic, the painted ladies of the parade – the Mary Magdalenes of the profession.*

*I hate it. I hate the concrete pavements, the neglected streets, the remnants of McAlpine Fusiliers who drink their dole and sing of a country that's long gone, of a land they'll never see again.*

*And in this time, this exile from Ireland, Davey's born. He learns to crawl, to walk, to show a smile that would break your heart.*

*He's mine, is Davey. He belongs to me. All the days that Michael is away, Davey shares with me. All those nights his firm little body lies in my arms and his breath softly fans my face.*

Like I said, I hated those three years in Kilburn but if I could call them back now I'd call them back forever. But in this here and now Gobshite comes home for tea and we make small-talk like any other middle-aged couple.

Gobshite says, 'Yer day? How was yer day?'

'Fine. How was your day?'

'Fine.' After this exchange he gets up from the table and switches the telly on and we don't talk again for another hour. Not until he gives me that look, yawns and says, 'It's been a long day, Mary.'

'Oh, are you tired, Michael? Do you want to go to bed?'

'Bed? What are you offering, yer fucking tart?'

The game has started again.

The next morning I'm up before Gobshite and I make him his breakfast. He comes down the stairs without his shirt. He's starting to run to fat and it ripples over the band of his belt.

But I know it's not only himself.

I stand in front of the mirror most days, take off my clothes, smooth my skin over my hips, lift up my drooping breasts, tense my slack arse.

You know, you'd have to look real closely to see any stretch marks, the signs that I carried my baby for the full nine months. But I search out these blemishes of flesh for comfort, for confirmation that Davey grew inside of me.

I cry then. I cry for all the wasted years. I cry for all I've got left in my life. I cry for the Michael that I glimpsed, for the Gobshite that's in his place, for the cold heart of the terrorist.

But most of all I cry for my Davey.


Later, I have a shower and try to kill time. Gobshite's going to be away for a couple of days and I'm between jobs at the moment. Well, not just at the moment, but for the last few months. I know I should be working because I need things to fill my days, but I can't seem to find the enthusiasm. Outside, the sky's grey and rain is washing the window and I'm thinking again of those dingy flats and the constant moving of the early days. I'm thinking of me in a strange city, me and my Davey and the quiet of the nights when Gobshite was away.


*And away he was with no notice, no warning. It might be a postcard with plane times, with ferry times. Or it might be a stranger in a pub sidling up to Gobshite and saying, 'Wednesday. Fishguard. Two thirty.'*

*I never asked, he never told, but we both knew.*

*But then there was the homecoming.*

\*  \*  \*

I let the phone ring for a long time and Gobshite, worse for the drink, says, 'I thought you were never going to fucking answer.'

I say calmly, sweetly, 'I was in the bath, Michael, and now I'm standing here with just a towel around me.' I add, 'Nothing else, just a towel and it's hardly covering me at all.'

Gobshite says, 'Jesus Mary, I wish you hadn't told me that. Yer fucking tart.'

And then I tell him what I'd like him to do when he gets home.

And I tell him because we only have each other.

And all we've got, all that makes life bearable, is this sex. It's our escape. My escape. His escape. I let it fill my head, fill my existence, make this living tolerable. Just tolerable.

I used to think that God would understand, make allowances for innocent involvement. But He brought no comfort, church brought me no comfort, and my confessions were incomplete. I stopped getting up on Sunday morning and I would scream at Michael, 'How can you go? After what you did, after what happened to Davey. How can you take the Communion?'

Michael says, Gobshite says, 'We need God with us in this struggle.' Then he says very quietly, almost to himself, 'And Davey is with God.'

So it's not love that keeps us together. It's hate, this perverted physical need that's never quite fulfilled. It's hate and secrets and grief. That's why we can never, never be apart.

Me and Gobshite forever or till death us do part.

Later, in the afternoon, I phone around the girls to see who fancies throwing a few darts at the board and the taking of a drink or two – or three. I want something to look forward to because all my memories are careering down a one-way street. I need something to put the brakes on before I go mad, before that terrible thought in my mind grows into a giant beanstalk.

# MONDAY NIGHT DARTS IN NOVEMBER
## THE BLUEBELL VERSUS THE DRAPER'S ARMS

*Maggie*

Ken's difficult to get out of bed this morning; he's hardly helping at all. I have to cajole and pester, help him to a sitting position – he seems to be getting heavier, flabbier, by the day – drag his pyjama trousers down and then slip off his top while he stares at the bedroom television, his pacifier.

Then I dress him, lead him to the kitchen and turn that television on. (It's a good job I don't have to buy a licence for every set in this house.) He watches the morning news – at least, I think he does – as I spoon-feed him his cereal. When he's had enough, he clamps his mouth shut.

'Come on, Ken, try a bit more.'

He doesn't speak; he shakes his head slowly from side to side, this man who should be enjoying his retirement within the world he's known, not this man whose eyes don't seem to recognise what's before him.

'Another mouthful, that's all, Ken.'

I nearly say, 'For Mummy,' because this is what it feels like.

So we're in the routine of a thousand days: these years of living with this. These years of broken sleep, of bed-wetting, of endless care and worry.

Around mid-morning, Kayleigh calls in for a cup of tea.

'How's Dad?'

'He's in the lounge watching telly.'

She gives me that look that tells me there's more to come.

'I didn't ask where he was, Mum, I asked how he was.'

'The same. Just the same.'

'Mum, he's getting worse by the week. You know what the doctor said.'

'They don't know everything.'

'Mum, he should be in a home where they can care for him.'

'I care for him.'

Kayleigh touches my arm, takes my hand, looks directly, softly, into my eyes.

'I know you do, Mum. But it's too much.'

'Soon, Kayleigh. We'll sort it out soon.'

I'm lying and she knows I'm lying and she can't say. So she changes the subject.

'I'll come about seven tonight, in time for your darts.'

My darts. My going out two nights a week for a few hours while Kayleigh stays with her dad. She'll sit and talk to him like I do, show him photos of when our life was normal. Show him pictures of sunny beaches, of snowy days and Christmas afternoons, of the three of us. The complete family.

'Do you remember this, Dad? What about that holiday? It was so hot.'

She'll try to see behind those blank eyes, to look into the mind of a father she once had. A father who can't wander down the garden path without getting lost.

Sometimes I forget that I'm not the only one in this situation.

Even now, after all of this, like Kayleigh, I look for something of the old Ken behind this shutter that's fallen over his mind, behind his grunted, unintelligible speech.

I still sleep with him, still hold him while he dreams. And I wonder if in those dreams he's the old Ken.

Once, I was in that limbo between sleep and waking and I'm sure I heard him say, quite clearly, 'I love you, Maggie.'

That woke me properly and all night I lay in the dark, hoping, wishing, praying that a miracle was taking place. So as not to break the spell I got up at my usual time, made him his usual breakfast, and, as usual, went to wake and dress him. But there was no miracle, no going back. His movements were slow and clumsy and he looked at me like he didn't know me.

Everything was as usual.

When this thing happened, when all the warnings could not be ignored any more, when all the telltale signs added up to a conclusion, it was this day; it was him saying:

'I stopped at the end of the road, Maggie. I couldn't remember what number we were.'

On his face is a perplexion of a smile, a bewilderment that creases his forehead.

'I don't know what's the matter with me.'

He talks of overwork, of tiredness, of stress, while I hold his *hand across the kitchen table. He wants a reassurance from me that everything is fine in our world. And I give him that reassurance even though inside me that coil of unease, of worry, starts to tighten.*

At seven, Kayleigh's knock is on the door.

'Mum, you there?'

Where else would I be? What else would I be doing this time of night? The same thing I've done over and over and over again till I want to scream.

So tonight I'm out with the girls. Before I go, there's the ritual of just checking Ken, of leaving him with a smudge of lipstick on his cheek: leaving my mark on him. For a few brief hours I'm stepping out of being a mother, a carer, an occasional lover.

I'm sixty-two years old and I didn't want my life to be like this.

I walk down to the Bluebell and I'm the last to arrive, to make it Six of the Best.

Pegs and Lena are on the oche. Scottie Dog is in the loo. Irish is already lining up her drinks, and Katy looks awful. She's smudged under her eyes and she looks tired out. She's sitting at a table with the Remnants – the team from the Draper's Arms – pulling out the draw.

'Maggie,' she says, turning over the cards, 'you've got Debbie.'

Just my luck to get their best player.

Katy goes through the list while I have a warm-up throw and grab a swallow from my half of cider.

Lena says, 'Have a vodka in it. Calm your nerves.'

She's dressed like she's up for a night on the town: short tight skirt, short tight top. And her hair – so much hair – curly and blonde; I'm sure it wasn't that shade last week. And her eyes, always flitting around the room. She's a flirt, is Lena.

'Anything in trousers.' Scottie Dog laughs.

'Better without the trousers,' Lena says. 'What do you think, Pegs?'

Pegs says quietly, 'I wouldn't know, Lena.'

'Wouldn't know? What about you and Dave Trinder?'

Pegs starts to say, 'But we ain't—' when Scottie Dog interrupts.

'Don't tell her a thing.'

But Lena persists. 'Haven't you, Pegs? Ever?'

Pegs is colouring up and Scottie Dog says meaningfully, 'Perhaps she's a bit fussier than you, Lena.'

'Cheeky cow,' says Lena.

'Moo,' says Scottie Dog, and Lena reckons she must be a Highland cow.

Even Katy laughs at this.


We win the team game for the odd point and then my single starts with the shot for bullseye and my dart sails in. I know people say I take it a bit too seriously, but I play another game in my head. Each throw becomes a wish: a wish for Ken. If I can score a ton there's a chance for him, a chance of regression out of the chaos of his mind. I know it's stupid, superstitious even, but I can't help myself.

This is for one of his rare smiles.

This is for walking out in the garden without getting lost.

This is for a clumsy attempt to kiss Kayleigh on the cheek.

This is for the miracle of 'I love you, Maggie.'

And this one is for coaxing him into loving.

Because I want to be loved; I want to be a woman, I may be over sixty but I still want. I want it to be like it was before all this.

But Debbie doesn't let me get away. She draws level with a treble nineteen and then clips the double top. I know she won't give me another chance and my ninety shot-out looks a mountain.

The girls have gone quiet and I'm glad the Motley Crew is having a night off. Even the jukebox is between records. It's in the pub silence that I hit the treble eighteen and skim outside the double with my second dart. I pause then, break my throw and concentrate, really concentrate. I'm thinking and praying and making the biggest wish of the night, of my life.

And it works. And the arrow flights into double eighteen. And the jukebox blares into life. And the girls are hugging me in turns.

'Good old Maggie.'

'Not so much of the old,' I say.

Inside me the wish is growing and I'd like to be home to see if that wish is working.

The Remnants are not giving up without a fight and poor Pegs is off form. The harder she tries the worse she becomes. She apologises after every throw and Irish tells her to 'Calm the fuck down,' which doesn't help at all.

So Pegs drops her game and Scottie Dog comes second and Lena's in one of her giggly moods. She loses a one-sided match.

Irish says to Katy, 'It's up to us then.'

Katy just nods. She looks too fragile, too hurt to be here, let alone win at darts.

Anyway, Irish blusters, drinks, swears, blasphemes – 'Jesus guide that bugger in,' – her way to victory.

'That'll give me something to tell Gobshite.'

So with the scores level there's only Katy can save us.


You know in some films when everything goes down to the wire? Well, this is nothing like that. Katy plays without smiling, without her usual exuberance, just drilling in dart after dart. Her opponent, Sandra, used to the Katy we all know, tries the odd joke, but Katy's not listening. She wins hands down and, still unsmiling, accepts a drink.

Looking at her face you'd think that she'd lost, that we'd lost. And looking at her you can see that what she's lost is weight. Her face is thinner and the plumpness is going from her body.

But it doesn't seem to have made her life any lighter.


Danny brings a plate of sandwiches around and Scottie Dog takes two before the plate's on the table.

Danny says, 'They're not all for you. What about the Remnants?'

Scottie Dog says, with her mouth full, 'The bread's stale anyway, yer tight sod.'

Lena says, 'I'm not having any. Want to keep my figure.' And she twirls around in front of an open-mouthed Danny. It's a good job he's put the plate down, cos I think he would have dropped it.

Pegs and Katy are sitting together and there's not a smile between them.

Irish carries the drinks over. 'Cheer up, girls, it could be wo . . .' She stops there because I don't suppose it could be much worse for Katy.

As soon as last orders sounds I'm ready to go.

I say, 'Anyone walking my way?'

No one is, not yet. I think it must be against their religion to leave while the pub's still open.

'Thursday for practice, Maggie?' Katy asks.

'Some of us could do with it.' Scottie Dog's already on her way to the bar. 'Just in case he really means last orders.'

I'm thinking that I just want to get home and slip into bed next to Ken's warm body. That thought is on my mind as I walk home, as Kayleigh slips out the door when I slip in.

'Okay, Kayleigh?'

'He's been fast asleep all night, Mum.'

I brush my teeth, go to the loo for a 'last-minute widdle,' as I used to tell Ken. Then I pull my nightdress on and sneak into the bedroom. I want to curl up beside him, hold him like I used to, feel his warmth in the dark.

But there's a smell in here, a gut-heaving stench that makes me retch.

And when I ease back the bedclothes, uncover my husband, it's over the sheets, over his legs, up his back.

'Oh Ken. Oh Ken. Oh Ken.'

I'm crying. I'm looking at this mess in our bed, this mess in our life, while Ken snores gently through it all.

And all my wishes have come to nothing.

I cry to myself, and it's always to myself, because no one else will ever hear.

# THURSDAY NIGHT PRACTICE
# IN NOVEMBER

*Pegs*

It's four o'clock and starting to get dark. I'm giving Dad an hour, helping him to sort the metals from the mountain of junk he keeps on his breaking ground. We're 'helping to keep the wolf from the door'.

Dad's in his T-shirt and his arms are smudged with dirt and rust and grease. He's still pretty much together, my dad: all those years of training and fighting, I suppose.

'Dad,' I say, 'don't forget I've got to get ready for going out tonight.'

He stops work, lights up a dog-end. 'Darts, eh?'

'It's Thursday, Dad. It's practice.'

'You won't be late back?'

'Dad!'

'All right. All right. You know I don't trust the Gorjers; they'd rob yer blind.'

'Dad, they're my friends.'

He laughs then; he loves winding me up. Sometimes he'll come in the pub, buy the girls a drink, flirt with Irish, try not to stare at Lena and offer to tarmac Scottie Dog's path.

'I couldn't afford you,' she says. 'And you'd probably steal the lead off my roof. That's why Danny's put those cameras in here; keep an eye on you.'

Then Dad'll have a pint with Pikey Pete and tell Danny his beer's rubbish on the way out.

He's handsome, is Dad, with his dirty blond hair and carefree manner. Maggie says she can remember seeing him when he was a young man.

'Could turn a girl's head, he could,' she laughs.

But all the same, people are a bit wary of him; they make room, shuffle along the bar to give him a place. Danny never keeps him waiting like he does some of his customers. Dad isn't exactly big; he's tall, all right, but he's muscular, not fat at all. He moves on the balls of his feet and sways past people, like he's in the ring. Only it's more than that; he has a presence, does Dad; folk watch what they say in front of him. I can't imagine anyone calling him a gypo to his face.

From out of the trailer, Mum brings a mug of hot meski for Dad and he flops into his old armchair – his outside comfort. He puts his feet up, spits out his soggy dog-end and rolls up a fresh tuv.

'This is the life.' He whistles Old Holborn into the early evening air.

'Spoilt, you are,' says Mum, 'sitting there like a rea rai.'

'Lord of all I survey.' Dad laughs.

And what Dad surveys is his plot of ground, his atchin tan: an area of concrete and tarmac, an acre of overgrown ground bushed with elderberry and patched with dock and horseradish.

There's a shed where his punchbag hangs, and a toilet and a shower building. Juk, our old grey lurcher, is lying in the dust by the trailer steps. Every now and then he raises his head to sniff the air.

'One day,' Dad always jokes to me, 'all this will be yours.'

He often tells me that I'm the son he never had. It makes me wonder why I'm the only child of Dad and Mum, why we're not a big family like the cousins that we meet at Stow or Appleby. All Mum ever said when I asked her was 'Bit of trouble' and she pats her stomach. 'We were lucky to have had you,' she says.

Mum perches on the side of Dad's chair and he wraps an oily, hairy arm around her waist and nuzzles her neck.

She struggles and hollers, 'Get off,' but she doesn't mean it because she's laughing at the same time.

And they're always laughing, Mum and Dad. I don't think there's anything that could come between their closeness.

An hour later I'm washed and changed and riding in Dad's old Transit van to the Bluebell.

'Give us a call if you want a lift back,' he says, knowing that I won't, knowing that he might be in bed anyway. All the same, he asks, 'Got yer mobile?'

'Yes, Dad.'

'Yer won't be late?'

'No, Dad.'

'Yer got enough vonger?'

'Yes, Dad.'

'Got yer mobile?'

'Oh, Dad.'

He might be a scarred koramengro who's not afraid of anything, but he's my dad.

Katy doesn't show tonight and it's not the same without her; she's the heart of the team and we play to please her as much as ourselves. Well, I do. But we all know why she's not here.

'Men: nothing but trouble,' says Irish. 'Should all be put down.'

Scottie Dog says, 'I knew a soldier from the Black Watch and he had some most peculiar habits. He had this thing about bottoms. What he liked to do was . . .'

Lena interrupts, 'You're putting me off my drink, Scottie Dog.'

'Let's get the darts going. Stop all this smut,' says Maggie.

We practise, seriously practise. I'm always better when it's not a real game; my hand is steady and I'm not nervous at all. There's a fiver from each of us in the kitty and it's to be the prize for the highest shot out of the evening. Scottie Dog's on the chalks, Danny's put the jukebox on free selection, and the Motley Crew are concentrating on their beer. The only fly, or flies, in the ointment are the two big mouths at the bar, Jackman and Robins. They're lounging in their work clothes, overloud, overrude, overweight and over-booted. And overlooked by Danny, who's giving them the evil eye. They're drunk, or 'mutto' as Dad would say. 'Beer in, sense out.'

I've known Jackman and Robins since my schooldays, since we came to stay with Gran. Even then they were chopsy to the teachers, trouble in lessons, and forever in detention. This is not their part of town. They're usually up the King's Head with all the no-hopers, the spaced-out cokeheads and the drowsy smokers.

Anyway, I'm waiting for Big Dave Trinder and I know they'll shut up when he comes in, studded leather jacket and hair down to his shoulders. Folk are wary of Dave – he's seen a bit of bother – but he's as good as gold with me, gentle as a lamb. Although he dresses like a biker, he drives a beat-up old Transit like Dad's: same make, same year, same dirty white; the most popular van of that year.

Gran would have liked Dave. 'A good man,' she would have said. 'A koorshti mush.' I can hear her voice now, making her judgements of people, telling me what she thought of them.

We could pass someone on the lanes, in the street, and she'd have an opinion of them in an instant. She was like that, my gran.

Sometimes she could be dozing in the sun outside her old vardo, dukal at her feet, and she might wake with a start.

'I dreamed Caleb was here.'

I knew – we all knew – that Caleb, whom we hadn't seen for a year or more, would soon be rolling up to spend a few days with us. Gran could read the tea leaves too. She'd look in Dad's mug, pucker her face, squint her eyes.

'You be careful, my Henry. I dik a Gorjer with no vonga. Empty morlers he's got.'

Then Dad would come home in a mood after working all day, topping trees or mending roofs.

'Fucking mush wouldn't pay.'

I'd look at Gran and Gran would look at me and nod her head to say, 'I told you so.'

\* \* \*

*I'm eleven when we come to bide here properly with Gran. I haven't seen her in the two years before we pull into her patch of ground on the edge of town. Well, it's more than a patch, it's this ragged overgrown acre of railway ground with a workman's hut and a square, block compound. An old Welsh cob is picking a meal among the weeds and an even older dukal is cocking his leg on our truck's wheel. There's a yog burning and a kharva's bubbling up to boiling, and Dad's out of the truck and he's put his arms round her and she's crying on his shoulder. Mum and I hang back until Gran and Dad let go of each other.*

*Gran turns to me and says, 'Oh Peggy, you've grown so big.' And then she holds me and I can smell rose scent and woodsmoke in her embrace, in her clothes, in her hair. And then she hugs Mum.*

*'Lydia,' she says, 'I'm so glad you're here.'*

This is one of the pictures I keep in my mind of that first day of our return, all of us sitting on foldaway chairs around the crackling yog while Gran questions us on who we've seen, who's died, and who's gone brick. The words tumble out of Gran; she talks real quick, even for a traveller.

Several times she catches Dad's hand; several times she says, 'I can't believe you're here for good, Henry.' She repeats it. 'For good. All of you.'

I sit with them until the sun goes down, the shadows creep in, and the stars are lighting the sky. I sit until I'm falling asleep and Dad carries me into our trailer to bed. He spreads a familiar heavy coat over me and I drift into dreams as my life begins to change.

\*　　\*　　\*

It does change; I go to school properly and Pikey Pete and I are the only two travellers there. He's picked up the nickname Pikey Pete for obvious reasons, and my Peggy is shortened to Pegs, because Gypsies make pegs and I'm a Gypsy.

So we stay here, settle on the edge of this little town, and bury my lovely gran when I'm sixteen and the cancer has burned through her body.

To this day I keep an old photograph of her on my bedside table, and in it she's a young woman like me. Dad says I'm the spit of her and sometimes I hold the photo to the mirror and trace her image into mine. Same small build; same thick hair: same dark eyes that see things that others can't.

We still go away occasionally, take the caravan to a family wedding or funeral, or a fight Dad wants to see, but it's not like it was. Dad says life on the road's too hard now.

'Those new-agers,' he says. 'They got travelling people a bad name. All that choreing and drug-taking. Everyone thinks we're the same.'

Mum laughs at him. 'You like yer beer and fags.'

Dad ignores this and turns to the foreigners. 'Taken all the land work, they have. At one time you could work from Kent to Wales. Look at it now.'

'Times have changed, Henry,' Mum says. 'And we're all right here, aren't we?'

Dad thinks for a bit. 'Yeah,' he says. 'We are, I suppose.' He's sitting in his chair, drinking a livvener and smoking a tuv and life is sweet.

And life is sweet to me now. Today. I've got Big Dave Trinder hopefully meeting me later, and the girls – well, except for no-show Katy – making the evening a good laugh. This is like my second home, the Bluebell. My second family, the girls. I suppose out of all of them I get on best with Katy. There's an easiness between us, almost like she's an older sister – I was going to say mother (Katy wouldn't like that) – to me.

Anyway, tonight I shoot out on treble twenty, single twenty and double top. I win the prize money for the highest shot out and I go to get a round in.

At the bar Jackman says, 'See you won the money. Gonna buy us a drink then, Pegs?' His words are slurred and I don't answer him; I don't like him.

Then Robins says, 'C'mon, Pegs, you can afford it. Get some of that gold out.' He tugs on my arm and that's enough for Danny. He leans across the bar.

'You're not upsetting my customers,' he says to the pair of them.

'It's all right, Danny,' I tell him.

But Danny's got his excuse to turf them out and he's not wasting it.

'Out,' he says. 'Out.'

Jackman says, 'We've been good enough to spend our money in here.'

Robins says, 'You can't make us go.'

Now the whole pub is silent, except for the jukebox playing 'Stand By Your Man' as Danny, spitting nails, picks up his phone.

'Move or it's the law.'

Jackman looks at Robins. Robins looks at Jackman, and you know that they're on the edge of kicking off.

Then Jackman looks at Danny pressing the numbers into his phone and shrugs in a conscious decision. 'Come on,' he says to Robins. 'Let's get out of this fucking dump.'

They barge past me – well, at least, Robins does, snarling out the side of his mouth, 'This is your fault, gypo.'

He twists his head and gives me a cutting glance, a nearly stare of mindless anger at his thwarting. And just when I don't want it, my gift kicks in.

It's like Gran's but not the same. Not exactly. Mine flutters like a butterfly: a little bit here and a little bit there, expected and unexpected. I can catch in a look, a peep behind the eyes, a person's life.

But most of the time I stop myself because I don't want, I don't need, to know. And I can play with the gift, I can ask for the good side.

Like I did when I looked into Dave Trinder's face and my thoughts were that I could love him and he could love me.

Like when Katy said, in my first week at the factory, 'You going to come to darts practice tonight, Pegs?'

There's a dartboard in the rest room and I've got a good throw. 'An aptitude for the game,' Katy says. It's probably because Dad and I play some nights in the old railway hut that's aged with creosote and dusted with cobwebs. We play for twenty pence a leg and Mum keeps the score and rolls the tuvs for Dad. She laughs every time he loses and the harder he tries, the more he loses, and the more she laughs.

'I used to be able to del a shoshi at thirty yards,' he says, and Mum laughs even more.

'There used to be a lot of things you could do better,' she says.

And that look passes between them, that look that excludes me.

\* \* \*

At this workplace, Katy's smiling at me and I'm thinking how nice she is, and then, without being asked for, her unhappiness leaps at me, asks me to take a glimpse.

'You going to come to practice, Pegs?'

Katy's puzzling as I'm stuttering an acceptance, as I shut the box, close the lid on something that unnerves me, something that tries to peep to me from behind Katy's eyes.

'*Look at me,*' it says. '*Look at me.*'

But I don't want to look, I don't want to know.

So I promise myself I'll never, ever, look again at Katy.

Or Dave Trinder.

Or Irish.

Anyway, what I see in Robins' heart is black and cruel. He's evil and he's marking me down on his hate list. It does scare me a bit but he's drunk and . . .

*. . . and there's a crushing pain crippling his body, holding him fast with twisted muscles of metal. And then there's the tang of hot plastic and a wisp of smoke.*

*And then there's the fire, the friendly dancing flames that wrap around him like a blanket.*

Behind the bar, Danny's watching them on the CCTV. He watches them go through the door, around the side of the pub into the smoking area. Here they kick over a couple of chairs and a table, and fell an umbrella.

'Prats,' he says to the screen and then turns to me.

'You all right, Pegs?'

I'm all right. I take the drinks back to the girls and we sit and chat until Danny's had enough of us.

'Come on, you lot, ain't you got homes to go to?'

So we say our goodbyes and Scottie Dog and I walk down to the end of the road together. It's starting to rain and she says that perhaps I should have phoned my dad, but I'm thinking that Dave'll be along any minute.

And Dad doesn't know about Dave, not properly. Not yet.

So I leave Scottie Dog and her 'Mind how ye go, Pegs' for the gusting wind and the patters of rain.

After the last streetlamp, and the last house, the road becomes a murky lane. I have to watch for potholes because the council don't tarmac down to us. They don't cut the hedges or clean the ditches because, Dad says, of who we are. There's a deep puddle right across the lane and I get a wet foot trying to hop across. So I pause for a minute to phone Dave, but I get answer service.

I give him the time and tell him I'm walking home and it's wet and cold and could he bloody well hurry up. He'll laugh at that.

I don't like this night, this lonely walk. It makes me think of Gran and the things she saw, the things I see, in the corner shadows. She keeps pushing into my mind lately and it's making me uneasy, like she's trying to warn me of something.

*The last time I see Gran, she's dressed in her favourite faded red dress and her hair is bunched under her headscarf. She's sitting on the steps of her old vardo with her stringy dukal at her feet.*

*'My Peggy,' she says. 'I just want a quick look round.'*

*I don't want to turn away, I want to hold her in my sight, in my life forever: my gran.*

*But my gran stands up, stretches her old bones, comes to me, wraps me in her thin, thin arms and kisses me.*

*And it's not a kiss from the dead, it doesn't taste of the grave. This is a kiss of love, of regret at having to go.*

*Then she's gone, drifted away on an evening breeze of summer, leaving a tang of woodsmoke and rose scent in the air.*

So that's why I don't like this uneasy feeling as I walk on into the night, down through the deep hollow, along the straight by Tuckers field until, just four hundred yards from our atchin tan, I'm near the derelict cottage and I dread going by here. Once I thought I saw a face from a broken window, and the door's always open like someone's inviting you in.

But I'm not going to hurry by this cottage because there's a glow of a cigarette in the road, in the damp night.

I'm thinking, hoping, that it must be Dad come to meet me.

'Dad?'

There's no answer and I stand stock-still. I can hear the drip of the rain in the hedges, the gargle of water from a broken gutter. And I'm praying for the sound of Big Dave's van, anticipating a sweep of headlights.

'Dad?'

But who answers, 'Who's standing on my path?' Jackman, that's who.

I can't see him properly, not in this light, but the second I hear his 'Why's a pretty girl like you walking home alone?' I go cold with fear.

It's afterwards, when I think about it, I'm sure that I must have heard something behind me. I must have. Maybe just a rustle in the grass or the scuff of a shoe on the road.

That's when I should have run. If I'd run then, got past Jackman, nothing would have happened.

But from behind me two strong, cruel arms grip me.

Robins says, 'You're going to like this' and a hand goes across my mouth.

Oh, I kick. Oh, I struggle but in this black night there's the strength of both of them, and there's not enough of me. They're half dragging, half carrying me towards the cottage and they're touching me all the time. Their hands are rough, coarse. They're pulling, tearing at my clothes; inside my clothes. They're groping, pinching at me, touching me there and there. I'm trying so hard to fight back but it's like they're animals, clinging, suffocating me. They get me nearly to the door of that cottage but I won't go there. I won't. I won't go in that evil place for an evil deed. I get a foot on the ground. I get a grip on the doorpost, half in and half out of hell. Robins' hand slips, paws again at my mouth. My feet are slipping, sliding, kicking and one of those kicks catches Robins between his legs.

'Fucking bitch,' he roars and then before he hits me, as he must be drawing his fist back, I scream. I scream at all the terrors of the night, loud and hard and deep. And then he hits me and there's a light in my head, stars in my eyes, and I'm lying outside that ruined house on the muddy ground, torn and dirty and hurt with blood in my mouth. But what's happened to time? Where does it go? Where have they gone? I'm on my own, on my back, and the rain is falling on my face, into my eyes. There's a throbbing rhythm of a diesel motor in the air and . . .

And Dave's bending over me, saying, 'It's all right, Pegs. It's all right,' as he's lifting me up, holding me to him, carrying me as if I was a chavi.

'It's all right, Pegs.'

But it's not all right. Now I'm kicking and screaming again in relief and hysteria and madness. I can't control my limbs and I've wet myself.

And this feeling of shame swamps me. It's like the tide coming in. Powerful. Unstoppable. All the time I'm struggling with Dave, I'm thinking, 'He won't want me now. He won't want me.' And then we're in the road and there's the headlamps of Dave's van lighting up the lane.

What Dad saw was me with torn clothes, muddy, dirty, struggling with Dave. What he must have heard were the cries of his only child in mortal danger. That's why I'm in Mum's arms and, in the lights of the van, in the shadowed, drizzling rain, Dad's hitting Dave and Dave's hitting Dad and then they're wrestling on the tarmac and I'm shouting, screaming at the top of my voice.

'Stop. Stop. It wasn't him, Dad. It wasn't him.'

They must hear, but there's so much anger in them, so much effort spent, that they're at a standstill, panting in the road like two buffaloes eyeballing each other as my words pierce Dad's terrible rage.

'Wasn't him?' he says. 'Not him?'

He mouths his frustration; he roars it like a bull.

'No, Dad, not him.'

'Who, my Peggy? Who?'

The names are in my mouth, ready to be thrown into the night, but something, something stops me. It whispers to me, *Not now, Peggy. Not now.*'

And it's because of him, because of Dad. Because he would kill tonight. So I cry out, 'I don't know, Dad. I don't know.'

Then Mum says, 'The gavvers, Henry. You must phone the gavvers.'

We're sitting in Mum and Dad's park home (Dad insists on calling it a trailer) waiting for the police. The rain's hammering down thick and heavy now, smacking onto the roof. It's like being inside a steel drum.

No one's talking, Mum's making a cup of tea, Dad's got his arm around me and I'm trying not to look at Dave. He seems dazed. He's got a split lip and a cut on his eyebrow. But it's as though he's out of place here, sat among the Gypsies. Not just because of what happened but because unease has settled on him. He's unsure of what's what. He keeps glancing at Dad, like he's expecting to go another couple of rounds, but Dad's beyond action, beyond words. I get up, I need to go to the bathroom, and while I'm in there I suddenly can't stand the touch of my clothes, these tainted clothes, against my skin. I turn the shower on full blast, pour a bottle of shampoo over myself. Then I peel off these soapy clothes, drag them off, and screw them into a wet heap of laundry. I stand under the shower and try to wash the night away and I can't hear the shower above the drowning noise of the rain on the roof.

No one can hear the shower.

So I try to wash Jackman and Robins out of my world with hot water and soap. And I wish them dead. With all my heart I want them smashed and dead. I want that fire and the pain and a death that's lingering.

There's me naked in the shower soaping the parts of my body that they touched, my top, between my legs. I'm wishing them dead and my anger is red-hot, burning, and I'd do anything for revenge. But all I can do is curse them. I curse them with the secret words that Gran taught me.

And the words are so hot they burn in my throat.

Mum taps on the door as I'm scavenging out the laundry basket, slipping into yesterday's clothes.

'Peggy, the police are here.'

The gavvers, a WPC and a DC taking up even more space in the small room, take a together look at me and then at each other.

The WPC says, 'You haven't had a shower?'

Mum says, 'She was soaking. Poor girl.'

The WPC says, 'But we need . . . How can we . . .?' She doesn't finish.

I realise then that I'm clean, that I've washed Jackman and Robins off my skin, off my clothes.

And that I might have washed them off the charge sheet.

So in this small room, in Mum and Dad's trailer, the investigation starts.

Dave Trinder says, 'I saw her in the headlights, she was lying on the ground.'

Dad says, 'She was struggling, least I thought she was, with the mush. Him.'

Mum says, 'My little girl was muddy and bleeding. You must get who did this.'

It's weeks later that Mum says to me, 'Someone knocked on the door, you know, That Night.' She always calls it That Night. 'Dad went out to see, but there was no one there, and that's when he heard you.'

\*      \*      \*

So now I'm at the police station for an interview in the incident room.

I'm with DC 'Call me Mike' Williams and WPC 'Call me Sue' Davies.

I'm here, but I'm not here. It's like I'm outside myself, like I'm watching myself sitting at a table with my head in my hands, in a room with no windows. I've been through the examination, the stripping of the secrets of my body, the taking of samples that will show nothing because they didn't get there. Not there. Not properly. Nothing will come out of this except bruises and lies.

I know this – they know this – as little old me, poor quiet Pegs, sobs into her hands as all those questions, over and over again, beat about her head.

I'm hearing my voice, my stumbling answers, my replies that don't sound convincing out loud. My story of Jackman and Robins; a story that they don't want to hear, that they don't want to believe. And then . . .

. . . And then, powerful and ice-cold with anger, the Gift comes to me, steals my voice.

And then it's so clear to me. I know what they're thinking, those gavvers.

Mike Williams, the one who's been so nice, is saying one thing to me but meaning another.

'When did you realise Mr Trinder was there?'

The voice in his head is saying, *The pikey girl and her bloke had a row, had a fight. There was no one else involved.*

'I don't know. It was dark and wet.'

'Your blood is on his shirt.' *It got out of hand and now she's lying, trying to protect him. Doesn't want her dad to know.*

'Why did you have a shower?'

'I was dirty. Muddy. I didn't think.'

*Like fuck.*

'You must have known that would wash evidence away.'

'I didn't think. I was dirty.'

*Like fuck again.*

'You must have known.'

'I didn't think.'

'Why did you change your clothes?' *You knew what you were doing. Had a bit of rough sex, did you?*

'Why didn't you think to phone your dad?'

'Because Dave . . .'

'Because you were meeting Dave?' *Clear as glass. She had a ruck with him. It got out of hand and now she's blaming those two lads from the pub.*

I'm thinking of all these questions, all these answers, time and time again. He doesn't believe me; they don't believe me. I can see Jackman and Robins with made-up alibis, with washed-off and washed-out clues on their side, walking free. They'll swagger the streets of the town, dirty my name, spoil my life because these two gavvers don't believe me. They'll conduct a half-hearted investigation because they judge me the Gypsy liar.

'Tell him,' the Gift says. 'Tell the Gorjers.'

And then me, gentle little me with all that anger that no one ever sees, tells that gavver what's in his head: that he thinks I'm making it up.

And then I tell him that his girlfriend, the policewoman sat beside me, isn't really interested in what's going on; she's counting the minutes to the end of her shift when they can drive up to the common.

He's stunned, his mouth drops open and he's saying, 'You dirty-minded little gypo. I can see why your boyfriend gave you a good slapping. I can see why . . .'

Policewoman Sue's face is scarlet with indignation.

'How dare you,' she says. 'How dare you. I'm a married woman.'

And I dare because I know this is as far as the investigation will go. The rain will have drowned traces, clues of evidence, into the ditches. There'll be nothing to find, nothing to be revealed in a half-hearted search.

There're other visits, of course, more questions, a social worker with a bulging briefcase and the manner of a missionary. She speaks to me in slow, deliberate words, like I'm thick, like I'm a *dinolow*. Like I made it all up.

She asks about Dave – she knows that the gavvers have knocked on his door more than a few times.

'Have you seen him since . . .' She pauses and almost whispers it, 'Since the incident?'

I tell her no; I haven't seen him. I don't want to see him, even though I think that it's the biggest lie I've ever told. So I don't pick up on his calls and I ignore his ringtones. Mum says men don't understand things like that. She says that they think a woman must be asking for it, must have sent out the signals.

I tell her that I didn't, that Big Dave Trinder is the only boy who ever kissed me.

And then I cry. I cry for what happened and what I've lost.

Mum holds me, comforts me. Says that one day soon we'll know who did this to you.

\* \* \*

The social worker, long skirt, long hair, long cardigan of a long-ago hippy era, says, 'We can help you through this. You can talk to a psychiatrist, clear your head.'

But I don't need to clear my head. I know what happened; I know what didn't happen. I know that Jackman and Robins have alibis, have sleazy friends who cover their backs, who belong to the brethren of the immoral.

All I want now is for it to be over. I want Dad to hitch the trailer onto his truck and for us to pull out onto the drom one early misty morning. I want all this to be left far behind. But I look at Dad and I can see a snake of hate twisting in his stomach. He holds me and I can feel this *sap* gathering itself to strike.

So at night I wish and dream for the smell of burning, for fate to hurry on, because my dad has a killer inside him, and my dream must come before that killer breaks out of prison. Before Dad finds out.

He asks me sometimes, asks me who it was, and I tell him I don't know. I lie to my dad because I'm so frightened for him.

I don't realise it's Monday until it is Monday. We've had a quiet day and it's not until seven and *Emmerdale* is on the telly that, from habit, I brush out my hair and crayon on my lipstick in the mirror over the stove.

Dad says, 'What are you doing, Peggy?'

'Getting ready, Dad.'

'Getting ready?'

'For the *kitchema*: darts.'

Mum says, 'You can't go, Peggy.'

'I've got to go.'

If I don't go now, I'll never go again. I'll shrivel up and die.

And then Dad looks at me like he knows why I'm doing this. He says, 'I'll take you.'

He takes me, but I won't let him come in with me.

I don't know what to expect when I walk into the Bluebell, but it's just like any other darts night. There's no pause in the hum of the pub. No sidelong glances. No whispering behind hands. No one knows. Yet.

Why would they?

The only mention in the local paper was, 'Alleged assault on young woman'. There were no names, no description. Hardly anything. Like they knew it was leading nowhere.

But in the background, so faint that I can hardly hear them, the jungle drums have started to slowly beat.

We've got an easy game tonight against the Fairmile Madams. They're triers but none of them are much good. They've propped up the league for the last two years and have only won a single game all season.

So this might be an easy game, but I don't win my match. My hands start shaking and Scottie Dog, who's chalking, says, 'Calm down, Pegs.'

But I can't and each chuck becomes more erratic. I drop one in the three, one in the seven, one in the five, while my old biddy opponent plods down to a double and out. It costs me a drink but I'm just glad when it's over.

Katy says, 'You're not yourself tonight,' and she puts an arm around my shoulders. It makes me want to hug her back, tell her my troubles. It's an urge that I curb, that I have to swallow.

\*     \*     \*

The rest of our team win well and we sit around our table and have a drink to celebrate. Danny turns the jukebox up a shade and Lena la-la-las along to the tune.

'One of my favourites,' she says, as if it wasn't obvious.

It's quite easy sitting here where everything seems to remain the same and, in spells of time, I forget what I never thought I could forget. But all too soon Danny's shouting, 'Last orders' and I realise Dad must be waiting outside. I dash down my drink and Irish says, 'See you Thursday, Pegs.' She's on a high tonight, but her laughter doesn't reach her haunted eyes and . . .

*No, I'm not looking. I don't want to see anything ever again.*

I say, 'Yes, on Thursday.'

It's the first time I've said that word, that day of the week that will never be the same again.


I'm leaving the Bluebell, stepping out from the bar into the entrance hall, reaching to push the brass handle of the big door. But someone beats me to it. Someone coming in stands stock-still at seeing me. Someone tall and strong with fading yellow bruises on his face.

'Pegs,' he says.

'Dave,' I say.

We look at each other almost warily and then he smiles a strange, sad smile.

'You're not answering your phone. I'm wanting to see you, Pegs.'

And I think, 'I'm needing more time.'

Aloud I say, 'Dad's waiting; I've got to go.'

Then he says so quietly that I have to strain to hear, 'I heard a rumour, Pegs.' He swallows. 'I heard it was Jackman and Robins.'

Just hearing their names stops my breath and a second's silence runs to ten. There's no denial from my mouth and the ten seconds of silence is my confirmation. And I can give myself the reason, the excuse, that it would be only a matter of time before Big Dave Trinder, with his low-life connections, found out anyway. And I know it's only a matter of time before Dad finds out, before he's taking his murder out on flesh and blood, not the old leather punchbag hanging in the shed.

Then Big Dave says, 'Is it done between us, Pegs?' And I can't say yes and I can't say no, and so I leave Big Dave standing at the door to the Bluebell. Unanswered.

# ANOTHER THURSDAY NIGHT
# DARTS PRACTICE IN NOVEMBER

## Lena

These are the best nights of the week; darts' nights with Six of the Best. I can't say that I don't enjoy the occasional break-out on a club night; the dressing up, the music, the lights, the drinking, the flirting, the sometimes dancing with a stranger; me and my mates pretending that we're single for a few hours.

I'm not being big-headed, but men look at me. They like my curves because I'm not some skinny girl, all legs and no boobs. Dandy says I look like a real woman and that pleases me, because I love Dandy with all my heart and what he thinks means more to me than anything else.

Tonight we're sat in the Bluebell listening to the Motley Crew putting the world to rights, while Paddy's killing a song about 'Smiling Irish Eyes' or something like that.

Danny shouts over, 'For Christ's sake, Paddy, pipe down. You'll drive everyone home.' Paddy's voice drops to a mumble, which isn't much better.

We're about to start practice and Scottie Dog and Pegs haven't arrived yet so we begin without them, just messing about, going round the doubles, trying to get our eye in. It's Maggie who mentions it first; she pauses between arrows, frowns and says, 'Did you hear about Pegs? Supposed to have been assaulted.'

Irish says, 'What do you mean? Beaten up?'

'No. Someone tried it on. In her lane.'

Irish says, 'Wish someone would try it on with me.'

Katy, usually the first to laugh but not lately, says, 'It doesn't sound funny, Irish.'

Maggie reckons it's supposed to have been – and here she drops to a whisper – 'two lads off the Mazes Estate, and we know what they're like there'.

I say, 'Well, she seemed all right on Monday. Apart from her throwing.'

'It can't have been that bad, then.' Irish gives a conciliatory nod towards Katy; she isn't unthinking all of the time.

Katy shrugs. 'Maybe. At least I'm not the topic of conversation.'

Katy's been like that lately, snappy and moody. Understandable really, seeing what she's got on her plate. That's the sort of thing Dandy says and it's sometimes his voice, his expressions, that I hear coming out of my mouth.

Maggie tries to smooth things over. 'We all love a bit of tittle-tattle now and then. Don't we?'

Just then Pegs comes into the bar and for a moment – only for a moment, mind – there is a sudden silence, like we've been talking about her.

Danny phones for a taxi for me at closing time. I'm not staying late tonight, but Irish and Katy are settling into a session. Katy's out for a ciggy every half hour, regular as clockwork, and this coincides with Scottie Dog's visits to the loo. She was a late arrival but she's more than made up for it.

'Bladder weakens a bit as ye get older,' she says.

I ask her if it's anything to do with whisky and water but she reckons she used to be able to drink a pint of the stuff without taking a slash.

She's got a way with words, has Scottie Dog.

Dandy's waiting up for me when I get home. He's sitting in the kitchen drinking a mug of cocoa. That makes him sound old, but he's only thirty-four and he doesn't even look that. (His hair is still jet black and he's still got all his own teeth, as he keeps telling me.) His eyes light up when I come in the door and he stands up and holds me. Then he kisses me because he loves me.

And I've loved him since I was fourteen . . .

*Mum's been different, happier, lately. Today when I come home from school she's singing with the radio as she's cooking up dinner.*

*Then she says, 'Lena, I want you to meet someone tonight.'*

*'Someone, Mum?'*

*I drop my school bag in the corner and prise open the biscuit tin.*

*'He's coming round for dinner,' Mum says as I stuff the first of several biscuits into my mouth.*

*All the time Mum's talking, she's watching the kitchen clock.*

*'He, Mum?'*

*'Andy. He's a friend.'*

*'A boyfriend?'*

*'No. Well, sort of. Yes.'*

*'That's why you've had your hair done.'*

*But it's more than a new hairdo; her clothes are smart-casual. She's got her tight blouse on and her even tighter skirt. And it's short, shorter than she lets me wear mine. Still, with my fat legs, plump body, and spotty face, I'm hardly a Cameron Diaz looka-like, so Mum's probably right.*

*Then Mum says, 'Watch the spuds, I've got to put my face on,' and she clatters up the stairs in her heels. High heels, mind.*

*So I'm watching the spuds and eating Jammie Dodgers when our doorbell rings. On automatic pilot and slowly munching like a cow on the cud, I open the door to a man standing on the door-step. He's tall and broad-shouldered and he's the colour of liquid honey. He's smiling at me and holding out his hand.*

*'I'm Andy,' he says, 'and you must be Lena.'*

*I shake hands with him and through a mash of crumbs, I splut-ter a hello. I can't even speak properly and my face must be scarlet. I suppose I'm staring, I suppose my mouth's open, I suppose there's biscuit and jam on my teeth. I suppose he sees a fat, ugly, red-faced, half-dumb girl who looks as if she is rooted in the doorway.*

*'Shall I come in?' he says.*

*I lumber aside and Andy introduces himself into our happy home.*

*That night at dinner, I look at him and Mum laughing and joking together. I can see this isn't one of Mum's temps; she's acting so vivaciously. Vivacious. I like that word; it reminds me of old-time film stars that I see on daytime telly when I watch with Mum. You know, like Vivien Leigh, or Lauren Bacall, or Olivia de Havilland. I love those films:* Rebecca, Jane Eyre, Gone with the Wind. *And that's what Mum's like: a film star. She's too pretty, too glamorous to be just a mum on our scruffy council estate.*

So at dinner she touches Andy's arm, touches Andy's shoulder, leans against Andy. He holds her hand, her slim wrist, her slim waist, while fat old me steadily chomps the meal away.

But that night the chunky fourteen-year-old has a dream that it's her, a new shapely her who's lost lots of weight, but who keeps her boobs and enough of her bottom to be interesting. It's her that Andy is holding, her ear that Andy is whispering into, her waist that Andy is slipping his arm around.

And the next morning that chunky fourteen-year-old has one slice of toast and a bowl of Special K for breakfast.

A new Lena is being born.

After a few months, I start to call Andy, Dad. I say it as a joke at first, something that's nearly funny. But Mum's pleased; she's desperately keen for me to accept Andy because this is serious for her; this isn't one of her escapades. This is real. Andy's not a one-night stopover. He's not a man's shoes in the hallway, or whispers in the night, or soft moaning from the bedroom. (Actually he is some of these things, but this time it's different.) So I start to call him Dad and he calls me a cheeky little madam because he's only nine years older than me. And he's nine years younger than Mum. But he's not exactly halfway between us because he's a month nearer to me than he is to Mum. I lay awake one night, working it out in my head. Like it was serious.

Like it was important.

But when Andy/Dad has been with us for about six months, Mum comes into my room, sits on my bed. She's always done this if we've had a row, or if I'm upset about something; or if she's upset about something. But we haven't had a fall-out recently and what she says is, 'You do like Andy, Lena. Don't you? Cos . . .' I hear her swallow, 'Cos you're going to have a little brother.' She pats her belly and smiles at me. 'How do you feel about that?'

How do I feel about that? I can't, I dare not, tell her how I feel because it's jealousy. Pure and simple. And it hits me, startles me, frightens me, with its suddenness. I'm jealous of Mum because of Andy; Andy who's brought Caribbean sunshine and easy laughter to our drab three-up two-down semi on a neglected housing estate; Andy who sometimes walks around with no shirt on; Andy who's tall and muscular and whose skin is such a warm, tempting brown. And it's Andy who sits with my mum, in my place on the sofa, watching mine and Mum's favourite films on Saturday afternoons. And it's me who sits like a cuckoo in the back of the car while they share their jokes.

So I'm jealous of Mum because of Andy, and I'm jealous of Andy because of Mum. I'm jealous of both of them. And before long I'll have a baby brother and it'll be like I don't exist.

It was soon after that I started skipping school, hanging out with the Wild Bunch, getting into trouble, getting into fights. Getting rid of my virginity.

So there's me, fifteen years old now, with the weight falling off me, and going downhill fast. I'm the same as a lot of other kids on the estate in what I do, but I'm different in that I've got a mum that worries, that waits up for me, that wakes me for school, that cooks meals I don't eat; a mum that touches my conscience, causes me guilt for what I'm thinking and doing.

And that guilt needs to be shoved away, buried beneath back alley knee-tremblers and White Lightning, and screeching cars *that burn rubber and go around and around the estate. I'm in with the In Crowd, escaping with the No-Hopers and the No-Carers.*

*'We smoke the dope, and chop the coke, and shag the night away.'*

*That's our refrain – it's partly true, well a little bit – and I can't say who made it up, but it sort of grew into a rap and every now and then we'd add a line to it.*

*Space adds, 'We're council trash and we're not flash and we booze the night away.'*

*Three days later Donna adds, 'We pick a fight, cos we are right, and we kick-arse the night away.'*

*A couple of days after that Chimpee adds, in his lisp, 'We own our time, because it's mine, and we waste our time away.'*

*No one said it had to be good, or make any sense, and a poet he ain't.*

*A week later I add, 'I'm not bad, and I love my dad, and I dream the night away.' The words just come to me out of the blue. I'm sitting on a swing at the park and we've drunk cider and vodka, and my head is starting to spin and Space's hand is sliding up my leg.*

*The others look at me.*

*'That's pretty tame,' says Hanny Scarecrow. She's on the high end of the see-saw, drawing on a cig the size of my thumb.*

*'It's pretty freaky, Lena,' says Blackhead. He's on the low end, holding Hanny Scarecrow up in the air.*

*Chimpee says doubtfully, 'Well, at least it rhymes.'*

*I say, 'I feel sick; I think I'm going to throw up,' and Space's fingers stop their slow crawl towards my knicker line.*

*I don't think it was then I decided to go back to normality; I'm sure it must have been in my mind for a little while, but this night, overfilled with cider and vodka, I phone Mum.*

'Lena,' she says. 'Are you all right?'

'Will you come and get me, Mum?'

'Mikey's playing up, Lena. I'll ask Andy.'

There's a murmur of voices through the phone.

'Andy says, "Where are you?"'

I tell Mum and she says he'll be there in ten minutes.

The others have been listening in.

'Going home?' says Blackhead.

'It's early yet, we were going up town,' moans Space, 'and then I thought you were coming back to mine.'

'Mine' is his dad's two-bed flat. I don't like staying there much because even if I go to the loo at two o'clock in the morning, I meet Space's dad on the landing. It's as though he's waiting, listening for me.

'After you,' he'll say, holding the bathroom door open.

I always put some toilet paper down the loo first, so as he can't hear me tinkle. Sometimes I'm sure he's got his eye to the keyhole, so I don't turn the light on. Anyway, I'm never, never ever, going to stay there again. Space keeps hinting at me to share his narrow bed, but he can take a running jump.

So tonight Hanny Scarecrow asks, 'You not feeling well?' She's fifteen, but she looks about twelve, and she's as thin as a rake.

In answer, I throw up. It's a gut-wrenching mess of cider, vodka, crisps, and chocolate that splashes over Space's new trainers.

'Jesus, Lena,' he says, 'I only just got them.'

He didn't just 'got them', we all got them: me, Blackhead, Hanny Scarecrow, Chimpee and Space. We got them in Arcade Sports on the high street at lunchtime, because that's when the trainee's on duty. He's a bit disinterested: he's got his MP3 player *stuffed in his ear, deafening him, and he's reading some lad mag on the counter. We go along the rows of trainers until Space sees what he wants. Then we crowd around him to block the cameras as he snips off the security tag and stuffs the trainers under his coat.*

*Then we leg it.*

*So this is the night I throw up on Space's feet.*

*This is the night when Dad comes to pick me up.*

*This is the night when I tell Andy I love him.*

*It's dark and warm in the car and the streetlamps are flicking by. I'm in two minds whether to call him Andy or Dad. What comes out is Dandy, and he laughs.*

*'You're getting your worms jumbled up,' he says.*

*He's like this; he can turn a drunken, smelly girl into a giggling wreck with a one-liner.*

*I put my hand on his arm, give it a gentle squeeze and all my feelings well up, swell up. And then I speak the forbidden words, the words I've whispered to my pillow a hundred times.*

*'I love you, Dandy,' I say, keeping to his new name like it belongs exclusively to us.*

*'Love you too, Lena.'*

*He's concentrating on the turn into our road and all of a sudden it's now or never.*

*'No, I really love you,' I say. 'I Really love you.'*

*He's stopped the car outside our door and turned the engine off, and there's a thick silence you could cut with a knife. Into it I say again, 'I love you.'*

*Dandy says, 'Don't Lena. You shouldn't.'*

*'But I do.'*

'Lena, you've been drinking; you don't know what you're saying.'

'I do. I do.'

And then I start to cry and he puts his arm around me.

'Look, Lena, we'll talk about this. Sort it out.'

But I don't want things sorted out; I want this gorgeous man to hold me forever. I want passion and love.

His hand is on my waist, high up, just under my boob. And I take it and I raise it onto my breast.

Just before he wrenches himself away as if I've scalded him. Just before he says in a stunned voice, 'Jesus, Lena, you're fifteen.'

Just before all of that, his fingers squeeze oh so slightly, oh so briefly, in gentle, forbidden, interest.


Inside, Mum says, 'You were a long time in the car, what were you talking about?'

'Nothing,' I snap at her. 'Nothing.'

Mum rolls her eyes at Andy and shakes her head. And Andy looks away like he's ashamed to meet her gaze.

Afterwards, I always call him Dandy and Mum laughs at my amalgamation of his names for her, not quite, toyboy lover.


That's how I'm leaving it tonight, lying next to Dandy.

Lying next to him and thinking of Mum and Mikey, and what I did to get what I wanted.

# THE LAST MONDAY NIGHT
# DARTS IN NOVEMBER

## Scottie Dog

Before I go out I feed the cats, my tribe of little friends. I feed them all together on the kitchen table. There's Elvis, Doris, Shirley, Bruce, Wallace, Posh and Becks, and Lady Gaga. And a right little madam she is with her soft purr, tortoiseshell coat and curly tail. I feed her on my lap because she's my beauty, my favourite. She follows me everywhere, sleeps on my pillow at night and cleans the egg off my plate at breakfast.

But right now all of them are yowling at the back door to go out into the garden. That means the neighbours will soon be twitching their curtains, sniffing their noses at my cats, my army of marauders. So I let them go, let them streak out, fan out, a dispersal of sharp-toothed killers searching out mice, voles, rats, birds on the roost. They'll scavenge in bins, search out scraps of meat, feast on . . .

'Shitting on my lawn again. Your bloody cat's shitting on my lawn.'

Molly Edwards' angry head is peering over the garden wall.

'Filthy bloody animals,' she says.

'Everyone's got to go sometime,' I say.

'Just the answer I expect from a Jock – fucking Scottish dyke.'

'Piss off,' I say.

'You wait. Just . . . just you wait.' Her words are spits of anger, stumbling words of frustration. She starts up again. 'You'll see. You'll see.'

I say, 'I don't want to see, if it means looking at your fucking ugly head.'

And I go inside, slamming the door behind me.

Scottish dyke, indeed; I've had more men than she's had hot dinners. I did try the other way once. Well, actually more than once, but I was young and pretty then and always in demand. 'Dundee Dors' I was called; figure like an hourglass and legs to die for. But look at me now; I could be one of the coven, more wrinkles than a prune, and pins like matchsticks. Father Time has treated me with nae respect. When I'm sat in the Bluebell some nights, and I'm counting out the money for the next round, I think, 'I used to get ten times that for an hour's work.' Mind, I never classed it as work; I liked it too much.

Mary, Our Lady (we didn't call her madam, that's for films and books) would say to me, 'You've got a real enthusiasm for this job.'

*She sits, plump flesh spilling out of her corset-tight dress, dyed black hair piled high on her head, and her features buried beneath scarlet lipstick, mascara and face powder. She sits on her stool behind the counter while the Punter, dusted with snow, slaps his hat in his hands. Our Lady, our Madonna of the brothel, warm and generous, smiling like the Cheshire Cat, greets him.*

'And what'll it be?' It's like she's serving drinks, not offering a contact of tender flesh for hard cash.

'What have you got?'

Our Lady opens the album on the counter, flicks through the pictures of her girls: us girls. (When I left I cut mine out, sliced that part, that page of my life, from the album. I've still got it, still look at it some nights and wonder what happened to me, what happened to my dreams. It's a good picture, me posing on a white rug with only a smoking cigarette for a prop. Mind, we're so made up that even our mothers, or our fathers, wouldn't recognise us.) But anyway, the Punter makes his choice, pays his money, takes his chance, and Our Lady rings her little bell and Maddy the maid leads him up the stairs.

'Not seen you here before, sir,' she says.

He grunts something like, 'Aye, I'm in town on business.'

Maddy shows him a door. 'The business is in there, sir.'

The Punter had asked for a no-frills hour, a girl tucked up in bed in a darkened room, with a no name, no talking, rule.

So he gets Lorraine who never says much anyway; in fact she hardly talks at all.

It's a quiet night, it's been snowing heavily, and the rest of us girls are in the salon warming our toes by the fire. We're sitting, having a chat, swapping stories of the pervs, when there's a God-almighty scream from Lorraine's room.

We spill out in the hallway as Our Lady, brandishing a wooden mallet, bounds up the stairs, armed and ready for action. But the Punter is already outside the room. He's trying to pull his trousers on and button up his shirt at the same time. Lorraine's at the door, and she's screaming and crying in a hysterical mess of noise.

The Punter is apologising to her. He keeps saying, 'I'm sorry, Lorraine. I'm so sorry.' His voice keeps breaking and he's almost in tears.

We're all wondering what – because we've seen, and done, just about everything – what he could possibly have done to her.

Our Lady is waving the mallet about, looking for something to hit. I think she's lining up the Punter's skull when Lorraine says, 'How could you, Dad? How could you?'

The mallet stops a foot from the Punter's head and Our Lady roars, 'Dad? You're her fucking dad?'

We're all agog in the hallway as the Punter, still struggling into his clothes, shouts back at her, 'It was dark in there. I didn't know. I didn't know!'

Then the thought strikes him, 'What's she doing here? Why's she in this place?'

Gemma, behind me, laughs. 'I think he knows why now.'

Anyway, the drama's over; the Punter scurries out into the snowy night; Lorraine goes back to her room and slams the door; we return to the warmth of the salon. There we do what we always do; we make light of it.

Anna reckons what happened is common practice in Wales. Teasy says the old boy should have got a refund; Petra reckons he should have paid a bit more because it's got to be an extra; Maddy reckons he was a tight sod cos he didn't even leave a tip.

Lorraine comes in later and sits with us. Her eyes are red but she's perked up a bit. Our Lady has made her the largest gin and tonic I've ever seen, a tumbler of spirit and quinine. She seems to be getting over the shock of it and we give her the seat closest to the fire. Petra lights up a fag and passes it to her.

*We pull in our company, close ranks, close to the warmth of coal and wood, while outside the snow piles up in the streets. We sit in our uniforms of desire: short nighties, smooth stockings and basques, sweating rubber and damp leather. We're pink skin, brown skin, red hair, fair hair, black hair. We're big, little, short, tall, but we've all got one thing in common; we're whores, we're tarts. We're on the game. We sell our minges for money.*

*We sit around the fire waiting for Our Lady's bell to tinkle, for Maddy to poke her head through the door and call one of us out; but trade is slow tonight. In the meantime, we're trying to cheer up Lorraine. Well, at least we were until Gemma, bit tipsy now, speaks up.*

*'Was he any good then?'*

*For about two seconds there's total silence and then Lorraine starts to snigger, and then to laugh.*

*'Good?' she says. 'Good? He was fucking hopeless. No wonder me mam left him.' She throws down the rest of her drink and lights up a cigarette.*

*The rest of us look at each other and then, like ripples in water, Teasy laughs, Petra laughs, I laugh. We all laugh.*

*But you know what? After this, all of us make sure we get a good look at our clients before anything starts. We don't want to make a mistake like Lorraine.*

*At least the others don't, but my mistake — why do I call it my mistake? — happened years before.*

*Och, it wasn't my fault. It wasn't. It was my dad's. That's who everyone would blame, but it takes two to tango.*

*That's all I'm going to say because I don't want to go down the low road now.*

\*　　\*　　\*

Today the papers are full of court cases, and the bookshops have shelves of misery memoirs all trying to outdo each other.

'Buy me' – 'my father started coming into my room when I was twelve.'

'Buy me' – 'my father used to come into my room and my mother knew what was going on.'

'Buy me' – 'my father started coming into my room when I was thirteen. But it's all right because he wasn't superstitious.'

I do this, turn the memory into a joke, turn the cliché into humour, push those remembrances back into the cellar with Josef Fritzel. (There, I've done it again.)

I'm last to arrive at the Bluebell, and Danny is chomping at the bit.

'You'd be late for your own funeral; important game this,' he says to me.

'I'll just a have a wee swift one then. Whisky and water.'

Danny scowls and hits the optics. 'They're all here waiting, you know.' He presents my drink alongside his scowl of impatience.

'Cheer up,' I say. 'You're still favourite.'

'Favourite?'

'Odds on for the ugly contest, Danny.'

'Ha fucking ha,' he says.

Tonight we're playing the Queen's Head. They're not the sort of women you might expect in a darts team. There're a couple of teachers, a manager, a social worker, a PA and the owner of Alwyn's Antiques. They keep a bit of distance, not exactly stand-offish, but not exactly friendly like the other teams. You know the sort: talk nice and have their little in-jokes with their in-crowd.

Irish whispers, 'Queen's Head? Couldn't imagine any of that lot giving head. The only thing you'd find in their mouth is a fucking silver spoon.'

Now, for the first time in weeks, Katy laughs. She laughs properly. And she looks better. The edginess, the brittleness, has drained from her and the Katy that we know is back in residence.

Lena says, 'Looks like someone's getting fed again,' and we all have a good chuckle at the innuendo.

But Pegs isn't laughing. I don't think she's smiled all evening. She looks a bit forlorn, sitting on the edge of our circle and nursing her drink. She still hasn't said anything; we're still none the wiser about what happened, or didn't happen, to her on that wet Thursday night. Also, we don't see Big Dave Trinder in here any more, and Pegs is volunteering nothing about that either.

We take the points on the team game; Maggie checks out on double sixteen and Irish – she can't help herself – calls out, 'Jolly well done,' in a piss-taking cut-glass accent that's politely ignored by the Queen's Head.

The Maggie of tonight seems tired, listless. There's black circles under her eyes and she yawns her way through the conversation.

'Ken keeps getting up,' she says. 'One o'clock, two o'clock, three o'clock. I hear him go around the house, turn on the taps, open the fridge, slam the doors.'

'When do you sleep?' asks Katy.

'When Ken does,' says Maggie.

By the state of her, it must be hardly at all.

Pegs is all over the place. She's playing the Social Worker: a patronising cow. Every time Pegs fluffs a shot, and the Social Worker – who's dressed like a middle-aged hippy – says, 'Hard luck, Peggy. Oh hard luck, that was close,' when it was nothing of the sort. Pegs is useless tonight and, what's more, halfway through the game she stops caring.

When the Social Worker shoots out on double sixteen she does it in an apologetic way, almost as though she doesn't deserve to win. 'Bad luck, Peggy,' she says again. 'Bad luck. That was close.'

Pegs still wants two hundred, so where she got close from I don't know. And another thing, after the game, when Pegs buys her a drink, she talks earnestly to Pegs; you know that close in-yer-face, smell-yer-breath, talk; head tipped sympathetically to one side.

I can't hear what they're saying, but Pegs is shaking her head and she turns and walks away while the Social Worker is still talking.

Bit rude, that, and not like Pegs.

They're not a bad team though, this Queen's Head lot. They're steady players, nothing too flash, nothing too loud. They plug away at the game and Irish, for all her tactics of pausing for a drink, stopping for a chat, can't distract her opponent. She loses without a throw at the double and, with bad grace, buys her victor a Diet Coke.

'Thought she'd be drinking champagne,' she mutters to me.

The rest of the games are close run, but we scrape through thanks to Lena playing a blinder – well, there're no interesting men about tonight, so she concentrates on her darts.

She shoots out on the twenties.

'I always go for the big one,' she says and winks at me.

I ask if that's why she's with Dandy and she says that would be telling, but it's true what they say about black – well, brown – men.

Anyway, we've won again, and Danny brings out a plate of sarnies for us as Katy 'Let me get my heroes a drink' celebrates our win. 'One step closer,' she says. 'Soon that cup'll be on my mantelpiece.' Then she laughs, 'That's if I still had a mantelpiece.'

Irish whispers to me, 'It'll be on Johnny James's mantelpiece, along with her knickers.'

Danny sets out the sarnies and then comes back with a big bowl of chips. 'There you are, girls, tuck in.'

Lena pouts. 'You'll spoil my figure, Danny.'

Danny says, 'I wouldn't mind having a go at that, Lena.'

I say, 'You two make me want to puke.'

Irish says, 'Try and miss the chips, Scottie Dog.'

Pegs says nothing, but she's watching the door as though she's expecting someone to come through: Big Dave Trinder, I would think.

Maggie says, 'I've got to go early. You know. Ken.'

Katy says, 'I'm going for a fag.'

She's already got her phone out and I bet there's a message halfway to Johnny James before she's through the door.

At the table next to us the Motley Crew have homed in on the Queen's Head and are helping them with their food. Paddy, mouth full of bread and chips, is telling Alwyn's Antiques that if he were 'ten years younger I'd be after knocking on your door'.

Pikey Pete reckons thirty years would be nearer the mark as he takes a fistful of chips from the bowl. He offers some, from his grimy paw, to the Social Worker who is trying, politely and gently, to leave. The teachers and the PA are sidling towards the door, shadowed by Jilted John, and Alwyn's Antiques is pulling slowly away from the table. Old Bob is in the bog, rattling the johnny machine. (As if he's got any chance. I bet it's not raised its head in years.) Pikey Pete sprinkles salt and shakes vinegar into his chips – still in his hand – in a distraction lengthy enough for the Social Worker to make her escape. As she passes our table she calls goodbye to Pegs, but Pegs is looking down at the table and doesn't answer.

We sit out the rest of the evening, a couple more drinks, a few more tunes on the jukebox while Pikey Pete grazes our leftovers. Katy goes for a fag every half hour and gets a text every five minutes.

'It must be love,' says Lena.

'It must be lust,' says Irish.

'It must be time to go home,' says Maggie, and I'm thinking, 'How does she keep going? She looks shattered.' Aloud I say, 'Anytime you want to pop round for a cup of tea, feel free.'

'I would,' she says, 'but you know . . . Ken.'

'Bring him as well.'

'I'll see, Scottie. I'll see.'

Maggie yawns her way out of the pub and Lena says, 'I suppose I better go.'

Irish says to her, 'On a promise then, Lena.'

'Always.' Lena laughs.

I tell Pegs I'm going now and she says her dad'll drop me back if I want, but I want to walk tonight, stretch my old – well, aging – bones. So I leave Katy to her texts and tobacco, Irish to her

'One for the road', and Pegs to Pikey Pete, who's trying to get up close to her quicker than she can back away. Danny calls out, 'Mind how you go, Scottie Dog. It's a full moon and there's a werewolf about.'

I say, 'He wouldn't frighten me.'

Danny says, 'I was more concerned for the werewolf,' and he laughs himself silly at his little joke.

Danny is right, it is a full moon; and it hovers above the houses on my walk home. There're deep shadows and black, dustbin alleyways, and I'm thinking that I can only see the moon because someone's been shooting out the streetlights. This town is becoming more like the Wild West every day. Anyway, I'm soon at my house and I go through to the kitchen to let my beauties in.

Usually they're waiting, milling around and ready to come in for their comfy beds. But when I open the back door, call into the night, there are no cats. No Posh and Becks, no Elvis, no Wallace, no Doris. No one. There's an emptiness in my overgrown garden. No rustling in the undergrowth. No mewings of welcome.

'Puss,' I call. 'Puss, puss, puss.'

Then, louder and louder, calling under the bright moon with my head thrown back. Me full of whisky and water and Danny's sandwiches, crying into the night,

'Puss, puss, puss.'

I'm still standing in the light of the doorway on the patio, still calling for my beauties, my babies, when Lady Gaga crawls into my sight. She drags herself to my feet. She's meowing quietly, pitifully.

And when I pick her up, she is bleeding from her mouth, from her nose, from her arse. Poison. Fucking poison.

And there, sliced and laced on my patio are the pieces of white meat: a deadly supper for my sleepy cats.

She dies, Lady Gaga, she dies in my arms. She twitches twice, a shudder runs through her little body, her mouth opens wide, and the light in her eyes fades away. It's almost as though she's waited for me to come home, as though she couldn't die until I was holding her. You know I haven't cried for years, but I cry now. I cry for all of them, for my company of cats. I sit at the kitchen table and I cry for my babies.

*I can see them, fussing, cleaning, pacing, twisting, turning; tails erect and twining together, ears pricked and listening for me. But then, from over the wall, comes a shower of tender chicken, a cascade of evil intent, an irresistible meal for the hungry horde.*

By the light of that bright cold moon I dig a grave for my Lady Gaga. I dig it deep and wide, I don't want her to be cramped, and I wrap her in my favourite jumper so she'll be safe and warm. I say a Catholic prayer from my childhood and I fill the hole with regrets, and sorrow, and anger as I Hail Mary with Grace. Then, after a minute's silence, I shout, scream at the top of my voice.

'You're bastards. You're all fucking bastards. Bastards. Bastards. Bastards.'

I shout and I shout until my neighbours' bedroom lights come on, a window crashes up, and Ed Edwards shouts out, 'Shut the fuck up. It's two o'clock in the morning. I'll call the police.'

'Call who you fucking like; you bastards murdered my cats.'

He speaks to someone behind him. Now there're two fat slobs framed in the open window.

'We murdered your cats?' Molly Edwards screeches. 'That's libel, that is. We'll have you in court.'

The window crashes down.

I sit on my patio all night on a kitchen chair, cloaked in a blanket and sipping Jameson from the bottle and, when it's light enough, I search the garden.

I find four more of my babies under the hedge where they have crawled away to die. Doris, Shirley, and Posh and Becks. Posh and Becks are touching in death, cuddled up together. That's all I find for now, but a week later there's a putrid smell from under the shed and I hook out Elvis. Like his namesake he's not composing, he's decomposing.

I don't find Bruce or Wallace; I just hope someone kind found them and gave them a decent burial.

Whisky and tiredness send me to bed and I sleep the day away. But as I sleep, I dream. And after all these years I dream of my father.

*He's holding me, kissing me with that love I thought was all mine. I can taste his aftershave on my lips. I can feel the tender strength of his arms. I can feel the stirring in my body and then . . .*

And then I'm awake and I'm lying on my bed, and I'm cold and hungry. And lonely: lonelier than I've ever been in my life. I'm thinking of an upstairs flat in Old Dundee. I'm thinking of my father. I'm thinking of Aubrey. I'm thinking that he's over fifty years old now and he might have grown-up children. I'm thinking that I could be a grandmother.

And then I'm thinking that they all could be fucking dead and I wouldn't know.

So I'll make myself a meal, force myself to eat, and then I'll go down the Bluebell, have a drink with Danny, a few more with the Motley Crew, and then I'll come home to this empty house. I'll put the music on loud and shake the shit out of those bastards next door.

# MONDAY NIGHT DARTS IN DECEMBER
## THE BLUEBELL VERSUS THE RED LION

*Katy*

This evening, I called in home – don't know why I call it that because it's not any more; not for me – to try and get things sorted out. Jerry says he's getting my name taken off the tenancy book. I tell him over my dead body and he reckons that would be the perfect solution.

I say, 'For Christ's sake, grow up Jerry.'

He smiles his self-righteous smile and says, 'It's not me who's shagging Johnny James.'

I don't bite back, don't let myself say, 'He's more man than you'll ever be.'

God how tempting is that. Instead, I ask for Laura. All I get is, 'She's fine.'

'But how is she?'

'I've told you. She's fine.'

'She doesn't answer her phone.'

'You can't expect her to.'

'You're poisoning her against me.'

He's standing in our lounge, on the fitted carpet that I took a loan for, with his 'I hold all the aces' expression sneered onto his face.

'She's old enough to make up her own mind.'

'Fuck you, Jerry.'

So there's a little bit of a stand-off: half a minute of seething on my part and Jerry waiting to obstruct my next question. Then, under the newspaper on the telly table, I can see the corner of a DVD case, or rather I can see a pair of long, bare legs with a hint of panties between them. I pick it up, read out the title. '"Raunchy Rena and Giant John REALLY get it on." Still wasting your money then, Jerry.'

'Someone lent it to me.'

He's defensive now and I'm still reading the blurb out loud. '"She knows what she wants and she knows how to get it."' Then I say, 'Me and Johnny, we could show them a thing or two.'

Jerry grabs my arm suddenly, viciously. He's white with anger and his grip hurts. 'Go, Katy. Just fucking go.'

So I go, and I'm tired now, tired of trying to sort things out and getting nowhere, tired of trying to talk to Laura to explain what she doesn't want to understand.

*'Don't even try, Mum.'*

*'But it's not like . . .'*

*'Whatever, Mum.'*

*She's looking to the ceiling and stifling a yawn with her hand.*

*'Whatever.'*

*How I stop myself from taking her shoulders and shaking her, I don't know.*

*I want to scream at her, 'It's not all me, Laura. It wasn't all down to me. I'm the one who carried you for nine months, who changed your nappy, who got up every night when you cried, while that fat, lazy bastard lay on his back snoring and farting. Sixteen years I cared for you, did everything for you and all I get is a fucking 'Whatever'.*

And now she won't talk, won't answer a question, won't take my calls. She's shut me out, and the worst thing is that she acts just like Jerry. She's got that same superior, detached look on her face that makes me feel like a shit. Or whatever.

Well, fuck her as well.

There. I've said it, but now it's two seconds later and I'm regretting cursing my own daughter. What kind of mother does that make me? What kind of mother would think those things?

*The kind of mother that throws away a family for a quick jump. Slut. Tart. Slag.*

I light up a ciggy, take a deep draw, and think it's not like that; I'm not like that. I think I'm in love with Johnny James and it's the most beautiful thing that's ever happened to me. The second man of my life makes me wonder what it was me and Jerry had all those years ago. I think of a teenage crush; of being picked up from school in Jerry's car; of the envious stares of Janey Hutching and Sonia Snell. Of being the only girl in my class who was doing *it* properly. And I could have, would have, lived and died without knowing about the Real Thing. That's until Johnny James looked me in the eyes and offered me something different. Something exciting.

And a voice inside me whispers, 'Does he mean more to you than Laura? Would you give him up for Laura and go back to that existence with Jerry? Could you do that?'

And my voice screams in answer, 'Never. Never. Never.'

\* \* \*

Mum watches me put my face on before I go to darts. She watches over my shoulder in the mirror.

'Any good, Katy? Did you see Laura?'

'No, Mum.'

'Give her time, Katy. Give her time. Remember we used to have our little upsets.'

I'm thinking that this is more than just a little upset, but Mum's always played things down. It was like when she left Jim/Dad (I see him in my head as that: Jim/Dad), she said, 'We just didn't get on.'

Didn't get on? He was a mean, selfish pig who kept her short of money, short of respect and short of love. But not short of a stinging slap, a backhanded blow or a right hook.

And he never liked me. Oh, I know I wasn't his, but when you're a kid you can feel if someone's shrinking away from you, or holding you stiffly, awkwardly, not really wanting you on his lap.

But Ellie. Now, he's relaxed with Ellie, his *real* daughter. His daughter who looks like him; who he can't wait to hold, to cuddle; who he gives his sly treats to.

Mum knows; Mum sees. But Mum says nothing because it'll only start another row.

*I come in from school and she's sitting at the kitchen table crying into her hands. In front of her is a red Huntley and Palmers biscuit tin.*

*'Mum? You okay, Mum?'*

*When she takes her hands from her face there's blood on her nose and her right eye is turning black.*

*'We have to go, Katy,' she says. 'Pack a few things; only what you really need.'*

'Where's Ellie, Mum?'

'He's taken her to her.' She spits out the second 'her' and I don't really understand.

'Taken her . . .'

Mum snaps, 'Taken her. To his bloody fancy woman. You're old enough to know what that means.'

It means we're leaving Jim/Dad and I'm glad. And then he's not Jim/Dad any more, he's just Jim.

So we go to the women's refuge, me, Mum and a couple of suitcases. This building overflows with snotty-nosed kids, cowed mothers and tears for the lonely. It reeks of cigarette smoke and dirty nappies. The front door is kept locked and the fourteen-year-old me must ask to be let out to go to school. When I come back I have to press a button, speak into the intercom and look up to the camera in the porch ceiling.

'It's me, Katy Jones.'

The door clicks open and for three months this is my – our – home.

And this home is a single room with a double bed where me and Mum snuggle up together at night. Apart from the bed, there's a wardrobe that's going to stay more empty than full, a table and three chairs, a grubby fridge and an even grubbier cooker. And a telly where we watch the soaps and all the shows that Mum likes. Here there's no, 'Turn that bloody rubbish off,' and a substitution of Corrie for a football match from someplace I'd never heard of. And here there's no long, angry silences that end with the fist and the boot and me screaming into the face of the beast.

After a few days Mum starts to relax a bit: she has a fag when she wants, sits with her feet up, cooks us biscuit treats. But of course she talks about Ellie, frets about Ellie. She goes to Citizens Advice, visits a solicitor, pesters the council for a flat. But for all of this going on, it's mine and Mum's time; we seem to have endless hours together. And if she cries into her pillow some nights, it's me that comforts her.

I see Jim with his new woman when I'm at the supermarket. She's big and blowsy with a couple of subdued kids and a screech of a voice that keeps them from moving an inch out of line.

'Don't touch. Don't look at those sweets; you're not getting any. Thirsty? You can wait till you get home.'

She's got a head of frothy blonde hair and lipstick that makes her mouth look like it's bleeding.

I avoid them, disappear down the next aisle and merge into the shoppers at the deep freezers. I study the frozen chips, the healthy burgers, the fish fingers; then I grab a bag of peas and head for the checkout.

So why does this happen? Why, coincidentally, should Jim and his new family tag onto my queue? Why does God let things like this happen?

'Hello, Katy,' says Jim.

We're separated by a young man and a couple who've seen better days.

I don't answer. I keep staring ahead, willing the lady ahead of me, who's fumbling in her purse, to hurry up. Hurry up. Hurry up.

'Not speaking then, Katy?' Jim calls down the line.

I do speak then. I say, 'I've got nothing to say to you.' Then in contradiction I add, 'Not after you beat Mum up.'

The queue has become suddenly silent and curious, and into that inquisitive silence, Jim says, 'I did no such thing.' In his voice is an appeal to be believed and it gives me a glimmer of satisfaction.

Then Frothy Head, sticking up for her man, bawls out in a foghorn of a voice, 'You lying little cow. Just like your mother.' She turns to Jim. 'No wonder you dumped her.'

I say, 'You don't know my mother.'

'I've heard enough about her.'

The audience is watching the exchanges like it's a tennis match.

'Don't you dare talk about my mother.'

Frothy Head says, 'You started it, you mouthy madam.'

This is going nowhere, except giving me a hot face. So I surrender the game. I drop the peas on the counter and walk out. I'm around the corner before I stop, before I lean against a brick wall and let myself cry.

I suppose that's why I don't hear the young man from the queue come by.

'Are you all right, Katy?' he says.

He has a shock of dark brown hair, but most of it will be gone before he's thirty.

It's very rare that Mum has a drink, but this night in the lounge of the refuge, when most of the kids have gone to bed, Mum sits with the bruised optimists and the worn-out no-hopers. There's a couple of bottles of cheap-looking whisky and a huge bottle of cola going the rounds while these women light up their fags, top up their glasses, kick off their shoes. They tell the tales of their life and forget about me sitting quietly in the corner.

About ten o'clock, I slip out of the room with my head full of images of fighting and yelling and cold, cold cruelty. There are tipped-over tables, smashed crockery and kids with fear in their eyes. There are wet beds and days off school and going without food. And always the shouting, and the red, red blood.

I go to our bedsit, curl into sleep and dream that Jim is beating up Mum.

I wake and it's really late, and I can see Mum sitting under the light with her Huntley and Palmers biscuit tin open on the table. But it's not biscuits she's pulling out of the box; she's dealing herself a hand of photographs, laying them out on the table like she's playing patience. It's only after she sniffs and wipes her hand across her eyes that I realise she's crying – crying and drunk.

I'm about to slip out of bed, put my arms around my mum, when I hear her half whisper, half talk. 'If only you'd come back sooner. If only I could have told you in time. It would have been all right; I know it would have been.'

There's a depth to her regrets that I can't interrupt; even the fourteen-year-old me can recognise tears for a secret.

In the next instalment of my life we get a council house and Ellie, just past her eighth birthday, comes back to live with us and, much to Mum's fearful unease, Jim arrives to take Ellie out every Saturday. Sometimes he's got Frothy Head and her two kids in the car, but he never once asks for me, never even nods in my direction. I know we've had our rows and I know what he did to Mum, but if he'd just acknowledged me, acknowledged that we shared ten years of life, it would somehow have made me significant, like I was worth something.

'Just because we fell out doesn't mean I can't see my own daughter,' he says to Mum.

I think 'fell out' is a bit of an understatement, but Mum says she doesn't want any more drama, and I'm to keep my mouth shut. She tells Jim that any sign of trouble and she'll have him in court. She says that because Jim's got himself a new woman he won't pester us.

At least she's right about that.

You can tell it'll soon be Christmas because Danny's hung a few strands of blue tinsel from the mantelpiece. He's even pinned bunches of holly in the tyre that frames the dartboard. Scottie Dog reckons he must have spent about a fiver.

Tonight we're playing the Red Lion Ladettes. They're a noisy, brash fashion parade who live up to their name. They love a drink and they love their darts and they're chasing the league with us. Last season, Danny had a ding-dong with their landlord – a chopsy short-arse – who visited with his team and moaned about the beer all night. That night, the Ladettes sneaked a win over us, and cost a reckless Danny a twenty quid wager. But Danny wants it back tonight. He wants a win on the board, and he wants to be knocking on the door of the Red Lion in the morning with his hand open. Danny says that he knows his girls won't let him down.

On our team, Pegs is her usual nervous self to start with – darts all over the board – but then she sucks in her breath, and a quick voddie, and settles herself down. Irish is fuelling up on G and T, Maggie looks half-asleep, Lena's under too much competition from the Ladettes, Scottie Dog is down in the dumps because of her cats, and me . . . Well, I'm starting to get used to my new life, my new man. I might try and sneak Johnny James into Mum's tonight; she's staying around Ellie's, and me and Johnny are due some loving.

Anyway, we go through the warm-up and then I chuck for nearest bull. I'm only just inside the treble, though, and the Ladettes' captain sneaks her arrow into the twenty-five. On her first throw she hits a ton and really knocks the wind out of my sails. The rest follow suit and they take the team game while we're still struggling in the hundreds.

I'm first on in the singles and Captain Ladette is still in good form; she hits another ton, then an eighty-five.

Maggie says, 'Settle down, Katy. She can't keep this up.'

But she does as I plug steadily away. Before every throw I take a big swig of my vodka and Coke to settle my nerves. It seems to start working as Captain Ladette splits double eight to double four to single two: all on the wire. Then she clips the eighteen, the twenty, but not the double one she wants. I've got fifty-nine on the board and a slip in a single nineteen and then the tops. So it's two darts and out.

Captain Ladette is a bit pissed off about that, and when I say, 'You should have won that,' she answers, 'I don't need you to tell me.' All the same she buys my drink.

Irish is next on and the Motley Crew are drifting over to see how we're doing and Captain Ladette asks for a bit of room and a bit of hush. All the same, it doesn't stop them shouting out the scores. Pikey Pete shouts forty-three. Paddy says, 'No.

No. No. It's forty-one. Yer see nineteen and twenty and two is forty-one.'

Irish says, 'Shut the fuck up and let us play,' and they take umbrage and wander back to the bar.

Jilted John says that they won't bother to help again and Paddy reckons that half the team must have PMT, and Danny, listening in, reckons that the other half must be on HRT.

Anyway, Irish wins – she usually does – and Pegs comes up third on.

Once Pegs is behind the oche she quickly settles into her game. This is a new Pegs – a couple of voddies seems to have steadied her up; she's calm and consistent, concentrating on every throw and not falling apart when a dart goes out of line. She's an easy winner, but she doesn't raise a smile in victory. I get that motherly–sisterly feeling towards her again, and I want to give her a cuddle, ask her if she's okay, put the grin back on her face.

The Ladettes never recover from these three games and we keep our noses in front to win the game. They leave a lot quieter than when they came in, and they also leave their sandwiches and chips, which pleases the Motley Crew.

Danny's over the moon. 'Well done, my girls!' he says (which I resent because they're *my* girls) and he pours the drinks for us. 'That'll rub the runt's (I think he said runt's but the bar is pretty noisy) nose in it.'

Pikey Pete asks if he could include the supporters in that round and Danny tells him to put his hand in his own pocket. Scottie Dog says, 'Don't encourage him, he's always playing pocket billiards.'

Irish laughs. 'He must be feeling cocky then.'

Pikey Pete, scowling, says, 'I'll get me own fucking beer then.'

Old Bob, who's not spoken all night, says, through a mouthful of cheese sandwich, 'If you're going up to the bar, can you get me a light and bitter?'

Pikey Pete uses the F word again and Danny says he won't have that sort of fucking language in his pub. Pikey Pete says he's sorry and it won't fucking happen again.

I go out for a fag and look at the stars beyond the lighting. It makes me think of when I was a schoolgirl, sneaking out into the back garden for a smoke on a frosty night. I'd go behind the shed, sit on the wooden bench, strike up, shield the match in the cup of my hand, and light up. I can still savour every draw from those stolen ciggies, that stolen time. No fags ever tasted as good.

*But from inside of my house comes the sound of raised voices and Ellie's wailing cry. So I sit out here, have another fag, feel my bum starting to freeze on the cold wooden seat. I sit until it's all quiet in my house. I sit and smoke and look at the stars and wonder if my life will always be like this.*

And it's not, is it? I've left my husband and I've got a daughter who won't even talk to me. I've got a job that I detest and I'm thirty-five years old and living with my mum. I sleep in a pull-down bed in the lounge like a temporary lodger in a temporary life. But this is my new life and I've made it this – not exactly intentionally – and the world hasn't caved in on me. I've been a schoolgirl lover, a much-too-young mother, a tied-in housewife going nowhere. And the thing that makes me feel guilty is that I don't want that past again; it's like I've outgrown it.

And in this new life I've got Johnny James, five years younger than me and darkly handsome, with eyes that can see straight into my heart. I'm thinking that tonight we'll be lying on my pull-down and he'll be saying, 'This bed's too narrow, I'm going to have to lie on top of you.'

And I'll say, 'Yes, please, Johnny.'

I'm thinking of all this as I walk back, but when I get there Mum's home; she's had a barney with Ellie.

'Rude to me, she was. Bloody rude. Too much of him in her.'

There's a sparkle of tears in her eyes and it seems Jim can still hurt her by proxy.

I go outside, light up a fag, park my bum on the garden bench, shiver, and look up at the stars. Then I text Johnny James and tell him our night of passion is postponed. He texts back that he could do with a rest, anyway; I'm wearing him out. He signs off with 'luv x jj' and I kiss the phone, kiss his message, kiss his name.

And I pretend I'm kissing him.

Back inside, Mum's made a pot of tea and she pours me a cup without asking.

'Do you want a sandwich?' she says. 'You're getting too thin.'

I take this as a compliment; Mum's been going on lately for me to eat a bit more. But I like this new me; I've got a figure I haven't had for ten years. I can go up the stairs without puffing and I can even run for a bus. I've had my hair shaped and I'm in a pair of skinny jeans with no belt of fat around my middle.

So I'm nearly satisfied with myself.

And I'm so nearly happy.

\*     \*     \*

Mum and I say goodnight and I set up my lonely bed and wait for sleep. But the late tea keeps me awake, keeps me thinking. My mind won't close down and I'm replaying tonight's game; then I'm meeting Johnny James and we're sharing a smoke outside the Bluebell and he's appraising me with those eyes: eyes that make me feel something special and make me just want to slip into his arms, into his loving.

*But then I'm a new mother tiptoeing into Laura's room, and she's lying on her back in her cot. She looks so warm, so peaceful that I want to lift her out and hold her sleepy warmth to me. From behind, Jerry has slipped an arm around me.*

*'She's beautiful,' he says. 'She's so beautiful.' There's a catch in his voice and his arm tightens on me.*

*And after this time, after these moments of tenderness, what happened? When did it start to change?*

It becomes one of those nights and I restlessly watch the time tick towards one o'clock. I can't turn the telly on, cos of waking Mum. Several times I've been on the edge of sleep and I've counted enough sheep to feed the bloody country. I open the window, lean out onto the sill and light up a fag. I have to stifle a cough that reminds me I'm well into my second packet of coffin nails. I go to the loo again, even though I have to squeeze hard to justify my visit. God, I won't feel like work in the morning. I check the time again; calculating the ever-diminishing window of sleep. I'll read myself to sleep, that's what I'll do.

Mum keeps a stack of magazines in the hall cupboard so I quietly select a few. At least that's what I'm intending to do but behind that stack of magazines I see something half familiar: a couplet of words on a biscuit tin.

Huntley and Palmers.

*I'm pretending to be asleep and Mum's crying into her hands in a refuge for the maltreated.*

*'If only you'd come back sooner. If only I could have told you in time. It would have been all right; I know it would have been.'*

I know I shouldn't be doing this, tugging the lid off Mum's secrets, prying into her life, but I can't help myself. It's late and the world is asleep and no one will ever know. At least that's what I tell myself.

And there's a curiosity tapping at my head like a woodpecker. 'Perhaps he'll be in here. Perhaps there'll be a clue. Perhaps I'll have a dad after all this time.'

So I sift through Mum's photos, through those months of her life that aren't in the family albums. I sift through pictures of an impossibly youthful Mum and a young man who's as thin as a rake.

There's one taken at the seaside. Mum has on a silly kiss-me-quick hat. She's looking adoringly at a man with dirty-blond hair, a man who has his arm around her waist. They're so close you couldn't get a fag paper between them. His skin is tanned, his shirt is open at the neck, his sleeves are rolled up and he looks a little bit wild. But this man – this boy, really – has a face that I'm sure I've seen before. It's the same feeling in the other photos. I hold them closer to the light, try to catch an expression, a clue of identity, on that young thin face, but it slides away from me.

Mum, in her thorough way, has dated each picture in the order of a seven-month romance from thirty-six years ago. I don't even have to check the maths to confirm what is obvious.

There's a photo that I nearly miss, that's bonded to one of Mum and – I take a deep breath and say the words – my father. I peel away a picture of a baby in an old woman's arms. This woman is cradling a child who is reaching for the woman's earring: one of those big hoops that used to be fashionable a long time ago.

On the back there is the giveaway date and my name. But who is this woman holding me, smiling down into my face?

Unthinkingly, I light another ciggie and puzzle over what I see. I spread out Mum's now not-so-secret past on my makeshift bed and put them in Mum's order of dates. Then I wonder what happened between Mum and the boy with dirty-blond hair and the woman with the big earrings.

I wonder at Mum's years of denials, of the 'not known' on my birth certificate. I really believed I was some sort of accident: not a virgin birth, of course, but that she really didn't know. How naïve was that?

I finish my fag, flick the dog-end out of the window, put the Huntley and Palmers biscuit tin back in the cupboard, turn off the lamp and slip into bed.

I suppose I lie in the darkness for about five minutes with all I've discovered, absorbed, floating around my head. I wonder how I'm going to sleep, but suddenly, so suddenly, I'm gone.

*I dream. I dream of Mum: so young, so pretty, so full of love for the boy in the photos. She's laughing as I've never seen her laugh. I can feel her happiness, touch it, taste it. Then her smile fades and she's walking the street with Jim. She's pushing a pram and her head is down and her shoulders are hunched. It's raining and the pavements are grey and the tarmac is shining wet. I'm watching her as she walks by me and I'm a small child, a child without a voice who tries desperately to call to her. But there's no sound from my mouth, nothing to turn her to me as she draws further and further away. I'm wet and cold and I'm crying on the cold pavement.*

*Then the dream has me walking away and Laura is the young child crying in the rain.*

I get up then, go into the kitchen, boil up the kettle, set the table. Tea and toast for me and Mum. It's still very early so I'm out into the garden for a fag and a cough. Mum's light comes on and then she's at the back door in her dressing gown.

'Katy, it's only six and you're on the fags already.'

I'm tempted to say that, after what I've found out, I should be on something stronger.

I've been composing in my head how I should confront Mum. I was thinking that I'd be angry, bitter, desperate for truth, but it's like I'm taking a first cautious step on a path of secrets. Leading I don't know where.

Mum's chewing slowly on her toast and she's beginning to look old: old and fragile. I add eighteen to thirty-five and come up with fifty-three. That's all she is, fifty-three, and worn out by life, and by that bastard Jim. And maybe me.

I know it's stupid, but on the way to work I find myself looking at men on the wrong side of fifty. I imagine one of them looking back at me, somehow recognising me, and saying, 'Katy? Is that you, Katy?'

Like I said, I know it's stupid. My dad, whoever he is, could be a hundred miles from here. He could be on the other side of the world: in Australia, in New Zealand. Anywhere.

Then the thought strikes me. *He could be dead*. And a terrible sense of being cheated settles on me. But then what if he's ill, or dying, and the chances of seeing him, perhaps knowing him even, are dripping away?

So I know what I'll do; on Sunday night I'll sit in with Mum and pour her a giant sherry. Then I'll tell her that I found this Huntley and Palmers tin in the cupboard, that I fancied a biscuit but found old photos instead.

'And I couldn't eat them, could I, Mum?'

Then I'll see what she has to say and I won't take any fobbing off. I'll sit with her until the whole story is out and I have a name.

# A FRIDAY NIGHT IN EARLY DECEMBER

*Irish*

When I come home, Gobshite is sitting at the kitchen table with a man I've never seen before, but who reeks of the Old Country. Gobshite says to me, 'Make yerself scarce, we've business to attend to.'

This man, much younger than Gobshite, brown hair spiked into fashion, doesn't speak but he has cold eyes that flick to and then disregard me.

Turned out of my own kitchen because of a fucking stranger, because of 'business'. And I'm making myself angry, trying to defer judgement with anger, while inside me a terrible realisation grows. I know what the stranger wants: it's that time again. After all these years, it's that time again.

*There's something big planned. Something really big to show the Brits that we're not finished. Not finished by a long chalk. Fuck the Good Friday Agreement. Fuck the traitors who signed it. One for all and all for Ireland's Thirty-Two.*

*The struggle goes on.*

\*    \*    \*

It's still early when Spiky leaves.

'Goodnight to you, Mrs O'Brian.'

He pauses in the hall, in front of the picture of Davey. He studies my boy for a moment and I don't want those cold eyes looking on my son.

Spiky shakes his head slowly and his gelled hair doesn't even ripple. He says, 'Such a shame. Such a shame, Mrs O'Brian. Fucking Brits,' and I'm thinking that my Davey isn't a fallen soldier shot in the line of duty; he's an innocent child. My child.

But Spiky gives him the clenched fist salute to a lost comrade and then he says goodnight again and adds, 'And a Merry Christmas to you, Mrs O'Brian.'

'And a Merry Christmas to you.'


Then he's gone. I know that Gobshite will follow his own pattern of preparation. It'll be the whisky bottle and the rebel songs and the dark, dark sex in that order. It will be the same every night until he says, 'I'm away in the morning; I've things to do.'

And very soon those things, that thing, will be in the papers, on the news.


The man has hardly left the house before Gobshite starts on the drink. He comes into the lounge with, 'Jesus, Irish, is this all we've got? Not enough here for an altar boy.'

He's waving a quarter-full whisky bottle at me and already that mood is in him.

I say, 'I'll go to the supermarket.'

'Now,' he says. 'You're to go now.'

'I'll go now.'

On my way out, in my ritual of leaving, I touch my lovely Davey. I kiss the tip of my finger, touch the cold glass of his face, whisper a mother's love to the dead child. Then into my head come my thoughts, words of solution to end a cycle of killings.

'I'll do it, Davey. I'll do it for you.' Then I add the bind that cannot be broken as I touch him again, trace the profile of his face.

'Mummy promises. Mummy promises, Davey.'

Then I'm out of the door into the street, into the chill of an early evening in winter. It was winter in Ireland when Davey was taken from me.

*Michael hardly said a word into his phone before he rests it back into its cradle and says, 'Mary, my name's come up. The Brits have a price on me.'*

*I'm changing Davey's nappy and he's putting up a hell of a fight. He's walking well and he wants to spend his life at his new height.*

*Michael says, 'We have to go. Quickly now.'*

*His voice is urgent, nervous, and the leaving has to be quick because the price on his head is the cost of a bullet.*

*There's a few clothes into carrier bags and in the car I strap Davey into his seat. He's still wriggle-arsing, and I say to Michael, 'He wants his freedom.'*

*Michael says, 'We all want our freedom.'*

*I sit with Davey in the back and he's grizzling at the restrictions on him.*

*We edge out into the traffic, into the flow to the suburbs, and along the old road to the border. The traffic becomes sparse and*

Michael relaxes a bit. He turns the radio on and says over his shoulder, 'We'll stop at the first pub in Eire and have ourselves a bucket of Guinness.' He laughs then, and before the laugh has left his throat, he says, 'Christ, what the fuck are they doing out here?'

Just around a sweeping corner the Brits have set up a road-block. A car is in front of us and another has squeezed in behind and there's the soldiers, cradling their rifles, standing each side of the car at the checkpoint. They keep the driver for a few minutes and then wave him through at the point of a gun. Now it's our turn and Michael is sweating and I'm sweating and Davey is still grizzling.

Michael says, 'Jesus Christ, I've got to go through.'

Now I don't know what he's going to do, I don't know what we're carrying. I don't know what's in the boot, what's in the glove compartment. All I know is that Michael is more nervous than I've ever seen him.

He rolls the car into the checkpoint slowly, gradually. He's casually winding the window down as a Brit is stepping in to meet him.

That's when Michael floors the accelerator and our vehicle clips the soldier, sends him spinning to the ground. Then we're away, weaving from one side of the road to the other as the back window takes a hit from the crack of gunfire and showers us in glass. There's a pounding on the back of the car like the devil himself is trying to get in and Michael shouts, 'Keep yer fucking head down.'

My head's down all right, I'm covering my Davey and I'm screaming like a banshee.

Then we're around a corner and we swing off the road into the maze of lanes and tracks that criss-cross the border. Michael knows the area, he's been using the smugglers' highways 'since I was a boy,' he says. 'They can't get us now.'

I'm raising my head and Davey's gurgling in my ear. His breath is warm, warm and wet and . . . and his mouth is full of blood. It's spilling onto his face, down his chin, onto his chest.

Oh no. No. No.

Davey, my beautiful Davey, is dying. The light is fading from his eyes, his arms are settling at his side. He's lolling like a rag doll, still strapped into his car seat: his safety seat. A seat for a baby who'll never grow out of it.

And that's it; that's how my child dies, with Michael on the run and a soldier's bullet in Davey's back.

We spend the night in a safe cottage in Free Ireland; me, Michael and our dead child. I don't sleep that long night, not for a moment. I've laid Davey on the bed and every few minutes I go in to check him, to see if a miracle has happened, but every moment of stillness is taking him further away from me. Michael spends most of the time on the phone and by morning his voice is hoarse, and his eyes are red-rimmed. He's talking to people, he's pulling strings, he's making arrangements.

And these arrangements take us to an early morning church-yard where a cold Irish drizzle is floating off the hills. It clings to our clothes. It clings to the winter trees, the baring hedges. It clings to the black-frocked priest who clutches the black-faced Bible of the Lord.

By the cemetery wall, in an overgrown corner, someone's dug a grave; someone's laid a child's coffin on the wet grass; some-one's made a wooden cross.

*We bury Davey here. I've washed his face, combed his hair, wrapped him in his blanket, kissed his cold, cold skin until my lips are numb. I stand by my baby's grave in a country churchyard and wish that I was lying in the damp earth with him, my arms around him, my heart next to his.*

*So we bury my Davey by the church wall in Free Ireland and Michael cries for the first and only time.*

*And alongside Davey I bury my reasons for living.*

It's winter in this English town, and it's winter in Ireland, and the leaves are drifting over a country churchyard. It's the time of the year for wanting to drown the remembering. Gobshite knows it too and he leaves the fresh bottle of whisky on the sideboard and says, 'Get yer glad rags on, yer Irish tart, I'll take yer out.'

We call a taxi because he'll be in no state to drive back and I'm fucked if I'm going without a drink tonight.

We visit a couple of bars until Gobshite decides he's hungry and wants a meal.

The restaurant we find is busy and we're lucky to find a quiet corner table.

Gobshite mutters as we sit down, 'Good of the English bastards to make a bit of room for us.'

I shush him. 'For Jesus sake, keep your voice down.'

He's like this, forever carrying that chip – more like a log – on his shoulder. I wonder there's enough room left for his head.

A waitress takes Gobshite's order of my gin and tonic and a whisky and soda for himself.

'And a Guinness,' he adds. 'Yer have Guinness?'

'Cans, sir.'

'Yer call that real Guinness?'

'It's all we have, sir.'

'It'll have to do then.'

He's starting to pick at things and I can see what mood he's building into. These are the signs I see from the old days, signs I haven't known this intense for years.

*Something big planned. Something really big to show the Brits that we're not finished. Not finished by a long chalk.*

So Gobshite drinks and eats and, under his breath, curses his hatred of the English. His eyes are wild and I pray to Jesus that I can pull him away from this, from exposure. There's been nothing, nothing for years. Not a phone call, not a postcard. Nothing. I thought that maybe, somehow, it was all done and the likes of Leary wouldn't touch us again.

Not after what happened to Davey.

But yer man's called and it's open season again. And once a patriot, always a patriot. Til the breath in yer body has gone.

Gobshite stabs at his food, drains his Guinness, bangs the table with his glass. 'Some service here for a poor Irish boy.'

We're being watched, the waitress and the manager whispering together in a head-down collusion of disapproval. If I don't get him out of here soon there will be trouble.

Gobshite, brutish and wild, and so full of bile it's almost choking him, has to be led by the nose. Like a bull.

I say to him, 'Will you listen to me?' Then, more loudly, 'Listen.'

'What do yer want?'

I lean across the table, so close to him my lips touch his ear. I whisper, 'I forgot to put my knickers on tonight.'

He hisses at me, 'Forgot to put yer knickers on?'

'Yes Michael. Forgot. I'm sitting here with nothing under my skirt.'

He looks me in the eyes; already the changing of his mood is on his face.

'Would yer like a feel, Michael?' I say, and I take his hand as though I'm going to guide it under the table.

Gobshite gulps his drink back and calls for the bill. 'As quick as yer like. And a taxi, will yer order us a taxi?'

There's no please or thank you with Gobshite, and we're shipped out quickly, and with some relief.

And so it's to home to the usual, to the dark sex that holds us together, to the losing of it all in the blind lust of the night. But this night there's a question rapping on my door.

When? How? Where?

Afterwards, after what it's always like, the questions won't go to sleep. It's in my head, it's in my eyes. I know that I've always been able to put it into that black box and bury it separately, so separately, from the memories that tear at me. But tonight there's a pure piping voice that slices cleanly through the haze of sex and alcohol.

'You promised me. You promised me, Mammy.'

So Gobshite sleeps the sleep of the just, of the righteous. He lives and breathes, even in slumber, the cause, the fight against the centuries of injustice.

'Yer see, Irish, we're still not there. It's got to be the thirty-two, not the fucking twenty-six.'

There'll always be a reason for a timer, a fuse, and the blast of a bomb.

\*     \*     \*

And now in the evenings Gobshite puts on his rebel CDs and he dies on the bridge with Roddy McCorley. Then, in a cell in Mountjoy Gaol, he's Kevin Barry waiting bravely for his last walk, for his last glimpse of the ragged blue sky.

Gobshite sings, 'Just a lad of eighteen summers, but there's no one can deny, as he walked to death that morning, he proudly held his head up high.' And then the moon's 'shining bright above the highway, where those men who fought for freedom now are dead.'

Then he's remembering the Boys of Kilmichael, 'those brave lads so gallant and true, who fought 'neath the green flag of Ireland and conquered the red, white and blue.'

Then he's the boy taking down the old Fenians' gun from above the mantelpiece.

Then he's all of these, rolled into one, but I'm thinking there's never been a song for a bomber: a whisky-soaked bomber who's slept for a long time in the country of the enemy.

When he comes up to bed I say, 'When?'

He says, 'Soon, Irish. Soon.' And tonight his head's hardly touched the pillow before he's gone. In his dreams he's a hero of Ireland and they will sing about him when the pipes are lit, and the turf fires are burning, and the stout's flowing like a stream.

They'll sing about him forever.

# A THURSDAY NIGHT PRACTICE
# IN DECEMBER
## CLOSING IN TO CHRISTMAS

### Still Irish

I don't much want to go to practice tonight, but Gobshite's pissed before six o'clock and looking for an argument.

'You'll be back early?' he says.

'I'll be back early.'

'I'm not waiting up half the night for you.'

'As soon as it's done, I'll be home.'

The phone rings then and he takes it to his ear, cowls himself around it. The only words he says are, 'Yes, yes and yes.'

The phone goes down and his eyes search out and hold mine. He says, with a clarity that belies his condition, 'Three months, Irish. It'll be three months.'

We have that moment of silence, of depth, of understanding without words. Then I leave him and, as always, I say goodbye to my Davey.

So I go to my darts, to a normal evening. I take with me the person of the dirty talk, the person that can hide behind the crudeness of language. I take the person that they expect to see.

I take the person that has true English friends and I take a mother who has made a promise to a dead child: a promise that cannot be broken.

And I pretend that the world is not going to change.

In the Bluebell bar Danny's improved – perhaps not the right word – on the seasonal decorations. There's now a Christmas tree in the corner and a 'Happy Christmas' lettered above the fireplace. Danny's sprayed canned snow on the windows, and a reindeer and sleigh are going nowhere on the sill. He must have brought a mile of tinsel because it's everywhere. Around the pump handles, around the optics and . . .

'Jesus, he's even wrapped it round the bog handle,' says Scottie Dog, coming out the Ladies.

At the bar Danny's talking up our chances of winning the league. 'I've put some money on you lot,' he says, and Katy whispers that he must have robbed the blind box.

Pegs reckons it's bad luck to bet on us and Maggie reckons it adds to the pressure. Lena says that she likes a man who spends money on her and Scottie Dog says that fifty pence won't go far.

Danny says that he wished he'd kept his trap shut. 'I was only trying to spur you on.' He looks a bit crestfallen. 'Willie at the Worlds End was shouting the odds for his team and I thought I'd stick up for you lot.'

I tell him that it's good he has confidence in us and he tells me I'm the only lady in the team. Then he adds quickly, 'And Lena, of course.'

Lena simpers at that one.

I know I'm drinking more than I usually do, and I even go out for a fag with Katy. We sit in the chilly winter's night on a damp bench in the smoking garden and Katy looks at her cigarette and says, 'I should be giving this up before it gives me up.' Then she says, 'What's with you, starting again?'

'Don't know.'

But I do know; I'm past caring what happens to me. I've got a numbness that's slowly spreading through my body and I can't wait for it to touch my brain. My head is seething with images of today, of the past. Of always. I can't settle, I can't sit for long, and Katy says, 'Are you on something, Irish?'

'Only fucking gin and tonic.'

Then Katy's phone rings and her attention's not on me any more and I dump my dog-end in the sand bucket and go back in to join the practice.

Tonight I can't hit anything. If I throw for a twenty I'll hit a one, if I aim for the nineteens I'll get a three. If I fell in a barrel of cocks I'd come up sucking my thumb. I'm almost glad when it's time to head for home: time to go back to Gobshite and a house without a soul.

Almost glad.

# MONDAY NIGHT DARTS, EVEN CLOSER TO CHRISTMAS
## THE BLUEBELL VERSUS THE FISHWIVES

*Maggie*

This morning, after breakfast, the usual bowl of easily spooned porridge, I tell Ken what's going to happen today. As I speak he looks at my mouth, my voice, with his blank eyes. I never imagined that I would be doing this to him, but I'm tired, so tired.

So today me and Kayleigh take Ken to the Cedars, the care-home of disinfectant and stale urine and carpeted passages. Tall square windows frame a soggy lawn that has captured a late scattering of leaves. In the lounge, the ubiquitous babysitter beams an endless stream of images into mindless minds, while Christmas carols trill to the season that doesn't sit comfortably here.

Depression is in this place, it sprawls in the armchairs, stares through the glass to an outside world that has ceased to exist, to be understood.

Ken, who can't possibly know, seems to know he's being left. For once he stands stock-still, empty and unsmiling in his new existence; he doesn't shuffle his feet or moan in his throat, he condemns with his stillness, with his silence. Even now, if he could utter one word of protest, I would take him back to our house, to my house.

Kayleigh tries hard to be enthusiastic.

'Look, Dad, you've got your own room, your own television.'

She tries, really tries, while I've got this cold heavy lump in my chest that weighs out my betrayal. After all I've said, all I've promised him, I'm to leave him alone among strangers.

'He won't know, Mum,' says Kayleigh.

And he won't. But still I look for the miracle, for a flicker of recognition on his face, for a return of the warmth of his voice. And what I'd give just to be held again, to feel his body against mine again. Loved like a woman again. But Ken's eyes are blank and mine are blurred with tears.

So I bring him to this place, this haven for the damned that's filled with ghosts shuffling out their lives.

'I can't bear it,' I say to Kayleigh, and Kayleigh says again, 'He doesn't know, Mum. It's for the best.'

'I can't let him stay here, among these people.'

And then she starts to cry as well. 'You must, Mum. You must.'

I know all the arguments, all the whys and wherefores that have been justified a hundred times.

I don't want to, but I must.

Kayleigh drops me at home and I go in and make a cup of tea for one.

Then I make dinner for one.

Then I make coffee for one.

Then I sing an old song to myself, to the empty house, about being alone and being lonely. My voice echoes around this empty house, and I'm three lines into the song, three lines, before I realise my cheeks are wet and my voice is broken.

It's darts tonight so I get myself ready, pretty myself up, and all the time I'm talking to Ken, asking him, 'Do you like this top? Do you like my new shoes? I won't be late back. Wait up for me, won't you?'

I pretend it's ten years ago, five even, and Ken is here and he's smiling at me. He's behind me in the mirror as I'm painting my face. He's slipping his arms around my waist. He's saying into my ear, 'You're as lovely as ever, Maggie.'

But then it's four years ago, and his words aren't fitting together properly, but I can just make out, 'Don't leave me, Maggie. Don't leave me alone.'

His face fills the mirror and his mouth struggles to form his meaning, and that fear of what's happening to him is haunting his eyes.

I recoil from that image of him; I tear it down and trample it into the carpet. If I try hard enough I can replace it with the old Ken, the handsome Ken, the Ken who would turn to me in the night, the Ken who'd laugh at daft jokes, the Ken who rolled on the floor with our sweet baby Kayleigh.

My Ken.


And it's now, this Monday darts night, and as I close the door, do I hear the words?

'Good luck, Maggie.'

I stand outside on the step, breathe in the night, listen for a sound from inside the house. I listen for the ghost of Ken; the complete ghost, not a shuffling shadow of what was once. I want a perfect ghost who will always be waiting for me.

I whisper 'Goodnight,' and I know he'll be there when I come home.

So I step into the street and that weight in my heart is falling away with every step. I'm making a new world, a bearable world for me.


At the Bluebell, when I walk in, Scottie Dog is at the bar giving Danny a bit of grief.

'You can't say that,' Danny says.

'I just did,' says Scottie Dog.

'It's racist,' Danny says.

'Fuck off, yer Sassenach bastard,' says Scottie Dog.

'At least I don't wear a skirt like your fucking men,' Danny says.

'Not in company, Danny.'

'What do you mean?'

'You should keep yer curtains drawn, Danny.'

Danny says, 'If you wanted a peep at the old man, you should have asked.'

Scottie Dog says, 'I'd need a magnifying glass to see it.'

Danny says something about a dustbin lid that I don't really want to hear so I go to the dartboard where Katy and Pegs are practising on their doubles.

'Maggie,' says Katy. 'All right?'

'Yes, fine.'

'And Ken. How's Ken?'

Well, they've all got to know sooner or later and it's a small town we live in.

'He's in the Cedars,' I say, and the image of that big old house with sodden lawns is in my mind.

Katy touches my arm. 'I'm sorry, Maggie.'

'It's for the best,' I say, and those words belong to Kayleigh.

Pegs says, 'I'll get you a drink?'

I was going to say the usual but then I think that I've no one to look after tonight.

'Rum and pep, please, Pegs.'

And it's the beginning of many on this first night of unwanted freedom.


By the time I'm on my second drink all our girls are here and the Fishwives are having a warm-up throw. Irish is taking the micky already; she's matching each of the Fishwives to a fish. She nudges me and names them in turn as they aim at the board.

'That one throwing, the one with pop eyes, she's a cod.'

A fat one's a whale. A gangly one, an octopus. Another, a long-nosed dolphin. Another, Irish's opponent, a pilchard. The last one, with buck teeth, is a shark.

Irish is full of it tonight, she's loud and brash and downing her drinks like there's no tomorrow. Even through her game there's an endless stream of commentary.

'Jesus, that was close.'

'For Christ's sake.'

'What about that, eh?'

And then a huge, drawn-out 'Yeees,' when she hits her double out. She collects a gin and tonic from the Pilchard and toasts her win with a slurping swallow. Then she flops down with me and Scottie Dog and Lena. Pegs is on the chalk and Katy's playing her game.

'With the Whale,' Irish whispers loudly and Lena snorts into her drink.

Scottie Dog laughs. 'They're not a team, they're a shoal.'

It's a good night and we all win. The food comes out and the Motley Crew appear like magic to dip into chips and sandwiches. Katy says, 'They can have mine.'

She looks like she's still losing weight.

It's funny with our gang, our team. We all get along, but we're not really close; we don't know much about each other. I know that Irish calls her husband 'Gobshite'. I know that Katy's left her husband, and there are rumours about Pegs. Then there's Lena, living with her mum's old boyfriend. ('Must like her sex in Technicolor,' one of Danny's less PC asides to me.) But I only really know what they bring to darts. Perhaps our reasons for being here aren't so different. Escaping our lives for these few hours.

Pegs says, 'You ready for another one?' She gathers the glasses together and looks at me. 'Maggie?'

Now, usually I'm ready to go by half past ten and my habit already has me reaching for my coat. Then I realise. I let my coat fall back on the chair.

'Yes,' I say. 'I will.'

It's warm and cosy in this bar and the six of us sit and talk and laugh. We talk about the darts, about the growing feeling that this could be our year. And then I'm thinking about the other years at the Bluebell, other faces in other teams. I'm thinking about a long-ago birthday present from Ken: three expensive tungsten arrows in a leather case.

*'Only the best for the best,'* he laughs.

This birthday was the last for us on our own; Kayleigh arrived soon after, and our family and my happiness were complete.

So I stay in this warmth and comfort of the Bluebell until it's pushing midnight and I really must be going.

Irish throws back her drink, gets up to go, and says, 'Me too. And if Gobshite's expecting some of the other tonight he's in for a master disappointment.'

We all have a chortle and we're still chuckling when Irish is pausing at the door, looking almost wistfully around the bar, looking back at us like she's fixing the scene into her mind. It's a fleeting thought and it must be my imagination – and the drink – that makes me think like this. Then Irish is gone and everyone at our table still has laughter on their faces. Everyone except for Pegs.

I'm next to leave and Danny says to me, 'Sorry to hear about Ken, Maggie.' He says it with meaning and he adds, 'If there's anything you need . . .?'

Without any thought, any bidding, those words are in my mouth again. 'It's for the best, Danny. Where he's gone. It's for the best.'

And if there's a shudder in those words no one seems to notice.

So I'm at the end of this day, half high and half depressed on alcohol, and I'm walking back up the street to my lighted doorway.

'Did I leave that light on? I don't remember. I wonder if Ken . . .? No. No, I mustn't go there.'

Inside my house the boiler is humming and the rooms are warm, and I make myself a cup of Ovaltine to take to bed. I prop myself up with pillows, sip my drink and think about this day. Then I think that after all this time there's a peace here now, like a quiet settlement, a conclusion that was inevitable from the first time Ken forgot our telephone number.

*'It's for the best, Mum. It's for the best.'*

Now those words are in my head as I drift into sleep. They're in my head as my dreams take me to the feel of gentle hands on my body, touching, warming, bringing me to a tingling . . .

And they're in my head as I realise the hands are mine.

# THURSDAY MORNING AT THE BLUEBELL
## CHRISTMAS DAY

It's half past eight and this morning is a bit on the chilly side, but the sun's bright and Danny's having a clear-up outside the pub. He's carrying a thick, green dustbin liner that flaps in the breeze and he's picked up discarded fag packets, several small, knotted polythene bags casually dropped from the early dog-walkers (*the Bag Swingers; the dirty bastards*), a large slippery condom, and a pair of see-through panties. He ponders on these panties for a while, trying to put a name to their owner; then he thinks that perhaps he's spending too much time on this fantasy, pleasant as it is, so he takes a pew on the grandly named smoking patio. Here there are stubbed soggy cigarette butts on the table, on the floor: everywhere except in the fucking sand bucket. Danny gives himself a few more minutes, until the chill of the wooden seat soaks into his arse, then he shakes himself into action, finishes his clearing up in double-quick time. All through this he's thinking of the day ahead: another Christmastime at the Bluebell.

Then it'll be yet another night that'll finish with him crawling up to bed in the early hours, leaving behind the ghosts of so many Christmases in the bar.

Danny loads up bowls of peanuts, bowls of crisps past their sell-by dates and scatters around a dozen Christmas crackers that he discovered in a box under the stairs. (*It's later when Paddy and Pikey Pete split one open in a drunken tug of war that the message 'Happy Christmas 1999' flutters to the floor.*

*Paddy says, 'Jesus Christ, Danny. They're not even this century.'*

*Danny says, 'There's no fucking pleasing some people.'*)

The Bluebell crowds up: the bar is heaving because every man and his dog have turned in to collect the once-a-year free drink from Danny. He moans that it's the only time he sees some of the buggers, and he wishes they'd piss off for their Christmas lunch. 'Lighten up a bit, Mr Scrooge,' says Irish. Danny mutters that Mr Scrooge had a point. Then Katy asks him what Santa Claus has brought him and Scottie Dog butts in with, 'Hair restorer wouldn't have gone amiss.'

Danny says that she could have done with a steam iron to smooth out her wrinkles.

So they're all here, the Motley Crew, Six of the Best – well, four of them anyway – and all the usual suspects. Most of them have been here since opening and they're nearly at the home truth stage. Then Katy tries to organise a game of Shanghai but the bar's too crowded, too noisy, and Jilted John walks in front of Irish as she throws and he nearly has his head pinned to the board.

She calls him a fucking eejit and he says if she gives him a Christmas kiss he'll forgive her for trying to harpoon him. Irish says she'd rather drink puke than kiss him and Scottie Dog says that puke'll taste better than Danny's beer anyway.

Danny is taking every drink that's bought him, and the more he drinks the more maudlin he's becoming. He's plucking events from the confusion of the twenty years he's spent in this pub, and the phantoms of those years are sitting by the fire, raking over the embers and shuffling an extra place for a newcomer.

There's one ghost who's young and pretty, with a smile to break your heart, and that one Danny sits in the corner along with the five years she was in his life.

But there's no Maggie here, she's spending most of the day holding the hand of a man who doesn't know her any more. She catches his eyes, holds them, but sees nothing in them. It's like looking into the empty sky, but still she looks and still she hopes for a miracle that can never happen.

There's no Pegs at the Bluebell either; she's at the railway site where a fire's smouldering in the yard, and Henry Smith is stacking up cans of Special Brew and rolling up fat tuvs. He coughs and spits into the yog in a hiss of phlegm. Pegs watches him, sees the *sap* twisting and turning inside of him and makes a wish that all this trouble will end very soon.

The afternoon's wearing on and even the Motley Crew are drifting away. At four o'clock there's only Scottie Dog propping up the bar and, when she's had enough for the road, Danny helps her on with her coat.

Scottie Dog laughs. 'You're a gentleman, Danny.'

He says, 'I'm just making sure you go.'

Danny watches her walk down the empty street on this Christmas afternoon; then he eyes up the optics, considers, selects, and pours himself a mighty rum.

He sits at the bar and surveys his domain: glasses herded onto tables, a scattering of beer mats, a floor that's screaming for a mop, a dying fire, a clock ticking away the day, windows that could do with a wipe over.

Danny takes a swallow of the rum.

'This is it. This is my life.'

The thought doesn't exactly cheer him up so he takes another swallow.

Then another.

Then he stokes up the fire, flicks the jukebox onto auto-select, dips out a pickled egg, tears open a bag of crisps, pulls the big armchair up to the hearth and settles down to his Christmas dinner.

Afterwards he lights up a cigar; his only smoke of the year. (Well, except for the one at New Year. And Easter. And his birthday.)

Danny falls asleep because the fire's warm, the rum's warm and he's warm. When he awakes, about nine o'clock, the bar's cold and his cigar has burnt a hole in the chair's armrest.

He mutters, 'Christ, I hate this time of the year,' and it's back to the optics and then a stumble up the stairs to an unmade bed. Danny sleeps until Christmas night is over and he pulls the curtains open to Boxing Day, to a new day. It's ten in the morning and there's already a sowing of little black bags lobbed onto his car park.

'The dirty bastards,' Danny curses to himself.

# A THURSDAY NIGHT
# PRACTICE IN JANUARY

## Pegs

I walk up the hill into the top woods with Dad this morning. It's still early and the mist is thick in places and the trees are dripping with the damp. Our dukal sets up two deer and they bound down the hill along the bor. Dad raises an imaginary rifle and says, 'Wish I had my yogga with me.'

I tell him he couldn't hit a barn door if he was stood next to it and he laughs. Then he says, 'Wish I had something else in my sights.' And my laugh freezes on my face.

And we're back in that place again.

Dad shakes his head 'Sorry Peggy, I don't mean to go on; it's just . . .'

He doesn't have to finish the sentence because it's all been said before. It's been worried over, sworn over, wrung to death in his strong hands.

And I feel guilty as though I've brought this curse to our family, as though I'm responsible for this sadness, this raging anger in Dad and Mum's silent tears.

All this trouble that can only be put aside after a retribution.

But Dad steadies himself, takes my hand like I'm a little chavi again and leads me down the hill. Before we're at the trailer, he sniffs the air, takes a deep breath of breakfast bacon rising to us on the breeze. 'Scran must be ready.'

This could be like any morning used to be. But it's not; nothing's the same any more.

After breakfast I sit in my room and listen to CDs. There's a country and western one that Big Dave bought me and when it starts to play . . .

*We're sitting in the front of his tatty white Transit and Don Williams is singing about a gypsy woman and Dave's saying, 'I always think of you when I hear this.' And I'm laughing and asking him what he wants from a scruffy didikai like me and he says, 'I'd like to show you.' And, still laughing, I say, 'Not in the front of this rusty old van.' Then he says, 'Where, then?' and suddenly it's become serious and I say, 'Don't, Dave.' And he's quiet for a while, and then he says, 'I think I love you, Pegs.' And my heart leaps into my mouth. And all this happens before Don Williams has finished singing about his gypsy woman.*

Now I've seen Big Dave twice since That Night, and the second time he says, 'You're still not answering your phone, Pegs?'

I don't say much, just shake my head and mumble that I've been busy.

'Busy doing what, Pegs?' He catches me with his eyes when he asks this and I can see the hurt in him.

'Just talk to me, Pegs; I'll make it right.'

But no one, nothing, can make this right. They mauled me, those two, made me feel dirty. *They touched me where I wanted you to touch me. Only you. What I was saving for you.* It's like I betrayed him, like I was unfaithful to him.

I so nearly say this, so nearly ask him to put his strong arms around me, but I've got enough to cope with with Dad. I'm full up.

'Please, Dave,' I say. 'When all of this is done.'

And Dave, lovely Big Dave, says, 'It's all right, Pegs, I understand,' although I'm sure he doesn't. Then he says, 'When you're ready, just call.'

And he makes me want to cry.

So I'm in my room playing that CD and hoping that soon everything will be fine. 'Fine and settled,' I tell myself. Then I get a strange feeling of apprehension and I have to go out and find Dad.

He looks at my face.

'My Peggy,' he says. 'What's the matter?'

I can't tell him, not properly, because there're these flickering images forming in my mind. It's like looking into the mist from the hill this morning.

I tell Dad, 'I just feel a bit odd,' when I'm sure that my Gift is mingling with my hate and the curse I loosed, and that the unavoidable is closing in, waiting to pounce. Dad's strong arms, like Dave's, are around me, protecting me, shielding me. And for now, I do what I always do; I shut off that part of my mind, draw the curtains on what I don't want to see.


The day goes slowly, and at half past seven, after Mum and I have watched *Emmerdale*, Dad drives me to darts. Tonight he comes in for a drink, sits with us girls – well, women – for a while. He pretends to be his old self, buys a round of drinks.

Danny says, 'You're splashing out, Henry.'

Dad says, 'Got to keep the heifers watered, Danny.'

Katy says, 'I heard that; cheeky sod.'

'I didn't mean you, Katy.'

Lena, hands on hips, boobs thrust out, says, 'What about me then, Henry?'

Scottie Dog says, 'Doesn't worry me, I've been called a lot worse than that.'

Danny says, 'I'm not surprised.'

Dad stays for another drink and Maggie asks him if he'll call round and clear a load of rubbish from her garden. 'It's just that I've let things go a bit lately.'

Irish, already on her fourth drink, says, 'My garden could do with a tidy-up; least, my bush could do with a trim.'

Danny, picking up glasses and poking his nose in, says to Dad, 'You'd need a hedge-trimmer for that job, Henry.'

Katy splutters into her drink and Maggie says, 'Wish I'd never asked.'

Then Scottie Dog asks how much he'd charge for a Brazilian, cos she's always fancied one, and Dad says he thinks it's time he was going.

'I'll be outside at eleven, Peggy,' he says to me.

*I'll be outside at eleven to make sure my little girl is safe and well.*

So our practice starts and I can't help watching Irish. She's flying high tonight, like she's on drugs or something. She's full of it, swigging back gin after gin, guiding her darts into the board with shouts of direction.

'Jesus, will you hit that sixty.'

I'm looking at Irish and she catches my eye and in that split second before she says, 'Will you be giving me some of that Gypsy luck, Pegs?' I see into her heart.

*I see a green, wet churchyard in the early morning and I can smell the freshly dug earth. I see a child's coffin, a baby's coffin, and I feel the terrible pain of loss.*

And then it's gone and Lena is saying to me, 'She'll be out of it at this rate, Pegs.'

'She's got troubles, Lena.'

Lena says curiously, 'How do you know that then, Pegs?'

'She just seems like . . . not herself.'

Lena squints at Irish. 'Suppose not, Pegs.'

I don't look at Irish again: at least, not like that.

Katy pairs me and her for a doubles against Maggie and Lena cos Scottie Dog and Irish now seem more interested in the Motley Crew. Irish and Paddy are crooning some soft lullaby and talking of the Old Country, about going back home. It's funny about the Gorjers, they don't seem to know how easy it is to pack up and go. It's like when Dad gets restless, Mum says, 'Henry, if you want to go, just go.' And Dad'll be off for a few days: maybe a week, even. He'll come back with a pocketful of vonger – 'No questions, mind' – and sometimes a black eye or a cut lip. But he's always got news of who's where, who's been lelled, who's run away with who. And if there's a wedding invite, Mum and Dad and I'll just hitch up the little wagon and we're off. It's like the Gorjers don't understand how easy it is to drift home and away. I know I've got a job now, but that wouldn't hold me. Nothing would stop me.

But then I think of Big Dave and suddenly I'm not absolutely sure.

At the bar Scottie Dog is telling Jilted John, rather loudly, that it's about time he got himself a woman.

'Och, yer not a bad-looking boy. Someone would be glad to snap yer up.'

Jilted John says women are more trouble than they're worth, and besides that he's 'the wrong side of fifty'.

Scottie Dog reckons he's nothing but a pup, but Jilted John says why should he give half his food away to get the other half cooked.

Then Scottie Dog says it's a waste of time trying to help some people and he's probably a fucking poofter anyway. And then Jilted John calls her a jock strap and Danny tells them that if they're going to fight they've got to do it in the car park, not in his bar. Scottie Dog says it was a private conversation and Danny should keep his big conk out of it and would he just pour the drinks like he's supposed to do?

Danny says, 'It's my pub and . . .'

And then Irish bawls, 'Where's my G and T? A girl could die of thirst in here.'

And Danny scowls, shrugs his shoulders in defeat and turns to the optics.

Me and Katy take a break from darts – Irish and Scottie Dog step up to the oche – and we sit down and have a quiet drink. Katy puts her feet up on a stool and tells me she's knackered.

'Been a hard few days at the factory, Pegs.'

It's actually been turmoil; we've been rushing a few late orders through and putting in some extra hours. Then she says, 'Are you all right? Only there's been a few rumours and . . .'

'Fine,' I say quickly. 'Everything's fine.'

It's perhaps too quickly and even to myself I don't sound very convincing, but then Irish yells that she's got her double out and she's ready to 'whup the arses off Katy and Pegs' and the moment when I might have said something is gone.

So Katy and I take to the oche again with Lena on the chalks and Irish tipping back and ordering Danny, 'One more before the game.'

Scottie Dog says, 'If I have much more I'll be on my back.'

Danny reckons that she's studied plenty of ceilings in her time and then Scottie Dog asks him if he still wears frilly knickers and does Jilted John find them a turn-on?

Danny tells her she's fucking sick.

So that's what tonight's like in this world of the *kitchema*: darts and drinking, swearing and joking. I even have an extra vodka more than I usually do and almost before I know it, last orders are being called and it's goodbye till Monday.

'Don't forget,' Katy calls to me. 'It's the Drum we're playing.'

Danny says, 'Well, you should beat them.'

Katy says, 'For God's sake, Danny, we hear that every time.'

Outside the Bluebell, the pavement's wet and shining. There's a freshness on my face and the night's breeze is in my hair. Dad leans across, opens the van door for me and I climb into a fug of Old Holborn smoke: comforting and familiar.

It takes me a while to drift off to sleep this night and I listen to the rain on the roof. It's a steady falling, a murmur of dampness soaking into the dark, while the bovel stirs in the rookers. It's not a night to be out walking the muddy lanes or . . .

*. . . walking home, down past the old cottage where the open door beckons. 'Come in here, Pegs. This is where we're waiting for you. Come in.'*

*They're standing there, those two, and they're smiling their fox grins, holding out their hands.*

*'Come on, Pegs; we know what gypo girls are like.'*

*But behind them, in the doorway, tapping on the windows of the derelict house, there are darting tongues of flame.*

I close my eyes against these pictures, imagine that I'm a young girl again in the times of nightmares and Gran is at my bedside stroking my forehead. Her hand is the cool hand from my childhood when the dreams, the visions, would pull me from my sleep and not stop with the waking.

'Hush my little one. Nantee. Let them go. Let them go.'

She smooths these images, magics them away. Banishes these things of the night.

And then it's today, it's tonight, and she's stroking away my worries: Dad's anger, that look in Mum's eyes, the distance between me and Big Dave Trinder. Then she strokes away Jackman and Robins, and it's like they never existed. I fall into sootee, into peace, for the first time in weeks.

Hours later, what wakes me? I lie in the dark and listen, and what I hear is a faint knocking, a gentle rapping on the trailer door. And you know what? I'm not afraid as I pull on my clothes and whisper aloud, 'Don't go. Please don't go.'

And then I'm in the lounge and the knock is still on the door, but it's more like a stroke than a rap. I'm reaching for the handle when there's a blinking of light and the ring of my mobile on the table. It's automatic that I snatch it up to shush it, that I dik the name that comes up calling: Big Dave Trinder.

'Pegs,' he says across the miles. 'Pegs, I need to see you now.'

His voice is softly hoarse and I say, 'Just come, Dave. Just come.'

Then I open the door and there's the swirl of woodsmoke and rose scent in the night air before the winter rain chills my face.

And when I turn back into our home Dad is standing there.

'Peggy,' he says. 'What's going on, my girl?'

Dad and I sit in the kitchen and he rolls himself a tuv and I boil up the kettle for meski. Mum's dead to the world; Dad reckons that she'd sleep through an air raid.

'Dad,' I say, 'Dave's coming here.'

'Here? Why? At this time of night?'

'I think there's been trouble.'

Dad scowls. 'Trouble? What trouble? We got enough of our own.'

'I don't know, Dad.'

But I do know. I heard it in Dave's voice.

So Dad has another tuv, drinks another mug of tea before we hear the van pull up and Big Dave Trinder steps back into my life. He's got a smear of grease across his cheek and his leather coat's tatty and in need of some blacking.

Before he can even speak Dad says, 'What's happened?'

'Give him a minute, Dad; he's hardly in the door. Let him sit down.'

So Big Dave drops down into our sofa and speaks so softly that I have to strain for the words. 'They're dead. Jackman and Robins. They're dead.'

Then, into a silence where I hear each raindrop tap on the trailer roof, Dad gets up, goes to the cupboard and takes out the brandy bottle and two glasses.

He looks straight at me and says, 'It was them, my Peggy. It was them.'

There's no question in his words, no asking of me, but I still give him, 'Avre'.

Then Big Dave's looking at me, holding my eyes. 'I don't know if I meant to do it, Pegs. I just don't know.'

Then his head is in his hands and Dad is saying gently, 'Tell me, Dave. Tell me everything that happened.'

Big Dave Trinder takes a great gulp of brandy, coughs, and starts to tell.

And as he speaks I'm looking again into his eyes and it's unfolding in front of me like a film.

*The night is dark and wet and Big Dave's on his drive back from the other side of Reddyke. The van's headlamps glisten on the road and the rain drifts across the windscreen as the wipers flap the miles away. Dave yawns, takes a deep drag on his roll-up, swigs a hit from a can of Red Bull. He's tired, he's done a long day's work and seen about another job, so he just wants to get home. But when he comes through Reddyke, he needs to stop in the car park for a lag. As he drives in, the sweep of his lights picks out Jackman and Robins getting into a red Fiat Punto. He knows the car, knows the number plate, and he swings around the deserted tarmac again to be sure, absolutely sure. But now their tail lights are disappearing into the distance and his Transit is too slow and old to gain ground.*

*'Shit,' he says, 'I was going to . . .'*

*Going to what? Going to take them by the scruff of the neck, drag them out of the Fiat, kick the fuck out of them, make sure they know what it's for? He wants to do all of this for me. Because of me.*

*Big Dave, smouldering and handsome, takes another tug on his tuv and tries to settle into the ride home.*

*Now he's thinking about me, wondering if I'm ready to see him, waiting for a call, a text, to break into my shame. This is in his head as he reaches the top of Hangman's Hill, dropping the van into third, feeling the brakes for the long downhill drop, when a red Fiat, that red Fiat, flashes by and cuts sharply in.*

*It cuts in so sharply that Big Dave Trinder stands on his brakes, blasts on his horn, and throws a string of fucks at the car. He flashes his lights and in return, in silhouette, he gets a turned head and two fingers.*

*Then the red Fiat slows down, speeds up, slows down, playing a cat and mouse game as the rain lashes the road and the wind buffets the van.*

*'Fucking prats. Fucking stupid prats.'*

*The Fiat slows down again and Dave whips out to overtake, but there's a taxi steaming up the hill and it's a near miss in the rain.*

*Just then the ember of a cigarette butt, flicked from the passenger window, arcs towards him, and dies on the windscreen as the brake lights flare up yet again. Only this time it's much fiercer and Big Dave hits the anchors a fraction later, a fag paper of difference than before. This time, the Fiat's braking for the sharp hairpin curve halfway down Hangman's Hill. It's braking hard because this is a deadly curve, an accident blackspot where bunches of flowers and scrawled cards spotlight lost control and violent death. But because he's angry, and because he's braking late, and because his pads are worn, Big Dave Trinder hits the back of the Fiat. It's more than that, it's a shunt; a shove that pushes the red car out of its line. That's all it takes, a dodgem collision, and the red car snakes once, loses it and flips. Tumbles off the road, in a shower of sparks and smoke, and shards of mirrors and glass, and popping windows, and screeching of metal on tarmac. And it rolls and rolls to land on its roof, smoking in the rain. Now it's thirty yards off the road and Big Dave is out of his van following the plough lines of the accident.*

*He's thinking, 'What am I going to see? What am I going to do?'*

*But he doesn't need to do anything because a flicker of flame dances inside the wreck. Then there's another, and another, until the motor's inside is lit up like a lantern.*

*And now the silhouettes are bent and twisted, and a hand is lifting and falling, lifting and falling. With every second that passes those tongues of flame grow brighter, stronger. They're feeding on plastic, on petrol, on flesh that oozes fat and melts at their touch.*

*They grow so quickly, so hungrily, so angrily.*

*Now this is what Big Dave Trinder doesn't want to hear, the sound that he will never forget: the screaming of the trapped, the screaming of the burning. The bonfire of the damned; the smell of roasting pork. He freezes, and his eyes and ears and nose fill to overflowing.*

*Then there's a dull thump of an explosion that blows out what's left of the windows, and a flaring of a bright intense light inside the carcase of the car.*

*There's no noise now except the crackle of the fire and the ping and rasp of metal in this parody of November the fifth. Big Dave is standing in the rain and it's too late to do anything, too late to save anyone.*

*Big Dave leaves the scene, climbs into his van with its crushed bumper and its scar of giveaway red paint. The front light's out and the indicator is smashed. He drives slowly, carefully, numbly, until he's off the road and into the back lanes.*

*Then he pulls into a gateway, rolls himself a tuv, lights up, takes a huge swig of Red Bull and phones my number.*

*I say, 'Just come, Dave. Just come.'*

*So Dave comes to me, drives his battered, guilty van through the wind and the storm onto our site, onto our atchin tan.*

Dad says quietly, 'Did anyone see you, Dave?'

Dave thinks, remembers the vehicle's roof sign.

'A taxi,' he says. 'A taxi.' *A full beam warning and the cursing of the horn.*

He looks at me, and his worry, his tiredness, is spread over his face. In spite of all this, of all that's going on, I'm glad he's here, sitting in our wagon.

Then Dad says, 'You're going to have to go home, Dave, before the gavvers get there.'

Dave says, 'I don't want to go anywhere, Henry.'

I say, 'Let him stay, Dad.'

But what my dad, my wonderful dad, is doing is putting together an exchange, a replacement of number plates: his innocent white van for Big Dave's guilty one in a swap of identical twins. Dad tells him to shower – God knows how he fits into that cubicle – and I'm thinking he's washing away the evidence like I did on That Night, and it seems like it's a sort of justice, an evening up of the score. So while Dad burns Big Dave's clothes and trainers he sits in our kitchen in Dad's too-tight trousers, too-tight shirt and too-small socks, and sips another brandy.

'I'll probably get stopped for drink-driving; that'll be a turn-up.' He laughs but it's a bitter laugh.

When Dad's done, Big Dave loads his tools, his paperwork, his cans of Red Bull into Dad's/Dave's van. Then, not caring that Dad's here, he holds me, hugs me, and he says, 'I love you, Pegs. Whatever happens, I love you.'

Then he kisses me softly, gently, and he drives away in his counterfeit vehicle. The rain's turned to a heavy drizzle and I watch him until his lights are out of sight.

Dad puts his arm around me. 'It'll be all right, my Peggy.'

I say, 'I know it will.'

And that's a truth, because I do know.


Mum sleeps through it all but she's awake at dawn when Dad's loading up Big Dave's van onto the low trailer. He's sheeting it over when Mum, rubbing her eyes and standing in the doorway asks, 'What's going on, Henry?'

'Lydia, there's been a bit of trouble.'

'Trouble? What sort of trouble?'

Dad tells her, spells it out to her: Dave Trinder's crash and the burning of the Fiat Punto, and Jackman and Robins. She listens quietly, hand to her mouth, cuts me a look at the mention of Jackman and Robins, at what's in Dad's voice. I nod and it's enough for her to know.

Then Mum, says wearily, 'And now, Henry? What now?'

Dad says, 'It's just this, Lydia, that's all. Just this one thing and it'll be done. It'll be koorshti.'

He puts his arms around Mum, holds her, loves her, calms her.

Just like Big Dave Trinder did to me.

So Dad takes the evidence to Isaac Stanley's scrapyard to be crushed into a cube of untraceable metal. There'll be no questions asked and it'll be in the furnace before you can turn around because Isaac Stanley's one of us, a *romanichal*, and blood is so much thicker than water. He'll look after us, cover for us, in the way of the Travelling People.

It's still early when Mum and I have a bit of toast and tea and I'm thinking that the police will be outside Big Dave's. They'll be looking at the van, looking at the front light, then the front wing for the damning of red paint. They'll be shaking their heads.

Then they'll ask: were you on the road from Reddyke last night, about ten?

Yea.

Did you see a red Fiat Punto?

Don't think so.

Only someone saw a white van driving dangerously.

Wasn't me.

There was an accident. Seems like the car was shunted off the road.

So.

Jackman and Robins. You know them?

Sort of.

Sort of?

You know why it's sort of.

Oh yes, your girlfriend. *Drawn out like it's a motive.* Anyway, they were killed. Burnt to death. Not nice that, is it?

Suppose not.

You wouldn't know anything about it?

No.

We'll be in touch, Mr Trinder.

Look forward to it.

They'll check out the van again, maybe sneak a sly look at the tyre treads; then they'll shrug, shake their heads, and go to the next on the list for a questioning. And they don't know that soon, very soon, Dad's/Dave's van will be joining its twin in the graveyard of vehicles.

Just in case.


They'll come to us in time, because of That Night. And they'll ask about Dad's van, of course.

'Scrapped it a couple of weeks ago. Got the ticket inside. All right?'

It's DC Williams and he's brought his swagger, and his dislike of the Gypsies, with him.

'Mr Smith, is there anything you think we should know?'

Dad reckons he should know to stop pestering us and try and catch some real criminals.

DC Williams says, 'If you're not careful I might have a good look around here.'

Dad says that we ain't got nothing to hide and he can do what the fuck he likes.

Mum says, 'Henry, please.'

But DC Williams has nothing. Even when he says, 'I'll be back,' like Arnie in that film, it's not a threat. Because when he's worked all of this out, when him and his girlfriend have found their way through the maze, the evidence will be in tin cans, steel beams and roofing sheets.

And DC Williams will make a point of calling round on any off chance that there might be something for him at our site. He'll pester for a while, sift over our scrap pile of lead and copper and cast iron; look for anything that might link us to crime. He's like the gavvers that used to move us on in the old days.

He's the bogeyman of the Travelling People.

# MONDAY NIGHT DARTS IN JANUARY
## THE BLUEBELL VERSUS THE DRAGON

*Lena*

Dandy says, 'You look nice.'

I'm putting on my make-up, leaning into the mirror, and I know he's giving my bum the once-over. 'Only nice, Dandy?'

'More than nice, Lena.' He's suddenly serious. 'You're beautiful.'

Then he says, 'I spoke to Mikey today.'

I'm painting on my lip gloss and my hand freezes into stillness.

'This afternoon the phone rang and it was Mikey.'

'What did he say?'

'He told me about school, about his football team.'

This is hurting Dandy, talking about the things he could be sharing. He's frowning now and the tell-tales of his age are crinkling under his eyes. But he's as handsome as ever; still as lean and as muscular as when he came through our door ten years ago.

'And Mum? Did you speak to Mum?'

'We said hello,' he says, 'and we said goodbye.'

Trapped behind his words is:

*Mum saying goodbye, a suitcase in one hand, holding onto a crying, bewildered Mikey with the other.*

*'I'll never forgive you,' she says to Dandy. 'Never forgive you.'*

*She spits the words at him, and there're the same words for me.*

*And then she's gone, leaving the door unshut behind her and all the neighbours' curiosity creeping in.*

*But what I'll never forget from that day is the look of utter desolation on Dandy's face. He loves her, he truly loves her and it's all done, all finished; the life with Mikey; the life with Mum.*

*And all because of me.*

So I'm ready to go and I know that I'm young and clean and pretty and, when I kiss him goodbye, he holds me close, tastes my lips, smells my hair.

'You're more than gorgeous,' he sings to me, 'and I'd do anything you want.'

This is our song and he did everything for me.

And to me.

As I'm walking to the pub that song keeps playing through my mind and each line brings back a scene from our affair, our loving time. It should have been a happy place, somewhere to keep my memories, but I keep seeing Mum with her head in her hands.

*'How could you, Andy? How could you, Lena? How could you?'*

I could say that I was young and foolish and that Dandy took advantage of me. But it wasn't him; I know that, and I think Dandy knows that. But we never talk about it, never mention the guilt that keeps us company in our house.

So he'll sing the song to me and I still get a delicious thrill at the words, and I'll know that I got what I wanted: the gorgeous man that Mum brought home.

I'm first at the pub and because it's quiet I sit at the bar and chat to Danny. He's funny, is Danny; he laughs and flirts with me, offers me a drink.

When I say, 'Go on then, Danny.'

He says, 'What's it worth, Lena?'

'What do you want, Danny?'

'What you offering?'

'Let me think. Mmm. What would please an old man . . .?'

'You're the one that'd be pleased, Lena.'

Danny looks but he never touches. Underneath his chat, his bluster, he's got a heart of gold.

The other girls turn up and we leave with Danny for the Dragon Inn. Katy calls it the Dragon's Den, and they have a team that doesn't lose very often. When we arrive they're practising hard and pushing each other on.

'Good shot, Sal.'

'That's the way.'

'Keep it up.'

'I bet that's what you say to your old man.'

'Mind I don't say it to yours.'

They're a lot like us, this team; this kidding, this laughing, this joking. This escapism of a Monday night.

Katy wins the toss and we play like a bunch of plebs to lose the team game by a mile. It doesn't alter Irish's manner; she's in a funny one tonight; she's laughing one minute, and snappy the next.

And drink! She pours it down her throat. She even buys herself one between rounds. It's a good job she's throwing first in the singles, because she'll be seeing double before she's down to a double.

How she wins, no one knows. Her darts float into the treble eighteen, the treble sixteen, then the double ten and out.

'One up to Saint George,' Irish laughs. 'One up to the Dragon slayer.'

Then she does a strange thing; she raises her glass in a toast and, in her broad out-of-place accent, she says, 'To Saint George and England.'

Scottie Dog says, 'You silly Irish twat, Irish.' Then she adds, 'But a drink's a drink and I'll join yer,' and she empties her glass.

Maggie slows down the action, plays her usual steady game and plugs away a win. Pegs loses a close one. Scottie Dog falls behind and never catches up. Every time she misses she calls the dart a 'fucking tart', and the next throw's even worse. So she's a hopeless case and suddenly we're behind; one down and two to go: me, and then Katy.

I go up to throw and I know that I've got to win to give us a chance of the game. I'm nervous as hell and my first throw only scores a twenty-six. I think that's bad but my opponent hits a seven. Her every score is below mine – her nerves are more shot than mine – and I smooth down to an easy win.

I'm loving this night with the girls. I'm loving the admiring glances from the lads. I'm loving the glow of winning. But I'm not loving the alcohol because my stomach's a bit queasy; it's soda-water and lemon tonight.

Scottie Dog says, 'Yer shouldn't swallow so much, Lena,' and laughs herself silly at her own joke, until Irish reckons Scottie Dog hasn't munched on anything since nineteen seventy-five and Scottie Dog says that was a vintage year, the last year they made real men. Katy laughs a strange, bitter laugh. 'That can't be true, it's the year Jerry was born.'

Then we have one of those silences when no one knows what to say.

It's three games each and we think we'll get a captain's game from Katy, because this is the new confident Katy: Katy with a new figure, hairstyle, a new purpose. And a new lover.

He's all right, is Johnny, but if I was to flash a bit of leg on the bar-stool, he'd have a good butcher's. Like all of them. Like the way Danny looks when I slide off the stool and show him a bit more than I intend.

'I can see next week's washing, Lena.'

Katy's darts are flowing. She's got winner written all over her, and Scottie Dog and Irish are celebrating two throws before Katy fires out.

'Yeees,' hollers Irish.

God, she's noisy tonight. I mean she's always been noisy, but lately it's like she's got to trying even harder to win the Gob of the Pub contest.

Dandy says that I think too much, that a pretty girl like me shouldn't analyse things so. I know what he means, but there's lots of things in my head that swim around . . .

\* \* \*

*My sixteenth birthday on this Sunday . . .*

*It's a lovely warm summer morning. I'm awake before anyone else and I go downstairs and put the kettle on. It's barely seven o'clock and already the day is bright. I make a cup of coffee, pinch one of Mum's fags, and sit outside the patio doors. From the open bedroom window above my head I hear Mikey stirring. He's nearly a year old and he's just becoming interesting. He still smells of poo most of the time, but he's trying to walk and he laughs at things I don't see. I think I've started to love my little brother. And Dandy really loves Mikey. He's always on Dandy's knee, in his arms. And he's a smaller, browner version of Dandy, like he's been buffed over with a darker cloth.*

*Dandy's voice drifts out of the window, drifts down to me. 'You have a lie-in, Mandy; I'll make Mikey's bottle.'*

*I hear him come down the stairs into the kitchen, hear the kettle clicked on, hear Dandy whistling the song that's always on the radio, the song that the girls at school sing behind the young English teacher: 'You're more than gorgeous and I'll do anything you want.'*

*Dandy doesn't know I'm outside, doesn't see me until I'm standing in the patio doorway. I know the sun's shining through my flimsy nightie. I know what I look like with cigarette smoke curling from my mouth. I know what I'm doing as I sing in my sweet, tempting voice:*

*'You're more than gorgeous and I'll do anything you want,*
*I'll save myself for you,*
*slave myself for you,*
*behave myself for you.*
*You're more than gorgeous and I'll do anything you want.'*

*I stop then and Dandy is looking, staring at me. This isn't a schoolgirl standing too close to him. This is me, someone who's loved and wanted him for two years.*

*And it seems that here in this summer morning kitchen, we're the only two people in the whole world.*

*Dandy says, his voice catching, 'You're gorgeous, Lena.'*

*But it's not me, it's him.*

*Then Dandy is holding me, kissing me. I can feel how much he wants me, wants to love me.*

*I think we would have done it there and then on the kitchen floor if Mum hadn't called down the stairs, 'Is Mikey's bottle ready yet, Andy?'*

*Dandy starts, pushes me away. Not harshly but gently. Regretfully.*

*'Lena,' he says. 'I'm sorry. So sorry. What was I thinking?'*

*But I'm not sorry and I know what I was thinking.*

*Dandy makes up Mikey's bottle and his hands are trembling. He spills powdered milk on the tray and nearly scalds himself with the kettle. Then he sits the bottle in a jug of cold water.*

*'I'll take it up,' I say, and he seems relieved.*

*Then he says, 'Lena, I love your mother,' and I say, 'So do I, Dandy. So do I.'*

*I take up Mikey's bottle and Mum has Mikey in bed with her. He's a wriggling little sod and he spots the bottle straight away and I tell him he'll have to wait; it's still too hot for him.*

*I say to my little brother, 'Have a bit of patience, Mikey.'*

*Mum says, 'You were just the same, Lena. Couldn't wait to get what you wanted.'*

*Then, as I'm leaving the room, she says, 'You should really be dressed, Lena; you're not hiding a lot.'*

*So me and Dandy are nearly there and I know it's going to happen and Dandy knows it's going to happen.*

I can look at this now and think what a cow I was to Mum but then my head was full of Dandy. I watched his every move, brushed by him in the hall, held his eyes in secret glances. It was like I was blind, like I had no concept of the future, of consequence. I couldn't see where it would end; I just wanted Dandy holding me, loving me.

I'm thinking this now and all I can see is him; all I can feel is that desire. It burns me up and Dandy only has to look at me to light the gas.

*I've had a bubble bath and I've wrapped myself up in a towel. I'm warm, scented and soft, and I'm drying my hair in the front room. The telly's on and Mikey's been tucked up in bed an hour. Tonight, Mum is going to Pilates.*

*'Do you think I'm getting my figure back?' she asks Dandy. She does a twirl in front of him but Dandy, lazing on the settee, has his head in the paper.*

*'Yes,' he says, without looking up.*

*Mum goes 'Men' and raises her eyebrows to me.*

*'Old men,' I say, and Mum laughs, and Dandy says, 'Watch it, madam.'*

*'Why, what are you going to do?'*

*He's looking up from his paper now. 'Don't tempt me, Lena.'*

*Mum says, 'You two, always teasing each other.'*

*Dandy says, 'She started it.'*

*So I go upstairs to dress and Mum goes to Pilates.*

*But I don't dress; I go back downstairs, still in the towel, and sit next to Dandy.*

*He says, 'You shouldn't, Lena.'*
*I say, 'Shouldn't what, Dandy?'*
*Then he says, 'Oh fuck it, Lena.'*
*And then the towel's on the floor and it begins.*


Irish says, 'I'd just as well be talking to the wall, Lena.'

'What?'

'God almighty, Lena; you were miles away.'

'Yeah, I was dreaming.'

'Well, fucking wake up, it's your round.'

Scottie Dog is falling asleep in the corner and Katy's texting Lover Boy, mouthing words that are almost readable. Maggie's looking at the door, waiting for Danny and our lift back to the Bluebell. Big Dave Trinder has turned up and he and Pegs are quietly sitting together, looking as if they're sharing a secret. She's squeezing his hand and shaking her head. It makes me wonder if she's up the duff. If she is, I can't see her father being too pleased: funny lot, the Gypsies.

At least they're out together, not like me and Dandy lately. We still have an occasional meal; he even comes to the Bluebell sometimes, but Dandy's not one for the high life. (That's one of the things Mum liked – loved – about him. He didn't put his wages up his nose or piss it up against the wall.)

So most of the time I go out alone. I laugh and drink and flirt, but coming home, slipping between the sheets, feeling Dandy's warm body beside me, means so much more.

And the thing is, that after these years together nothing's changed; I still want him all the time. I really can't wait to go home.

I really can't wait to tell him the news.

*       *       *

He's in bed when I get back, and he moans when I switch the lamp on.

He sits up, rubbing his eyes. 'For God's sake, Lena, I've got to be up early in the morning.'

'I've got to tell you something.'

Just those half a dozen words and his manner instantly changes.

'Lena, what is it? What's wrong?'

'Not wrong, Dandy. Right. It's something right.'

All the same, the words crawl out of me. 'Pregnant, Dandy. I'm pregnant.'

Dandy looks at me and I can't read his face, not properly. I wanted him to hold me, to share this with me, but he sits there and it's like he can't grasp the meaning of what I've said.

He says, 'Your Mum, who's going to tell her?'

And all my joy freezes in my body and it makes me wonder if Mum ever left this place, if she ever left Dandy's heart.

Later, Dandy does turn to me in the night. His arm slides around me and his voice comes out of the dark.

'I'm sorry,' he says. 'It was a shock.'

I don't tell him that it's been a strange few months and my monthlies had been a bit odd, almost non-existent really and the shock was just as much for me.

Although I hadn't *exactly* known, I must have suspected because I'm in the bathroom after Dandy's gone to work, throwing up my breakfast, and I've started piling on the pounds and eating like a horse, and . . . *and all those things I didn't want to see in my second great betrayal of Mum.*

And then there's Dandy, and into this night I'm thinking that because of me he lost Mikey, and now I can give him back the same. Like repaying a debt; well, not exactly that, but it sort of evens things up between me and him.

And Mum? I'll have to tell her; I know Dandy can't. Or won't.

# THURSDAY NIGHT PRACTICE IN JANUARY

*Scottie Dog*

I don't like sitting in on these dark stormy winter nights now I'm an old – I mean, elderly – woman. The night never used to worry me; the dark was for warmth and comfort, and sometimes passion. And mostly for concealing.

Even when I was a little girl, plain Marie Stewart, I'd lie in bed, listening to the Scottish gale seeking out the loose tiles on our roof. They'd rattle and clap like . . .

*'Like Mrs Delaney's false teeth,' Mam says and laughs.*

*Mrs Delaney is our neighbour and her teeth are always slopping around her mouth. Occasionally, the top set will pop out and she crams them back in with an 'Och, the little devils are alive.'*

*Mam laughs again and I always see her, remember her, like that; smiling, laughing; the happy-go-lucky Mam of no consequence. She's pretty, I suppose, in a brassy way, like Elsie Tanner in Coronation Street. (Years later, the first time I see the programme, it's Mam on the screen with brown hair and a Manchester accent.)*

\*    \*    \*

On this night of long ago, Mam's getting ready to go out – dressing up to the nines. She's straightened her stockings, fluffed up her hair and painted her face. She looks glamorous, attractive. Just how I'd like to be.

'Now, don't answer the door to anyone,' she says, and kisses me goodnight. Then she holds me, hugs me. 'My bonny wee war baby.'

I remember the warmth, the smell of her, to this day, and I remember what the two words 'war baby' meant then. It meant no father. Before I realised the impossibility of it, I used to imagine a rich, handsome American turning up in one of those huge gleaming cars. He'd park in the street, ring on our bell and I'd answer the door to:

'You must be my little girl.'

He'd pick me up, throw me into the air and we'd drive to an ice-cream parlour (in Dundee!) and he'd order me a huge knickerbocker glory and a tall glass of soda pop, like in the films.

It's funny, Mam was never in those daydreams; it was just me and him.

And all she says when I ask about my father is, 'He was in the army. He was away too much,' and her face hardens into one of those 'no more questions' expressions.

Mam says, 'I'll not be too long.'

The 'not long' will happen when I'm deep in the Land of Nod, but for now, as soon as she's gone, I go to the window and watch the street by the lamplight, watch Mam walk the length of this road, watch her disappear around the corner. I can almost hear the tap of her heels on the pavement. From up here, in our rooms above the ironmonger's, I turn off the light and watch the night-life of the town begin.

It's nineteen fifty-three, I'm ten years old, and the Scottish rain is sweeping the Dundee streets. In my street, from my window to the world, the bright door of the Jolly Sailor swings open and shut; people spill out into the rain, people spill in from the rain. There's deep male laughter, high-pitched giggles, and always the glow of cigarettes. A dulled tinkle of a piano snatches half a tune through the gale. These sounds are subdued, distanced by the wet, thin glass and the curtain of rain. There's a lonely cyclist pedalling by, head down, wrapped in a yellow cape, wobbling against the wind.

I'll watch from the window until my eyelids start to droop, then I'll go back to bed and pull the covers up to my eyes and imagine the wind on the sea, the collision of white wave and shore. I'll imagine until I fall asleep.

I won't hear Mam come in, but when I wake in the morning she'll be lying beside me. She won't stir as I slip out of bed, go out to the kitchen, make myself a bowl of hot milk, bread and sugar. She'll still be sleeping as I pad down the stairs and let myself out into the street to join the weaving band of kids playing their way to school.

And this is my life as I grow older, stronger, taller. There are other flats, other rooms, and once even a two-up, two-down, with a proper bathroom. But we're never anywhere for long. Because of how Mam earns a few bob when we're in a tight spot, I suppose.

She ships me out when she has a male visitor. She'll give me a half a crown and say, 'Get yourself down to the chippie for . . .' she'll look at the clock, look at the man kneading his hat in his hands, ' . . . for an hour.'

And Mam's hours merge into nights, into awaydays, into lost weekends, and for me into long hours watching and waiting from the window.

At twelve years old, I might come home to mashed tatties and neeps topped with a melting knob of butter, peas and two thick slices of Spam for tea. Or there might be burnt sausages and baked beans, because Mam tries, Mam really tries, but she's a bottle blonde in a tight skirt who can't resist the bright lights. She can't resist a drink. She can't resist company. She can't resist men.

But sometimes when I come home there'll be nothing to eat, and no one there.

And most of the time when I'm thirteen pushing into fourteen, there's no one there.

Bedtime no longer exists. I can stay out until dusk, until the streetlights start to burn. I'm a part-time orphan, and I join the other orphans who walk the twilight town until a policeman sends us on our ways, sends us to our houses. Then I can let myself in, slip a shilling into the gas metre and warm my feet by the fire. I can listen to the wireless until I fall asleep, or I can sit at the window and watch the world slow, watch the streets empty, until no one walks the lonely pavements.

So was it this that made me vulnerable? Was it because I was on my own when Denny Adams knocked on the door?

It's a Saturday morning, the sky is grey and it's raining again. I'm thinking about going down the arcade. I like it there; I like the penny machines, the laughing policeman, the crane where you grab a toy and drop it into a chute if you're lucky.

*I'll say one thing for Mam, she never leaves me without money now. (She's doing well – or being well done.) In fact, I can tell how long she'll be gone by how much is in the purse under the mattress. The going rate is five bob for each day and I've got fifteen shillings left, so sometime on Monday she'll be back in my life. She'll flop down in the chair and I'll make her a mug of hot milk, feed her a couple of aspirins, light her a cigarette.*

*'Marie,' she'll say, 'you're a good girl, a good daughter.'*

*Then she'll fall asleep and I'll drape a blanket around her.*

*She'll sleep until the clock strikes seven, then she'll wake, yawn, stretch and start to get ready for the night.*

*But now it's Saturday and Denny Adams is knocking at the door, asking for Mam.*

*'She's not here.'*

*'I'll wait.'*

*'You can't come in.'*

*'I can,' says this infrequent visitor, and he pushes open the door, shoves me to one side, and then he's up the stairs with me following close behind.*

*'Where is she?' he asks in our sitting room.*

*'She's not here.' I'm a little wary now, wary of this young man in pale-blue jeans, white T-shirt and leather jacket. His Brylcreemed hair is greased back into a duck's arse and he leaves a cigarette smouldering in his mouth as he talks. He's good-looking in a cruel way.*

*'What do you want?'*

*'Your mother; I paid her for something I didn't get.'*

*He settles into the sofa, puts his feet, his pointed shoes, on the coffee table.*

I say, 'She won't be back for ages yet.'

He's looking at me now, looking me up and down, and I can't quite meet his eyes.

'I wouldn't say no to a cup of tea.' Then he adds my name, 'Marie,' and he laughs. 'Tea. Marie. I'm a poet and I don't know it.'

So I boil up the kettle, brew the tea, put it into his hand. But he sets it by his feet on the table, makes no attempt to drink.

He's looking at me again and he says, 'You've really grown up lately, Marie.'

I'm conscious of him eyeing me up and down. He pats the sofa.

'Come and sit by me.'

I pretend not to hear, but there's just the beginning of a strange thrill shivering down my spine. I should be thinking, 'Just make him go. Just make him go,' but somehow the words won't form in my head.

Denny Adams pats the sofa seat again.

'Come and sit by me, Marie.'

His voice is soft, cajoling, and he's smiling at me like he's a friend.

'C'mon, Marie. I won't bite you.'

He reaches out, takes my hand and pulls me down.

So I sit there unprotesting while he gently unbuttons my blouse, lifts my skirt, slips down my knickers.

Why do I let him? Why do I let strange curiosity close my mouth and cloud my brain?

This makes me sound like some sort of goody-goody seduced by a predator, but it's not like that. I've not gone the whole way before, but I know men look at me; I know what's in their minds.

I know what Mam does to make a living. I've had to avoid the odd drunken lurch towards me, the 'My yer a pretty young thing, Marie.'

But like I said, I'm no goody-goody and I've shared hot wet kisses in the back seats of the Odeon, fumbled at love in night-time doorways, and discovered those touches for relief.

And now with Denny Adams it's the time, the time for me.

There's a young girl on the sofa and this youth with her has kicked off his pointed shoes. His pale-blue jeans are down to his knees and the young girl is trembling under his body. She is staring to the ceiling and her eyes are blank, uncomprehending, like she isn't here. Like she's looking into somewhere else. Like she's in another world.

The hands on the clock have ticked by less than ten minutes before he stands, pulls up his underpants, his jeans, and buckles his belt as the young blonde girl lies with her legs splayed out on the sofa.

'We better keep this quiet,' he says. Then he adds, laughing, 'Tell your Mam I'll be calling round to collect what she owes me.'

The girl doesn't say anything, just carries on staring at the ceiling.

The youth shrugs his shoulders, lights a cigarette, pauses at the door, flicks her the packet in a parting gift.

'Just tell her that. Only that, mind,' he says and then he is gone, whistling down the stairs.

Like nothing has happened. Like nothing for five cheap fags in a cardboard carton.

\*     \*     \*

*Later, before I try to fill my head with sleep, I'm watching from*
*the window at a building Dundee gale. The wind's veered to the*
*west and the rain's falling in sheets. Mam's still not come home*
*and I'm thinking that the flat sounds hollow. There's a feeling*
*creeping over me that I need someone to cuddle: someone safe.*
*There's a feeling I've gone over a threshold, done something I'm*
*not sure of, so I make the sign of the cross and tell Jesus all my*
*troubles. I don't know why I do because I never go to church,*
*never make a confession or take Communion, but in the dark,*
*wet night I talk to someone who listens because the world has*
*changed for me.*

*Then I wait for Mam to come home.*

*And you know what? When she does, that bastard Denny*
*comes around for his money's worth, saunters in like he's cock o'*
*the walk.*

*And I suppose he is, in this house.*


That's enough for now. When I relive those days, they drain me.
They pull all the strength out of me. So I pour myself a stiff
whisky and toast myself – 'Here's tae me' – and knock it back in
one hit. Then I pour myself another. Then I pour myself a hot
bath and, when I'm undressed, I stand in front of the mirror and
smooth out the wrinkles, peel the years from my old body,
remember what it was like to be young and firm.

And beautiful.

And then to fill my head, like I always do, I count the cats of
my life; right from the first kitten that I was given for my eight-
eenth birthday.

*'Now you're really one of my girls,' she says after the busiest*
*Saturday in months.*

By the time I've put my cats in order of time and place it's a quarter to eight and the Bluebell is calling and I've reached Posh and Becks.

It ends there.

At the Bluebell, Danny says, 'You're late on parade. Thought you needed the practice.'

I suppose we do, we had a shit result last week against the King Charles – Charlie's Angels – and it's nice of Danny to remind me.

I say, 'Cut the cackle and get me a whisky.'

Danny says, 'Charming, yer miserable Jock.'

He milks the optic and then slides my drink across the bar like they do in the western films. 'Hope it chokes you.'

'You'd miss me, Danny.'

'Like I'd miss a hole in my head, Scottie Dog.'

I tell him if he doesn't watch his gob that hole's going to appear pretty soon.

The girls are practising on the dartboard and I sit down with Maggie. I get on well with her – she understands about my cats.

'I'm thinking of getting a pet,' she says quietly. 'Maybe a dog, it'll be something to keep me company at night.' The next thing she says is, 'I saw the piece in the paper.'

I saw the piece as well. I tore it into bits and flushed it down the loo. I know where it came from; I had a reporter come sniffing around, knocking on my door.

'Mrs Stewart,' he says, 'I've heard you've had a problem with your cats.'

I tell him there's no problem now because they've all been murdered.

'Murdered?'

He's really interested now, this man standing on my doorstep, waiting for an invite in, waiting for a cup of tea and a juicy story dressed up in a cosy chat.

'If you really want to know what happened . . .' I pitch this in just above a whisper, and he leans forward with his head cocked and his little piggy eyes bright with anticipation.

'If you're really interested,' I say in barely more than a whisper. He moves up another step and I shout loudly, suddenly, into his face, 'Ask those bastards next door.' Then I slam the door on him.

But then you know what? The slimy little toad wrote a story about a lonely widow who'd lost her only friends. He even quoted those bastard neighbours saying how my cats had been my whole world and how they missed them as well. Fucking Pinocchios.

Maggie says, 'I expect you want to get another cat.'

I'm thinking that it's the last thing I want because my old heart couldn't stand another hurt.

This is a good night in the Bluebell; we're playing the Busy Lizzies from the Queen Elizabeth. (We call them the Busybodies because they seem to know everything that's going on in town and more.) They're a middle-aged team with middle-aged spread and they sit in the middle of the league. And they play a middling game, not giving any of us too much trouble – well, except for Lena, she's really off-colour. Her hair is straggly and she's hardly bothered with make-up. She doesn't want a drink, keeps running off to the loo, wants to sit down between throws. Her match takes so long she pisses off the Busybody she's playing.

'God, we're going to be here all night at this rate.'

Irish says, 'Wake me up when they're done.' But she goes to the bar and watches from there as she slots in a drink between rounds. Even Katy, who's chalking the scores, is stifling yawns. We're all hoping that it's a quick check-out on the double, but the Busybody has lost interest and her casual chucks are wide of the mark. So it's Lena who eventually drops into her number.

There's a half-hearted cheer and her opponent offers a congratulation, 'Thank Christ for that.'

Lena flops down beside me. 'I thought that would never end.'

I say, 'You weren't the only one.'

Then, as Pegs is at the oche, I look around this pub. There's the yellowed ceiling, dated adverts, fading photographs of the Motley Crew on pub outings from the eighties, nineties, noughties. They've gone from young men in flares, with wide collars and big hair, to plump, and skinny, and balding, and fashionless.

I look around and I count the years like I counted my cats. Twenty years I've been coming here, twenty years of Danny behind the bar, of darts on a Monday and practice on a Thursday. Twenty years of being carried home every Hogmanay – Christmas is all right for the Sassenachs, but New Year belongs to us Jocks. And lately I've missed all things Scottish. I've missed the summer rain, the winter snow. I've even missed hearing Mr Brown's dour accent.

And now I'm going to miss this team, my friends, this town. I'm going to miss the Bluebell and joshing with Danny.

Because it's time to go home before I die.

Because there was blood in the toilet again this morning.

\*    \*    \*

Lena says, 'I'll buy this one,' but I tell her she's been on lime and soda all night and so I'll get the drinks instead.

At the bar, Danny says, 'What's up with Lena tonight?'

'Upset stomach. She must have eaten one of your sandwiches.'

'Ho bloody ho.'

I bring the drinks to our table and unload a gin for Irish, a whisky for me, a cider for Maggie, a brace of vodka and Coke for Katy and Pegs, and Lena's much softer drink. But Lena's buttoning up her coat.

'Your soda,' I say.

Lena says, 'Sorry, Scottie, I'm going home; I feel like shit.'

She's burping and swallowing and I think she might throw up, so I move out the line of fire, give her a clear run to the door.

After Lena's scurried away I say to Katy, 'She's been a bit odd lately.'

Katy reckons that Lena looks pregnant to her and it seems to fit, so there's a discussion between Katy and Maggie about how uncomfortable the carrying is, what with spewing down the toilet, the wind, and worse.

'Longest nine months of my life,' Katy says.

Pegs is contributing nothing to the conversation and Irish not much more until she turns to me and says rather quietly for her, 'Have you ever popped one out, Scottie?'

Then I say quietly, 'Aye I have, Irish,' and they all shut up and look at me. But I just pick up my whisky, take a sip, and keep my mouth closed, because it's my secret, my story, and I don't want to share it with anyone.

\*　　\*　　\*

Now you would think after the Denny Adams episode my life would be changed. But what's to change? Mam's the same; I'm the same – apart from being a bit sore for a few days.

So things stay in the status quo of my existence.

But I'm not a lonely kid, even though I spend a lot of time being alone; I have friends from school, friends like Connie Smart, Lennie Dalgish, Pete Macoy and Mickey Broyne.

We share cigs, we share cider, we share light and heavy.

And we share growing up.

That was when I found I had a weakness for men – well, boys at the outset – and though the first was Denny Adams, after him it was easy. So easy.

I'm fifteen when the Welfare call – it wasn't Social Services in those days – and they've come to school to collect me. Now this is a school I like, because we've been at the same address for over a year now, and things have become familiar to me.

I'm sitting in class and we're trying to memorise the capital cities of South America. I'm pretty good at this and I'm quicker than the rest. While Colin Smith is struggling with Venezuela, I whisper across to him, 'Caracas'. Then, for Ollie White, 'Brazil – Rio de Janeiro.'

Then there's an interruption when one of the first-formers brings in a note for Sir.

Sir studies it, frowns, looks at me and then says, 'Marie Stewart, Headmaster wants to see you. Straight away.'

All eyes are on me as I scrape back my chair, and Colin Smith says, 'Who's been a naughty girl, then.'

As I pass him in the aisle I slip him the V and mutter that he'll have to answer his own fucking questions now.

On my way to the office I wonder what I've done, if the headmaster is going to give me a pep talk about my schoolwork? He's called me in a couple of times before. 'If you tried – really tried – you could go places. You could have a career.' Then he tells me that he knows my home life isn't ideal. 'But you have a quick mind, Marie and . . .' He pauses. 'And I hate to see waste.'

But this isn't going to be a pep talk. This is the interfering busybodies of the Welfare State and they're sitting, puritan straight, on rigid-backed chairs. They're the couple that you see in the crumbling mansion: the creepy housekeeper and her butler accomplice in a shadowy horror film. In unsmiling, disapproving disclosure, they tell me that Mam's . . .

That Mam's stepped out of a pub and under a lorry.

They don't exactly say that, they say 'traffic accident', but later I find an article in the paper about a Mrs Stewart who 'believed to have been drinking in the Rose and Thistle, walked into the road without looking'. The lorry driver, 'A Mr Arthur McBain, stated to the police that, "The lady was laughing with a companion, and she just didn't see me."'

After, a long time after, I like to think that Mam died with a smile on her face and a drink in her belly. I like to think that she died happy, unknowing.

I'd like to die like that.

But now Housekeeper and Butler tell me that they'll take me home to pick up my belongings and then it's into care for me.

The headmaster, who's been sitting quietly through this, says, 'I'm sorry, Marie,' and he says it like he means it, but he frowns like the sentence isn't enough said.

\*     \*     \*

All my clothes, all my things, fit into a suitcase and a hold-all. That's all I take, apart from the photo on the mantelpiece of Mam and me. She's got her arm around my waist and we've got the same smile, same figure; we could be sisters.

I don't know about the next few days – they're not the proverbial blur – they're more like a realisation that sinks slowly in. Fuck it, I don't want to try to put it in words because it's all in impressions.

Me lying in bed in the attic dorm of the Home and seeing the bright moon fill the skylight, a huge eye peeping in at me.

The other three girls softly sleeping, softly snoring in the warmth of their beds.

Me the stranger, a story they all want to read at the breakfast table.

Me thinking that it's all been a mistake, and soon Mam will be calling to take me home. She'll have a pocket full of money and a head full of dreams.

'My little girl,' she'll say, even though I'm not little. 'Things are going to be better now.'

But she doesn't come and, here in this time, there's no one to talk to – it's not like today when a counsellor's on your doorstep if you so much as sneeze.

Because I'm fifteen, grown-up and about ready for the world, no one bothers me. On most days, in this week of waiting, I sit in the attic room. Sometimes I go down for a meal, sometimes to listen to the radio, and sometimes I don't.

Mostly I watch the Dundee rain through the window, blowing in off the sea. I think about Mam and I have a cry to myself.

Then I dry my eyes and carry on in a foretaste of what my life's going to be.

On the day of Mam's funeral, Housekeeper and Butler come to take me to the church. We catch the bus from the bottom of the road, and I'm in a borrowed black coat with my fair head covered with a chiffon scarf.

'We'll see you to there; we won't be coming in to the service,' Housekeeper says.

She looks to her partner. 'We won't be coming in,' Butler says in a confirming echo.

At the church there's a polished hearse pulled up and a coffin's being shouldered through the door by four men in charcoal suits. I follow, not sure of what I'm meant to be doing, if I should sit to the left or to the right.

There are people here, perhaps twenty, no one I recognise though, and there's a priest with his back to the altar. He smiles and nods me to my place with Catholic care. Then an organ begins a hymn, and priest and player launch loudly into voice. They're joined by a mumbling, ragged congregation.

'We shall sleep, but not forever,
There will be glorious dawn.
We shall meet to part, no, never,
On the resurrection morn.'

I'm listening, but I'm not really hearing because I'm studying the nameplate on Mam's wooden box.

Eileen Stewart 1923–1955

I'm counting the years, taking the date of birth from the date of death. Then I take my age away, and Mam's seventeen and she's carrying me.

Behind me one of the — I suppose I should say mourners — is having a coughing fit. It goes on and on even when the service ends, and we're following Mam out into the graveyard.

So the priest says a few words, and Mam's lowered into the stony soil, and everyone stands stock-still for a few moments except the poor bugger who's still coughing. Someone says to him, louder and more shrill than intended, 'We'll just as well leave you here, too.'

It's then that I take notice of this group, this dozen mixture of men and women who drank with Mam, who plied their trade with Mam. Who lived in Mam's world.

There's too much perfume, too much make-up, jewellery, and fake fur, too many bulging waistcoats and florid faces. They come up to me one by one to pay their respects.

'She was a lovely dear, your mam.'

'She'd give away her last penny.'

'Heart of gold she had. Heart of gold.'

There're no introductions, no names. Just a few words and then a return to the flock. Then there's one man, fifty if he's a day, towering over me, who takes my hand and says, 'If you ever need anything, you ask for Ben. Big Ben of the Beagle. Landlord I am. Thought the world of your mother.'

He leans forward and pulls me to him in an embrace close enough for me to smell the drink on his breath. He holds me slightly too long and in my ear he says again, 'Big Ben, my dear. Don't forget. Anything you want, come to the Beagle.' Then he does let me go and he returns to his companions.

And again there's that shrill, cutting voice. 'Och, her mother's hardly cold and you're pestering that slip of a girl.'

But I didn't think that then, that I was being pestered. I'm unaware of anything in my state and it wasn't until a few years later, when I was really in – or on – the Game, that I understood the attraction of grief to a man.

The last person to come to me is a man who's been standing in the background talking earnestly with Housekeeper and Butler. Now he walks over, tall, dark-haired and smart, so very smart. He's what Mam would have called a handsome man. There's a purpose to his approach and a half-smile of greeting is forming on his face. I can remember every detail of these moments when I first met him, as he takes my hand gently in his, looks straight into my eyes.

'Marie,' he says, 'I'm sorry for your loss.' The accent is a thick, harsh Glaswegian. Then he says, 'You should know, Marie, that I'm your father.'

And although I didn't know it then, ahead of me were the happiest and the saddest days of my life.

But now I've got to shut the door, shut down all that I know will happen. I'll leave it to laugh over, to cry over like the sad, exiled Scot that I am.


It's tonight and we've had a fairly comfortable win with only Irish losing. She's played like she doesn't care and she's got right up Katy's nose.

'You better pull yourself together for next week,' Katy says to her.

'Sure everyone has an off night.'

'Doesn't mean you've got to have everyone's,' I tell her, because I can't keep my nose out.

Irish says, ''Tis only a fucking game; it's not life or death.'

Maggie says quietly, 'I love our nights out; let's not spoil it.'

And that shuts us all up because no one would want to upset gentle Maggie after what she's been going through. Is going through.

It's later I ask her, 'Ken. How's Ken?'

'All he does is stare, Scottie. He stares at the television, he stares out of the window, he stares at me.' Her voice breaks just a little. 'But he doesn't see anything.'

Then she says, 'I keep the Ken I knew at home.' She touches her heart with her fingertips. 'And in here, Scottie. And in here.'

I don't know what to say, so I wait a few moments and then start to call the drinks in.

No one seems in a hurry to go tonight, well, except for the opposition. We, Six of the Best, sit and jaw, clean up the sandwiches, insult Danny: things we've done for years. There's a comfort to it, a familiarity. I suppose this is what Maggie meant when she said, 'Let's not spoil it.'

And she's right.

I make the mistake, when I get home, of pouring myself a large nightcap, but what I thought would help me sleep keeps me awake. I'm tossing and turning and I'm thinking that what I need is a good, strong man to curl up to at night.

Then I laugh to myself because who would want an old fleabag like me, withered, empty tits and as dry as a bone in you know where.

I'm thinking about getting up to make a cup of tea when I hear a sound like a meow. I stop breathing, listen. There it is again. Clear. Distinct.

Meow. Meow. Meow. Long and plaintive and coming from the back of the house, the patio.

You know what? I'm shaking because it can't be, not after all these weeks. But all the same a prayer, a fucking prayer, is forming in my head.

When I'm downstairs he's there, one little runaway who escaped the slaughter. He's pushing himself against the glass, squinting at the light. My own holocaust survivor come back to me.

My own Robert the Bruce.

And I forget – for now – about the blood in the toilet bowl.

# THURSDAY NIGHT PRACTICE – FEBRUARY

*Katy*

It's Thursday night and I should be having a drink and laughing with the girls, but I'm driving back to Mum's in Johnny James's car. I feel like I've been kicked in the stomach and the only thing I want tonight is some honesty from Mum.

I'm thinking that an hour ago the world was nearly a settled place and one thing, just one thing, has opened a can of worms.

Earlier Johnny James says, 'Take my car, Katy, pick up Pegs and I'll come down to the pub later, drive you home.' He gives me that look that makes me think I'm the only girl in the whole world.

I say, 'What if I have an accident?'

'You don't drive fast enough to do any damage.'

'Cheeky sod.'

He kisses me then, wraps his arms around me so tightly you'd have to peel us apart.

'I bet you'll be *really* grateful for this,' he whispers. My man's breath is warm and the taste of him so tempting and . . . and if I don't go now I never will.

And later I wish I hadn't.


It's dusk when I drive down the narrow lane into the site. I say 'lane' but really it's a rough track. Mum says that when she was a young girl it was a proper road to the station, but now the hedges have spread and the verges have closed in.

Mum says, 'That was before the Gypsies came.'

Johnny's car is a low-slung Beamer and it glides over the humps and through the potholes like it's on the highway. This motor is Johnny James's pride and joy. He keeps it spotless and I tell him it's clean enough to live in.

He says, 'Why not? We've done everything else in it.'

He nods towards the back seat.

It's this way about him that makes me laugh: his directness. No smutty porn for Johnny James; he wants the real thing.

Like when we were having a smoke together outside the Bluebell and he just leaned forward and kissed me.

And started all of this.


Now it's dusk and I'm pulling onto Pegs' site and I get that feeling of déjà vu, but it's beyond the times I've been here before. It's something distant, something older that slips away from me. You know how something puzzles you sometimes and you don't quite know why, but so, so, nearly do? Well, it's like that.

When I knock on the door Pegs isn't ready and her mum says, 'Come in, Katy, and wait.'

I haven't been in their home before but I've seen the inside of Gypsy places on the telly, so I'm expecting lots of cut glass and ornaments, like on *Big Fat Gypsy Wedding*. But this park home isn't cluttered up; it's quite roomy. Well, apart from a wall of framed photographs that's crowded with people.

Pegs' mum shouts through the bathroom door, 'Katy's here, Peggy.'

Then she takes two cans of beer out of the fridge and says to me, 'You all right here? Henry and Big Dave are working in the shed. I better take them a livvener.'

Then it's like she corrects herself, like she's given away a secret word. 'Beer. I mean take them a beer, Katy.'

She leaves with the cans and I can hear Pegs singing softly to herself as she gets ready for our practice night. She sounds so happy, not a care in the world.


I've never been too good at sitting still, and after a few minutes I have a nose around. Not prying, just curious, I look down the wall of photos.

There's pictures of old-fashioned caravans and tethered horses.

There's a family sitting around a fire, where a big pot is hanging above the flames, and they're giving the camera a broad-grinned thumbs-up.

There's a picture of an old lady with a basket of bunched flowers.

Then there's another one of her holding hands, caught in a walk with who I think must be a young Pegs.

This old lady's hair is in two long plaits and she looks like a Comanche off the reservation. But she also looks slightly familiar, and then I think that I must have seen her years ago in town, maybe.

I scan the rest of the pictures and, just when I'm nearly done, I hear Pegs open the bathroom door.

'Katy,' she says.

Now if she'd have stepped out a fraction of a second sooner, I wouldn't have seen the framed photo at the end of the bottom row. But she doesn't and I do.

It draws me in, this close-up of the same *old lady with hooped earrings, cradling a baby*.

Behind me, Pegs says, 'Katy?'

I don't know what she must think when all I can answer is, 'Who's this?' I've got my finger on the picture. 'Who's this, Pegs?'

Pegs is looking at me quizzically. 'You all right, Katy?'

'Yes. Yes. Who is it?'

Pegs says, 'That's my gran.'

'Your gran? And the baby. Who's the baby?'

'What's the matter, Katy?'

I don't know what's the matter. I don't know anything. I only know that it's the same photo that's in Mum's Huntley and Palmers tin.

Now Pegs is speaking slowly and she's not looking at me. It's as though she doesn't want to see me.

She says, 'Gran never said. Reckoned we'd meet her one day. Gran was like that, talking in riddles.'

Then she says, 'We should get going, else we'll be late.' She laughs. 'I spent too long getting ready. Was it worth it?' She laughs like she's nervous of something and then little, gentle Pegs revolves in front of me, in front of that picture.

We climb into Johnny James's Beamer and we head for the Bluebell. My mobile rings on the way and, although I know it's him, I don't answer it.

Me and Pegs hardly speak at all.

\* \* \*

When we reach the pub, I buy a round for the girls. Then I leave them all to their simple fucking lives and do what I should have done months ago. I'll do like I promised myself; I'll empty that biscuit box on the kitchen table and I'll sit Mum there and make her answer every question.

But when I get home, Mum's not in and there's a note on the worktop.

*Gone with Moira to bingo. Might be a bit late back.*

I get out Mum's photos, make myself a cup of tea, light a cigarette and dip into the box. I lay these pictures out in order of date and look for clues. But they tell me nothing and I shuffle them like cards, lay them down again and again. I do it time after time but there's not anything given away.

I've smoked three cigarettes and drunk two cups of tea before the door opens behind me.

I'm turning around as I say, 'Mum, I want the truth and I won't take no for . . .'

But it's not Mum.

Laura says, 'I didn't think you'd be here. Where's Gran?'

'Bingo.'

'I'll go then.'

'No, Laura. Stay. I'll make you a drink.'

She hesitates, half in and half out of the night.

'Can I have one of your fags?'

She's never smoked in front of me; she knows my illogical disapproval.

'Dad lets me,' she says.

It's all there, isn't it? A 'no' and she'll be gone. A 'yes' a victory won and she'll stay.

I say, 'Okay,' and she lights a cigarette and takes a deep exaggerated drag. I half expect her to blow the smoke into my face.

We sit in silence for a while, with me frantically searching for some common ground. All I come out with is, 'How's your father?' and this sounds so formal, like I'm talking about a stranger.

She's straight onto it.

'Your father,' she mocks. 'Your father. Don't you mean your husband? As if you cared how he is anyway.'

I'm thinking that feeling sorry for someone is caring, but I can't tell her that because it won't make things better.

'How's school?'

'I go sometimes.' She adds, 'When I feel like it.'

My daughter, this young woman in her time of puppy-fat and too-tight jeans, is perched on her kitchen chair, trying to be detached. She's drawing on her cigarette and showing the attitude of her age.

*But it's me I see there, like I was. And I'm seeing me with Mum's eyes.*

*And I'm saying, 'But I love Jerry; we want to be together. You just don't understand.'*

I purse my lips and whistle a plume of smoke into the air.

Then Laura says, 'What are you doing anyway? What's those?'

'Just some of Gran's old photos.'

'Can I see?'

I pass her the one of Mum on the seafront in the 'Kiss me quick' hat, where she's wrapped up with her young man.

Laura studies it.

'Is it Gran? She was a looker. And he was a bit of all right.'

She laughs at herself for this description, studies it a bit more. 'So who is – was – he?'

My head's whirling with all the questions that I have, and now I'm being asked to explain. All of a sudden I've had enough. I've had enough of trying to explain, I've had enough of being denied. I've just had fucking enough.

'It's my dad.'

'What?'

'He's my dad.'

Laura's mouth hangs open. 'Your dad?' she says disbelievingly. 'Your father? But how?'

But then I've got to get out before I scream. I need space and air so I walk out then, leave her with her mouth gaping open.

'Ask your gran,' I say over my shoulder. 'She might tell you more than she ever told me.'

I drive around for a while in Johnny James's car until my mobile rings and it's him, asking where I am, whether I'm looking after his car. Although I've pulled over, I tell him I can't talk for long because I'm on the motorway and the police are trying to get by me.

I tell him this and he's laughing and I'm laughing.

And then I'm crying, just like that, and I'm saying, 'I need to see you, Johnny. Now, please, Johnny.'

'What's the matter, Katy? What's happened?'

'Fucking everything,' I say.

'Just come and get me, Katy,' he says, and I love him so much it nearly chokes me.

But later, when Johnny James is softly, lovingly, questioning me, why do I tell him that it's just because I saw Laura?

Afterwards, Johnny drops me at home, reclaims his beloved car.

And when I walk through the garden gate the kitchen light is shining onto the path and I know that Mum is waiting up for me.

She's waiting up all right, the Huntley and Palmers tin is on the table, and her face is set into 'I'm going to give you what for, Katy'.

But I pre-empt her. Before she can even open her mouth I say, 'You know what I saw today at Pegs'?'

'Look, Katy, I can't have you sneaking into my things. You've no right.'

'I saw that photograph. You know, the one with the old lady. The one that you keep with my dad's.'

'Your dad's? Oh Katy. You've no right, Katy.'

'I've got every right, Mum.'

I pull up a chair, sit opposite her: mother and daughter across the kitchen table.

'Mum,' I say. 'I've got to know. I have to know. No more covering up.' I was going to say 'lies' but that word is too harsh to say to Mum.

She goes white. 'Please, Katy. Please. You don't know where this is going.'

And I don't, do I? I'm trembling and I've got to have a fag. But when I fumble one out of the packet, Mum wipes her forehead with her hand and says, 'I'll have one, Katy.'

I light it and pass her the cigarette, her first one in five years and then I dip the photographs from the biscuit tin, lay them out, and say, 'Tell me, Mum. Please tell me.'

And when Mum tells, each picture is a chapter of her long-ago love affair and she talks it from beginning to end.

\*　　\*　　\*

And it's the early eighties and Mum's sipping her Coke in the disco. Marvin Gaye is wanting some sexual healing and Mum's waiting for her friend to come back from the Ladies. Then this boy's there and he's leaning to Mum, asking for a dance. Even through the fan of flickering lights she can see his smile.

'Lovely he was. Lovely.'

Anyway, one thing leads to another and he offers her a lift home, and in the car park he opens the door of a Transit pick-up. The back of the vehicle is loaded with old fridges and washing machines and Mum suddenly puts together this stranger and his occupation, his quick way of speaking and his accent. And when he tells her that he's staying with his mother at the old railway yard she knows for certain.

He drives her home, stops at the end of her road, comes around and opens her door like he's a chauffeur.

'Manners he had. Such manners.'

Then he kisses her goodnight, soft and gentle, and she's lost, and this is the beginning.

They never go out locally and she keeps him a secret. There'd always been trouble in town with the Gypsies coming and going, and her father wasn't the most understanding of people.

'Bloody pikeys. Don't pay no taxes. Steal anything that isn't bolted down. I didn't fight a war for the likes of them.'

Mum's got a friend in Weston-super-Mare, and that's her excuse for a bank-holiday weekend away. Mum's eighteen and he's twenty, and they sign in a hotel as Mr and Mrs Smith, and he laughs because that's his real surname.

'Common as muck, I am,' he says and Mum laughs.

\*　　\*　　\*

But his Christian name? What's his Christian name?

'Henry,' Mum says, and I begin to go cold. I pick up a photograph, hold it close, and study his face for a confirmation.

*At Weston he buys her the kiss-me-quick hat and they have their picture taken for a quid. Mum reckons that it's the happiest she's been in her life and she wishes the weekend could last forever.*

'But nothing does, Katy. Nothing can.'

*He's a Gypsy boy and there's business to be done on the summer rounds, and the briefness of a three-month affair is over. Of course there're the promises of waiting, the clinging together in a long goodbye, but she can feel the restlessness in him.*

'I cried myself to sleep for a week, but I was young then and you soon get over these things.'

*But Mum didn't get over it, because when That Time of the Month came, nothing else did. And it was the same the following month, so she went to see Dr Andrews, although she already knew she was pregnant.*

'I was going to have an abortion, everything was arranged, but I met your auntie Doreen in the street. Her little Sammy was in the pram and she looked so small, so helpless.'

Mum, eyes brimming, looks at me. 'I couldn't do it, Katy. I just couldn't do it.'

I'm crying now, and then I'm holding Mum and we're sobbing together.

Then I make a pot of tea, give Mum another cigarette and let her catch her breath before she starts again.

In the bright kitchen of her council home, she tells me of leaving home, of walking out of her parents' house to live with a girlfriend on the other side of town.

'I couldn't have stayed at home, what with Dad . . .' She sighs. 'Well, Dad was Dad, and Mum wasn't going to cross him.'

So Mum cuts herself adrift, works at the supermarket till her waters break and then goes on the Social. It wasn't much in those days, but she was good with money and she managed.

She used to wheel me out in the lanes around the town.

'Because I didn't want to see anyone, Katy; I didn't want any questions.'

One hot summer's day she's wheeling me past the lane to the railway yard, and sitting on the verge in the sunshine is Henry's mother, Mrs Smith.

Mum didn't know her then, of course, just knew there was this Gypsy woman, sitting with a shopping bag and a Jack Russell at her side.

She gets up, stops Mum, pulls her into a conversation about the weather.

*'But she kept looking at you, Katy, and then she took an old coin, a half a crown, and put it into your hand, closed your fingers around it.*

*'She looks at me then, right into my eyes, like she could see inside me, and she says, "I'd like a picture of this child. A picture, that's all I'm asking."*

*'But I'm spooked then, and I mumble something about getting back and hurry away as fast as I can.*

*'But the next week when I'm passing she's there again, sitting in the same place with her dog by her side, on another hot, sunny afternoon.*

*'She says to me, "You must be thirsty, my dear." She's all kindness and concern and it makes me feel a bit ashamed of rushing away before. She fusses over you in the pram and then she says,*

"Come and have a cool drink," and when I hesitate she says quietly, "I'm Henry's mother."

'I walk with her down to the railway yard where she goes into one of the sheds and comes out with a bottle of lemonade and two cracked cups. We sit in the sun by her old caravan and I'm thinking it must be lonely, scary, here at night, and she says she loves the peace and quiet, like she's read my thoughts.

'She tells me about Henry, about his marriage in the spring, about him being in the Border counties. "He doesn't know," she says, "about the baby."

'It's afterwards I think, "How did she know about me and Henry?" I suppose it's possible someone could have seen us, put two and two together; or Henry could have given it away, but we'd been so careful cos of Dad and everything. Anyway, she knew.

'But what's filling my head is how to tell Henry. I'm thinking of his wife, newly married and looking forward to life; she might even be pregnant herself. Would she leave him? And if I told him would he come to me, settle down and get a proper job, a council house, be a bird in a cage?

'I knew in my heart that he'd never want me enough, hadn't loved me enough. He was with his own kind, his own people, and nothing else could work.

'"I don't want him to know."

'I say it out loud and Mrs Smith says, "It's for the best." There's a sadness in her voice and she says, shaking her head slowly, "All this will pass. One day there'll be a right time."

'Then she goes into her caravan and comes out with a camera. It looks so old and dusty I don't know if it'll work. She says, "Take a picture of me and Katy."

'She lifts you out of the pram and cradles you, and you try to grab her earrings and she's smiling at you; and a few days later this picture is pushed under my door in a white envelope, and then we don't go there again; and then I meet Jim, and then . . .'

And then Mum cries like her heart is breaking.


Well done, Katy, you wanted to fucking know and now you do. So what are you going to do with it? Go storming up to the Gypsy site and demand thirty-five years of fatherhood? You going to throw a family's life into turmoil?

And then it really sinks in. Am I going to put my arms around Pegs and call her sister?

And then there's the memory of the Christmas before last in the Bluebell.


*The bar is heaving and we've been on it all day and some silly sod is holding a sprig of mistletoe above Henry Smith's head, and Irish is going to me, 'For God's sake, give the man a kiss, Katy.'*

*He's laughing and I'm laughing, and I put my arms around his neck and kiss him short and sweet and, for the briefest of moments, I'm so tempted to dart my tongue between his warm lips.*


Now I'm so glad that I didn't.

# MONDAY NIGHT DARTS IN FEBRUARY
## THE BLUEBELL VERSUS THE INSTEADS

*Maggie*

I'm getting used to my new life. I don't like to say it, but it's better than before – I mean after Ken got ill. I've got my own routine sorted out now, and he's no trouble at all. I'm not talking of that shell at the nursing home, I'm talking about . . . Well, it's not something that's easy to explain. Least of all to Kayleigh.

She called today at lunchtime and she saw that I'd set the table for two, like I had for nearly forty years.

'Mum,' she says, 'you shouldn't. It's not healthy.'

I clear Ken's plate away. 'It's just that I forget sometimes, Kayleigh.'

She looks at me sharply then, looks for the signs we first saw in him.

I laugh. 'No, not like that, Kayleigh.'

'Then how, Mum?'

'It's a comfort, Kayleigh. It's like he's still here.'

'Oh Mum. Don't. Please don't.'

I'm tempted to tell her then, to let her into my secret, into my world. But instead I promise myself to be more careful.

Kayleigh says, 'Me and Mike have been talking. We're worried about you living here on your own.'

I know what's coming next and to forestall it, I say, 'I'm all right; there's no need to worry. I'm all right.'

It comes out a bit louder than I've expected and that gives the words an ungrateful edge.

Kayleigh looks hurt. 'Okay, Mum,' she says. 'Okay.'

She leaves soon after that, and I put Ken's plate back on the table and pull his chair in.

I cut some of that thick ham he likes and slice some tomatoes on top; that, with a nice crusty roll, is his favourite. I make him a cup of tea and take it through to the lounge and switch on the telly for the afternoon racing. I've ticked off my choice of runners and I flap the newspaper out onto my lap and say, 'Now what about yours, Ken?'

We've always done it this way, relaxing on the sofa on a wet afternoon.

'This one, Ken?'

I mark them off for him, from the one o'clock to the five o'clock race, and then settle back to watch the meeting. And you know what? Three of his selections come in, giving him a treble and three doubles but, as always, we've never put a stake on. It's our little game and I laugh. 'We could be worth a fortune now.'

Now, in here, it feels so warm, so comfortable.

So right.

So why does this knife stab at my heart?

\*　　\*　　\*

Later, when I've had a bath and smartened myself up I let myself quietly out of the house and head for the Bluebell.

Katy and Pegs are already on the board warming up and, like Cilla used to say, 'surprise, surprise', Scottie Dog and Irish are at the bar. Lena, looking a bit green around the gills, has just shot into the Ladies.

Our opposing team, the Insteads from the Homestead pub at the top of town, are putting their drink orders in and shrugging off their coats. They're a family team, all related in one way or another; you can see it in their faces.

Last time they were here Irish nicknamed them the Inbreds, they weren't amused, but I couldn't help laughing. When I got home I told Ken about it, but he wasn't well then and didn't get the joke. I explained it a dozen times, hoping a smile would break on that bewildered face.

There's football on the telly in the other side of the bar and the Motley Crew are refereeing the game. They're supporting Spurs – God knows why – against Aston Villa and their team are incapable of committing a single foul, or even straying offside. The Villa goal should have been disallowed and Spurs should have had at least three penalties. Old Bob offers the linesman his glasses and Jilted John says the ref must be pissed. Paddy reckons you've only got to breathe on a Villa player and he falls over.

'Bunch of bloody poofs,' he says.

Paddy can remember when slide tackling was legal and the elbow was part of the game. He says it's enough to drive a man to drink: 'Thank God.' So they bawl at Danny for three more pints and he bawls back that he's busy and can't they wait a poxy minute.

Our darts fixture is a game and a half tonight. It's a bit like the football – end to end stuff. We pick up the team leg and the first single with Katy, but then Irish plays the worst game I've ever seen her in. It's like she doesn't care; she hurls her arrows, and her curses, at the board like she's trying to do it serious damage. Irish ends her losing game with a 'so what' shrug of her shoulders and not even a 'Well done' to her opponent.

Scottie Dog says to Katy, 'What a load of shite that was,' as she warms up for her game. Irish, wiping off the chalkboard, turns to say something but Katy, reading the signs, strikes up with, 'We all have our off nights,' and Scottie Dog says, much more quietly, 'Och you're right there, Katy,' and takes a big slug of her whisky: 'to calm me nerves down.'

It does more than calm her down; she misses the twenties, she misses the trebles and she hits five instead of double top. Her opponent is straight out and then Lena drops her game and suddenly we're a point behind.

Tonight I feel so relaxed, I can't put a foot, or a dart, wrong; everything is going right for me and I shoot straight out on double nineteen. So it's three all and Pegs has to play the oldest of the Insteads who's eighty if she's a day.

Scottie Dog reckons the old lady'll be lucky to see the game out. 'Probably leave here in a hearse.'

'You won't be far behind her,' Irish says and Scottie Dog calls her a bog-trotting bitch who should be buying a round, not slandering decent folk. They're still arguing when Pegs takes the oche.

Katy says, 'For God's sake, shut your faces and give Pegs some support.'

This little exchange makes me think that everyone, everyone except me, seems a bit on edge. Pegs has been biting her nails and staring into space, Irish is in a funny one, Scottie Dog is as cutting as a knife. Lena's pregnant. And Katy? Katy's up to her neck in it.

On the board Pegs is nervously starting her game. She's slotting one in the sixty, two in the sixty, three in the sixty, and then looking like she can't believe it. Katy, chalking the board, calls out, 'One hundred and eighty,' and she sounds like she can't believe it either.

Granny Instead, peering at the board like she can't see it properly, says, 'I did that once, long time ago mind.'

Then she realises it's her go and everyone's waiting. She slowly sets her throw and looses her darts at the board. Too loose, because one drops out and she can't reach down far enough to pick it up. One of her own team comes to the rescue and stands on duty to pluck Granny's darts from the board. Irish reckons it's like an old people's home in here and Danny, who's clearing up glasses, mutters something about having to provide pissing care in the community. But Pegs is home and dry because the old lady will never shoot out in a month of Sundays.

When it's done, Katy says, 'I'm glad that's over,' and takes her drink in the relief of a single swallow. It must be murder being captain; it's not a job I'd want.

It's getting late now, Lena's gone and I'm ready for my bed, but Irish has insisted on buying yet another round – it's like she's in no hurry to get home. Danny has already called time and it's only because he's included in the circle that he serves them up. Katy clinks my glass, laughs, and says, 'We'll have thick heads in the morning, Maggie.'

Katy could well be right; it only takes a sip to tell me I've been served up a double shot of rum and pep and I'm already at the light-headed stage. Scottie Dog, raising her glass in a toast for Irish's generosity, asks Irish if she's come into some money?

Irish says loudly and a bit aggressively, 'Sure and can't I buy my old friends a drink?'

In this late hour we all sit around a table and go over the evening's darts' show. There's a bit of moaning, a run through the rest of our fixtures, and a weighing-up of our chances for the rest of the season.

And then Irish, even louder now and bright-eyed with drink, says to Pegs, 'C'mon Pegs. Use yer Gypsy magic; tell us if we're going to win the league or not?'

Pegs shakes her head and Irish says again, 'C'mon Pegs. Let us know.'

Danny says, 'You're meant to cross her palm with silver.'

Irish says, 'Are you her fucking agent?' and calls Danny Mr Ten Per Cent.

But Irish is like a dog with a bone. She asks Pegs again and it's another shake of the head. I'm beginning not to like this, this pushing onto Pegs, and I'm quite glad when Scottie Dog says, 'Give it a rest, Irish. You're getting on my pissing nerves.'

But Irish isn't giving it a rest. She thrusts her hand, palm uppermost, across the table until she's almost touching Pegs' nose.

'Tell my fortune, Pegs,' she says.

Danny says, 'Tell her she's going to end up in bed with a handsome landlord and have the best time of her life.'

Katy snorts a laugh and suddenly it's like it's fun again and Pegs is taking up Irish's hand. I don't think anyone else is paying much attention to this at the moment because Scottie Dog is noisily calling for yet another drink – I don't know where she puts it. She thinks that it's time that Danny put his hand in his pocket and Danny says that his hand is always in his pocket and Scottie Dog says she's not talking about him playing with himself. But on the table Pegs had said something, whispered something, to Irish and Irish has snatched her hand away from Peg's like she's been scalded.

I think it must only be me – and Pegs – who hear Irish mouthing 'Fucking witch,' to Pegs.

At least that's what I think I hear, and then Irish has gathered herself together and formed an abrupt, 'A goodnight to you all,' and she's gone.

Katy says, 'And what's the matter with her?'

I say quietly to Pegs, 'What happened with Irish?'

But all Pegs does is shake her head slowly and say, 'I better be going; Dave's waiting for me.'

She pushes her drink towards Katy. 'You have that,' and Katy says that she'll be on her arse at this rate.

We wind up shortly after this; it's been a strange old night and I'm not sorry to put on my coat and say goodnight to the Girls. Outside the streets are quiet and it's a lonely walk home, but I don't mind because the porch light will be on, and the radiators will be warming the lounge.

But it's not like that, not at all.

The central heating must have tripped out – again – and, inside, the house is cold and empty. There's no soul in here, no breath of comfort as I stand in the hallway and listen to the silence, to the loneliness.

'Ken,' I whisper into the darkness. 'Ken, are you there?'

And of course he isn't, he's lying in that Home, in a bed with a rubber sheet under him. That Home where his eyes don't know me, where he isn't mine, where he's forgotten he ever was.

I sit on the stairs in the darkness and I cry for his memory. I cry until there's no tears left and then go to bed with all the usual questions crowding into my mind.

*Why do I do this? Why do I tell myself these lies? Why do I pretend?*

I'll go over and over these questions until they're a mantra in my head, until the rhythm of the words become less harsh, become more gentle, more soothing; words to fall asleep to.

I'll sleep and dream of a perfect world where a lifetime of happiness doesn't end at an institution's door.

In the morning I'll wake, stretch, yawn, get up, go to the bathroom, put on my dressing gown. In the kitchen, I'll push bread into the toaster, put water in the kettle, lay the table. For two.

# GOING HOME ON THE SAME MONDAY NIGHT IN FEBRUARY

## Irish

I'm walking slowly home. I've got a head full of gin and my stomach churns like a washing machine. The euphoria of earlier has disappeared; I've left Irish in the pub and it's Mary O'Brian now who is counting the steps home to Gobshite.

I'm lingering in the street, in the cold winter breeze. I'm dragging my feet like I used to on school days in a lane in County Meath. I'm wondering what my life would have been like if Gobshite had never come to our little town.

But what's done is done and, as he's fond of saying, 'There's no going back, Irish. There's no leaving this club; this is for life.'

He's right. I've seen too much; I know too much. I don't want to be buried in a lonely grave on the hillside, but that's the only way they'll let me go.

Then, as always, I'm thinking of Davey. I'm thinking about the way he would cling to me, the grip of his small, chubby fingers, his snotty kisses, his wonder at seeing something new, his first crawl, his first steps.

His last breath.

I'm sobbing to myself because this life is too hard, too painful to live. It cuts into me, dicing my feelings into measures of love and hate and cowardice and lust. I weigh my strengths, my weaknesses, and the scales tip heavily away from me.

And on the night wind my promise, my vow, whispers to me: 'This time; it has to be this time.'

Then I'm outside our house and it's hushed and the windows are black, but I know that in the darkened bedroom Gobshite is waiting.

He hears me come in, hears me slide the bolt behind me. He calls down, 'Is that you, you fucking Irish slut?'

I climb back into Irish, put her mask on my face. I call up the stairs, 'I hope you're full of it, sir; I've got a big itch to scratch.'

'Get yer arse up here and you'll soon see. Fucking prossie.'

I go up the stairs slowly. I'm undoing my blouse, loosening my skirt, unclipping my bra, because that's how he wants to see me. I hear him flick the bedside lamp on and I tap on the door. He calls out again.

'Is that you, you fucking Irish tart?'

I say, 'Are you ready for me, sir?'

'Ready? Ready? Get yerself in here, you'll soon see if I'm ready or not.'

In the bedroom he's stretched out on the bed. He hasn't a stitch on and his face is flushed against the paleness of his body.

'What have you got for me?'

I lift one leg onto the bed, give him a flash of stocking and more.

'I thought maybe this, sir.'

As I answer I reach for the bedside cabinet, slide open the drawer, take out the handcuffs and the manacles.

'So it's for the teasing,' Gobshite says.

'You won't forget this one, sir.'

So Gobshite's crucified to the bed, eyes closed and overfilled with the wanting. He's arching his back and his words are of the gutter, the crudeness of the trench, the cursing as the pick rises and falls. He's desperate to be touched, desperate to begin, desperate for the tongue and the mouth.

But I don't.

'A second,' I say. 'I'll be a second.'

I move slowly away from him and his eyes snap open.

'Yer bitch,' he says. 'Yer can't go.'

He's thinking that this is part of the game, a delicious suspension just for him.

'I have to get something, sir.'

'You'll be quick.'

'I'll be quick, sir.'

So I leave Gobshite spread out on the bed and I go down to the kitchen and, from the rack by the side of the sink, I take out the longest, heaviest knife. Then, when I kiss the cold glass of Davey's picture, I hold that knife behind my back; I don't want him to see.

In our room Gobshite says, 'Yer fucking slut, this had better be good.'

I sit on the bed and I say, 'It's got to stop; it's got to end.'

Gobshite says, 'What? What the fuck are you talking about? Let's get started.'

I show him the knife and he says, 'Jesus, Irish, this is different.'

He's thinking that we've never taken it this far before and when I touch the skin above his heart with the point of the blade, he is suddenly still. But his eyes are locked onto mine.

'Jesus, Irish,' he says again. 'Jesus.'

And now the moment is in me, a time of contrivement, of opportunity that may never occur again. I've got both my hands on the knife and I push down into the living flesh of his body.

I push down for all the wasted years.

I push down for all the years of human bondage.

I push down to kill a killer.

Gobshite gasps, 'What the fuck are you doing, Irish?'

His eyes, locked onto – into – mine are suddenly startled, suddenly bewildered and he's trying desperately to wrench his body away from the knife, to break away from the cuffs.

And now this is a nightmare because I must be on a rib; the blade won't go in. I bear down with all my weight, thrust with all my strength and I'm virtually lying on Gobshite. And his eyes, those eyes, hazel green and flecked with grey, are inches away from me.

'Jesus, Mary. No. Why, Mary? Why?'

Then the knife graunches off the hardness of bone, plunges into soft flesh with a suddenness that brings our faces into touching. My lips are on his in a perverse kiss. I can taste his breath, the breath of a dying man losing its warmth in my mouth. I can taste his words, unsure and unbelieving, on my tongue.

And my knife is in his heart and I can feel the pump of his blood matching the beat of my heart. Then he jerks like a marionette, retches like a dog.

Dies like a dog.


So that's it then; Gobshite emptied of blood, drenched in scarlet, lies on the bed, manacled to the four posts like a victim of the Spanish Inquisition. I free him; I give him some dignity. I lay his arms by his side, pull his legs together, slide the knife from his body, put the eiderdown over him, close his accusing eyes, turn off the light.

I'm in the dark, in a silence of a dream where the unbelievable is believable.

I suppose I should cry, sob into the deathly silence, but I can't. It's like I'm dry inside.

I shower, wash his blood, his taste, from my body. Then I go down the stairs, quietly, unsurely, drop the weapon of the killing into the kitchen bin. In this night it's like the house is listening for me, tracing my passage in its rooms.

There's a shaft of moonlight cutting through the hallway window and it's shining onto Davey. I can hear his voice now, the voice I've imagined in my darkest hours, and it's in the soft lilt of the south of Ireland.

'Mamee,' he says, 'I've missed you.'

I tell him that we're going to be together, that we're going home. Then I take down his picture and hold it to my chest, let him feel the beat of his mother's heart, of his mother's love.

I play out what I've rehearsed a hundred times in my head. I gather up my everyday items of intent. There's a bottle of Plymouth Gin, (only the best for this special occasion) some tonic water – cool from the fridge – and there's pack after pack of blistered paracetamol. And then there's my album of the past, of the innocent years before Gobshite stole my life. And Davey's.

It's cold in the lounge and I click on the gas fire, pull the big easy chair up to the warmth of the glow and pour myself a tumbler of gin and tonic. I pop out a hundred paracetamols and start to feed them slowly to myself in a pattern of five tablets and a swig of my favourite tipple. Then with Davey in my lap, I open the photo album and show him the picture of Mammy and Da and the green of County Meath. I can feel the shape of Davey in my arms and the sweetness of his breath on my face and . . .

*And I'm drifting away down a country lane in County Meath and Da's dogs are barking and Mammy's at the window of the house. The sun is warm and bright and the swallows are rising and falling from a clear blue sky. I know I must reach the house before my strength dies, but it's like I'm treading water, pushing against the current.*

*At the gate my da is standing with his hand on Davey's shoulder. And Davey is all I ever dreamed he'd be; he's tall and strong and blond and he's smiling a shy smile at me. And it's like they can't step forward to help me, like they're in a different world and it's me that has to step into theirs. But I'm so weak, so weak, and I've got this terrible feeling that I'm not going to make it, not on my own. I pray then, I pray to a God that deserted me all those years ago and then suddenly it's like a miracle.*

*There's a strong arm on mine, taking my weight like the Good Samaritan in the Bible.*

*But then the harsh words are in my ear.*

*'Yer fucking Irish prossie. Did yer think you'd get away that easily?'*

*Gobshite has a hold on me now, the iron grip of the possessor, and he's turning me away from all I love, pulling me back, and . . .*

. . . and there's a plastic mask on my face and I'm after feeling as sick as a pig. And I just want to die.

Let me die. Please God let me die.

\* \* \*

But they don't let me. They sedate me. Watch me. Sit by my bed. And there's a priest, a Catholic priest, who tries to hold my hand and tells me that God saved me.

I tell him I don't want fucking saving and that it was his fucking God who took my Davey.

But what really saved me – if you can call it that – was our nosey neighbour.

*Mr Evans has more than a touch of flu and he's finished his night shift very early and he's dog-tired. He's half-asleep and he's trying to reverse his car into his parking space. This pale dawn light doesn't help him and it's a bit of a tight fit. And the rear window's steamed up. And he edges back and back until – 'Shit' – and there's a crunch of a bumper putting a dent into the wing of Gobshite's motor.*

*'God all bloody mighty.' Poor Mr Evans, his flu really starting to bite, doesn't need this. All he wants is a dose of hot Lemsip and to curl up in his warm bed.*

*He gets out of his car, surveys the damage and, being the upright citizen that he is, comes to knock on our door. And he knocks and listens for the sound of movement. But what he hears is the beep of the fire alarm. Then he smells smoke and opens the letter box and bellows for Mr O'Brian and Mrs O'Brian. Well Gobshite's not going to hear anything and I'm in a limbo world between the living and the dead. So our little fucking hero breaks into my house, batters the door open and rescues me to a fate worse than death. He drags me out onto the cold grey of the concrete path, phones for the fire brigade and the ambulance and then gives me mouth to mouth. (I bet he liked that, me all warm and pink and offering no resistance.)*

*But he's not going to rescue Gobshite because Gobshite is long past rescuing.*

*It's not a bad fire. In fact, by any standards it's a fairly minor conflagration – more smoke than flame. Two hunky firemen (missed out there) drag out a half-burned rug, inspect the scorched floorboards, and pull the charred edges of my album from the hearth. This album must have slipped from my unconscious self, slid down my knees, and perhaps toppled onto the gas fire. Anyway, that seems to be the consensus, confirmed with a knowing nod between the uniformed men. It seems simple enough to them. That combined with a near-empty Plymouth Gin bottle and a scattering of little white tablets to complete the scenario.*

*But then something drips onto one of the firemen's helmets. A drip of red blood from a wet, glistening patch on the ceiling.*

And all of this is why I'm here in this secure unit for the unfit of the mind in a bare, locked room where a bored orderly on suicide watch checks me out every ten minutes.

But I know that somewhere far away it's a warm, sunny day and I'm walking up the track to my da's farm where my Davey is waiting for me. And I know that as soon I can, as soon as the opportunity arises, I'll be on that road.

# WEDNESDAY EVENING AFTER WORK

*Pegs*

Big Dave has picked me up from work and he's having a bite to eat with us before me and him go out for a quiet drink. Mum has set the table and Dad is in his big chair by the wood burner, warming his bare feet. I ask Mum is it cheese on toast for tea cos the smell is mighty strong in here?

Dad says, 'Watch yer lip, young lady.' And then he says, 'We heard something down at the market today,' and he calls out to Mum in the kitchen, 'didn't we, Lydia?'

'What?'

'Heard something about Irish.'

I'm going cold before they even start to put the story together for me and Big Dave.

Mum comes in wiping her hands on a tea towel and says, 'She mullared her mush with a shiv. Chinned him deep, Pegs.'

Her words are slow and regretful. She touches her forefinger to her temple and shakes her head. And in my head, my sane mind, is the touching of Irish's fingers on Monday night and the clear, jolting image of a blood-smeared knife, before Irish snatched her hand away like she'd been electrocuted.

*Fucking witch.*

Later I lie in the darkness, listening to the bovel sighing in the rookers, and trying to sleep. I've a wishing that Big Dave could have sneaked in here, held me like only he can, do the things we're dying to do, but even that imagining can't settle me. In the finish I get up and put a pan of sugar and milk on the stove. Then I curl up on Dad's comfy chair in the middle of the night and sip my drink – if I smoked, I'd light up a tuvla – and try to put Irish out of my head.

But Gran's voice is here now and she's saying, 'It's no good worrying, Peggy. You can't change anything. It's either happened or it's going to happen.'

But I had tried with Irish; I'd whispered to her over the table at the Bluebell Inn, 'Whatever it is, Irish, don't do it.'

But she did do it, had to do it, because what's written can't be unwritten.

And I've known that since I first reached my teens.

*I'm thirteen years old and I've been a woman for two weeks, and me and Gran are having a 'wander' as she calls it. Even at her age she can't rest for long and most days me and her'll take a walk. A long walk. And this afternoon me and Gran are at the edge of town in a posh area: a mature estate of gravelled drives and lawned gardens. Real Gorjer country she calls it. And she talks, my gran. She talks non-stop sometimes and it's not as though she lives in the past but she certainly spends a lot of time there. I don't mind cos I'm interested to hear* about the old days, the stories about the pea-picking, the bean-picking, the endless hoeing out of sugar beet and the plucking of the hops in the county of Hereford. But sometimes it'll be about the granddad I never knew; 'Henry's the spit of him,' she always says and it's with a sadness that's never left her in the forty years since Granddad did. Since he died.

Anyway this day it's starting to drizzle and Gran reckons we've got to get a move on else we'll be drenched before we're back home. But our getting a move on is interrupted because a taxi stops in the road and a youngish, smartly dressed woman, bag of shopping on each arm, steps out and hurries to the pavement. But she doesn't make her step up over the kerb because she catches her toe on the edge and goes a gutser. She's fallen just in front of us and her shopping spills from her bags. Gran's onto it straight away and she helps the lady up – there's already blood dribbling down the woman's knee – and I shove her shopping, her purse with it, back into her bags for life.

But when this lady tries to stand she sucks in her breath, winces, and Gran says, 'We better get you inside, dear. Get you sat down.'

The lady took the tumble outside her house and we go into it through a side door, a kitchen door, Gran, with the Hobbler, and me following with the groceries. Gran settles her into a chair and the lady says, 'I can't thank you enough. Now you must have something for your trouble.' She's white-faced and still seems a little shocked from her fall. She reaches for one of her bags and rummages about until she finds her purse and unzips it. I look at

Gran and she catches my look and we both know that the woman's checking that I haven't chored any of her vonger, 'Cos you can never trust a gypo, can you?'

Some colour is creeping back into the lady's face as she holds out a ten pound note to Gran. Gran shakes her head, 'No. It's all right, dear.'

'Take it. Please take it.'

Gran shakes her head again, 'Can't take money for helping someone in distress,' she says. But the lady is adamant and the offer of the ten pound note isn't withdrawn.

'Please,' she says.

So Gran takes the money, plucks it out of the lady's fingers and says to her, 'For this, my Peggy will tell your fortune.'

Me? Me who hasn't said a word up to now has to look at the lady's palm and tell her future.

Gran says quietly to me, 'The time is right for you, my Peggy.'

And in this modern kitchen on this exclusive estate with the promised rain beginning to tap on the window, and with a woman who's becoming nervous at our presence, I take her hand and turn her palm to my eyes.

Gran says softly, as though there's only me and her in the room, 'Just rocka what you dik, my Peggy.'

I take this bruised housewife's hand, load up the patter in my mind: the talk of love and good fortune and whatever else she needs to hear. (To tell you the truth I'm not really that interested; I'd much rather me and Gran were jaulen back to our atchin tan; it's going to be a long wet walk and already there's a nibble of hunger in my belly.) Now it's not as if I haven't done this before, this dukkering – Gran's been a good teacher – but this time it's suddenly, instantly, so different.

I'm looking at the lady's palm but I'm struggling to see the heart line, the life line. My vision is shifting, blurring. This room, the housewife's kitchen, is fading, receding, pulsating. Then it's like a jolt, a bolt of lightning, passing between me and the woman who fell in the street. It's light and it's dark and I'm here and I'm not here. And I'm thirteen and the Gift is woken in me for the first time.

'Gran?' I say and my voice has an echo to it. A frightened echo.

But now Gran's voice is a whisper in my ear. Gentle. Insistent. 'Tell what you see, my Peggy. Tell what you see.'

And what I'm seeing now is our new friend in this same kitchen. And it's a room that's light and bright and shining with happiness. And she's holding a child, a baby, close to her heart, a newborn that's nuzzling inside her open blouse. A future baby.

I must be saying the words, I must be telling what I'm seeing, because the woman's face is searching into mine and there's tears brimming over her eyes.

But now Gran's clutching my arm, pinching me, hissing at me urgently, 'Nantee, my Peggy. Nantee.'

And now the woman's snatched her hand from mine and she's sobbing out, 'How could you? How could you say that?' She's crying out to me. 'How could you? I can't have a child ever – never – and you come here with your Gypsy lies.' Then she screams at us, 'Get out. Get out. Get out.'

We leave then and Gran asks me how I feel and I tell her that I'm a bit shaky, bit blurry, and she says that it's sometimes like that. But I also feel that there's now something inside me, something that flickers between me and Gran. On our way back to Station

Yard Gran says for me not to worry about the lady and at least we got a tenner out of it. And of course that's not an ending because a year later Gran leads me to the same lady's house, to knock on the same lady's door on another wet afternoon. And this time there's no telling us to jaul, nor screams of Gypsy lies. The woman simply says quietly, 'You'd better come in.'

And we sit in that kitchen of twelve months ago and she's nursing a child she thought she'd never have and she's saying to me, 'How did you know?'

How did you know?

Fucking witch.

That's how I knew.

# THURSDAY NIGHT (THE NEXT NIGHT) PRACTICE IN FEBRUARY

*Lena*

Dandy comes in from work and he looks knackered. 'What a day; I'm glad that's over.' He sinks into his chair and I fetch him a beer from the fridge.

I say, 'I'm going down to the Bluebell now, Dandy.' I'm dressed and ready to go.

He says, 'You sure you're up to it?'

I laugh. 'I'm only pregnant; I'm not ill.'

He laughs then. 'Tell that to the toilet in the morning.'

Then I ask him if he thinks I'm as fat as I feel?

'You're gorgeous,' he sings.

'Still?'

'Always.'

I call him a soppy old man and he calls me a babe and then he asks very quietly, 'Did you speak to your mum today?'

'This afternoon. We talked this afternoon.'

Dandy takes a swig of beer and tries to sound casual. 'And?'

But what he means is, 'How did she take it? What did she say? Is she all right?'

I say, 'I don't think she was too worried.' And I add, 'She's got a new boyfriend. It sounds serious.'

Dandy says slowly, drawing out the words, 'Well, as long as she's happy.'

'She's fine. Don't worry, Dandy. And Mikey, he sends his love.'

This is what I tell him because the truth would have me in tears again.

What I didn't tell Dandy was that I did more than talk to Mum and I didn't go to work this morning; I went to see her instead.

*I've taken Dandy's car and driven the fifty miles to Mum's. And now I'm standing outside her door, rapping on the knocker and I can hear Mum say, 'See who that is, Mikey.'*

*The door opens and this skinny nine-year-old I've only seen erratically over the last eight years is staring at me with his liquid brown eyes as Mum calls through, 'Who is it, Mikey?'*

*His face comes alight and he shouts back to Mum. 'It's Lena, Mum. It's my sister.'*

*Then Mum's at the door and her face is hard and unsmiling.*

*'I suppose you'd better come in, Lena,' she says.*

*There are no hugs, no kisses for her errant daughter.*

*We sit in her little kitchen waiting for the kettle to boil and she says that Mikey should be at school today but he'd complained of feeling sick this morning.*

*'I think he used the old fingers down the throat trick. You know, like you used to, Lena.'*

*She says this like a recrimination to me. There is no humour, no allowance for me in her words.*

*The kettle boils and she gets up to make the tea. Even though it's still early, Mum's hair is done and her make-up's on. She doesn't look anywhere near her age and her features are sharp and pretty. She's still slim, much slimmer than me; but then she always was and everyone else seems to be now. It's so obvious what Dandy saw in her and a stab of jealousy jolts me.*

*I say, 'You look good Mum.'*

*She says, 'You've put a bit of weight on, Lena.'*

*Then all the words I carefully prepared a hundred times in my head are drowned by my snap reaction, 'That's because I'm pregnant, Mum.'*

*These words are out before I can even consider them and then it's like everything is frozen in this room and I say, 'I need to talk to you.'*

*Mum tells Mikey to give us a minute. Then she sits across from me at the table and says, 'Tell me, Lena.'*

*And it's the way she says it like someone whose last hope has just crumbled in front of them. Like she doesn't really want to hear it.*

*And as I tell her she just stares into my face as the tears trickle down her cheeks.*

*So just when I thought things might be better, that this might bring us closer again, all I've done is to cut deeper into her heart.*

*She says, 'I think you'd better go, Lena.'*

*'Mum, I . . .'*

*'Go, Lena. For God's sake just go.'*

*'But Mum . . .'*

*Mum screams at me. 'What did you expect, Lena, that I'd be happy for you and him? I could never have imagined my tart of a daughter would be carrying his bastard.' She spits out the last word.*

*But now Mikey's come back in and he's looking from me to her in bewilderment.*

*'Go, Lena. Go,' Mum says and I do.*

*That's how I leave the house: Mum upset, crying; Mikey scared and quiet.*

*I sit behind the wheel of Dandy's car and, for the briefest of moments I almost wish I wasn't pregnant.*

*So I don't let Dandy into the truth, I pretend that Mum's coming round, that she's living her life, and that one day it'll all be okay. I don't say, because he'd only worry, fret that nothing's ever going to change.*

*At least that's what I tell myself for my reasons of invention.*

And now it's evening and I'm putting my face on and Dandy's gone quiet; he always does when we talk about Mum and Mikey.

I say, 'It'll be all right, Dandy.'

I sit on his knee, slip my arms around his neck, hug him tightly, whisper into his ear, because he's mine, all mine, and I don't want to share him with memories.

But the local news is on the telly and Dandy's craning around me. He says, 'Shush a minute, Lena.' Dandy's tone is serious so I shush and I listen. And the voice on the gogglebox is saying that the dead man was a Michael O'Brian and that his wife, Mary O'Brian, is in hospital suffering from the effects of smoke inhalation. Then there's a picture of a house with white-suited men going in the door, and the voiceover is saying that the man is believed to have died from knife wounds and that the police aren't looking for anyone else in connection with his death.

Dandy says, 'Christ, that's only the other side of town.'

But now I've put a name to a face, to someone who swears like a trooper and drinks like a fish.

Dandy's saying, 'It's got to be her. She must have done it.'

'Done it? Irish must have done it?'

'Well, it figures,' says Sherlock, 'she must have done it if she's . . .' Dandy says and starts to explain, like I'm a bit slow on the uptake.

'No, Dandy, it's Irish. It's who we play darts with.'

But I can't really believe this. My mind can't seem to take it in. I suppose I must look stunned and Dandy is full of concern.

'Irish? Lena, are you all right?'

'It must be a mistake.'

I'm still sitting on his lap and Dandy's stroking my hair.

'Don't go tonight,' he says. 'It's shaken you up.'

I was thinking that things couldn't get much worse after this morning's episode with Mum, but this . . . well, I don't know.

I say, 'It's all right, Dandy; I'm all right.'

When I'm not.


It's time to leave and I kiss Dandy like I'm not pregnant, like there's not a bump in the way. Then I slip – well, not exactly slip, more of a lumber – off his knees and button up my coat.

Then I go to meet Six of the Best, only it isn't six now, is it?

It's five. Five of the Best.


The Bluebell is quiet and the girls are sitting at our usual table. At the bar, Danny says, 'You heard about Irish then?'

'Just. On the news, Danny.'

He pours my orange juice and shakes his head. 'Can't believe it. Who would ever have thought?'

I'm shaking my head in unison with him and I'm still doing it when I sit down with the girls.

'You got a nervous twitch?' says Scottie Dog.

Before I can get an answer in, Katy scrapes her chair back, stands, and says just one word for a sudden, complete silence. 'Irish.'

She holds her glass out in a toast and we all touch drinks together over the table.

Then we talk about it, go over it a hundred times, dissect it into a thousand pieces.

We drink, or rather the rest of them – minus me – drink, and the darts are left in their cases and the chalkboard stays clean. It's Irish this and Irish that and I realise that we're talking about her like she's dead. And in a way perhaps she is to us.

Danny comes to sit with us and reckons that Irish must have had a brainstorm or something like that.

He says, 'No one could turn that quickly without a sign.'

Scottie Dog, taking a large swig of her whisky, says, 'Nothing surprises me any more; it's what people do.' And she sounds bitter, like Irish has somehow betrayed her.

At this wake everyone's got an opinion except Pegs who's even quieter than usual.

All she says is, 'He must have been a bad man,' and then she mutters a word to herself that sounds like *mukado*. A Gypsy word, I suppose.

I say, 'He must have done something awful to set her off.'

Katy wonders if we'll ever know and Danny says she'll be kept in the loony bin for the rest of her natural.

'Shame,' he says. 'She was a good-looking woman.' He adds, perhaps a bit louder than he intended, 'Well put together.'

Then Maggie asks, 'What are we going to do on Monday? We'll be a player down.'

Katy says, 'I don't want to think about it yet.' Then she goes outside for a fag.

Danny says, 'I could ask Big Nellie; she throws a mean dart.'

So we sit for another hour until everyone's had enough and then we say our goodnights and Katy says she'll have a think and let us know over the weekend.

When I get home, Dandy's already gone to bed and I make myself a hot chocolate and then I take a cigarette and slide open the patio door. I know I shouldn't be doing this, but one fag's not going to hurt, is it? I've been through a lot today.

Outside, there's a cold moon in the sky and the air is clear and still. It's late now and there's only a sprinkling of lights across the town. I'm shivering and drawing on my cigarette at the same time. I sit on a freezing plastic chair, filling my lungs with smoke, and wondering why Irish did what she did. It seems so unreal; I half expected her to walk in the pub tonight and ask, 'Why all the fucking long faces?'

And then I don't want to think about it any more and I lean back, close my eyes and empty my head. What intrudes is a bright summer morning when I was sixteen, with smoke in my mouth and love in my body. A time of eight years ago.

*It's a wet afternoon in the summer holidays and I'm revising in my room for my college course. I'm not really interested and I've read the same page on hair care three times and not taken a word in. Mum and Mikey have gone to Aunt Edna's and she's left me instructions for tea. The rain's tracking down the window and I'm feeling as miserable as sin when Dandy's car pulls into the drive.*

*I'm watching him as he climbs out of the car. His shoulders are damp and his hair is flattened to his head. He looks really pissed off.*

*So I'm watching him and I'm wanting him and when he steps into the hall I'm on him like a Doberman.*

*'Jesus, Lena. Your mum . . .'*

*'She's at Edna's and I'm fed up with revising.'*

*'I'm wet through, Lena. I'm dripping.'*

*But he's kissing me, hard and needing.*

*I squeeze against him and say, 'You have a nice hot shower and I'll make you a cup of tea.'*

*'Five minutes,' he says. 'Give me five minutes.'*

*He slips his shoes off and bounds up the stairs and it's times like this that he forgets – that we forget – about Mum. We shut her out of this world we've created; this exclusive place that exists for just the two of us.*

*I give Dandy two minutes and then go into the bedroom, slip off my skirt, my blouse, my bra, my pants, and quietly open the bathroom door to surprise him.*

*Really surprise him.*

He's in the shower, behind the steam-streaked glass, singing softly to himself, and I tap on the panel, let myself in.

Dandy says, 'Lena. Christ, you shouldn't,' but I've put his soapy hands on me and am drawing them over my body.

All over.

We're still wet when we're on the bed, too hungry to dry, too ravenous for love. It's like nothing on earth could prevent us. I'm gasping, moaning, almost breathless with this wanting for it to last forever.

Then Dandy stops, freezes. Turns to ice. Melts inside me.

'Dandy?'

But before I've even finished saying his name, I hear Mum's voice. She's standing there looking at us. She's crying, she's sobbing. 'On our bed, Andy. On our bed. How could you? She's only sixteen, Andy. Sixteen.'

There's a broken heart in her voice, in her words. There's Mum with such hurt on her face that it starts a pain, a jolting physical pain into my heart. There's Andy desperately trying to say something that isn't a lie. He's looking at me, willing me to explain, to make Mum understand it wasn't him, not really him; it was me, teenage temptress me, of the long legs and big boobs. Me who shouldn't have used the power of transition, of the signals of availability. Me who shouldn't have squeezed by him in the narrow hallway. Me who shouldn't have been sitting opposite him after a bath, skin all soft and pink and hair carelessly, carefully, dropping, curling and wantonly, onto my shoulders, so that he can't help looking, can't help following each shift of my body, each shuffle of my legs.

And Mum saying time after time, 'For God's sake, Lena, put some clothes on.'

*Did she know, did she suspect, that I was trying to . . .?*
*Trying to what? Attract her man, steal him from her?*

I don't know; even now I don't know. I didn't think, not deeply. All I could see was this man whose every word meant so much to me, who I wanted to please. Who I wanted to tuck me into bed at night.

And then climb in with me.

*But now in their bedroom Dandy's standing, sheet clutched around his waist and I'm still sitting on the bed with my legs together and my hands across my chest.*

*Dandy just says her name and he says it like it's the saddest word he's ever said. And now this room is suffocating with hurt and guilt and Mum won't look at me, doesn't say anything to me. Instead she launches herself at him, hits his face with her clenched fists again and again. Blood trickles from Dandy's nose, smears his lips, and, although he flinches with every blow, he doesn't raise a hand to defend himself. Then Mum stops, wipes her eyes with her bleeding knuckles, and turns to me.*

'You better get dressed,' she says.

'Mum?'

'I don't want to talk to you,' she screams into my face, 'and I don't want you for a daughter,' and she's out of the room while downstairs Mikey has started bawling for his tea.

Me and Dandy look at each other. His face is full of shock, of disbelief, of blood.

He says, 'What have I done, Lena? What have I done?'

I say, 'We. What have we done?'

I go to him, go to hold him, but he pushes me away, turns away, stumbles into his clothes as I watch the beginning of an attempt of salvage for him and Mum.

'What are you going to do, Dandy?'

'Going down to her.'

'What about me?'

He says, so tiredly, 'She's hurt, Lena. She's so hurt,' and then he's treading down the stairs.

I sit on the bed, dressed now, as below their voices ebb and flow between recrimination and tears. I listen for an hour and then I go to my room, put on my coat, take some money from my emergency fund and creep down the stairs.

Outside it's still blowing wet and the early evening light is only just into fading as I start to walk the streets. I walk past the familiar, the grey pavements and the bright shop windows, out to the edge of the town. I can hear her, feel it, screaming in my ear.

'You're not my daughter, Lena. Not my daughter.'

But through all this I'm thinking about Dandy, loving him from this distance. Still wanting him.

I suppose I'm crying, my hand's to my mouth, and I'm cold, and the wet is squelching in my shoes, creeping down my neck, and I must get out of the rain. So I walk into the next pub I see.

Inside there're only a few people drinking, and a log fire is burning in a big old grate and I stand in front of it and let the heat soak into me. I must cut a strange figure, straggly-haired and red-eyed.

Then there's a voice, a woman's voice cutting across the bar room. 'Will you be after looking at that girl; she's steaming.'

Then she comes over to me, stares me up and down, this woman with a G and T in one hand and a cigarette in the other. She says, 'Are you all right?'

I can't say anything, I just nod. At my feet a puddle is forming and she puts her hand on my sleeve and says, 'You're wet through, my lovely.' My clothes are sticking to me and my bra is showing through my blouse.

She yells across to the bar. 'Danny, a warming drink for this poor mite.'

He shouts back, 'How old is she?'

'For Christ's sake, just get her a brandy. And if you're asking, I'm paying.'

She drags up a chair. 'Set yourself down.' Then she says to me, 'Boy trouble?'

I find my voice. 'Man trouble,' I say and she laughs. ''Tis usually so.'

Then she says, 'Christ, here I am and I haven't even introduced myself.' She holds out her hand. 'Mary. Mary O'Brian, but everyone calls me Irish. Now, let's get yer poison cos it's all shit that he sells here anyway.'

She nods at the bar and tells Danny to stop drooling and serve up my brandy and says that if he can manage to take his eyes off my tits for long enough she'd like another gin and tonic.

Danny says that it's nice to have a customer who's young and pretty and not the wrong side of forty. He adds, 'And a bit too well fed.'

Irish says he needs to take a look in the mirror and mutters about pot and kettle and is that a bad smell coming from behind the bar?

Then she turns to me and says, 'Do you play darts? Cos we're short of a player.'

I'm finishing my cigarette and shivering in the dark, and Irish is . . . is what?

Locked up? Banged up in the nuthouse?

I can't believe what she did.

And then I think that Mum couldn't believe what I did, probably never would have if she hadn't seen it with her own eyes.

I flick the cigarette butt into the garden and then I go up to bed.

To Dandy.

# SAME NIGHT – SCOTTIE DOG AT HOME

As soon as I'm at home I open a can of Whiskas for Robert the Bruce and pour a whisky for me – it's a coincidence that our sustenance sounds the same. Well, almost. He eats his on the floor, purring away, and I drink mine in my big chair, worrying away.

I can't help this, can't stop my fingers searching my stomach, pressing here, pressing there; feeling the things that aren't right.

I've got a doctor who won't look me in the eye, who says, 'I'll make you an appointment with Mr Hope.'

I tell him that's a good name for a hopeless case and he coughs and says that nothing's certain and I shouldn't worry and I must be checked out. But something outside the window has caught his attention as he speaks, draws his gaze from me again.

And his diagnosis is in his avoidance.

I don't want to be pushed about, prodded about, cut open, filled with chemicals. I'm too old, too tired, to fight. I feel it in my body, in my bones, and it makes me wonder how long I've got. Weeks? Months? A year?

All that time for this pain to grow, to make me catch my breath.

All that time before it becomes unbearable and whisky and painkillers come out of the cupboard.

But have I got enough time to take the train to Scotland, the train to home?

A voice whispers in my head:

*If you go now.*

Have I got enough time to get to Glasgow?

*If you go now.*

Will I find Aubrey? Will I see him?

Silence. Deep, deep silence. The silence of the grave, of things long gone, long buried.

Like Mam's funeral on that afternoon of fifty-five years ago.

*'Hello, Marie,' he says. 'I'm your father.' And a wonderful smile crinkles his face. Then he takes my hand and we stand on the brink of Mam's grave.*

*'Lovely,' he says. 'She was so lovely.' He turns me to him, strokes my face with his fingers. 'You're so like her,' he says. Then he stoops, takes a handful of soil and trickles it into that black hole, onto Mam's coffin. As we walk away, leave Mam to God, he slips his arm around my waist.*

*And it fits so well, so comfortably, this embrace from my father the stranger, that I want to stop and hold him. I'm trembling slightly and he grips me tighter and I can feel the strength of his hand, the muscles of his arm, as we walk from the churchyard.*

He just took me then, just put me in his car, drove me to the Home, waited while I packed my case, grabbed Mam's carrier bag of mementoes, and left by the kitchen door. Then we picked up the old A road to Glasgow and we were on our way. He never really said, 'Come with me.' He just led and I followed.

That's how it was.


*On the road he says, 'Light me a fag, Marie?'*

*There's a packet of Capstans in the glove compartment and I light one up and pass it to him. It seems like a familiar gesture, something close to this unknown man who's my father.*

*'You have one,' he says. 'If you like?' He flashes a smile at me.*

*I do like, I'm used to smoking, and for a while we sit in silence while I study him from the corner of my eyes.*

*His hair is black and thick and I'm thinking he must be around Mam's age; the age she'll be forever.*

*He says, 'I never expected you to be so grown-up, Marie.'*

*'I'm fifteen,' I remind him, 'and I'll be sixteen before Christmas.'*

*But that he thinks I look so grown-up has pleased me, warmed me.*

*We stop at a crowded roadside café and while he goes to the Gents I order up two teas from the flustered server and find us a table. I'm daydreaming, staring out of the window, wondering if Mam is watching me, wondering at an explanation that left so much unclear. Unsaid.*

*('Marie, don't pester me. He was no good. He made his choice.'*

*'What did he do, Mam?'*

*'Och, he liked the women too much.'*

*'But Mam . . .'*

*'Aye, and I liked the men too much and there's an end to it.'*

*'But Mam . . .'*

*'An end, Marie.')*

But it's not an end because I'm here with him, I'm going to his home, I'm going to meet his wife. I'm going to live with them.

The end was for Mam.

I want to cry then but I bite my lip, suck in my tears. I don't want my new dad to think I'm not grown up.

He comes to the table and lights a cigarette, while the woman behind the counter furiously beckons me to her.

She snaps, 'It's no waitress service here; I've got other folk to see to. Yer'll take yer boyfriend his tea.'

To tell the truth, I'm a wee bit flattered that she thinks some-one as handsome as that could be my boyfriend. But that doesn't stop me saying that the tea's too strong and could she give me some more milk?

She says it's how it is and I say that when the farmer comes to milk her later, he should give her tit an extra squeeze.

She calls me a cheeky madam and I call her a stupid cow and go back to Dad. When we leave, I can feel her eyes boring into my back and I stretch my hand behind me and give her the Vs-up.

So Dad and I take the road to Glasgow, to a stepmother I never knew existed.

To a life I never knew was waiting.

A life with Canny and Davina in a nice house in the better part of town.


Dad calls her Diva and she calls him Canny. 'Like he's bright or something,' she laughs, but the smile doesn't quite reach the eyes of this slim, black-haired woman.

We're sitting in the kitchen and she's made us a plate of ham sandwiches and opened a bag of crisps. This room is clean and tidy: no cobwebs in the corners, no pots in the sink, no shoes in

245

*the doorway. But it's a warm, comfortable cleanness, not the Spartan coldness of the Home.*

*'I'm sorry about your mother, Marie,' Diva says.*

*I'm sorry too, but I don't say that, I just mutter a thank you. Then Dad says he'll show me my room and it smells of fresh paint and wallpaper paste.*

*'I had a week to smarten it up,' he says, 'after I heard.'*

*He turns me to him, puts his arms around me.*

*'I'm sorry,' he says, 'sorry for all the years.'*

*He's holding me so lovingly, so close, that I can taste the smell of him. He strokes my hair and tells me again that I'm the image of my mother. Then he says, 'Get yerself a good night's sleep, Marie,' and he gently releases me.*

*'Dad,' I say, and I savour the word. 'Dad?' But he puts his finger to his lips and says, 'Tomorrow, Marie. We'll talk tomorrow.'*

*Before I go to sleep, I do what I always do. I go to the window to look at the street outside. There's a new window, a new scene, a new life, and as I'm watching I'm thinking of all the times I was on my own, all the times when Mam was away. All the times my face was pressed to the cold glass.*

*I'm watching the street for a big American car and a flash Yank who'll buy me the tallest knickerbocker glory in the world. I'm watching and waiting and when he comes he just drives by without even a glance up at me.*

*I'm not his any more.*

I pour myself another dram, top it up with tap water, and see myself in that new, clean room all those years ago, warm in my new bed, flattered by Dad's attention, unsure of Diva, wondering if she'll become the wicked stepmother; she with her black hair and black eyes. But most of all that first night, I'm missing Mam. So I have a few tears to myself and ask that faraway God to let her into Heaven. Because she wasn't that bad, was she?

Then I sleep and not a single dream disturbs me.

But tonight, here in this southern town, I'm going to relive it all again: this bitter-sweet story of unbearable love. There's just me, Robert the Bruce, and the best part of a bottle of Bell's to hear the song being played through once more.

*Dad and Diva run a nightclub and, after a week, I go to work with them. The club is a shuttered-up building in an alley just off Sauchiehall Street. There's broken glass on the cobbles, blood on the wall and a padlocked grill over the door.*

*Dad says, 'It can get a bit rough sometimes.'*

*Inside there's a small dance floor lit by two square skylights, a tiny bar, a seating area with a dozen tables. Diva and I mop the floor while Dad stocks the bar with beers from the cellar. We're working together like a family, like we all belong together. A record player is wired up to corner speakers and Diva sings along to Ruby Murray, 'Softly softly turn the key and open up my heart', as we mop and rinse, clean up the spilt beer and the dog ends. She has her hair tied back in a headscarf, like a Gypsy. She's dark and slim and I'm blonde and curvy; least I think I am. We must look complete opposites.*

*Dad laughs, calls us his 'bonny lassies' and reckons that we should be able to pull the punters in.*

*'Of course, when you're a bit older, Marie.'*

*Diva, warning, says, 'A lot older, Canny.'*

*Later, when she's gone to the warehouse, I'm polishing glasses with Dad and, because it's just me and him, I ask the question because now I'm confident enough; I think I know him enough.*

*So I say, 'Why did you never come to see me?'*

*He shuffles glasses onto the shelf, looks away from me.*

*'Dad?' I'm still savouring that word and it takes the bite out of the question.*

*'Dad?' I say much more gently, squeezing myself in front of him, holding his eyes, making an answer unavoidable.*

*'Marie,' he says, 'I didn't even know until I came back from the war.'*

*What he didn't know was that the girl he left behind with a bellyful of white mice was pregnant.*

*He puts his hands on my shoulders, holds me away to look at my face. He says, 'She was lovely, just like you, Marie.'*

*Then he kisses me softly on my cheek and slowly draws his lips down to mine, and I'm so thrilled.*

*So thrilled.*

You know what, I can still taste the beauty of that first proper kiss across all these years; I can still put myself into that dim club in that dank Glasgow alleyway. I can still be fifteen years old and tell Robert the Bruce to close his ears, not to listen to this tale, but he lies in my lap and cocks his ears every time I speak.

I call him a dozy little moggie and he nudges my hand and purrs. I'm going to miss my little friend when I leave. *When I'm gone.*

Anyway, now I'm going to take another mouthful of Bell's, close my eyes and become young again.

Young and fiery and still missing Mam and bored out of my skull.

*Dad and Diva are at the club and I'm sitting in the lounge. It's Saturday night and they won't be home until the early hours. I've* taken a sip of spirit from every bottle in the cabinet and I'm restless for excitement; it's barely nine o'clock and I want a bit of life. The windows are open and I've pulled the curtains back, but it's still hot, sticky hot, in this room. All day the city sun has been blazing down and I'm missing the cool sea breeze of Dundee around my ears, the familiar streets, the café where we'd all meet up. I'm missing people like me: the waifs and strays of broken marriages, broken homes. Young people. Wild people. Orphan people. My people.

So I loll on the settee, pull my knees up to my ears, hum along to Radio Luxembourg, light up another cigarette and realise that, in a strange way, I'm homesick.

But I've also got a yearning in me; I want to be held in that way, held close and feeling the whispering of warm breath on my body.

I've hardly been out on my own; I go shopping with Diva, work with Dad and Diva; I want to be able to stretch my wings, explore this town. But Dad . . . well, he keeps an eye on me.

'There's bad folk here,' he says, 'and you're an attractive girl.'

Diva's not in the room, so mouthy, restless me snaps, 'What, like Mam?'

'Yes,' he says quietly, 'like your mam.'

Instantly I wish I hadn't snapped like that, but that's me. Big boobs, big arse, even bigger mouth.

A quietness sits between us and I can't stand the silence so I perch on the arm of his chair, put my arm across his shoulders, around his neck. He reaches for my hand, holds it gently. Then there's this feeling of such closeness, of such loving that I want to cry. A sob catches in my throat.

'Marie,' he says, and I slide onto his lap.

We just hold each other as my tears trickle down my face, spot the front of his shirt.

And I don't know how long we're like that, how long I'm lost in this place where I really shouldn't be. It's only when Diva says, 'Tea's ready,' that this spell is torn.

She's standing in the doorway and she's not smiling.

'Shepherd's pie, Marie,' she says. 'I hope you like it.' Never taking her eyes out of mine.

But this night, this hot sticky night with thunder rumbling in the distance, I can't bear a moment more indoors. I close the windows, leave the door on the latch, and I'm out onto the street in my bright summer dress. On my arm is Diva's white handbag and on my feet are her white, tight shoes. They make me four inches higher and I reckon I must look the bee's knees, clipping along the pavement and pulling on a cigarette.

In this part of town the pubs spill out into the road and wolf whistles feed my ego. Maybe I do swing my hips just that little bit more, tighten my stomach, breathe in deeper, hold it longer. I know I seem older than I am, I know that I'm well developed, and my long blonde hair draws the stares, the comments of the lads.

'Hi, gorgeous. D'yer fancy a drink?'

I stop, turn around.

'Who's asking?'

There's a group of Teddy Boys lounging on the warm evening. One detaches himself and says, 'I'm asking.'

He's the leader, this one. He's tall and strong-looking, and so, so confident. He's drainpipe trousers, drape jacket, a D.A. with long sideburns, and crepe boots. He's big and handsome and dangerous.

'Well,' he says, 'do you want a drink or no?'

'Aye.'

'We'll go somewhere quieter, away from the crush.'

Then he takes my arm like he owns me and pulls me gently into a side street, into a smoky pub where old folks sip their drinks and click dominoes on the tabletops.

We claim a corner seat and Teddy boy says, 'A drink, what'syername?'

'Marie, and a gin and tonic, what'syername?'

'Tony,' he says.

So this is a hot summer night with a dark-haired boy who looks more Italian than Scottish. He laughs at my 'soft Dundee accent' and he says he'll teach me 'real Glasgee' if I give him the chance.

But all the time he's talking to me he's looking at my lips, at my mouth, at my body.

And I've seen that look before.

And I know where it's going to lead.


He's walking me back when the first patters of rain smack heavy and wet onto the pavement. Then there's a terrific flash of lightning and a crack of thunder that leaves my ears ringing. The street lamps flicker and go out and already we're running for home.


What was I then? A confused girl? A little tart? A contrary little madam?

I think I was more like Mam than I knew and, like her, there were things that I needed, that I would always need.

Just like she had.


Outside this house of just me and Robert the Bruce the rain is starting: cold winter rain that taps on the glass and drips down the chimney. This is the steady soaking of the season, not like the cloudburst of that long-ago night when I was so young.

*There's no lights on anywhere: in the streets, in the rows of windows. It's like the blackout in the war and, by the time we reach home, I'm out of breath and drenched through and still the thunder rolls and lightning slashes the sky.*

*But once inside, I light the gas fire and then we're fumbling at each other, clutching, touching, clinging. There's to be no nice-ties, no waiting here. We're beyond impatience.*

*I say, 'Have you got something?' because although I'm like Mam I don't want to end up like her.*

*'I'm a boy scout,' he says. 'Always prepared.'*

*We're voices, shadows on the couch. Shadows struggling in the gaslight, dressed in wet clothes and passion.*

*And that passion is brief. In fact it's over before I've hardly started and it pisses me off that he starts to get dressed while I'm still not properly undressed.*

*He lights up a cigarette and I see his face in the darkness. 'I think we can still make closing,' he says. 'You coming?'*

*I tell him he can go on his fucking own, and he laughs and says that if I fancy a repeat performance I know where to find him.*

*I say after that performance he's not getting an encore and he laughs again and calls me a funny girl.*

*He's still chuckling as he steps out into the night.*

*With nothing better to do, I go up to bed and later, much later, the electric clicks on and the landing light floods through my door: that and the sound of Dad and Diva clumping up the stairs.*

\*     \*     \*

We always have breakfast at ten o'clock and this morning I don't get up till then. I'm glad of the lie-in because, to tell the truth, I've a little bit of a hangover.

Dad grunts 'G'morning Marie' over his paper and the teapot, yawns and lights a cigarette.

'Late night, Dad?'

'Early morning,' he says.

He's sitting opposite me with his hair uncombed and blue stubble on his chin. But he's handsome, so handsome. He's in a summer shirt and his arms are lean and muscular, hard and strong. He lowers the paper and says, 'You're bright-eyed, Marie.' When I'm obviously not.

'Good night's sleep, Dad.' When I obviously hadn't.

Then from the front room Diva says loudly, clearly, 'The dirty cow.' Then she's standing in the doorway, pinching between thumb and forefinger a wrinkled, soggy, dangling French Letter.

In this moment I look at her, I look at Dad. I look at what's on their faces.

Diva's is grimacing distaste.

Dad's is like he can't believe what he's seeing. His face shows the workings of his mind.

She says to Dad, 'In the front room, on my best carpet. She must have had some boy round when we were out.'

I'm thinking that she didn't have to do it like this; she didn't have to tell Dad. She could have pulled me to one side, given me a pep talk, but she wants him to know, wants him to see what I'm really like.

Her expression is one of sly triumph and I would love to scratch that face, those ever-watchful eyes. But I sit still in this horrified silence while my heartbeat drums in my ears.

She says, 'Well, Marie?' and, as though to prompt my answer, she gives the johnny a little shake, the fucking bitch.

Then Dad just says, 'Oh, Marie.' And there is such a sadness in his voice I want this to be a bad dream, a terrible nightmare. I pinch my thigh, squeeze the flesh as hard as I can. I squeeze the top of my arm. I squeeze and squeeze and squeeze.

But nothing changes and it's ten o'clock and I'm still at the breakfast table and Diva is still dangling that johnny like she's won first prize in a raffle.

I get up, go to my room, sit on the bed and say to myself, 'Why have I spoilt it? Why didn't that fucking creep just slip it into his pocket?'

Then I pack my case, have a cry – that's all I seem to do lately – then I wait.

They leave about one o'clock, shutting the front door quietly behind them like they don't want me to hear. But I watch them from the window, see Dad's car drift away down the road: him and that fucking bitch.

I give them five minutes, smoke a fag, and then carry my case downstairs. Off the hook I take Diva's favourite coat and then I'm to the door, saying my goodbyes to an empty house, thinking that I'll get away as far as I can. Then I think I'll leave a note, just a few words to Dad telling him I'm sorry, and leaving my love.

So this is what I'm doing when the door swings open and he's standing there looking at my case, looking at me writing my goodbyes.

'Marie,' he says. 'What's going on?'

Then he says, 'You can't go, Marie.'

'I can. I'm nearly sixteen.'

'You're too young.'

'Mam wasn't too young.'

I know this is a lie, I know Mam was a year older than me but it's a smart thing to say, and it cuts into Dad.

He says, 'That was different, Marie,' in a smack of an answer.

And it's a different Dad; he's edgy and nervous and he's saying that he came back from the club to talk to me.

'I don't want anything to change ...' He hesitates. 'After what's happened.'

After what I did, he means.

I say, 'And Diva?'

'She'll come round. In time.'

So we're in a kind of truce, with me feeling a bit ashamed and now only pretending about wanting to run away.

'Dad, I'm sorry.'

It seems I'm saying it as though I betrayed him. I say I'm sorry again and then he says, 'Come here, Marie.' He holds me fast and hard and strong but with – I can't explain how – such tenderness.

And with love.

And I don't care because it's what I want, what I need.


I'm going to take a breather now because this pain, this gnawing in my stomach, is making me catch my breath. It twists me double and I have to wait until it's done a lap of fucking honour before it passes. Then I pour myself a double Bell's.

Robert the Bruce has slid off my lap and he's studying my grimace, so I lift him up again and settle him on my knees, while outside the wet night gathers strength.

Then I close my eyes and let the past drift over me.

And what a thing this past is, where wrong is right and that wrong fills me up, burns me up, takes me by the hand and leads me into the misunderstood.

*After the johnny episode, it's a week before Diva speaks to me properly, politely. She serves up breakfast with a curt, 'Here you are, Marie.' Then as she and Dad leave for the club, she says, 'Don't forget the washing-up. Oh, and the kitchen floor.' And at the front door she calls back, with a toss of her jet-black hair, 'The dirty washing's in the basket.'*

*Dad, following her out, raises his eyes and blows me a kiss. I blow him one back and he gives me the conspiracy of a smile and if only he could hold me now, kiss me now, and not stop for the world.*

*And do what we did before.*

*I'm on a curfew which includes even helping at the club, but Dad says give it a few more days and we'll be back to normal.*

*So I start my chores, my penance for sinning with a Teddy boy who didn't even try to hide the evidence.*

*And Dad's never mentioned this sinning. But for a few days afterwards, in the way he looked at me, I expected him to say, 'You're just like your mother.'*

*And he would have been right, wouldn't he?*

*For now I'm in the house on my own, pissed off again, and thinking that I'm only a fucking skivvy here. But I also think if I rush through the washing-up, the floor cleaning, the laundry, I could catch the bus to the market and lose myself for a couple of hours and no one would know.*

*I light the gas boiler, light up a cigarette and, as the water's warming, I sprinkle in some soap flakes and sort through the washing. I sort whites from colours, Dad's shirts from his socks,*

Diva's bright skirt from her white blouses and white slips of knickers; all the clothes of a week to go into the tub.

I boil up the whites, stir them with the paddle, let them bubble away while I have another cigarette and nurse my resentment of Diva.

Sodding cow, always bossing, always hanging on Dad's arm, always snuggling up to him on the settee like she owns him. Well, if only she knew.

But she won't, because it's our secret, mine and Dad's.

All the same when I look at those knickers, bubbling pure and white in the wash, I suddenly have this image of Dad peeling them slowly down from Diva's narrow hips. Then this image becomes one of them lying together in their bed at night, lying together like they belong together. Pressing together.

And then I'm angry with both of them and it's with the anger of the helpless in the last year of childhood.

Fuck them. Fuck them. Fuck them.

Slowly then, I drop, one at a time, Diva's tight red sweater – the one she thinks makes her look like Lana Turner – plus Dad's blue socks, a yellow tie; an armful of colours into the boiler. I chuck in my dog-end for good measure, and I stir the cauldron like a witch. I stir my growing resentment faster and faster, till the suds slop over the side and hiss onto the gas ring.

I'm a little bit uneasy when, on the draining board, Dad's cream shirt is now a pale shade of pink, his vest exactly the same. But I can't help laughing to myself that at least they match.

I laugh even more that Diva's favourite pale blouse is no longer pale and her white brief knickers are streaked red and blue like little union flags. But my uneasiness is growing.

Then I think of what Mam would have said. 'What's done is done, Marie. Worrying's not going to change anything.'

*And she never worried in her life. Well, only about the next drink. Or the next man.*

*But she never had to answer to anyone, did she?*

There's a fuss, of course, when Dad and Diva come home.

Diva says, 'How could you?'

'I slung the lot in together. Wasn't thinking.'

'You'd need a brain to think.'

Dad says, 'She said it was an accident.'

'Don't stick up for her.'

Dad says sharply, 'It's done, Diva, give it a rest.'

She looks at him as though she's about to cry. There's shock on her face and her mouth drops open. 'You must see what she's doing, Canny.'

'You've had your knife in her ever since she got here.'

'Canny, I haven't. It's not me, it's her.'

But Dad's had enough; he's out of here, slamming the door behind him.

Diva screams at me, 'We were all right before you came.' She raises her hand and slaps me hard across the chops.

'You little bitch,' she says.

But I've had a tough upbringing and I slap her right back.

That does Diva and she stands stock-still, with tears filling her eyes and the mark of my hand burning her cheek.

'I'll never forget this, Marie,' she hisses. And there's more threat in those quiet words than any I've heard in my life.

I say, 'Bollocks to you, Diva.' And then she turns without another word and leaves me alone in the kitchen with the mess of the laundry heaped on the floor.

\*    \*    \*

Sometimes I catch my reflection in a shop window and I can't believe what I see: a skinny pensioner, lined and so old. A bag of bones. A Scottish refugee who's spent too long in the soft South. That's what I see. What I look for is the image of that busty young blonde that life couldn't cower; young and firm and so in love that blindness and carelessness surely had to follow.

I can trace all this now, as clear as yesterday. As clear as dawn breaking over this wet town that's been my home for twenty years in my exile.

As clear as that terrible attraction that, once started, was like a drug.

Yes, I can see it, feel it, touch it, but I'm not sorry for it.

And I'm not sorry for the trouble I caused that cow Diva; in fact, I relish every time she felt her heart break, because mine was broken just the once. Because of her, and forever.

*After the laundry episode – seems my life's made up of episodes – it's three days before Diva acknowledges me again. She comes into the kitchen, and I hear her take a deep breath before she says, 'You're to come to the club with us this afternoon.' She adds, 'If you like?'*

*I reckon she's trying for Dad's sake, because she's being extra nice to him, calling him 'darling', pouring his tea, buttering his toast. But it's more than that, she adores him. Those dark eyes follow him everywhere and she's grateful for his attention, for his thank yous. If she were a dog, she'd be a lovesick spaniel.*

*'Well,' she says, 'are you coming?'*

*I tell her yes, smile brightly at her, as she purses her lips.*

*'At three,' she says. 'Be ready at three.'*

*The afternoon finds us in the dim indoors of the club, and it's this club that, as Dad says, puts the bread and butter on the table.*

*It also pays for the car and the nice house, for Diva's clothes, and for keeping me, I suppose.*

*We do the usual cleaning up from the night before: mopping the floor, wiping the tables, stocking the shelves.*

*Dad's told me that if I help I'll be on the payroll.*

*'Can't afford too much, mind,' he says.*

*Diva starts to laugh, starts to tell him he's a tightwad, but then remembers that this is about me and she clams up. She's not going to forget what happened in a hurry.*

*But she's given me a glimpse of what it was like between them, probably still is when I'm not there, and I'm seeing it through green glass.*

*Our shared life goes on in this uneasy world, in this uneasy truce. It passes through the end of a hot listless summer, a wet autumn, and a winter that dusts the streets with snow before November is out. I've now turned sixteen and, despite Diva's protests, Dad lets me serve behind the bar. I'm good at this, flirting and pouring beer, or stretching up to the optics aware of the eyes that look, the long glances that give away interest.*

*And sometimes I'll turn and it'll be Dad.*

*And sometimes I'll turn and it'll be Diva with her cold, cold eyes.*

*I take a break about midnight, go and stand by the door with Bert the Bouncer. He always offers me a cigarette, tells me how pretty I am and wishes he were ten years younger.*

*'Twenty,' I say, and he laughs a gummy laugh, this toothless, scarred giant of a man.*

*He says, 'You're right, I'm getting too old for this game.'*

But he keeps the door for Dad two nights a week and spreads out the rest to the highest bidders. Dad says that Bert's a legend and he'd have been a top pro if the war hadn't taken away his best years.

'Like all of us, I suppose,' he says, and it's in a wistful way, as though those years of conflict had stolen much more than his time. Which they have, when I think about it.

Anyway, tonight's quiet and by midnight Bert the Bouncer has made tracks and Diva's sitting with a couple of stay-ons. Dad and I are at the bar having a drink and he's had a few already. He pours me a whisky and halves it with water and I see Diva's head flick around like she's got a radar, so I raise the glass like I'm toasting her, and Dad, not missing a trick, says, 'Don't aggravate her, Marie.'

'Can't help it, Dad.'

'It doesn't help when we're all living together.'

I dare to say it then, say what I've been dreaming about for weeks. 'We don't have to.'

'Don't have to?'

'All live together. We could leave her.'

'I couldn't, Marie.'

'But, Dad, we could go away. We could . . .'

'No, Marie. No, I couldn't.'

'But no one would know who we were.'

Dad's looking hard at me now. 'Marie,' he says, 'everything I've got is tied up here.'

He says it as though he wants it to be the final word and I button up my mouth.

For now.

*　　*　　*

*The next morning Diva's gone off early to do the shopping and Dad brings me up a cup of tea. He sits on my bed, strokes my hair and tells me not to worry.*

*And when he slips in beside me, holds me, loves me, I don't.*

*I don't worry.*

*But I do worry when, a month after Christmas I'm sitting in the doctor's feeling sick as a dog with a sample of pee clutched in my hot little hand.*

Well, that's made you prick up your ears, Robert the Bruce, and I'm still only halfway through my story, halfway through this night. Monday evening the girls'll be down the Bluebell – well, except for Irish – and I shall be in Glasgow. I should be feeling guilty about letting them down, leaving without a word; but this part, retracing the beginning of Aubrey, tears open my heart.

And I can see the bewildered girl I was then, desperately trying to keep a secret that could never be kept. I tried to hide it away, shut it away, pretend it wasn't happening. Those times I dragged myself to work when all I wanted to do was leave my head on my pillow; all those times I needed Dad, his warmth; and yet I couldn't let him near me because he would notice my swelling belly, my fuller breasts.

All these times are going around in my head, and there's young, unsure me remembering that once, when he was holding so tightly, so closely, it was Mam's name that whispered from his mouth.

But this limbo world ends when Diva, ever watchful, corners me in the loo of the club.

*'You've put on weight, Marie.'*

*'I haven't.'*

'You have, you know.'

This isn't a friendly nose, it's got an edge of inquisition.

I say, 'I don't think I have, Diva.'

She stands in front of me, slim and dark. 'It only seems to be here.' Her hand is on my stomach before I can flinch back.

She says, 'You are, aren't you?'

Her fingers have felt my firmness and triumph is smeared across her face, because she thinks I've really fucked up this time.

I say, 'At least I'm not a barren cow like you.'

She smiles her smug smile. 'Wait till your dad finds out, it'll be the shock of his life.'

I very nearly say, 'More of a shock than you'll ever know,' but I hold my tongue, swallow those words that could condemn him, condemn us.

'So, whose is it?'

'None of your business.'

'I bet it's that dirty little toerag who left his johnny on my carpet.'

'Can't say for sure.' I pause. 'Might even be Bert's.'

Diva can't take this winding up; she's no sense of humour. Well, at least where I'm concerned.

'We'll have you put in a home,' she spits at me.

'Not Dad,' I say, and she knows I'm right but she still says, 'We'll see,' before she leaves me in the Ladies.

I stay for a while, look at myself in the mirror: the bulge under my dress, the bags under my eyes. So much for the bloom of pregnancy. I light a cigarette, blow smoke at myself and think I should be telling Dad before she does; there can't be any more putting it off, as much as I dread it.

\* \* \*

*Dad's in his usual place, elbows on the bar, watching the couples smooching on the floor to the tinkle of a lone pianist. Diva is playing mine host, flitting between tables and drinkers.*

*At the bar in this lull of punters needing drink, I catch him.*

*'Dad.'*

*He says, 'Marie, where've you been?'*

*I just say, 'I need to talk to you, now.'*

*I'm literally trembling and my words stutter out.*

*Dad says gently, with such concern in his voice, 'Marie, what's the matter?'*

*I'm frightened I'm going to break down, my legs buckling beneath me, but then Dad is by me, his arm supporting me. Diva, missing nothing, guessing everything, doesn't need to be beckoned over.*

*'Are you all right, Marie?'*

*She looks at me like she cares and then she says, 'I'll mind the bar, Canny; you mind Marie.'*

*Dad takes me outside into the shadows of the winter alley. There's no Bert the Bouncer tonight and, because it's so late, there's no one else about.*

*'Marie,' Dad says, and I slip into his arms. 'Marie, what is it?'*

*We're close like we haven't been in months, not since I knew, and I just want to feel him around me again.*

*'Marie,' he says again, and then I take his hand, hold it onto my belly.*

*'It's there,' I say. 'It's there.'*

*'What's there?'*

*In the cold shadows of this winter alley I show him child and grandchild.*

*All in one.*

*So there I am, gaining weight through this cold, snowy winter, living and loving in this strange closed world of me, Dad and Diva.*

*Me, young skin stretching as Aubrey grows.*

*Dad, nervous and edgy, snapping at Diva, snapping at me.*

*And Diva desperately wanting to see the back of me, wanting her life – their life – returned to her.*

*That's how it was for that winter. But there would be times when Dad and I would sit by the fire on a dim afternoon and, sometimes, he'd talk about Mam.*

*'Och, she was a beauty.' He puts his hand to my face, turns me to him. 'Just like you,' he says, and kisses me softly, gently on my mouth. Then he kisses me again and . . .*

And I can't bear this part of the remembering. I'm crying into my hands and Robert the Bruce, thinking he's a help, is purring around my legs.

But now I've got to put this away for a little while, because after all these years it can still scorch me. It's late and my eyes keep slipping shut.

But when I wake it's getting light and there's hardly time to grab my case, visit the toilet (*don't look back, you know what's in there*) and put my trusting Robert the Bruce into a cardboard box, leave him outside the cats' home and catch the eight o'clock train to the North.

## MONDAY NIGHT DARTS.
## STILL IN FEBRUARY
### THE BLUEBELL VERSUS THE BELL RINGERS

*Katy*

I'm at the bar and it's nearly time for the game and still there's no sign of Scottie Dog. All I get on her mobile is the bloody answer-phone with its daft 'Will ye no leave a message, yer Sassenach bastard'. Christ knows what's happened to her, but we'd have surely heard something by now if it wasn't good.

Danny says he hasn't seen Scottie Dog since last Thursday and she was a bit odd then. 'That was nothing out the ordinary, mind,' he says.

I think that Irish was never out of her ordinary, and look how that turned out.

'Danny,' I say, 'where am I going to find another player now?' There's a few in tonight and I'm looking round the bar for a sub.

'Pikey Pete's mum used to be a tidy player,' Danny says. He nods towards the Motley Crew, where Ada Pikey is sitting with a half of bitter and laughing like a scruffy old crow.

I'm thinking that there must be someone else. Anyone else.

But of course there's not. 'Fancy a game of darts tonight, Ada? We're a player down.'

She looks surprised, this plump woman with gold in her ears and a cardigan that's seen better days, and hair in desperate need of a good brush-through.

'You must be short, my dear, asking me.'

Pikey Pete says, 'Go on, Mum, you'll enjoy it.'

So Ada joins our team for Scottie Dog, and Big Nellie, sitting in the corner like the pub chucker-out, is in for Irish, and it makes me wonder where this'll all end, these changes to the team, to my life.

It also makes me wonder what we'll be nicknamed by the other teams, what with two didikais in the team, probably the Bluebell Gypos.

But then I realize it's not just two Gypsies in the team because I forgot to count myself in.

And I'm in because I gained a father I didn't know I had.

Anyway, the Bell Ringers arrive at the bar and Danny cracks his usual corn.

'It should be a ding-dong of a game tonight,' he says loudly and the Bell Ringers – Irish had always called them the Bell Enders – groan like a choir.

They're an unlikely lot, this team; most are from the Mazes estate in town – all on the social, and mouthy, bare-armed, tattooed and bovine. Like Pegs' dad would say, 'A herd of heifers.'

Like my dad would say.

So we have a few practice throws, make the draw and start the game.

\*       \*       \*

I'm right about the piss-taking because it starts straight away from the Thomson sisters in the team game. Rita Thomson just misses out on the double and Ada Pikey, taking a keen interest in the proceedings, says, 'That's bad luck, my dear.'

Carol Thomson – captain of the Bell team – says, 'We came here for a darts match, not to have our fortunes told.'

Well, they didn't come here to win because Lena shoots out on twenty-two and Ada smirks to Carol Thomson in payback, 'I knew that was going to happen.'

Then, pissed off with the defeat, Rita Thomson says that Danny should rename the pub the Appleby Arms because it's full of tinkers.

But Danny's listening from the bar and he bawls out, 'Any more of that and you're out the door.' Then he mutters to me, 'It's didikais anyway, not tinkers.'

Carol Thomson says that Danny should be more careful who he lets in. Danny says he usually is but it seems he made a mistake with her.

That shuts her up, along with everyone else, and Pegs – who's looking a bit pissed off – plays to the music of the jukebox for five minutes. And it's long enough for a tight-lipped Pegs to cruise in the points.

Then Big Nellie, who I don't think has said a word all night, steps up to the oche and grunts, 'You chalking this one, Katy?'

Now Big Nellie's been all right in practice, but now she's on it. Her darts, between swigs from her pint pot of ale, hit the board like bullets and the Bell Ringers, lowing support for their captain, watch another one go down.

Then Lena, swollen belly and just reaching the waddling stage, scrapes through by the skin of her teeth. Hers has been a low-scoring, boring, lengthy contest and because of that I'm almost sure I can hear Irish say:

'If this game goes on for much longer she'll be having the fucking baby on the oche.'

That's as far as we go tonight because me, Maggie and Ada Pikey ('Didn't see that one coming Ada, did you?' says Rita Thomson) drop in quick succession and it's only the team game that's seen us through.

They're not happy, this team the Bell Ringers, and Scottie Dog would have lapped up this win against them.

And that reminds me when I go outside for a smoke to try Scottie Dog on the mobile. But again I get that dozy answerphone, so I sit on a damp bench, at a damp table, under a dripping umbrella, smoking a soggy fag, and promise myself that Johnny James and I will call around her place tomorrow. Then I blow a kiss to the camera and go back inside for last orders.

But later this night, after Johnny James has loved me, after the soft burr of his snoring lets me know he's in the Land of Nod, I wonder if Jerry and Laura are sleeping just as soundly in the darkened house of my past.

And I'm back to yesterday afternoon and I've gone to that house to try and make peace with Laura.

*Johnny James says, 'You sure you want to do this, Katy?'*

*We're sitting in his Beamer outside my old home and we're sharing a cigarette. There's a gentle rain falling and he flicks the wipers on.*

*'Last try, Johnny,' I say.*

He says, 'I'll wait, Katy,' and he leans across, looks at me with those *eyes*, and kisses me properly.

But then he always kisses me properly.


This doesn't seem like my house any more. The front path's swept clean of leaves and there's no dog-ends on the step and the curtains are neatly drawn. I'm heading to the back door, but from around the corner there's a drift of smoke, a tang of wood and plastic.

And Jerry is poking a bonfire to death in the back garden.

He says, 'I'm having a clear-out, Katy.'

'In the rain?'

His hair, what there is of it, is curled on his head and his damp clothes are hanging on his frame. But that haunted look is off his face and he laughs to me and says, 'I'm getting rid of my girlfriends.'

He's watching the flames as his Luscious Linda, Daring Debbie, and Randy Rhoda DVDs curl up in the heat, their beautiful bodies changing to melting plastic and charring paper. Then he turns to me and says very quietly, very gently, 'I probably shouldn't say this, but I'll always love you, Katy.' He pauses, pokes the fire again and Sex-starved Sarah blisters and bursts into flames. He looks at my face, my give-away expression. 'Please let me say this, Katy.'

Then he tells me in a slow clear voice, like he's rehearsed it a hundred times, 'I know it's done. I know you'll never come back. I've thought about this night after night and all I've been doing is making it worse.' He pauses again and a spatter of rain hisses in the bonfire. 'So this is it for me; goodbye to Katy.'

We stand in silence for a minute of respect for a dead marriage.

'Might have to get myself a couple of Thai girls now.' He

*gives me a mock-shy, mock-guilty, smile. 'You know, to help with the housework, or maybe to play ping-pong.'*

*I laugh then because he's turning this situation into his show and the old Jerry, the Jerry from a long time ago, is coming back. I feel a sense of relief, like I'm not being blamed any more.*

*'Jerry,' I say, 'I'm sorry. Sorry for it all.'*

*I put my hand in his and squeeze. He squeezes back.*

*'It's all right, Katy. I should have seen it coming. I needed a good kick up the arse; pity it had to be this way.'*

*I say, 'Laura, Jerry? What about Laura? She hates me.'*

*Jerry says quietly, 'When she knew you were coming, she wouldn't stay in. I'm sorry, Katy.' He pauses. 'Sorry again.'*

*And so am I.*

*So I walk away down that familiar unfamiliar path out to Johnny James in his posh car and I don't realise I'm crying until he says, 'You all right, Katy?'*

*And I don't know if I am or not.*

It's two o'clock in the morning and I can't sleep, so I slide out of Johnny James's warm bed, wrap a coat around me, and go out for a fag. It's still spitting with rain, but between the clouds the moon's to trying poke its head out.

It's funny how I always seem to end up in a lonely garden in the middle of the night, but I don't mind with a cigarette, or two, for company – even if it's a bit chilly out here and I've got nothing on under my coat. (Johnny James always likes the thought of that.) I'm shuffling along the path across the lawn, puffing on my fag, thinking I'm no nearer to reaching Laura, no nearer to making it something like it was. Before all of this.

\* \* \*

271

Laura on a high, voice bubbling with excitement, because Barry Wood had asked to meet her after school.

'Oh Mum, what'll I wear? Can we' – she means me – 'buy that . . .?'

And for several trips to Matalan 'that' was a skirt, a coat, a pretty blouse, a pair of shoes. I even put in some extra Saturday morning shifts to help pay for it all. (Jerry couldn't see the sense in buying 'even more clothes when there's plenty in the wardrobe'.

And for me and Laura there's a giggling together, a clutching of my arm. An impulsive hug. Sometimes it's like I'm the teenager, like I'm the fourteen-going on fifteen-year-old with a headful of stars.

There is a month of this Laura in her first love, this Laura tearing out of the house, coming back much too late at night, sitting on my bed – when she should be in her bed – and reliving everything that Barry had said, everything that they had done; well, perhaps not everything. And then there's a night of Laura not coming back at all because she said she was staying over at a friend's. But after that night there's a slow tailing off of Brilliant Barry; and then there's hours of Laura moping in her room, bursting into tears at the slightest upset because . . .

'He's dumped me, Mum. He's dumped me.'

Then Laura finds out that fickle Barry has latched onto Tanya Jones, who's a year older than Laura and wears minute skirts and fake tan. Her family 'own their own house', and 'have a new car', and 'holidays in Spain'. And, apparently, they're not trailer trash – or the council house equivalent.

And suddenly life's so unfair and somehow it's all my fault.

\*　　\*　　\*

Well it wasn't then, but now . . .

Mum says Laura'll come round. 'Give her time; look at all the trouble I had with you, Katy.'

I don't say it but I think that I had more trouble with her: her and poxy Jim.

It's the thought of dads that leads me back to Henry Smith and – I take a deep drag on my cigarette – my secret sister, Pegs. It's strange with her, because although we talk together, play darts together, work together, there's this thing between us. It's like we're nearly close, only inches away. Sometimes I catch her looking at me, really looking. *Like she knows.*

I've been through them all, sitting here in the night, stoking up the fags, trying to make sense to these twists and turns of my life.

But I haven't been through them all, not quite; because there's still my other sister, Ellie, Jim and Mum's daughter. I wonder what the stuck-up cow will think when she finds out there's dids in the family. That'll be one in her snotty eye.

That's if it ever comes out.

It's getting cold out here and the kitchen light's gone on, so Johnny James must have missed me. He's getting a drink of water when I open the door, then open my coat and show him what I've got.

'You bloody tart,' he laughs but he still has a good butcher's and it puts him in the mood again; I'll be knackered in the morning.


I'm late, as well as knackered, and everyone's already in their white overalls and hairnets.

Pegs is back in the fold and we have a quick chat about last night's game.

'Miserable lot, the Bell Ringers,' I say.

'Bunch of dinolows,' she says. (I think that's what she said – least that was what it sounded like.)

But she's been doing that a lot lately, sort of popping in the odd Gypsy word to me. Some of them stick in my mind, but I can never follow the conversations she has in the pub with Ada or Pikey Pete.

Danny'll ask, nodding towards them, 'What do you think that lot's on about?'

I pretend to listen and then say, 'They reckon your beer's shite and you're tight as a duck's woskit.'

'Very funny, Katy,' he says, 'and there's me thinking they were discussing hedgehog recipes.'

We're both laughing then and it's a little while before I realise my laugh has turned a shade guilty, because I'm sort of laughing at my own kind.

Anyway, today I'm glad when five o'clock comes around and Johnny James is picking me up in his car. Lately we've been going straight back to his place after work and I've cooked us a meal.

'We're like an old married couple already; you'll be washing my boxers next,' he jokes.

I'm opening a can of beans and I tell him that his boxers can crawl into the washing machine on their own. But his words have made me wonder – not the bit about his underwear – but about us being an old married couple. It makes me think what the future will be for us.

Will I always be in Johnny James's kitchen cooking tea for two, or will those eyes of his be stealing someone else's heart?

And you know, sometimes the five years between us seems too many. I worry; I look in the mirror at my face, at the giveaway signs of ageing. But then Johnny James will come in, tell me I'm the best thing since sliced bread, and all those worries will be out the door.

After tea we drive around to Scottie Dog's house and I bang on her door. There's no reply so I call through the letter box. But my voice echoes into the house like it really is empty, like there's no one breathing in there. I'm back to knocking and getting worried when the neighbour's door opens and I see a woman who looks like she's just got out of bed.

'She's gone.'

The voice of explanation is like the screech of an owl.

'Pardon?'

'She's gone. Her and her suitcase and her sodding cat in a cardboard box.'

'When?'

'Friday morning, and good riddance if you ask me.'

'Where's she gone?'

'Don't know; hopefully back to Jockland.'

This caring neighbour scratches her head like she's got nits and slams her door shut.

'Thanks,' I say to the door.

So Johnny James and I drive to the Bluebell where there's only the Motley Crew in listless midweek conversation. They're sitting around the fireplace, beer in hand and moaning about the weather.

'Hi, Katy. Hi Johnny,' is muttered in a ragged subdued chorus. Danny says he didn't chuck 'em out till two o'clock last night and by then Paddy was Off to Dublin in the Green, Pikey Pete was throwing up in the bog, Jilted John had run off home with the runs, and Old Bob had fallen asleep in the chair.

'I thought he was dead so I left him there. Gone this morning though.'

I tell him about Scottie Dog and he says that it's strange, what with Irish doing what she did and now Scottie Dog's packed up and gone.

'I'll miss the old bird,' he says, and I'm thinking that the pub won't be the same without them.

Johnny James and I have a drink and then go outside for a fag and I try her number and I get that bloody answerphone welcome again. But her voice is really clear, like she's standing beside me, talking in my ear.

And then I'm so stupid because I start to cry, to sob like a schoolgirl, and Johnny James asks me what's the matter and I can't answer him. I can't tell him that I'm crying for Irish, for Scottie Dog, for Jerry, for Laura, for a dad who doesn't know me, for a sister I never knew I had.

'It's nothing, Johnny. Nothing.'

He holds me in such a comforting way and I'm still crying because the thought of losing him would be the worst of all things.

# THURSDAY NIGHT PRACTICE AT
# THE BLUEBELL – EARLY MARCH

## *Still Katy*

I didn't feel like coming tonight but Johnny James said he'd drop me and pick me up.

'You can stay at my place, Katy.'

I'm thinking that my problem is with me and my fucking insecurity, because I read that like he's making a point to me. *His* place.

I say, 'It's okay, I'll stay at *mine*,' when it's not really mine, it's Mum's.

So sod everything again. But Johnny, lovely Johnny James, quick on the uptake, says, 'I want you to come back to *the house* tonight, Katy. After you've been to *the pub*.'

Despite my mood, I have to laugh and he says, 'That's better, Katy.' Then he kisses me slowly, lovingly, and I'm getting out of his car and he's saying, 'See you later, lover,' and he guns the BMW out of the car park like Steve McQueen in one of those old chase movies.

\*     \*     \*

The Bluebell is pretty quiet. Danny is reading a newspaper on the bar and Big Nellie is nursing a pint by the fireplace. She's absent-mindedly pushing a log into the grate with her foot and there's a tang of burnt shoe sole in the air. Danny, looking up and sniffing, says, 'She don't feel pain; I'm waiting for her to set her leg on fire and I bet she won't notice till it reaches her . . .' He thinks better of it and turns to get my drink.

Then he says, 'Still no word from Scottie Dog then, Katy? Anyone know why she's gone?'

'Search me, Danny.'

'Is that an offer, Katy?'

I call him a pervert and take my drink over to Big Nellie. She grunts a good evening and I'm hoping the other girls'll turn up soon, else there won't be much conversation.

Pegs is the next to arrive and the first thing she says is, 'What's Danny burning on the fire?' Big Nellie is now tapping her foot on the hearth like she's stubbing a fag out.

Maggie comes in, and then Ada Pikey, and that's it for practice because Lena is growing fatter by the hour and we won't see her tonight.

So we have a knockabout and a few drinks for an hour. Then Maggie reckons she's due an early night and Big Nellie lumbers off. Then Ada Pikey yawns and tells us she's got to be up before six.

Then it's just me and my secret sister and we have a quiet drink and I ask her how things are going.

We sit cosily together in front of the fire and she tells me about her and Big Dave Trinder, about what they're planning and how it's not difficult between them, even though they're different.

'You know what I mean, Katy, about him not being one of us.'

I'm still thinking about what she means by *us*. Then she says, quite unexpectedly, 'You should pop in sometime; Dad was saying he'd not seen you for a while.'

This comment's innocent enough so why does my paranoia start ticking louder?

Why do I imagine she's looking for a reaction at the mention of Dad?

At the mention of *us*.

And why do I imagine that her glance into my eyes is seeing into my soul?

Or do I imagine it?

Christ, what's happening to me?

I'm really glad that just then Johnny James turns up. He calls to Danny, 'Two more voddies for the lovely ladies.'

Danny asks, who does he mean? And Johnny says Danny must be blind. Danny says it would help in his job, cos he wouldn't see the ugly mugs the other side of the bar.

Johnny James reckons it's a wonder he's got any customers at all, and Danny reckons it's only his charm that makes the Bluebell the best pub in town. Then Johnny James brings our drinks over, pulls up a chair, and we sit around the fire like three kackers at a travellers' camp.

Well, two anyway.

And we're still keeping the fire warm when Laura and a couple of her friends – at least girls she knocks about with – come loudly into the bar. They're dressed in short black skirts and long black coats and enough make-up to keep a clown happy. Laura scans the room in a quick flick-over and deliberately, oh so deliberately, ignores me. She won't catch my hello.

Danny serves them – they look old enough and I'm not going to poke my nose in and say who they are.

They crowd the table near us and it's obvious what they're in here for; I'm now getting black looks instead of ignoring ones and Laura, flanked by her witchy friends, is staring me down. Then she stands up with purpose painted on her face and expectations on the coven's. It's two strides to me and, 'Still shagging him, then.'

She spits the words at me, and sneers at Johnny James.

'Have a bit of respect, Laura,' he says. Then he adds, which doesn't help things, 'No need to show off in front of your mates,' like she's a little girl.

This put-down fires her up even more and she thrusts her face into mine, inches away, eyes skunked and saliva on her lips.

'Slag,' she says. 'Fucking slag. That's what you are.'

From behind her comes another titter of laughter from her moronic mates.

'Laura,' I say. 'Don't, please don't do this here.'

She's not listening, and she throws into my face again, 'You're a slag.'

I stand up and our noses are nearly touching in this scene that could have been lifted straight from *EastEnders*.

'Laura, not here.'

Now my voice is a lot firmer because, to tell the truth, I've had enough these last few weeks. My head's full of trouble and I'm starting to tremble. Then Pegs is beside me and her hand is on my arm and she's saying, 'Don't, Katy. Don't.' There's a some-thing in her voice that makes me think that perhaps I should button my lip and sit back down.

Now if only Laura had left it there, had turned on her heel and stormed out of the Bluebell. But she doesn't, she leans right into my face again, so close I can feel the warmth of her breath, the taste of dope smoke.

'Slag,' she says to me, 'fucking slag,' and her gormless friends titter in the background like my life is for their entertainment. And I think that's what does it: their tittering. I don't think I even draw my hand back, I just seem to hit her hard and open-palmed across her cheek without any thought at all. It's a deep resounding slap and it stings me so God knows what it does to her. Then there's utter silence, cut-the-air-with-a-knife silence, and in that silence I'm sure her eyes cloud with shock, with wounded hurt.

I'm sure I say, 'You asked for that,' before I walk out the pub, before I'm choking with consequence.

I'm sure I'm halfway across the car park before Johnny James catches up with me, holds me like I'm a hysterical bitch.

Then I'm sure he sits me in his car, takes me home, whispers to me in his warm bed all night long.

Then, in this whole fucking mess, I'm sure he loves me.

And if that's all I've got, the only thing I'm sure of, I'll manage.

# MONDAY NIGHT DARTS IN MARCH
## THE BLUEBELL VERSUS THE DAIRY MAIDS

*Lena*

Dandy says, 'You don't have to go, Lena. Phone Katy, she'll understand.'

I say, 'It's an important game, Dandy; I can't let the team down.'

All day my stomach has felt like it's going to explode and now I've had to put on my tracksuit for going out; it's the only thing that's big enough for a baby elephant like me.

I tell Dandy I look like trailer trash and he tells me I'm beautiful and he doesn't mind that there's a bit more of me to love now.

'Especially your boobs,' he laughs.

And that makes me even more conscious of them.

So tonight Dandy runs me down to the Bluebell and from there we've got to get a taxi to the Old Dairy public house because Danny is more than half-cut. Katy reckons he's been on it all day, him and the Motley Crew.

In the taxi Maggie says, 'What's the occasion then?'

Katy reckons it's an anniversary, something to do with Danny's wife running off with the drayman years ago.

'Danny always says he misses him so much.'

Big Nellie says that Danny's wife was a pretty little thing but he treated her like shit, and no one really blamed her for leaving.

'Except Danny,' she says.

I think it's the most I've heard Big Nellie say in one go.

Then Ada Pikey tells the taxi driver to get a move on because she's dying for the loo and if he doesn't hurry she'll wet her knickers.

'You'd think there'd be a bucket in the back,' she says, and I'm so glad there isn't.


In the Old Dairy bar I've only been standing a couple of minutes, playing in the warm-up, when my weight catches up with me, drops me into a chair. Pegs sits down beside me and I pat my belly and say, 'I'll be glad when this is over.'

Now I say that but really I'm terrified. Lately I've been waking in the night, listening to Dandy's peaceful, easy breathing, and sometimes I want to pound him awake. I want to scream at him, 'You have this.' I want to pass over my pregnancy to him; I want him to understand this fear of being torn open, of seeping blood and splitting pain. And I want . . .

I want my mum and I can't have her because of what I did.

Pegs says quietly, 'It won't be long, Lena; it might even be tonight.'

Well, I don't think that's likely because I've still got four weeks to go and my midwife says she's never been wrong.

Anyway, I'm first on in the team game and I'm just glad to take my throw and then sit down again. Maggie buys a still water and a packet of crisps for me while Pegs and Katy have their vodkas and Big Nellie drains a pint glass. I feel I'm spilling over my chair like I'm an obese invalid.

Pegs must be a size zero – put her in a school uniform and she'd only seem like a fourteen-year-old. Even Katy, who six months ago was decidedly plump, is now so slim she could be called skinny.

It's all right for her with a new figure, new hairstyle. New man.

I take that back, it's not a fair thing to say, but that's how I've been lately: pretty unreasonable.

I've snapped at Dandy, picked him up on petty little things and, to tell the truth, I've said some nasty things to him, like what's he 'doing with me when he could be with my beautiful mother?'

He just says, 'Don't, Lena. Don't speak like that.'

And for the first time I see him angry.

'Never bring your mother into this.'

'Why, Dandy? Why?'

'Because,' he says, and his voice is hard and cold, 'because none of this is her fault. It was me and you, Lena. Me and you.'

I storm off to bed then (well, waddle really, because you can't make a proper exit when you're thirteen stone of blubber) and cry myself to sleep. Dandy comes up much later and we sleep back to back.

But in the morning he's bringing me a cup of tea and he's whistling up the stairs:

*You're gorgeous. Yes you're gorgeous and I'll be a slave for you.*

Then he sits on the bed and I tell him I'm sorry and he says he's sorry and then I want him so badly that my tea's left undrunk and my big fat body's wobbling with pleasure.

We're loving each other and if I think I can see a shadow in his eyes, I ignore it.

Anyway, tonight at the Old Dairy Big Nellie sits down beside me and I don't feel quite so bad in size comparison, but then some lads push by to feed the jukebox and they don't even look at me. Not a glance, not a flicker of interest, and that kicks my hormones up in the air again.

Then I wish I hadn't come tonight because I'm so uncomfortable and my darts go to pieces and I can't score or get a double for love nor money. And I have to heave myself off to the toilet every ten minutes.

It's a good job the Dairy Maids – all slim girls – are sitting at the bottom of the league because the rest of our team struggle and it's only a fluky treble one, double one out from Ada Pikey that wins our first game. That sets the standard for tonight and the rest of it is dire; any other six would have wiped the floor with us.

This night drags like hell and we sneak a lucky four-three victory with no thanks to me or Katy or Pegs. I've never been so glad to finish in my life and all I want to do is curl up next to Dandy in our warm bed.

Katy says in the taxi back to the Bluebell, 'Not many games to go, Lena. Reckon you'll last it out?'

I tell her I think so because although I want it over, I've still got a month to go. Another month of dread.

In the Bluebell, Danny's behind the bar and he's in a right state. God knows how he manages to take the orders and give the change; habit of years, I suppose.

He says, 'My beauties, how'd it go?'

Katy tells him we scraped through by the skin of our teeth.

Then he says to me, 'You're looking well.' But I can feel his eyes on my enormous boobs.

I say, 'You'll go blind, Danny,' and he laughs. 'Looking can't hurt, Lena.'

I say it can if I lump him.

Suddenly I'm feeling a lot better and I think I'll leave it for a while before I phone Dandy to pick me up. The only thing missing is a good, long drink and I tell Katy that as soon as baby's shown his face, we'll be wetting his head.

'As soon as little Andy's here,' I say, patting my belly.

Pegs says it's bad luck to name a child before it's born and Maggie tells her not to be so superstitious. Katy says that I shouldn't listen to old wives' tales and everything will be fine.

'You're as healthy as a horse,' she says, and I half expect someone to say I'm as big as one. Irish would say that if she were here.

Or Scottie Dog.


I'm sitting in one of the easier chairs in the bar. Okay, the armrests might be a little bit sticky and there might be more than a whiff of staleness to it, but it's comfortable for me. So I lie back and it's like I'm drifting off, listening from a distance to the prattle of Danny.

Danny says, 'So I says to her, "You're not going like that."'

Pikey Pete says, 'Like what, Danny?'

Old Bob says, 'To the fancy-dress party, Pete. His wife was going to a fancy-dress party.'

Danny starts again. 'She's come down the stairs with nothing on except some black gloves and a pair of black socks.'

Pikey Pete says slowly, pondering – perhaps savouring – the image of a near-nude woman coming down Danny's stairs, 'Nothing except gloves and socks? What was she going as then?'

Danny's laughing out loud and he splutters the words out.

'The five of spades, Pete. The five of spades.'

There's a pause and then Pikey Pete gets it.

'You're a fucking twat,' he says to Danny.

I'm laughing now, long and hard, cos suddenly it seems the funniest thing in the world. I'm laughing in this old-style pub, in this tatty old chair with the sticky arms and the damp cushion under my bum, and Katy is looking at me, at the floor where a puddle is forming, and she's saying, 'I'll phone Dandy for you, Lena.'

Dandy comes, leads me out of the pub to the car.

'The seat, Dandy; I'm all wet.' I think I'm crying.

Dandy says, 'It doesn't matter, Lena. It doesn't matter.'

Then, as we drive, he asks me if I'm all right. Then he asks again and again and then I tell him Danny's joke and he laughs and doesn't ask any more.

Then I say, 'Have you phoned Mum?' and he says he has and she'll try and get over. Then I want to ask him what was it like speaking to her after all this time, telling her that her daughter was going to give birth to your child.

But I can't. I couldn't.

Now I've probably seen too many programmes about childbirth on telly. It seems there's always a lot of screaming and a lot of blood and it's always touch and go. But now I'm in bed, in hospital, and I'm not worried like I was. Although I haven't got Mum, I've got a nurse and a midwife and Dandy. Dandy, always conscious of the years between us, jokes that the nurses might think that he's my dad. I tell him that would be really weird considering it's his baby – and I'm the wrong colour to be his daughter – and this makes me laugh again and I think I've laughed more tonight than I have in a long time.

And so I give birth to Andy, little Dandy.

Okay, I know it drags on for hours and it's painful, but it's not a screaming, screeching pain. It does make me grunt a bit and bite my lip and it is so undignified that I don't think Dandy will ever fancy me again.

Then it's done and I'm holding a slippery, mucky bundle of life that latches onto my huge boob and sucks like Dandy does. That thought makes me feel a bit odd and it seems pervy to imagine it now, but I'm already thinking about getting my figure back, getting me back. After all I've just lost four and a half pounds in four hours.

Then there's the midwife and a doctor and they're giving little Andy a bit of an examination, listening to his breathing, taking his temperature. The midwife is saying that because Andy's four weeks early 'He'll need a night or two in the NICU, Lena.'

It's like the midwife is talking from a distance and I'm tired, so tired my eyes won't stay open, and Dandy is kissing me on the forehead like I'm the child and it's bedtime for me.

Then Dandy and Andy leave me to a dreamless sleep that I wake from guiltily, with an urgent need to see my baby.

I'm in a wheelchair with a towel between my legs and a nurse is pushing me along a corridor and she's saying, 'He's in here.'

And behind the glass window 'here' is the unit: four incubators of sleeping offspring. Right in the corner, with the light falling on them, are Dandy and Mum. I can see her slim figure, her perfect hair, and how close she stands to Dandy.

And I can see that her shoulders are trembling, like she's crying.

Their backs are towards me as they lean over child and grand-child. Now they're huddled together like they're sharing a secret and, as I'm watching, Dandy's hand slips around Mum's waist.

And then it's their hands, their fingers, twining together, weaving into each other. It could be their bodies, their flesh, and that thought kicks the breath out of me.

I can't, I won't see this. I say to the nurse, 'Take me back.'

She says, 'But your baby . . .'

'Please, just take me back.'

She hears what's in my voice, my voice that sounds on the edge of unreason, and she turns me to my bed.

It's there I wait until Dandy and Mum come and sit each side of me. Like piggy-in-the-middle, big fat me is between slim, lovely Mum and so handsome Dandy.

And then Mum finds my fingers, squeezes my hand – the first time she's actually touched me in all these years – and says that this is a flying visit just to see I'm okay and she can't stay long because Mikey is on his own, and Dandy says he'd better walk down with her because it's dark in the car park and you never know who's about this time of night. And Mum says she'll come to see me when I get home. And then she and Dandy leave, together.

289

# MONDAY NIGHT IN A GLASGOW
# HOSPICE IN THE MONTH OF MARCH

## Scottie Dog

It's a Monday night again, only a few weeks ago I was in the Bluebell with the girls. Now I'm in this fucking hospice in a ward of no-hopers; a six-bed team of players with nothing left to play for; I suppose we could call ourselves the End-of-Liners. (Irish would have had a chuckle at that and made some crack that this new team will be dead certs to reach the final final.)

In this room there's moaning and groaning and the young woman opposite me sobs forever to herself. Most of them can't make the bog any more and there's always the whiff of shite in here. I'm plugged into a morphine drip and I give the line button a quick press every time that cowing pain shoots through my guts.

It's raining on this Monday night, sweeping fine Scottish rain that gathers on the window and dribbles down the glass, like it used to all those years ago in Dundee. When I watch the rain I could be there again, nose against the cold pane, waiting for Mam to come rolling home.

But I'm not that girl with all my life in front of me; I'm loose skin, a scrawny neck and red rims for eyes that forever weep; I'm a bag of old bones only fit for the knacker's yard.

There's a crowd of visitors filtering in and that means scraping chairs and inquiries of 'How yer feeling?' as if a fucking miracle could happen. They all have visitors, these wasting people. I have to look away when the young woman's children, not more than bairns, climb onto her bed. Her husband – he only seems to be about twenty – holds her hand and she starts to cry again.

I've had enough of this and I ring for the nurse and ask her to pull the curtains around my bed.

She says, 'No one comes to see you, Marie?'

'Haven't got anyone, Katja.'

She's foreign, this nurse; I think she's Polish, and she'll always have a chat. She seems to want to talk. I tell her she's practising her English on me.

She laughs. 'I thought you were Scottish.'

We're inside our curtained room, shut away from the ward, and Nurse Katja says again, 'You sure there's no one, Marie?'

Now, in this Macmillan hospice there's time for all of us: sitting-down chats, tea and biscuits when we want (when we can still eat), and time is relaxed here, drawn out to fill the last weeks of life.

So Katja asks me if there's anyone and I tell her that there's no one I can find. And then I say I had a son once but it was a long time ago.

Katja says softly, 'Tell me, Marie.'

And I shall tell her because nothing really matters now.

Before I came in here – was brought in here – I searched for Aubrey. I walked the streets of that time and found that semi in suburbia. I knocked on the front door and asked for my past.

*But all I get is a blank look from the man of the house and he says, 'You're talking about before I was born. I canna help ye.'*

*The accent is Dad's and I try to peep by the man to see into the hall, to see if there's any remnant of that lost time.*

*But this man's giving me a strange look and he's closing the door on me as a woman's voice calls out, 'Who is it, Jamie?'*

*I just catch, 'Some daft old bat,' before the door slams shut.*

*The night comes early this far north and by the time I've made it back into town the streetlamps are on and the shop windows are lit up. But now the pain in my guts is cutting me in half. Every now and then I've got to stop, catch my breath, lean on a wall. This pain is bad, a devil twisting a knife in my stomach, slicing me from the inside. I'm thinking hospital; I don't want to die in the street. Then a taxi drives slowly by, ignoring this drunken old lady hanging onto a brick wall for support. I try to wave him down but he's not stopping.*

*'Bastard,' I mouth at his tail lights.*

*Then my bones turn to rubber and I sink onto the pavement with the whole of the night swirling around my head.*

But in this now time Katja says, 'Tell me, Marie.' She settles onto my bed, this fair-haired nurse, who can't be much more than twenty-five.

'Och, it's all a long time ago,' I say. 'It's too late to find him.'

Katja talks about the Internet, about Facebook, about a world

I don't understand. 'It's not difficult now, Marie. It's not like it used to be.'

But she's losing me and, above the curtains, the ward clock is pushing half past eight and I'm thinking it's Monday night and the girls – well, except for Irish and me – will be down the Bluebell getting a few drinks under their belts before the game. These thoughts make me maudlin; I'd give anything to be lining up on the oche, listening to Danny chopsing behind me, or Irish cursing the cartwheel every time one of her darts bounces out.

*'You'd think the tight bastard would pay for a decent board,'* she says loudly for Danny's benefit.

*Danny mutters that if she don't like it, why don't she fuck off back to Paddyland?*

*Irish says if he doesn't watch his mouth she'll send him a letter bomb.*

*Danny reckons she's too thick to spell his address properly and Irish says she'll just write 'Cunt' on the envelope and it'll be sure to find him.*

I'm laughing now, thinking about this, and Katja asks what's so funny. I tell her it's an old joke and then she's straight back onto my case, like I'm her mission in life.

'About your son,' she says.

About my son, my Aubrey, whom I knew only for the briefest of summers before my big mouth determined all our futures. You know, I can still feel his warm, firm little body, still feel his eyes following me around the room. Still see that first smile on his face. Christ, I'll be making myself cry in a minute, then I taste the salt on my lips and realise that I am.

This is what I tell her; this is the story. Of course it's told in half an hour, but this is what I say, and in the telling the time is real, the hours are real.

And the loving and the hating and the hurt are real.

*Again, I'm sixteen years old and it'll soon be spring in the city, and mine and Dad's little secret isn't so little any more. It wakes me in the night, plays football in my belly.*

*So there's Diva's silent treatment of me, and Dad, unsure of his status in this strange household, spends most of his time at the club; sometimes he even sleeps there.*

*And sometimes he sneaks away from Diva and holds me and tells me that he loves me.*

*'You'll always be mine, Marie.'*

*He's got his head on my belly, my swollen, naked belly, and we've been sharing a slice of afternoon delight. I'm drawing my fingers through his black hair and thinking that if only this hour could last forever and ever. But of course it can't and Dad, with one eye on the clock, starts to get dressed.*

*'You too, Marie,' he says nodding towards my clothes discarded on the floor, and adds, casual like, 'Diva'll be back soon.'*

*And he says it like a father, not a lover.*

*It fires me up and I tell him to bog off and I'll get up when I'm ready, and if he's worried about his precious Diva finding him in my bed perhaps he ought to . . .*

*'Whoa,' he says.*

*'Don't whoa me, I'm not a fucking horse.'*

*He laughs at my anger, says I'm like my mother, and that makes it worse and I say that I don't give a shit if Diva does find us like this. I just don't care.*

294

Dad says it's got to be a secret, a secret forever, and I say that if we moved far away where no one knew us we wouldn't have to hide.

And then for the first time Dad doesn't give me the reasons not to, he just says, 'We'll see, Marie. We'll see.'

My heart's in my mouth and later those words wake me in the night. I repeat them to myself, this promise of considering, then I drift into a dream of me and Dad and the bairn (he's not Aubrey yet) and of me being a housewife and Dad coming home from work to tea on the table and me rocking Bairn in the pram. So he's promised and I hug that promise to me so tightly that I must be stifling it.

I bring it out for comfort when Diva's in one of her sharp moods, when she's pissed off. She's always saying, 'Do I have to do everything around here? I'm not a slave.'

With Dad there she softens, she watches for his moods and curbs her mouth about me. To him it's, 'Canny, let's go for a meal tonight.'

It's a Tuesday and the club is closed midweek and, although it's only six o'clock, Diva's dolled up and ready to go.

Dad says, 'What about Marie? She's . . .'

But Diva's into that like a polecat.

'I'm sure she won't mind staying in. Will you, Marie?'

Of course I mind. I mind her treating Dad like he belongs to her, but he's looking at me and saying, 'You sure you'll be all right, Marie?'

Off they go, dressed up like a couple of film stars, and when I watch them from the window Diva's arm is tucked through Dad's.

I give them an hour, just to get settled, then I phone the restaurant and ask for Dad.

'Marie,' he says,' what is it?'

I make up some cock and bull story about pains in my stomach and I say, 'I'm frightened, Dad; I'm scared.' I suck in my breath, put a tremble in my voice.

'Please come home, Dad. Please.'

Diva isn't best pleased and she cuts me daggers as soon as she steps in the door. When Dad hugs me I look over her shoulder and give her the sweetest smile I can muster.

She can't help herself then and she snaps.

'You seem all right now.'

I tell her I feel a lot better and again I smile smugly at her, like she smiled at me earlier.

Her mouth twists out a silent 'Little cow' to me before she slams out of the room and up the stairs.

I say, 'I didn't mean to spoil your evening, Dad.' And he says, 'Didn't you, Marie?' But then he's kissing me, holding me, and it's delicious, this taste of him.

Upstairs Diva is crying herself to sleep while in this front room in a Glasgow semi Dad and I are loving as only we can.

And this is my life, our lives, as that long-ago winter ends.


Aubrey, my beautiful baby boy, is born on the tenth of March and, because he's a first child, I have him at the hospital. He's born with a full head of his father's hair and skin so smooth I want to lick him like an ice cream.

Dad comes at visiting time – Diva never does – with a couple of magazines and a box of chocolates. Aubrey – he is Aubrey now – is asleep in his cot by my bed.

Dad stands over him, watches his sleeping son/grandson. On Dad's face is a strange, strange look. It's like he's shocked, like he's just realised something terrible has happened. He looks at me, looks at Aubrey and he whispers, 'My God, what have I done, Marie?'

It's not what he's done, it's what we've done, and I'm glad, so glad, because now he has to be mine, not hers; that skinny cow with her dark eyes.

At least that's what I tell myself.

But all the same, when I'm feeding Aubrey in the middle of the night, my mind leaves that quiet ward and wanders into their house, into their bedroom where they're curled up together, sleepy and warm.

And I have to imagine that for ten long nights, and each night I hate her more.

I come home after that time and straight away Diva starts her chipping at me, talking about the cost of keeping me and Aubrey, about the stench of nappies in the kitchen, and tutting every time Aubrey cries for his feed.

'For God's sake, Marie, give him some milk.'

I tell her she could take a turn if she had any tits and she tells me I'm a coarse tart, so I call her a barren cow and she says at least she's married and not a mother to a little bastard. I think it's a good job Dad comes in then because I was ready to draw her one off.

He's heard half of what's been said and he says can't we get on because we've all got to live together?

My big mouth jumps in with, 'For now, Dad.' And Diva says, 'What do you mean, Marie? For now?'

She's asking me but she's looking at Dad and then he does a terrible thing; he shrugs his shoulders like he doesn't know what I'm talking about.

*I go mad. 'Tell her, Dad. Tell her.' My voice must be approaching scream level and Diva's taken a step back.*

Now in this present day, in this ward of cancer sufferers, I pause for breath and a swig of cool water. Katja says, 'You don't have to go on, Marie.'

But I do. I need to put myself back into that place for the last time. To be that girl again with a baby in her arms and a lover who's turned his face from her. With my sixteen-year-old thinking as twisted as a snake, all logic and consequence forgotten. Yet I held such a power in my young hands and I didn't realise it.

Power that I threw away and that Diva caught.

*Diva says 'Tell me what, Canny?' Her voice is so soft, so quiet, so sad. She's on the edge of tears and it's like a question she knows the answer to but doesn't want to hear. I almost feel sorry for her. Almost.*

*Then Dad, shaking his head like he's in a terrible dream, says to Diva, 'I can't. I can't tell you this, Diva.'*

*And Diva says, 'Then don't say it, Canny. Just make her go. Make her go.' The sadness is out of her voice now and it's fear and panic that scrabble from her mouth.*

*'Make her go, Canny.'*

*Dad says, 'I can't.'*

*Diva, desperate Diva, says, 'You must. You've got to.'*

*Her nose is dripping and her eyes are flooded and she clutches at Dad. Her face is into his face.*

*'Whatever it is, Canny, it's her fault. You've got to make her go.'*

So this is where my big mouth comes in and I say, 'He wants me, Diva, not you.' I add, 'He wants me; me and Aubrey.'

There, I've said it and it's done; the unsaid has been said.

Dad gasps, 'Marie.' And Diva fumbles for the chair behind her and then her face is in her hands.

'No. Oh no.'

Her crying is more like retching and she says over and over again, 'I knew. I knew. I knew,' as though this is all her doing.

I must be a hard-hearted bitch because there's a core of happiness glowing inside of me and I'm already planning for her leaving. There'll be me, Dad and Aubrey: a bonny little family in our own little home.

Then Diva stands up, slips away Dad's arm like she's peeling off her cardigan, and heads up the stairs. Dad doesn't move, I don't move, as we hear her drag out the suitcase from under their bed. Then, in minutes, she's down the stairs and the front door is closing gently behind her.

'Dad?' I say and he says, 'Not now, Marie. Not now,' and his voice is choking him.

In the quiet after the storm Aubrey starts to grizzle for my milk and Dad says he's got to open up the club. It seems he's shocked, dazed, and he leaves without a look to me, or Aubrey.

So this evening, after all that's happened, I sit alone with my baby and the radio for company.


Dad comes home late and I know he's pissed because he scratches for the keyhole, clatters the milk bottles off the step, and stumbles through the door. I wait for his footsteps up the stairs, across the landing, the pause by my door. I'm so quiet I can hear him breathe. But then he says, 'Oh fuck it,' and he's past my room *and into his, the door slamming loud enough to make Aubrey stir.*

*I lie awake for another hour, waiting to see if there's going to be a soft tap on my door. Once I even put my feet to the cold lino, almost make the running. If it's his guilt that keeps him away, it doesn't last long because two nights later we're loving like Bacall and Bogart. And it's a desperate, clutching love that afterwards has him cradling me in his arms like the child I'm not.*

*He talks gently to me, tells me how much he loves me and Aubrey in a soothing of words. I'm looking up at him, his so handsome face, and watching his mouth talk.*

*But then I'm listening, really listening and I'm stiffening in his warm strong arms because he's saying that this is wrong, that what we're doing is wrong, and we must stop.*

*I'm saying, 'No, Dad. No.'*

*And then he says, 'No,' and it's like he shuts the arguments away, pushes them out of his mind, and he's stroking my hair and telling me I'm beautiful and I look so much like Mam.*

*And for a while we're safe here in this world we've made, closed off from all other life.*

*But two weeks is all we get, just that before paradise ends.*

Back in this hospice for the dying I take another swig of water – the morphine seems to dry my throat – and I want to hurry this part, this fortnight that's oh so sweet and oh so bitter. And I want to draw the curtain behind the telling, rolling up the past behind me for the last time.

But I can't stop the images, the pictures of a sixteen-year-old me nursing my beautiful wee bairn, with Dad's arm around my shoulders, sitting there for hours on end as daylight fades into evening.

I'm crying now, crying for a past that's been dead for well over fifty years, but Katja's not asking if I want to stop, is she? She's listening to me; she wants to know this story in my life.

She takes my glass away, wipes my mouth and waits.

*Dad's at the club when Diva comes in the front door. I'm mopping the kitchen floor and the windows are open and a warm breeze is drifting through the house. Aubrey, my lovely Aubrey, is asleep in the front room. I've tied my blonde hair back with a scarf and I'm humming along to the radio.*

*So she's in the house, with a newspaper in her hand, and she's saying, 'I need to talk to you, Marie.'*

*She's skinnier than when she left and her eyes seem darker, bigger.*

*I say, 'I don't want to talk to you.'*

*Then she looks at her watch and says, 'Your dad'll be here in a minute.'*

*That throws me. 'Dad. Why Dad?'*

*Diva says, 'We've got to sort this out.' Her lips are tight together and they hardly move when she speaks.*

*She's baffling me, but in my heart there's a whisper of dread.*

*I hear Dad's car and I'm at the threshold and hissing, 'She's here,' before he's even in the door.*

*'I know,' he says and he sounds so tired and he looks beaten; it's like he's shrunk.*

*'Dad, what's the matter?'*

*'Marie,' he says and he hugs me tightly, lovingly, and I can feel a trembling in his body.*

*In the front room Diva says, 'We've got to be civilised about this, Marie.'*

*Dad says, 'Please, Marie,' like he recognises what's coming.*

*I'm looking at them, knowing they've been meeting, talking, deciding, and that whisper of dread is growing louder and louder.*

*Dad starts to speak but Diva says, 'I'll do this, Canny.'*

*She's moved to the table and she opens the newspaper and taps the headlines of the page.*

*'See this, Marie.' She prods the words:* Man found guilty of incest: jailed six years.

*There's a whole story underneath but it doesn't need telling because it's all in those few words.*

*'Is this what you want, Marie? Do you want this for him?'*

*Aubrey is grizzling in his pram and I'm thinking that this is his feeding time and I should be changing his nappy and . . . and doing anything except hearing all this.*

*Dad's slumped in a chair and I'm going over to hold him, to stroke his hair. I take a step, just one step, and Diva starts, 'No, Marie. You've done enough.'*

*There's a difference to Diva; she's not the woman who dragged her case from under the bed and crept out the front door; she's filling this room and she's pinning me like a butterfly.*

*Dad just sits there, not saying anything.*

*Diva says very quietly, 'If you don't leave us, Marie, give us our life back, I'll get the police. Then we'll see.'*

I need to catch my breath. Who would have thought that talking could be so tiring? Katja passes me my glass of water and I say, 'I wish it was something stronger.' She laughs and calls me a hopeless case and smoothes the sheet around me. You know, if I'd had a daughter I would have wanted her to be like Katja.

But I didn't; I had a beautiful baby boy who grizzled in his pram while Diva decided our lives. And now I'm lying in this bed and reliving that time, and I can't plead the innocent; I knew what we were doing, what we did, but once we'd started there was no stopping. And this is what Diva knew, that there would be no broken promises, because there were to be no promises.

Now I must go back to that sunny afternoon with a warm breeze sifting through the house where they're waiting for me.

*Me with a scarf tying back my blonde hair.*

*Dad, with his face in his hands.*

*And her: queen of the dance, belle of the ball, with cruel right on her side; the law on her side.*

*I know what's coming.*

*I say, 'Dad?' and he says there's no other way. That it's got to be like this.*

*And there is such sadness, such acceptance, in his voice that I scream at him, 'No, Dad. No.'*

*'Yes, Marie. Yes.'*

*Diva is nodding to his words like she's pulling the strings. Then she starts again, saying Dad could be put away for ten years. All it would take was for her to say something, then there would be the police, a blood test and I'd be in a home and Aubrey would be taken.*

*But if we do it her way, the only way, the secret stays just that, and if I don't agree she'll tell because without Dad her life means nothing.*

*'If I can't have him,' she says, 'then no one will.'*

*She means it; there's a black flame flickering in those calculating eyes and her face is set.*

*I hate her then and I know I'll hate her as long as I live.*

*But on this warm sunny afternoon she's not finished destroying my life. She wants Dad and she wants the child she never had. She wants my family. She wants my Aubrey, so it really is all or nothing for her.*

*This is it, she says.*

*'Is this what you want, Dad?' Now I'm crying, sobbing. 'Is this what you want?'*

*Dad says that there's no choice and it sounds like a plea for acceptance, like he's cutting me adrift.*

*I say, 'Not Aubrey, Dad. Not Aubrey.'*

*I know that I'm shaking my head and my voice is breaking into fragments and my hair is tumbling down my face.*

*Diva says, 'It's the only way,' and it's hard and unyielding.*

*I say, 'For you. For you two.' Then I realised I've paired them, put Dad and Diva together.*

*Then Diva says the words that are on her face.*

*'All or nothing for me or you, Marie.'*

I say to Katja, 'And that was it.'

'It?' she says.

And it was it. I walked out of that house the next morning with twenty-five pounds in notes and the clothes I stood up in. I didn't take a suitcase and I didn't take my baby.

But I took the train to Dundee to Mam's old haunts, to Mam's old friends, to Big Ben, to Mam's old life. I became Mam for thirty years. These are the words I say to Katja and I cover that time after in the blink of an eye, because I don't want to explain the drag of the years, the peeping into prams, the watching of children through the school gates. Or the long, long nights that men and drink couldn't dull. Oh, I could tell a hundred tales of rooms that reeked of perfume and smoke and sex.

I could tell of a life apart.

I say to Katja that I've had enough for now, that I want to sleep.

And sleep I do, and I dream of Dad and Aubrey, and in that dream there's no Diva; she's not in my life.

When I wake it's late and the bed opposite me is empty and at visiting time there's no boy-husband and no young bairns clambering on the covers. It's done for the young wife; another one ticked off the list.

I look around the ward and wonder who's going to be next, whose will be the next empty bed. And then I think I've got as good a chance as anyone and that sobers me up.

When Katja comes she asks me if I'd like Father O'Hallaron to come and talk to me. I tell Katja that it's too late to save my soul, and that I'm too old to be abused. She laughs and squeezes my hand and then she says, 'I shall miss you, Marie.'

It's not going to be that much longer; the grey on the edge of my vision grows deeper, closer each hour. It's starting to cloud in on me like it's shutting down my sight, my life.

You know, I never thought dying would be like this; slow and quiet, and with more morphine in my veins than blood. I always said I wanted to go with my boots on and a glass of whisky in my hand. Quick. Sudden. But it's not that bad, gently unfolding my memories, closing the door on each one in turn. Och, I've had a life: good and bad, sweet and sour.

I lose time, all sense of it; a minute could be an hour, an hour a week, and every now and then I hear Katja, see her blurred face.

'Hold on, Marie,' she says. 'Just a little longer. Hold on.'

I can feel her softly squeezing my fingers.

'Marie, can you hear me?'

I squeeze back because words are difficult to get out now and in my head there's a strange sound, like water slowly dripping into a deep well.

Drip. Drip. Drip.

'Marie.' Katja's voice is ebbing and flowing and . . .

*And then I'm a young girl and I'm seeing the waves drive up the beach and then there's a pause and then they fall back and the shingle's singing and Mam and I have wet feet and Mam's laughing fit to burst and she hugs me and says, 'Marie, my bonny little hussy.'*

*She takes my hand, leads me up the pebbles and onto the sand of the beach. And on that sandy beach there's Dad and he's sitting with a dark-haired toddler on his lap.*

*Mam has her arm around Dad's shoulders and she says, 'Say hello to Aubrey.'*

*The boy turns, looks at me, and then says so clearly out of his child's mouth, but in Dad's voice, 'Hello, Mam.'*

*But then this world jolts, freezes, dies . . .*

. . . and I'm back in my bed in the Macmillan Hospice and Katja is squeezing my hand.

'Marie, can you hear me?' Her voice is soft and distant. 'There's someone here.'

I feel a different grip on my hand, a hesitant grasp on my fingers, and then a thick Glasgow accent says, 'Hello, Mam.'

If I could cry I would cry now because all this is too late, much too late, and my window on life is closing over, and then I can't feel his fingers on mine. I can't feel anything and this night is as black as pitch.

And then there's nothing any more.

And it's all done.

All finished.

# A WEDNESDAY NIGHT – FOR
# A CHANGE – IN MARCH

*Maggie*

I've had this mood on me all day. Kayleigh reckons I've become a real grumpy gran.

'Honestly, Mum,' she says, 'it's about time . . .'

'About time what, Kayleigh?'

'I don't have to say it.'

And she doesn't because it's all been said before a dozen times. But she's wrong, because it's not about Ken, not about getting used to being on my own. It's not that.

I tell Kayleigh that I'll have a hot bath and an early night and she says that's a good idea; it's freezing outside and the talk is of heavy snow sweeping in from the north.

We share a pot of tea and then Kayleigh goes home, and my house sounds so quiet, so empty.

I take the radio into the bathroom and while I'm soaking I listen to an hour of depressing news that makes me yearn for a bit of laughter, some light-hearted humour. So while I'm getting dressed I switch on the telly, but it's *EastEnders* and someone's been murdered, someone's been beaten up, and the rest of them are wearing faces as long as horses'.

I give myself a pep talk and decide I need to get out of the house.

I'll go down to the Bluebell, see if any of the girls are in. Even Big Nellie will do for company tonight.

When I step out, a blast of bitter wind hits me, and before I'm halfway to the pub snow starts to fall. It's not much to begin with, but by the time I reach the Bluebell it's swirling like a mist in the light of the streetlamps. God, I'm cold, and I'm looking forward to warming myself in front of Danny's fireplace.

And inside the empty bar the fire is blazing away and Danny's got his back to it.

'Just warming my ars . . . bum,' he says, smoothing his trousers behind him.

I ask for a shandy, but he says I need something warm inside me on a night like this. He serves me a rum and pep and says, 'On the house, Maggie.' Then he says, 'I think I'll join you.' And he joins me in a drink and pulls up a chair to the fire as well.

I say, 'Thanks,' and he says he's got to look after his only customer.

We sit for a while, talking about the darts and our chances of winning the league, and I buy another rum for me and him and he asks how I'm managing. I tell him it's hard at times and he says it must be because I'm still a fine-looking woman. I don't quite know what he means by this but the rum's warming me inside, and it's so nice to have someone to talk to.

Danny goes to the window, says he doesn't think we'll see anyone else about tonight. I tell him I'll drink this one up and then I'll go and he says, 'There's no rush, Maggie. I'm glad of the company.'

He says it in a way that makes me think there's a depth of truth to it.

He must be younger than me but he's got that lived-in face of too many late nights, too many years of enjoying a drink too many. He's still got most of his hair and . . . Stop there, Maggie.

I've been doing this a lot lately, sort of looking at men – not like that – but sort of considering them. Kayleigh said I was staring at the butcher the other day and gave me a sharp nudge.

'Mum, he'll think you fancy him.'

I tell her it's no such thing and I was thinking about his offer of a Weekend Special Sausage. She raises her eyebrows at this and we both have a snigger.

Anyway, here in this snowbound pub Danny picks up my glass and says, 'Another one, Maggie?'

I say that I shouldn't really and he laughs and says he won't tell if I don't.

He's turned off most of the lights. 'Can't waste electric when there's no bugger here.' He sets the jukebox on play and he asks me if I've any old favourites.

I say, 'Something from the seventies, Danny.' (I'm worried that seventies came out sounding like the sheventies, but if it does he doesn't say.)

Then, as we sit by the flickering fire, the first lines of his choice sift gently into the bar.

It's a song about the realisation of loving, of a *moment captured in emotion and stored away for forever and a day*. I know it's corny, but it belongs to a time and place that's long gone. I wish Danny had put anything on but this because this tune, these words, wrap themselves around me and . . .

\* \* \*

I'm twenty-two years old and Ken and I have treated ourselves to a meal. We're sitting in this bistro in town and we're looking for the cheapest dish on the menu; the mortgage is due next week and we really shouldn't be here. That's what Ken says.

'We can't afford this, Maggie. We should have gone to the pub and got some chips on the way home.'

In the corner of this restaurant there's a guitarist plucking out bits of tunes, strumming some bars of this and that, quietly singing a few lines. He's dressed like a Spaniard, red open-necked shirt and too-tight black trousers, there's even a sash around his waist.

I'm saying it's a special occasion and it won't hurt just this once, and Ken wants to know what's so special that it costs a fortune.

I say, 'I'm pregnant, Ken.'

I say it and I'm worried because of our new house, a job I won't be able to keep, Ken's erratic subbing on the building sites. It all sounds too much with a baby on top as well.

Ken just stares at me. He's open-mouthed and I'm already trying not to cry.

This wasn't a good idea coming here, but I wanted him to remember the moment. I know it sounds soppy and we can't afford it, but I did want it to be so special.

Then into our bubble of silence the guitarist–singer starts, 'For forever and a day' and Ken's face breaks into the broadest of smiles.

'Really, Maggie?' he says disbelievingly. 'Really?'

He reaches across the table, takes my hand and squeezes it.

'I'll always remember this moment,' he says and then laughs. 'And that awful song.'

\*　　\*　　\*

And now, all these years later, I'm sitting in the Bluebell with Danny. I'm full of rum and pep and I'm crying again because of that song. And this is not a choked-back sniffle, this is a proper sobbing because my heart is breaking for what's gone, what's finished and can never come back. Outside the snow is still sweeping in on an iced wind, but inside Danny is holding me, drying my tears.

And then I do it. Oh, I can blame the booze, blame this close situation, blame whatever I like, but I'm a sixty-two-year-old woman and in this flickering, softly deceiving firelight I bring my face up to kiss Danny.

And he kisses me back gently, slowly. And I'm desperately pleased and desperately worried at what's going to happen next.

What happens is that Danny gets us both another drink, puts a few more oldies on the jukebox and we slow-dance to ballads of the seventies. I stifle guilt, lock the door on Ken in his nursing home, hide Kayleigh's disapproving face.

Then Danny says, 'Let's go upstairs, Maggie.'

And this is how it begins, mine and Danny's Wednesday nights secret. I know he's not the catch of the year but on his own he's different to Danny-behind-the-bar.

He's a nice man and that's all I want; a nice man to hold me on a dark night.

That's all I need to help me through this life until forever has come and gone.

# THURSDAY NIGHT PRACTICE IN APRIL

## *Maggie*

At six I ring Katy to check practice is on and she reckons that nothing will keep her from a vodka and Coke tonight. Not the rain and . . .

'Not even Johnny James.' She laughs. 'See you there, Maggie.'

As I'm leaving I stop at the hall mirror, brush through my hair once more, try to see if there's any grey growing from my roots. Then I touch up my lipstick, dab a bit of scent to my throat (*just in case, Maggie*) and give myself a guilty smile and leave my house.

When I get to the Bluebell, the girls are practising at the board and Danny's behind the bar.

I order half a cider and Danny winks at me and says, 'I thought it would be a rum and pep, Maggie. Or is that only for special occasions?'

I say, 'Only on Wednesdays, Danny,' and he gives me the loveliest of smiles. And when he passes my change over he gives my hand the slightest of squeezes.

Over at our table the girls have had enough of practice and they're having a team chat about missing Lena.

Ada Pikey says, 'It'll leave us one short for Monday,' as though Lena's being inconsiderate.

Pegs says, 'She can't help it, Ada, she's had a baby.'

Katy says, 'I've been looking. So if anyone knows anyone handy?'

Big Nellie puts down her pint pot and says, 'I might.'

We wait a moment because she's a bit slow at coming forward. Then she adds, 'My sister. She can play a bit.'

Katy shrugs. 'Well, bring her along on Monday; we'll give her a try-out.'

I'm thinking that we're only half the team we started out as. Lena won't be coming back this season, and Irish, who, according to Ada Pikey, is locked up in the madhouse with all the other nutters, will be lucky to see the inside of a pub ever again. And then there's Scottie Dog, and she's just vanished without trace.

Pegs, as if reading my thoughts, says, 'Makes you wonder who's next, Maggie.'

She does that sometimes, Pegs; catches your thoughts like she can see inside your head. Well, she'd have a shock if she looked into mine after what happened with Danny.

It's about half past nine and I'm yawning. I tell the girls that it's an early night for me. There's a lull at the bar and I say goodnight to Danny.

'Already, Maggie? The night's still young.'

I say, 'But I'm not, Danny. I need my sleep.'

He says, 'You must have been overdoing it, Maggie.' And it's the way he says this, with his knowledge of last night, his knowledge of me.

Then he says quietly, seriously, so that only I can hear, 'Wednesday, Maggie?'

'Wednesday, Danny.'

Then he whispers, 'I'll stock up on the Viagra,' and I leave the pub laughing to myself.

Outside, the roads are wet and the gutters are running with rainwater. It's damp and cold and windy. It makes me glad I left the heating on. Ken always said it was a waste warming up an empty house but now, although money's tight, it's a luxury I'm allowed. That and the electric blanket.

As I'm getting into bed I hear Ken's concern. 'Now remember to switch it off, Maggie.'

I laugh at this because I know I'm going to hear his chiding until the day I die.

'Goodnight, Ken,' I say and when I shut my eyes I'm into sleep quickly, deeply. And I'm into dreams, vivid and real. These dreams are of a middle-aged woman with a girl's yearnings and a surprise lover.

I dream of Danny, and next Wednesday suddenly seems a long time away.

# MONDAY NIGHT DARTS IN APRIL

*Katy*

We're playing the Gatehouse Groupies at their pub tonight and Johnny James drops me at the Bluebell.

'See you 'bout eleven,' I say.

He laughs. 'I'll count the seconds, Katy.'

I call him a soft sod and he blows me a kiss as he drives away. I light up a fag and watch him go out of sight and I'm thinking that nothing seems to faze him, not the trouble with Laura, not my being married, not me being a wreck half the time. I don't stand outside smoking for long because it's bloody cold and wet in the car park.

Inside, my team are at the bar and Big Nellie grunts at me and says in an introduction, 'This is Tina. We call her Tiny.'

She's shoved a dainty blonde towards me who doesn't look old enough to be in here – still that wouldn't worry Danny as long as she can down a few.

I say, 'So you've played a bit?' and she says that she's just finished at uni and she was in the team there. She talks really nice, posh almost. Nothing like grunting Nellie.

'Big Sis said you were a player down, so if I can help?'

I'm wondering how she could be related to Big Nellie; she's less than half the size and as pretty as a picture. Alongside, and looking down at her with a sister's fondness, Big Nellie reads my mind, 'She takes after Dad; I'm more like Mum.'

Now, I don't want to let my imagination go there, do I?

Lately we've been getting a taxi to the aways, but tonight Danny runs us over to the Gatehouse and, soon after eight, we're straight into our warm-up. Because we're second in the table we're a target every week and this team of Groupies have been dying to have a pop at us. They're several points behind and looking for glory, so we could really have done with Irish or Scottie Dog to lighten the load a bit.

And they're serious, this lot. On the team game they crowd the oche and yell for each of their players. It pisses me off because it unsettles Tiny on her throw.

I ask their captain to put a sock in it and she says it's part of their game and I should like it or lump it, but then Big Nellie loudly interrupts to tell them to 'Shut the fuck up while my sister is throwing,' and the whole pub is suddenly silent.

Danny mutters to me behind his hand, 'Christ, she even scares me.'

Then I have to take a second look at him because he looks so smart; not the usual rumpled Danny. His hair is slicked back, he's clean-shaven and even his shirt is ironed. And he's left Paddy looking after the bar, which is risky to say the least. I tell him the Motley Crew will be off their faces on his beer and he gives me a sickly grin. Then he buys us all a drink and sits next to Maggie who perks up at a bit of attention.

We edge the game, with Tiny scraping through and Big Nellie

watching guard over her like a minder. As soon as we're done I sneak out for a fag and I phone Johnny James.

I say, 'We won.'

He laughs. 'You always do.'

Then he tells me he'll pick me up from the Bluebell and I tell him to give me time to have a drink with the girls.

'Not too many,' he says. 'I want you conscious.'

I say, 'I just want you.'


Back at the Bluebell, Danny ushers Paddy from behind the bar and checks the till. Paddy says, 'I've still got two pints in, Danny.'

Danny reckons he's the one who's been had over and Paddy says that next time he'll charge him the going rate, not just a few beers.

Danny reckons that would be cheaper and Paddy reckons that Danny wouldn't acknowledge a favour even if it jumped up and bit him in the arse. He takes his pint and stomps away to the furthest corner of the bar room.

Danny says to me, 'What the fuck's up with him, Katy?'

I tell him I haven't a clue and Danny mutters something about Paddy being an ungrateful bastard.

I buy the girls a drink and go for a fag. Outside, in the smoking area, there's a shine of wet on the patio chairs and a drift of rain across the Bluebell sign. I light up my cancer stick and text Johnny James:

*Come and get me, lover boy xxxx*

It's quiet out here and although I can hear the noise of the bar it's muffled and distant. And I can see the red dot that gives away the CCTV camera, which turned a chance kiss into a catalyst.

Christ, who'd have thought one little kiss . . . but it was so much more than that and it makes me think of the Katy I was just a short time ago.

Katy Jones, plump(ish) mother of a devil daughter and wife to porno-loving Jerry. Unhappy. Unsatisfied. Pissed off with her lot.

Look at me now: I'm slim and I've got a daughter who won't speak to me and a father who doesn't know I'm breathing.

This is what I dwell on as I blow smoke to the bright, cold moon. I so badly want him to know. I want him to know me.

Back inside I've time to slot in another voddie, so I join my team for a quickie. I'm sitting next to Pegs (my secret sister) and I ask how things are. I mean with her and Big Dave Trinder, but she says her mum's okay and her dad's taking things easy for a day or two.

'Got a cold,' she says. 'Thinks he's dying.'

I laugh at that and then Johnny James sweeps into the bar like he's Prince Charming and carries me off in his BMW.

On the way back to his place Johnny James says, 'You're quiet, Katy,' and before I answer he says, 'Laura again?' and I say it's different than that.

He asks, 'What?' and I go quiet and he doesn't ask again.

What I can't tell him, in the comfortable warmth of the Beamer, is that I'm practising the words I'm going to say to Henry Smith.

If ever chance and courage coincide.

On Tuesday night I go round Mum's to pick up a few more of my belongings, what there is of them, because I'm really living at

Johnny James's now. He's even bought us a new bed, and I've also collected several things from . . . I was going to say 'my house' but it's not my house any more, it's Jerry and Laura's house. It still hits me hard, these little bits of realisation. Anyway, Mum and I sit and have a cup of tea and she asks how things are going with Johnny James.

'He's the best thing that happened to me,' I say. 'I wouldn't have got through all this without him.'

Mum says quietly, 'None of this would have happened without him.'

I say, 'I wasn't happy before, Mum,' and that makes me feel guilty for what I've got now.

I'm thinking that Mum's had a shit life and it's like it's over for her. She looks worn out. There are deep lines on her face and her shoulders are hunched and her hair is grey. Then I think of how that bastard Jim treated her, how she must have struggled bringing up me and Ellie.

I see myself at sixteen, knowing it all, gobby as fuck. I see Mum turning away from me after yet another row, shaking her head slowly, tiredly.

*'Just do what you like Katy. Do what you like.'*

And I did. So, Mum and I, Laura and I. What's the difference?

I put my arms around her then.

'I'm sorry, Mum.'

She says tiredly, 'So am I, Katy. So am I.'

I go into the spare room and empty out my drawer in Mum's cupboard. I fill my hold-all with the underclothes I brought here – God, did I really wear those passion-killers and that granny bra? It's a bit different to what I'm wearing now, flimsy and soft to touch. That's what Johnny James likes.

Anyway, I pack my bag and then, devious me, because of what's in my head, take *those* photos from Mum's tin and I bury them beneath my grey, obsolete underwear.

# THURSDAY NIGHT DARTS PRACTICE IN APRIL

## Katy

When I get to the Bluebell, Maggie's already at the bar – Christ, she seems to live here lately. Pegs reckoned that when she and Big Dave called in for some baccy last night Maggie was settled by the fire like a comfortable farmhouse cat. So I suppose there must be something here for her, and I wonder if one of the Motley Crew is feeding her. I'll ask Danny later; there's not much escapes him.

We pair up for practices: me and Ada Pikey versus Pegs and Tiny, with Maggie chalking. Big Nellie calls the scores and Danny keeps reminding us to win on Monday. He's cleared a place on the shelf behind the bar. 'For the trophy,' he says. 'I can just see it up there. The Bluebell team, Six of the Best, winners of the Ladies' League.'

Ada Pikey says he shouldn't count his chickens and Tiny says he shouldn't count our chickens.

Danny reckons it's no sweat and the Battersby Babes will be a pushover. Then I say they beat the Pelicans the other week and they were third in the table.

'A fluke,' he says. 'Couple of lucky darts.'

I'm thinking that's all it takes sometimes, a bit of luck.

Me and Maggie are getting the drinks in and I order up my vodka and Coke and a rum and pep for Maggie. Danny says it seems she's developed a liking for that drink.

'Keeps the cold out, Danny,' she says. 'Warms me up.'

Danny says, 'I could do that, Maggie,' and I tell him he's a dirty old man, and he says he'd make me an offer, but he's become a bit fussier in his advancing years.

I say I've never fancied old age creeping over me anyway, and he says that it's my loss.

Then alongside us Paddy snorts, 'Will yer look at the pair of them?'

Jilted John is sitting in the far corner of the bar room with a woman who's a bit younger than him, a lot heavier than him, and certainly as drunk as he is. They have their arms wrapped around each other – well, his don't exactly reach – and they're singing along to the jukebox. Tuneful it's not.

Paddy snorts again, 'Will yer look at the pair of them?' I think he's miffed because he's worried about losing a drinking partner.

I ask who she is and Danny, earwigging over the bar says, 'Josey something. From Wales, I think. He met her on the Internet.'

Paddy says, 'She's come a long way for a shag.'

Then Pikey Pete, who's just come out the Gents and is still doing his flies up, gets the gist of the conversation and nods in the direction of Jilted John and his new girlfriend. He says, 'Well, you know about women over forty?' He waits a second, puffing himself up like an end-of-the-pier act, 'They don't yell. They don't tell. And they're as grateful as hell.' He's saying it like he's just made it up and he's killing himself at his humour. But what I'll remember is the sly wink that Danny gives to Maggie, a woman well over forty.

Christ, surely not them?

I guess I won't be grilling him about Maggie after all.

# SATURDAY MORNING IN TOWN

*Katy*

I'm in the supermarket this Saturday morning and I hate shopping. I always have, so I go into the café for a cup of strong coffee before facing the aisles and shelves. I've just sat down with my drink when I see Pegs and her mum, Lydia. Pegs says, 'Don't mind if we join you, Katy?'

As Pegs sits down Lydia says, 'I'll get us a cup o' tea, Peggy.'

Lydia heads towards the counter and Pegs says, 'On your own then, Katy?'

I tell her Johnny James wouldn't be seen dead pushing a supermarket trolley.

'Nor Dad,' Pegs says. 'He always finds something to do at home.'

'Busy, is he?' is straight out of my mouth.

Pegs says, 'Him and my Dave got a drive to do next week. Dad's sorting out the roller.'

I've drunk my coffee before Lydia brings their drinks over and

I say I must get on. I leave them to their tea and KitKats and abandon my trolley in the aisle.

Within ten minutes I'm driving down the rough, pot-holed road to the Station Yard. My hands are trembling on the steering wheel and my head's full of what I may or may not do or say.

And nestling inside my handbag are Mum's pictures of the past.

I'm out of the car and into the yard and, in front of Pegs' static, there's a smouldering fire with a hanging blackened kettle, softly steaming. On an upturned crate there's a brown teapot, a plastic bottle of milk, a bowl of sugar and a couple of mugs. Henry Smith's stringy grey dog noses me from behind, at my behind, and makes me jump. Johnny James would have laughed at this.

I stand by the fire and call out a feeble 'Hello'. I don't know if I really want anyone to answer, but at the sound of my voice the grey dog starts an almighty racket.

Then Henry Smith's at the door of the static and yelling at the dog to shut up. Then he says, 'Pegs ain't here, Katy.'

I say, 'It's you I came to see, Henry,' and my voice is so small and quiet.

'Are you all right, Katy?' He pauses, frowns in a question, and says, 'Come inside, Katy.' He nods me in.

And then it's like I'm in a dream. I seem to see myself go up the four wooden steps (am I really counting them?) and into a Gypsy's home.

Henry Smith says, 'Sit yerself down. Now what can I do for you, Katy?'

I perch on the sofa and I'm confused; I don't know where to start. All the words I've practised in my head seem to be wedged in my throat.

He asks, slowly and curiously, 'Are you all right, Katy?'

I tell him yes, I tell him no, and then I stumble out, 'Will you look at this for me?'

From my handbag I slide out the picture of the baby me reaching for those hoops of gold from all those years ago. I pass it to him and watch a puzzling smile freeze on his face.

'What's this, Katy?'

He seems to stare at it forever and then to suddenly realise its twin is hanging on the wall of family pictures. He holds out the photo, compares it to the other, and shakes and then nods his head.

'It's Mum,' he says, 'and the chavi we didn't know and . . .' He stops and then, still puzzling, 'Where did you get this, Katy?'

'She . . .' I don't know what to call her. 'Your mum gave it to my mother.'

'Your mother?'

Then I tell him Mum's name, her maiden name cos he's only known me as Katy Jones, and he becomes stock-still. Then he says so quietly it's almost a whisper, 'Tell me, Katy, tell me what you came here for.'

So I take all of Mum's photos of their pictures together, and I pass him over a love affair from thirty-five years ago. The images are there and the dates Mum so carefully, so lovingly, wrote on them are there too.

And he's there. He's there as a young man with the sun in his face and love in his eyes.

*　　*　　*

Henry Smith picks up each photo, puts it down, picks it up, rolls himself a thick cigarette, lights it. (This is the cue for me because if I ever needed a fag, I need one now.)

I say, 'I'm sorry, Henry,' and he says quietly, 'You've nothing to be sorry for, Katy.'

Then he says, shaking his head, 'I never knew.' And then he tells me that times were so different then, no mobile phones, no letters to find them, and he was half the country away, and he, they, were always on the move.

I want to ask what if he had known . . .? But that's too personal, too close a question.

Too soon.

I say, 'I only wanted to know, Henry. To be sure,' when I'm so sure already.

And there's no denying from him, no excuses.

He says, 'All this time, Katy. All this time.' There's a wistfulness in his voice.

And then his arms are around me and my head's into his shoulder and I can taste the scent of him. He smells of the caravan, of tobacco, of woodsmoke, of the man I so desperately wanted to tuck me up in bed and kiss me goodnight.

He smells like my father should.


I don't stay long after that, I don't want to be here when Pegs and Lydia get home but, when I step outside, Big Dave Trinder is sitting on the crate by the fire and sipping a mug of tea.

He says, 'All right, Katy.'

'All right, Dave.'

I want to say, 'Don't tell anyone I was here,' but I can't, can I?

Anyway, Henry Smith at the door says, 'Goodbye, my Katy,' and I drive away in Johnny James's Beamer.

I'm almost home before I realise Henry said *my* Katy. It's like he's already claiming me. Like the Gypsies are claiming me.

*My* Katy.

I say it to myself a dozen times before I get back to Johnny James. And when he asks where the shopping is I burst into tears. Then he makes me a cup of tea, lights me up a fag and says, like Henry Smith did, 'Tell me, Katy.'

And Mum's secret, so carefully, so lovingly kept for all that time, is given voice again.


For the rest of the day Johnny James treats me like an invalid. He supplies me with more fags – lets me smoke in the house – and more tea, and about five o'clock he asks if I want something to eat. I'm wondering what's in the cupboard, since I didn't do the shopping, and he says he can do me some toast, but we're fresh out of hedgehog pâté and badger rissole.

He makes me laugh out loud.

Anyway, he goes out to pick up an early Indian and I set the table and make sure there's lager in the fridge. Then I take out Mum's photos again, and see my dad as a young man and my mum as a pretty girl. I've never seen her as happy as she is in that kiss-me-quick hat with Henry's – I whisper Dad's – arm around her. All those years ago, a lifetime, *my lifetime,* is trapped in a beach photographer's lens on a long gone summer's day. I look at these pictures, shuffle them over and over, until I hear Johnny James's key in the door.

As the lock turns, the enormity of what I've done, what's been realised, rolls over me and I think of Mum with these pictures spread out on the table at the refuge. I see her with her head in her hands, crying, sobbing for a boy, for a life she never could have had.

And it's that thought that starts me off and it's my eyes that are running.

*Then Henry Smith says, 'Don't cry, my Katy,' and because he says 'my Katy' I cry even more.*

# MONDAY NIGHT DARTS –
# THE BEGINNING OF MAY
## THE LAST GAME OF THE SEASON:
## THE TITLE DECIDER

### *Still Katy*

Johnny James wishes me – us – good luck and drops me at the Bluebell. Before I go in I take a deep breath and kick a bit of mud off my knee-length leather boots. (A Johnny James present to me. And for him.)

Inside, my team are already warming up on the board and at the bar Danny's pouring me a vodka and Coke.

'Get this down your neck, Katy,' he says. 'Calm your nerves.' But he's the one clinking the ice as he passes it over.

I'm not feeling nervous, not at all, and I really can't wait for the game to begin. It's like it's the last thing I've got to do, to settle, because my marriage is dead and buried and I might have lost Laura for now, but I've gained Johnny James and Henry Smith.

So winning tonight would be a bonus for me and I would love to do it for the ones that aren't here: Lena, Irish, Scottie Dog.

It's strange how Scottie Dog just vanished, stepped out of our lives with not a word to anyone. Makes me wonder if she's sitting in some pub calling up another whisky and moaning '*go fucking easy on the water*'.

Danny says that he'll keep the pub open all night if we win.

'And,' he says, 'if we lose I'll stay open anyway to drown our sorrows.'

I tell him he's just after our money and Danny looks pained and says, quietly for him, 'It's not for me, it's for the pub.' He says it as though he's talking about a loved one but you never know with Danny.

I wait for a crack, a comment, to wing over but it doesn't come.

At the oche, I join my girls in taking turns to throw at the board. Ada Pikey hits a bull and swears blind that she aimed for it, and Big Nellie grunts that there's a first time for everything. Ada Pikey opens her mouth but then thinks better of saying anything. Tiny, looking like a little blonde fairy, dances up the mat to retrieve her darts, and Maggie, with a new hairdo, carefully throws at double one because she reckons she'll end up on it anyway. That only leaves Pegs and she's even quieter than usual. In fact she hardly said a word at work today and it makes me wonder if Big Dave Trinder told her I was at the site.

The Battersby Babes come in right on eight o'clock and we let them have the board for a quick warm-up. They're stunning this lot, really living up to their name: all long legs, short skirts, shapely, fresh, young. Christ, I'm sounding like their fan club and we haven't even got Lena to offer them competition.

Anyway, we can't compare – our ragged team of Little and Large, rejuvenated Maggie, and us three, the Didicoys. Christ (again), am I already changing sides?

So we start the game against Diana, Charlotte, Catherine and the rest. Even their names are glamorous, even the way they throw their darts is all poise and pose. But they aren't only Yummy Mummys; they're not up the league with us for nothing. They're cool and keen, and soon in front of us in the team game. I'm wishing for an Irish or Scottie Dog to unsettle them when Ada Pikey says that you can't move in the car park for Chelsea tractors. This image suits this team so we all have a snigger. But the Babes still win the team game pretty convincingly and when a nervous Tiny drops the first single she looks like she's about to burst into tears.

'Sorry, Katy,' she mumbles.

I tell her not to worry but I do a bit because we're not used to being two points down. Ada Pikey, with a throw like a spear-chucker, whacks home a double sixteen to bring us back a leg and then Pegs gets stuck on double five and her opponent shoots out with her second dart. Now the Babes have got their pretty tails up and they cheer in tune, like they're a sweet-voiced choir.

I say, 'Bad luck, Pegs,' and she shrugs and says she had her chances. Then she says so quietly, it's almost a whisper, 'It'll be down to you then, my Katy.'

And that *my* is casual, natural, familiar. And I'm wondering if the tale's been told down on the site, if the secret's out.

Danny's left the bar and he's standing behind Maggie watching the action. I don't know if anyone else has noticed, but you couldn't get a fag paper between them, and I keep expecting her to put her hands up in the air cos he must be prodding her in her back.

So the score's three to one and Big Nellie's on the oche. All the game she doesn't say a word; she throws her darts slowly, with grim determination, and grunts her way to a convincing win. A disappointed Babe – Catherine, I think – pulls a face behind Big Nellie and rolls her eyes.

I need another voddie before the next game and Danny's half-way through serving Jilted John and grousing out the order, rushing it through with impatience.

'Well, does she want a single or a double?' He's asking for Jilted John's girlfriend – the Josey from Wales. (Or Josey the Whale as Paddy now calls her.) Jilted John ponders. 'Um . . . uh . . . um . . . a . . .' and Danny, becoming even more impatient, makes the decision for him.

'A double.' He pushes up the optic and mutters to me, 'Shouldn't think a little one would be much use to her.'

Then Pikey Pete calls across that Old Bob has thrown up in the bog and blocked the pisser.

Danny says, 'Jesus bloody Christ,' and tells me to help myself to a drink and it's not as though he hasn't got enough to fucking do.

Anyway, Maggie's started her game and she's lagging a bit. She knows we've got to win this to keep us in with a chance and she keeps plugging away to a double. The Battersby Babe has first poke, misses, and then Maggie lines up for her double four. Everyone's shushed down and as Maggie takes her throw the only sound is a loud belch, and a curse of Danny's gassy beer, from Paddy.

Maggie throws and drops in a single four and then a single two. She pauses now, takes a deep breath and pins the double one.

'Told you I'd end up there, Katy,' she laughs, all the tension out of her face.

My girls are loudly whooping and Danny's sneaked out from the bar again and he gives Maggie a hug of congratulations.

Ada Pikey moans that he never does that to her when she wins, and Big Nellie says she wouldn't want him to.

Danny says that some things are beyond the call of duty anyway.

I whip outside for a quick fag and I give my text messages a checkout.

Johnny James has sent two of the usual – beyond porn – and there's another one from . . .?

*Mum please give me a call.*

Well, I'm only Mum to one, and the last time we met she called me a slag and I slapped her face. That's a thought that flashes through my mind as my fingers tap in her number.

'Laura?'

'You at darts, Mum?' She sounds quiet, subdued. Civil.

'Yes but . . .'

'Will you call round when you finish?'

I get out, 'Yes but . . .' again, and she says, 'It doesn't matter what time it is; please come.'

This isn't the chopsy little madam with a log on her shoulder; she sounds small and frightened.

'Laura, tell me what's the matter.'

She's quiet for a few moments and then I hear her suck in her breath.

'Oh, Mum,' she says, 'I'm pregnant,' and her voice goes hoarse.

I take a choking pull on my fag and say, 'Oh, Laura, I'll come straight over.'

In that same tight little voice she says, 'You've got your darts, Mum. Come later.'

'Laura . . .'

'Please, Mum. Later. An hour's not going to make a difference now.'

She sounds so tired and so suddenly grown-up. 'Love you, Mum,' she whispers.

And then she hangs up.

And then Ada Pikey's bawling to me across the yard, 'Come on, Katy. We're all waiting for you.'

I'm standing on the oche, darts fanned in my hand, leaning forward slightly, focusing on the treble twenty and thinking how could it have come down to this: the game we need to win for the title, the game that's standing at three to three? Christ, it's like a corny film.

I weigh my dart between my fingers, draw back my arm.

And throw.

I throw for Irish, for Scottie Dog, for Lena, for Laura, for everything that's gone on this season.

And then I throw for me.

# CONTINUING IN THE BLUEBELL PUBLIC BAR

And so the last game of the last game of the season begins between Six of the Best and the Battersby Babes. The audience comprises of the players, the ever-present Motley Crew and a few more customers who've wandered in off the street on this Monday night. Oh, and not forgetting the landlord of this salubrious establishment, Danny, who'll be craning his neck from under the optics.

The public bar is a hushed set except for the jukebox plaintively wailing a country song about a cowboy's dog that's much more faithful than his wife. Against that background, Katy starts first and she throws with intent, notching an admirable sixty. After a few snatches of 'Well done,' 'Steady darts,' and the like, the hush returns for the rather gorgeous Battersby Babe to step up to the oche. From the speakers, the faithful dog is now waking up the cuckolded singer with a good licking every morning. (You can almost hear Scottie Dog remarking that if only the cowboy had woken his missus like that she wouldn't have fucked off with his best friend. And Irish would be telling her she's got a dirty gob for an old bird.)

The Battersby Babe, all perfect poise and concentration, knocks out an eighty-five to put her pert little nose in front, and then Katy leaves a treble twenty on the floor as she hits the wire. (Irish would be saying, 'For fuck's sake Katy,' – then a pause for a mighty swallow of gin and tonic – 'get yer arse in gear.')

That's how it goes, this game: a good throw, a bad throw, until it's neck and neck approaching the final furlong. Well, it is until Katy chucks a lowly thirty-seven and the proceedings lose their momentum as the chalker – a Babette since she's several years younger than the rest of her team – hits a blank with her subtraction. She's staring at the numbers with the chalk in her hand and bafflement on her face before the score slowly clicks into place. But not before Scottie Dog would have said, 'Fucking hell, yer daft cow. Thirty-seven off a hundred and sixteen leaves seventy nine.' Which it does for Katy.

The Battersby Babe is down to fifty-five – a single fifteen and double top shot out – and the way she pushes so confidently to the oche you'd think she'd already taken the game. Her first dart is smacked centre of the fifteen and then she takes her time, takes a deep breath, and lines up the highest double on the board. And it's so nearly the perfect shot, but it just snicks the wire and sits above the target. And that's as close as she gets – her third dart's a mile away – and Katy finds herself in with a chance after all.

Seventy-nine.

Pegs can't look and Ada Pikey, who's never won anything in her life, is wreathed in nervous anticipation. Maggie, not used to all the tension, has cut off to the Ladies to change her Tena and Tiny has her head buried in Big Nellie's shoulder.

Seventy-nine.

Katy needs the treble thirteen and then the steal of the Battersby Babes' double top.

Bang. Bang. Just like that. And that's how Katy does it. Just like that. And it's finished and she holds her arms aloft and the chalker's confused again and half the pub are also trying to match the darts to the score. (Behind the mayhem, the song on the jukebox has finished with the cowboy's wife, realising her mistake, crawling back home wanting to give the marriage another try. The dog sees her off the premises.)

The celebrations start – high fives and clinking glasses – and Danny, wide grin on his face and flushed at the success of his team, has left his post behind the counter. He's almost lifting Katy off the ground with his enthusiasm and he says loudly, 'The drinks are on me,' and there's a big cheer and such a rush for the bar that no one hears the single word of the rest of his proclamation peter out with 'team'.

After a while the bar's quietened down and the food's been dished out – cheese and onion and egg and cress sandwiches and a large bowl of crisps. The Motley Crew have raided the plates and loaded up their grubby maulers with free food. The Battersby Babes have taken their runners-up spot out of the pub with their tails between their long shapely legs, and now Six of the Best are sitting around the table and having a team time. A winning team time. A reflective team time. A team where there's two players – not counting Lena – missing.

A whisky and water and a gin and tonic fill the empty places at the table. Katy scrapes her chair back and stands up, raises her vodka and Coke and says 'To Irish and Scottie Dog'. And there's a toast to those who no longer belong to the land of the living. Or the sane.

And it's Pegs who reaches across the void, who taps glasses with the ghosts of the past as she echoes, 'To Irish and Scottie Dog.'

At the bar there's a bit of a rumpus developing. Danny, through gritted teeth, is impatiently explaining to Paddy, who's been on the ale for the best part of the day, that he meant, 'A free drink. I said I'd give out a free drink. Not free fucking drink all fucking night.' Paddy says free drink means free drink, and Danny says that doesn't Paddy understand plain English. Paddy mutters under his breath that nothing's much changed since the potato famine.

Then Old Bob chips in with, 'I thought you said three drinks, Danny?'

Jilted John, tapping his empty glass on the bar, says, 'It doesn't fucking matter just get 'em in cos a man could die of thirst waiting here.'

Paddy says it's Jilted John's round anyway so he can fucking get 'em in. Jilted John swears blind it's not his shout and Old Bob says it can't be his because he's spent all his pension and he can't see why he should buy Jilted John's financee – or whatever she is – one every time when she don't buy one back. Paddy says that the girl could swallow for Wales. Danny says that if there's any more dirty talk like that he'll throw the lot of them out. Pikey Pete, returning from a visit to the bog, says no one's going to throw him out of 'his' pub. And then, Danny, having enough of it all, rings the bell for closing time and tells them all to piss off anyway, and if Pikey Pete wants a dap on his hooter he's only got to ask.

It's later and the Bluebell Inn has emptied – nearly – and there's glasses crowding the counter for the washing. Maggie's sharing a nightcap with Danny and she's looking at the clock and the hands have ticked well past the midnight hour.

She stands up and says, 'I'd better go, Danny.'

'Stay tonight, Maggie.'

'I shouldn't, Danny.'

'Go on, Maggie. No-one will know.'

Danny puts his arms around her, slides his hands down her body and puts his face to her face and kisses her gently.

'It's not one of our Wednesdays,' she laughs, hardly pauses, and says, 'but I'll make an exception tonight.'

The offer of a warm bed and a bit of loving is too tempting for Maggie because what's at home for her? (Plus Maggie's had more than a few celebratory drinks and it's gone straight to her hot spot.)

Danny flicks the lights off and leads Maggie up the stairs.

*Irish says, 'She didn't take a lot of persuading.'*

*Scottie Dog says, 'The hungry must be fed.'*

*Irish says, 'Jesus, I wouldn't mind a portion of what she's going to get.'*

\*    \*    \*

Then Danny's back down the stairs, flicking on the lights, scratching his receding hairline, nosing around the bar room on lily-white legs topped with black boxers.

'I could have sworn I heard voices.'

He checks the bogs and shakes his head and thinks he might be going senile. Senile or not, he spots a whisky and water on the counter among the jungle of glasses.

'Be a shame to waste that.'

He downs it in one swift gulp, takes another glance around the bar and then it's lights out and he's up the stairs again.

*Scottie Dog says into the darkness, 'My fucking drink; the cheeky bastard.'*

# THE BLUEBELL VERSUS
# THE LAMB CHOPS
## A SEPTEMBER NIGHT – THE FIRST
## GAME OF THE NEW SEASON

### *Katy*

I'm last to arrive and my girls have settled into pre-match practice on the dartboard. I go up to the bar and Danny says, 'What
do you think of that then, Katy?'

He's showing me the latest site of the highly polished Ladies
League Winners' cup. Over the last few months it's been on every
shelf in the pub and at present it's residing above the row of optics.

I say it looks fine, but Danny cocks his eye at it and says, 'I
don't know, Katy. Perhaps it was better above the fireplace.'

I say that I think it looks good where it is and I'm sure that if
Scottie Dog was here she'd have told him where to stick it long
before now.

Anyway, I buy a round of drinks.

I buy a voddie and Coke for me, Katy Jones – imminent grandmother: thirty-six years old, slim and madly in love, and desperately trying to give up the fags.

For Ada Pikey: mother of Pikey Pete, a mouthy gypo, but
pretty good with the arrows, a half of bitter.

For Maggie: a rum and pep, and a wink from Danny that she thinks no one notices.

For Big Nellie: a pint of best as she watches over our team like a minder.

For Tiny: a baby doll of a girl, a dry Martini and lemonade and the chalk cos she's good at maths.

And then there's Pegs, my sister who shares my taste, but not my capacity, for vodka and Coke. And she's the one who wishes me '*Koorshti bok*' before I take my throw.

And cos she's teaching me the lingo I know what it means.

# ACKNOWLEDGEMENTS

I'd like to thank Peter Buckman at Ampersand for keeping the faith and to Hannah Black at Coronet for all the hours of patience she's applied to this novel. Thanks also to Fiona Rose, Joanne Myler and Rebecca Mundy at Coronet for their involvement and expertise. Another thank you is to Karen Hayes for her much-needed enthusiasm throughout the writing of this book.

I'd like to include some family and friends in this acknowledgement, namely: Sarah Woodhouse, Carrie Woodhouse, Angie Cassidy, Sharon and Scott Mitchel for their knowing, and unknowing, help in bringing this project to fruition.

And a last, but by no means least, a very special thank you to my wife Debbie whose help and understanding made everything possible.